The
Folded Notes

The
Folded Notes

Inspired by True Events

Mandz Singh

Matador
9 Priory Business Park,
Wistow Road, Kibworth Beauchamp,
Leicestershire. LE8 0RX
Tel: 0116 279 2299
Email: books@troubador.co.uk
Web: www.troubador.co.uk/matador
Twitter: @matadorbooks

ISBN 978 1788035 521

British Library Cataloguing in Publication Data.
A catalogue record for this book is available from the British Library.

Printed and bound in Great Britain by 4edge Limited
Typeset in 11pt Minion Pro by Troubador Publishing Ltd, Leicester, UK

Matador is an imprint of Troubador Publishing Ltd

In loving memory of my grandparents, who took those bold steps to move to East Africa after the Second World War and the Partition of India.

For that time at Golden City (Geecees), Ballarat, for it inspired me to carry on with the completion of this book.

It takes a moment to be infatuated, an hour to like someone, a day to fall in love, a lifetime to forget a love.

Anonymous

Ascot, England
June 1889

Prologue

It was a perfect summer's day at Ascot Racecourse. The British flag was flying high, perched above the grandstand in the warm breeze. The oak trees were all covered with a green canopy of leaves in full growth. Punters were milling outside trying their luck; the ladies were flaunting themselves, eager to be seen as elite members of the upper class. The brass band was playing, adding a unique ambience to the whole event. Everyone felt important.

Inside the grand pavilion, lunch was nearly over.

Sir William Mackinnon, who had set up the Imperial British East Africa Company, was a close associate of Lord Rosebery, and over the past two years, he had pleaded with the Foreign Secretary to make the British establishment see through his eyes what a profitable future he saw for the empire.

Mackinnon was shrewd, energetic, empire-minded and had learned through his mistakes and failures never to give up. He had a vision of exploiting further the shipping routes along the East African coast and the interior.

"The increasing German presence and influence in East Africa is of great concern," Mackinnon said as he wiped the last residue of dessert from his lips with a napkin. "You must be aware of the effects occurring at present due to the ten treaties that were signed by that ruthless German Karl Peters with the Sultan of Zanzibar six years ago," he added with concern.

"It has been observed that the German influence is greater than before around Tanganyika and the rest of the East African coast," Rosebery added, raising his eyebrows.

"We, the British, cannot sit still and see the Cape-to-Cairo vision just disappear."

"Mackinnon, I am as concerned as you are and I also know that your shipping routes are threatened along that coastline."

"The Imperial British East Africa Company, of whom I am a chairman, do not have the resources to develop the whole territory for the British." Mackinnon paused for effect. "If it were not for my effort in securing the fifty-year concession with the Zanzibari Sultan over two years ago, the German government would be making a mockery of us!" He fumed under his breath.

"Things are changing here in the government. I can assure you that very soon it has plans to make at least part of East Africa a British protectorate." Rosebery leaned closer and whispered, "Not only that; there are patriotic private British investors interested in Kampala who are putting pressure on the establishment."

"Kampala! That is hundreds of miles from the East African coast." Mackinnon had a confused expression on his face, not quite understanding. "Are they aware that the land across is hostile, inhabited by the fearsome Masai, and totally unforgiving?" he grunted.

"Why not concentrate on the coast initially instead of Kampala? I have been made aware that it is fertile; the source of the mighty Nile rises from there and it will be a strategic post for us against the French." Rosebery leaned back on the green leather-backed dining chair, reached into the inner pocket of his tweed jacket and removed his cigar case. "Would you like one?" he offered politely.

"No thank you," was the reply.

Mackinnon saw a sudden elated expression on Rosebery's face. Was it the temporary satisfaction of the cigar as a warm rush from inhaled tobacco spread through his body, or was it the fact that he had caught the middle-aged lady seated across looking coquettishly towards him?

It was neither.

"Well, my friend, I am about to divulge extracts of a confidential document that may interest you!" Rosebery spoke softly as he satisfyingly exhaled circular wisps of cigar smoke.

"What might that be?"

"We are in the final stages of implementing one of the most enterprising projects in East Africa – one that you have been pushing for, and will not only benefit the empire but also you."

"Could it be what I am thinking of?" Mackinnon asked, with impatience in his eyes.

"Yes! How does the building of a railway right from the port of Mombasa to Kampala sound to you?"

That statement surprised Sir William Mackinnon.

He had put forward this idea to the British government for some time now. He knew that the shortest route to the area that the Nile flowed from was through this remorseless land that only a few explorers like Thompson had ventured to.

His company, the British East India Company, had been contracted to provide mail services between Aden and Zanzibar. The contract also included distribution of mail to other remote parts of the Indian Ocean.

The mail contract in itself was not an attractive business proposition, but it was the vision of the trade that his ships could do in this area of East Africa, which was in the early stage of development, that had made Mackinnon push for greater involvement of the British government. Although he had business interests in Uganda, he was aware that if the British government did not financially back his company, he would have had to pull out from there.

"Finally, I see that my proposals have been taken seriously."

"You have many powerful friends in important positions." Rosebery smirked and further remarked, "Despite the opposition of some Members of Parliament, it will be made sure that this passes."

"When will the project begin?"

"I acknowledge that it may take two to three years for the building of the railway to actually start. There are various issues to solve till then. Sir Gerald Portal has been commissioned to investigate the matter and prepare a report. Let us keep this meeting and conversation between the two of us for now," Rosebery stated as he got up and ran his left hand over his tweed jacket, straightening any creases he thought were there.

Mackinnon stood up, his legs trembling slightly at the news he'd heard.

With a glint in his eyes, Lord Rosebery drew forward his hand to signal the end of the meeting.

"Start your preparation, Sir William Mackinnon," he said as they shook hands.

LONDON, ENGLAND
FEBRUARY 1890

"England to expand empire further!" shouted the young paper vendor on a frigid, dull and foggy morning in Fleet Street, London, as he tried to sell as many papers as he could.

In Parliament, the Foreign Secretary Lord Rosebery was making a statement in the Commons.

"It is of great importance that we maintain the lead in the expansion and the protection of the British Empire. We cannot stop at the Suez Canal. Strategically, East Africa is now extremely important in relation to Egypt. It has been confirmed that the area around Uganda has vast, untapped resources that would benefit the British public in every way," he exclaimed with an air of authority as he gazed over his reading glasses and looked directly at his fellow members of Parliament. "It is our moral duty to implement the abolition of slavery that we have worked tirelessly for."

"Aye!"

The House of Commons roared in agreement with Lord Rosebery. Prime Minister Gladstone nodded in agreement, endorsing what his Foreign Secretary was saying.

"Nay." Some MPs shouted, especially Henry Labouchère, who had always opposed this idea, which, according to him, was lunacy.

Everyone in the House of Commons knew that the Treasury was concerned about the increasing cost of subsidies for transport development in the empire at this time, and this was the kind of announcement that all wanted to hear.

Lord Rosebery had always had strong imperialistic leanings and was convinced that Britain had to expand overseas, and was outspoken in his views about a British Uganda.

MOMBASA, BRITISH EAST AFRICA
11TH DECEMBER 1885

As chief engineer, George Whitehouse was given the responsibility of overseeing the building of the railway by the British government. It was December 11th 1895 when he arrived in Mombasa aboard the *SS Ethiopia*, which was one of the British India Steam Navigation Company's 2,000-tonne ships.

He knew that the task that awaited him was huge and the timescale given to him by the government left no room for error. The Germans were already building a railway line 350 miles south of Mombasa, hoping to pass through the town of Bagamoyo before heading north towards the great lake. They already had a head start.

The humidity took a toll on Whitehouse when he disembarked the ship, but he was glad to see that he did not have to walk to the government offices on Vasco da Gama Street.

The British East India Company had laid a flimsy network of rails within the town, but instead of a train there was a Toonerville pushcart driven by African manpower that ran on the rails for the benefit of the few whites living there.

A few hundred yards from Vasco da Gama Street was a corrugated iron bungalow amongst palm trees that was the residence of HM Commissioner of the British East Africa Protectorate, Sir Arthur Harding. Whitehouse was to meet Harding here and discuss the final details of the civil project. Harding was the official communications link between Whitehouse and the British government. They were discussing the Macdonald report.

Macdonald's report was the endorsed record used by the government to reduce any difficulties anticipated in the building of the railway and included all the details that were thought essential for making the project a success.

Part of the report stated that the building materials required, as well as their transport, were going to be a colossal part of the project.

Inside the bungalow, Sir Arthur Harding read part of the report out loud to George.

"To reach the great interior lake, a total of 600 miles of track needs to be laid; this would involve over 200,000 individual thirty-foot lengths of rail tracks that weigh 500 pounds each. A total of over a million sleepers are needed, all steel. The wooden teak sleepers will be useless, as they will be infested with termites. To hold the rails on the sleepers, over 200,000 fishplates are required; 400,000 fishbolts and five million steel keys are needed!"

He let out a sigh. "This is staggering!" he exclaimed as he removed his reading glasses.

"We have accomplished huge projects before in India and I have the confidence that we can achieve the same here, sir," George said.

"Apart from this, there are unknown issues like materials required for constructing an unknown number of viaducts and bridges. Then, there is the matter of transporting the materials as well as the workers," Harding stated, pointing his glasses at George.

This, according to Whitehouse's calculations, necessitated at least thirty locomotives, brake vans, goods wagons and passenger carriages for the project to begin.

"Sir, the locomotives and goods wagons, as well as the workers, are all procured from India and will be here on time. Rest assured," George Whitehouse stated confidently.

"A truly astronomical effort will be needed to achieve this," Sir Arthur Harding commented.

This was the British at their best and the expansion of the British Empire was the end product of the expansion of the railway network in the colonies.

The report was discussed in depth and a final strategy was formulated. The meeting concluded with Sir Arthur Harding and Whitehouse shaking hands.

Part 1

Bath, England
January 1898

1

Faint wisps of fog were beginning to shroud the limestone plateau of the southern Cotswolds. The River Avon had a surreal silver shade that appeared to melt within the fog. There seemed to be no separation between the surface of the river and where the fog began.

The evening was a typical crisp winter's scene. The trees were devoid of any leaves; just bare, lonely branches that looked frail. It was frigid.

Just reading the sign outside the diminutive building in the centre of Bath was enough to feel a sense of warmth.

HOT MINERAL SPRINGS of BATH

The building was constructed on the corner of York Street and Stall Street, had opened six years previously and was the newest addition in Bath. It was called the Douche and

Massage Baths; a spa that utilised the hot water springs for therapeutic effect.

The complex contained a New Continental treatment suite, a Berthold vapour bath suite, an inhalation room, a pulverisation room and a general massage room. These rooms were lit up under the arched ceilings and had beautiful Roman tesserae as flooring.

As an extension of the Royal United Hospital, the baths were utilising the reputed healing properties of the water from the hot springs, which was at a constant temperature of 120 degrees Fahrenheit, to treat various conditions from stiff necks and muscular rheumatism to Scrivener's palsy and hysterical paralysis.

Catherine Rose walked through the high-ceilinged corridor on her way out, wearing a satisfied smile. *That was relaxing, as always*, she thought, adjusting her small, high, steel-blue hat.

There was nothing wrong with her health. Her father, Gilbert Rose, was a doctor who had worked at the Royal United Hospital and also at the spa three years ago, and it was because of him that she could occasionally visit and have a relaxing massage at no cost.

Everyone who knew her always cited her visits to the spa as the reason for her glorious smooth skin. She modestly offered her parents as an explanation for her features, but the truth was that she was blessed by having the best traits of both her parents.

She approached the door leading out.

"Goodnight, madam," the stout doorman greeted her as he lifted his hat and opened the wooden door for her.

"Goodnight," was her reply as she donned her white gloves on her feminine hands and stepped out onto the uneven pavement. Her scarf covered her silky ash-brown curls.

She let out a sigh that misted in the cold air and straightaway adjusted her winter cape, which was tailored from winter-weight Melton wool cloths and quilted on the inside to provide warmth.

Looking to her right, she saw the four-wheeled black brougham carriage stationary on the cobbled road.

"All ready to go, dear?" the familiar voice of her mother said.

"Nice to see you again, Mother, and thank you for coming to pick me up."

"Hop in carefully. Watch your step," Ethel Rose instructed her daughter in a concerned tone.

"It is a rather cold evening," Catherine commented as she huddled close to her mother in the carriage.

"True. We will be home soon and a hot supper will be ready for us when we get there."

The driver flicked the leather reins and the carriage jerked suddenly as the horses began their trot.

"You must be missing Father now that it has been one year since we last saw him," Catherine remarked.

"I do, but I have accepted your father's life and the man he is, although it is not easy." Ethel paused. "He can be obstinate."

Gilbert Rose had been posted in India for the past three years. He had always had an ambition to work abroad somewhere in the British Empire and experience a totally different way of living. At present, his work differed from a normal doctor's in the sense that he was a teaching practitioner at the Medical College in Lahore, which was linked to the Punjab University. It had been a difficult decision for him and his family but the opportunity to do much more than what he was doing in England was too good to miss. Dr Henry Freeman, a surgeon and friend who had worked with Gilbert at the Royal United Hospital in Bath, had informed him of the vacant teaching post in Lahore.

Gilbert had hoped to take his wife and daughter along with him to Punjab, but it did not work out. Thinking in great depth, both parents concluded that Catherine had to carry on with her studies in England before she could move abroad. The thought of leaving her by herself, although she would have stayed with her aunt in Rugby, was heartbreaking, especially for Ethel.

It was a dilemma with no clear path out of it, but, eventually, Ethel had persuaded her husband to pursue working abroad while she offered to stay with Catherine while she completed her education.

At first, he had declined, but with persuasion, he had reluctantly agreed, promising to visit them every year whenever it was possible.

This kind of situation was not unheard of. Anglo-Indian mothers knew that at one stage they would have to choose between living with their children in England or their husbands in India. It was a very unnatural way of living.

Some of the British who lived in India, mainly from the upper classes, sent their children back to England to study. They were afraid that, if educated in India, they might be pampered growing up surrounded by the ayahs and become spoilt, dictatorial and obese, or develop the high-pitched Indian accent.

There were all sorts of stories told about the British Raj in India, both enticing and dreadful. This was what created the mystery around the grand lives of the British living in the vast empire – a temptation.

"I cannot wait to see Father. I have missed him and it will be an exciting time there." Catherine beamed as she gently clasped her mother's arm.

"Yes, dear, although I'm a little concerned about how we will cope with living in a new place surrounded by new people with different cultures and—"

"And warmer weather as well," Catherine interrupted gleefully. "I am very much looking forward to visiting India."

"That does not surprise me." Ethel leaned her head and gazed straight into Catherine's eyes. "You have always had an interest in travelling, because of your father. Every time he took you with him as he travelled all over England, he unknowingly further sculpted your inner love for travelling."

Their conversation was suddenly muffled by the loud gallop of hooves on the street. From the adjoining Milsom Street, four men on horseback rode past their carriage at great speed, shouting and laughing.

"Drunken idiots," Ethel scoffed. "Some things just never change."

Coming from an upper-middle-class background, as well as having married into one, Ethel despised such behaviour. To her, it was rather unnecessary and showed the true social colours of a person.

In the early part of the 18th century, Bath was a resort full of charm, freshness and urban splendour. Every trendsetter was hoping to be associated with it.

After the crash of 1793, depression set in and new investment into the area dried up. Unemployment increased, resulting in the formation of Bath's slums in the low-lying southern part of the city. Vice dens sprung up, and with them the emergence of beggars and dipsomaniacs.

It was only in the last fifty years that the revival of Bath had recommenced and it was the coming of the railway in 1841 that started it.

"There is one last trip your father intends to make before he finally retires and returns home to England."

"Another place for me to visit, then?" exclaimed Catherine eagerly.

"No, I do not think that it will be a place for you or me."

"Why? Where does he want to go now that his contract is coming to an end in Punjab?"

"East Africa," Ethel replied scornfully.

"Now, that sounds even more adventurous! I will bear that in mind and talk to him… Tell me more about that."

"Not now, dear, we will discuss this another time, but whatever your question, the answer is a firm no."

The puffing of the horses became rapid; it was hard work

for them pulling the carriage as the incline increased as they approached the Roses' residence at the Royal Crescent.

The Royal Crescent was a residential road of thirty houses of beautiful Georgian architecture, all built to look like one huge building laid out in a crescent on a hill beyond the edge of the city, overlooking the vast communal lawn framed by the hill.

The carriage pulled up right outside Number 2, which was at the end of the cobbled crescent. The chill in the air had a numbing effect; even the door handles and leather seats in the carriage were now feeling harsh. The fog still lingered.

"There is nothing like the feeling of arriving home," remarked Ethel as the thought of a warm fireplace sent a comforting feeling through her.

"I cannot wait for supper." A sense of hunger hit Catherine's belly as she stepped out from the carriage.

"Have a good night, ladies," the driver wished them. Both mother and daughter lifted their dresses ever so slightly to keep the frills at their hems from getting dirty as they walked over the two stone steps leading to the door of their home.

The entrance hall was covered with wallpaper that replicated marble, as it would have been too costly to import the real thing. The pretty cornice ran through the entire hallway and the flagstones were all symmetrical. At the end of the passage was a tall wooden grandfather clock.

Catherine went straight up the wooden stairs that were on the left of the hall leading to her room, while her mother walked straight into the kitchen to instruct the cook to prepare supper.

Should I have told Catherine about her father's trip to East Africa or should I have waited until we are all together in India? Ethel pondered, not too sure how she felt about revealing her husband's possible future plan. *She would have found out eventually*, she tried to reassure herself as she watched the cook prepare supper.

An hour later, a dinner consisting of roast pork, potatoes and glazed carrots was over. The fire was crackling and Catherine was at the polished oak dining table, while her mother had just settled on the wooden chair next to the fireplace.

"So, Mother, tell me more about Father's next posting in East Africa."

Ethel remained silent. She did not want to have this conversation with her daughter at this very moment. Catherine stood up, walked towards the fireplace and tilted her head slightly to the left, placing her hand on her hips.

"Mother, you have not answered."

"We were meant to discuss this as a family." Ethel let out a deep sigh. "It was hoped that your father would be present as well."

"Do not worry, Mother, I am sure that Father would not mind."

Catherine was the only child in the family. Her birth had been difficult and complications had arisen. Although the Roses had intended to have more children, they never could. No one knew whether it was an unfortunate consequence of childbirth or not, but it did not matter. Catherine was the love of their lives and made up for any initial longings for more children that her parents might have had.

Despite her father working away from home, it did not affect their relationship; the distance made them closer as a family. Gilbert Rose always made sure that he visited his family as often as he could.

"When is he going to Africa, Mother?" Catherine asked inquisitively.

"As soon as we leave India for our return trip to England. Although he may change his mind and come with us before he takes the ship to the East African coast, if that works out."

"What is he going there for?"

"I think he has been offered work in some hospital. If he takes up the position, he will be responsible for the health of workers involved with some sort of civil engineering project that is backed by our government," Ethel replied as she stoked up the fire with the poker in her right hand.

"It seems like a harsh place compared to India, from what everyone says." Catherine paused for acknowledgement.

"I admit I am weary of your father working at that post. It is not easy, but with the realisation of the fact that it will be his last posting before he retires, I have come to terms with it."

Catherine gently walked towards her mother's chair, knelt down and gave her an affectionate hug.

"Everything will be fine, Mother, do not worry."

Lahore, Punjab, India
5th January 1898

2

It was a cold night. The still air of the day was overcome by the gentle breeze that blew across the field, causing a sudden chill for Kharak as he admired the starlit sky.

He rubbed his hands together for a little warmth as he walked back to his village, Rahmanpur, from the neighbouring village where he had been asked to take sweet rice – *jerdha*, the local dish – to his paternal uncle and aunt by his mother, Seva.

Kharak, being an affectionate eighteen-year-old, got on well with his Uncle Jaswant and Aunt Beas, who were a part of the close-knit Sikh community living in Lahore. Slim with a regular build, wheatish skin and a symmetrical face, to anyone else he would have seemed average, but he had a striking aura that drew people towards him. His hazel-brown eyes had a soft, disarming effect.

At night, the appearance of the fields surrounding Rahmanpur, which were three miles south of the walled city of

Lahore, was in contrast to how they looked during the day; the green hue of the early seedlings of wheat shooting in the golden sun of northern India versus the grey-silver carpet-like tufts swaying under the moon.

"I adore the beauty of this land," he mumbled to himself as he walked along the dirt path that separated the vast fields. "Such a shame that a lot of blood had been shed over the years for this freedom and it's still not over."

In the distance was an orange-yellow pin-like dot in the dark. A feeling of comfort swept through him as the light of the oil lamp from his house became visible.

As he approached his family home, he heard a familiar voice.

"How were Uncle and Aunt?" his father, Mann Singh, asked in his clear, statesmanlike voice while holding the lantern.

"They were fine and enjoyed the *jerdha* very much. Aunty was applying *takor* to Uncle's sprained ankle," Kharak replied.

Takor was the traditional therapy to help heal any injury on the body. It involved slicing a lemon in half and using one half draped in a cotton cloth. Oil and salt were heated on a flat steel pan, in which the lemon in the cloth was immersed for a few minutes until hot and then applied to the swollen or bruised area to help with the healing.

"He works too hard; it is not good for his health at his age. He needs to be more careful at the quarry," Mann Singh commented as he sat down on the *manji*, a traditional bed made from a wooden frame on four legs with two-inch-wide tweed belts weaved in an interlocking pattern right across the four sides to form the lying surface.

"He is very skilled at masonry, Father, and I have learned a lot from him. He is a proficient teacher," Kharak said proudly.

"Keep on learning your skills, son, it is your path forward," Mann reassured his son as he looked directly into Kharak's eyes with pride.

Mann Singh was tall with broad shoulders and a pointed Roman nose. His long, dark beard covered his rugged square jawline and his dark complexion gave away that he worked for prolonged periods in the sun. By donning a navy-blue turban, his dignified appearance was made complete.

"Father, you are a skilled carpenter and the time I have spent learning woodwork from you and stonework from Uncle is valued and I appreciate it."

"At the same time, don't neglect your training at university." Mann smiled as he massaged his masculine hands, which showed the telltale signs of his work.

"I'm honoured at being able to go to the Punjab University in these times when the British determine everything that happens around us, and I will make sure that these skills are complemented by learning new foreign concepts," Kharak replied in a thoughtful tone.

At this time, Lahore was becoming a centre of excellence and achieving what the British wanted: a class of people who were Indian in blood and colour but British in taste, opinions, morals and intellect. As a result, a Medical College was established in 1860 and thereafter the Punjab University was established in 1882.

Kharak was fortunate enough to be able to gain admission to the University of Punjab thanks to the achievements of his grandfather Ram Singh, who was a clerk to the district officer responsible for revenue collection in Punjab, and who in turn was appointed by Sir Henry Lawrence, one of the Board of Commissioners who were responsible for the administration of the region.

"Is everyone awake?"

"No. Your mother, brother and sister are all in bed after a long, tiring day in the fields. You got a bit delayed at your uncle's," his father pointed out.

"Sorry, I got carried away with Uncle's stories of life."

"Never mind, just be careful of the time in future, especially late at night," Mann answered as he got onto the *manji* and pulled up the blanket to cover him. "How is Uncle getting on with his current job with Mr Stanley? He is a difficult man to work for, you know."

"Methodically, as usual, but he does get fed up with all Mr Stanley's interference and fussiness," Kharak replied in a muted tone.

"He does work your uncle extremely hard, especially now that the foundations of the house are being laid," Mann added.

"It is like the more work he does, the more work he is given to complete. That's unfair," Kharak stated.

"That is how things are. When you work for someone else, this often happens. Well, you'd better go to sleep now and we'll talk in the morning."

"Goodnight, Father."

Kharak was the eldest of three children. Being born into a religious, stable and loving family, there was no sibling rivalry and his parents had made sure of a sound foundation in the long journey of life for all their children.

His younger brother Saran, who was twelve years of age, was from the same mould as Kharak, but still had that juvenile look that his brother did not have.

Neina, the baby of the family, was only ten. Adorable, talkative, full of love and always had a spring in her step. Kharak and Saran were always protective of their younger sister.

3

23rd January 1898

Lahore at this time was taking an important step as an administration centre in Punjab after over eighty years of Sikh rule, during which time it gained a great revival due to peace. Its eminence in the trading and manufacture of silks, woollens, carpets, swords, leather goods, arms and boats was growing.

The historical facts, stories and legends about the huge difficulties and sacrifices that were made by the great Sikhs of generations before were passed on from parents to their children.

Kharak was no exception. His grandfather Ram, in particular, had always made his grandchildren aware of this history while they were growing up.

One particular fact was etched in Kharak's mind. It was as vivid today as it was the day his grandfather had made him aware of it a few years back when he was a young boy.

He recalled that hot summer's day in Lahore. Kharak and his grandfather were sitting under the soothing, cool shade of the mango tree on their land on a blistering hot day, narrating the history.

"Kharak, grandson, today you and I would not be here if it were not for the unbelievable sacrifices that Sikhs of your great-grandfathers' era made. It was on February 5th in 1762 when the Afghan tyrant Abdali attacked the Sikhs in Kup. The Sikhs fought bravely and ferociously for their survival despite being heavily outnumbered," the barrel-chested Ram uttered passionately, his flowing grey beard following the movement of his mouth as he spoke.

"We were outnumbered, we had women and children to protect, and had fewer weapons. It is thought that ten to thirty thousand Sikhs lost their lives!" he added with regret in his voice. "It is known as *Wada Ghalughara*, or 'Great Disaster for the Sikhs.'"

Kharak was stunned.

"Two years later, in December, Abdali attacked our most important spiritual temple in Amritsar. There were only thirty brave Sikh soldiers in the temple at that time, who fought right to the end," his grandfather said with anger and pride. At the same time, Kharak saw his fist clenching. "Those evil people threw dead bodies in the temple's surrounding pool of water and made a pyramid of Sikh heads to try to scare us."

"Why is there such evil?" Kharak asked with a confused look.

"My dear child, that is life. There is always evil that tries to overcome good," was the prompt reply. "And good always overcomes evil," he reassured Kharak as he lovingly wrapped his big arms around him, giving a warm and secure hug.

Kharak had great adoration for his grandfather, who always had interesting facts and folk stories for him. They would laugh together and Ram Singh would always be playful with his grandson.

For two days afterwards, Kharak did not sleep well due to the emotional highs and lows the story provoked within him. He

16

later realised it was part of growing up and facing the challenges of life.

That was the third and last time that Abdali desecrated the sacred Fountain Temple, and that time the Sikhs avenged the horror by finally forcing the Afghans out of India and Punjab for all time.

It was in April 1765 that the Sikhs vowed to take Lahore, which was the Afghan seat of authority in Punjab. After a swift military action, the Sikhs accepted the surrender on 16th April 1765 and declared sovereignty over Punjab, and thus began the next phase of the revival of Lahore.

Now under the British, there had been rapid expansion, linking Lahore with the surrounding areas. There was a railway station now, which was a focal point not only for the travellers, but for the local people, who would spend their free time looking in amazement at the steam trains that would frequent it.

It was a grand work of British architecture. There were round bastions and tall machicolated towers, giving the station an imposing look. The architect had made sure it could be fortified into a colossal bunker if the need arose to deal with any uprisings of the locals.

Not very far from the railway station was the prominent building that was the Punjab University. Established in 1882, it was an exquisite building designed in the Muslim South Asian style of architecture, with red facades that were similar to some of the other British-built buildings in Lahore.

It was here that Kharak studied English and technical studies. He had spent two and a half years there, and those years had been fulfilling in every respect.

It was there he had met his great friend, Lal. They were enrolled on the same course, were of the same age and had an amicable understanding. Lal was a Hindu whose family had a tiny shop selling groceries in Anarkali Bazaar and, like Kharak, lived in the village of Rahmanpur on the outskirts of Lahore.

Kharak and Lal were now in their final months at the university and approaching a crucial point in their lives. As had been their daily routine for a while, they ambled through the narrow dirt street towards their university.

"What are your plans after we complete our studies?" Lal asked Kharak.

"Cannot say for sure. There is a huge pressure to get married, as I am way over the normal marriageable age due to my studies. I should have got married two or three years ago," he added with a slightly embarrassed look.

"Do not worry," Lal chuckled. "I'm in the same boat as you. Has your family found a bride for you?" he asked, as he put his hand over his forehead to protect his eyes from the morning sun, which was rising high in the clear sky directly ahead.

"No one at the moment that I know of."

Kharak knew that his family would find his lifelong partner. This was how it worked. It was tradition that his parents would choose which family his bride came from, and he would accept their decision.

"I intend to settle down soon," he said slowly, kicking a stone on the dirt track as he broke into a momentary skip.

"What about work? What will you do after you complete your studies?

"That's straightforward: I hope to join my father in woodwork and hopefully there will be plenty of work available."

"That's true; the British are developing Lahore and there are very many of them coming from England to live here. They will need to live somewhere," Lal added.

"What about you? What are your plans?"

Lal tilted his head, gazed at the sky and took a deep breath. "I want to travel and see newer places, maybe find work somewhere far away," he replied as he brushed his hair with his hand.

"Are you serious?" Kharak asked, furrowing his left eyebrow in surprise.

"Yes, I am."

"Well, good luck with that."

Kharak knew that his friend was very ambitious and had competitive streak in him. He could not see him running his father's little shop with its stall in the future.

"What will your parents say about all this travelling?" he asked.

"That I do not know, but as long as it is sensible and will improve my prospects, it should be fine." There was a pause. "As long as the family name rises with honour, that's what matters to them."

"Then you will have to be extremely careful with every decision you take." Kharak smiled.

They were emerging into the city from the narrow alleys, right into the centre of Lahore. The horse-drawn rickshaws were already busy on the roads. They were wooden, two-wheeled and decorated with a variety of colours and ornaments, like peacocks displaying their majestic feathers. Some had canvas roofs to provide relief from the unforgiving summer sun or a deluge of rain during the monsoon season.

"Let's purchase one of these rickshaws. You could ride it in the morning and I could ride it in the afternoon," Lal suggested cheekily.

"That might be your kind of work, but it's not mine."

"Don't take it so seriously," Lal laughed as he patted Kharak's shoulder in mischief.

After another twenty minutes of brisk walking, they crossed the dirt road and were heading straight to the Punjab University entrance.

The terracotta stone building stood magnificently with a definite presence in the morning sunlight, its white clock standing out in the main dome tower.

"What field experience are you planning to undertake for the last three months of our course?" Kharak wanted to know.

"Most probably the aspects of railway engineering," was the ready reply.

"Mmm…" Kharak rolled his lips inward in contemplation. "What about you?"

"I have thought about it for a while and narrowed it down to two options." Kharak gazed up at the blue sky as they approached the entrance. "Either irrigation and canal engineering, or, like you, the railways."

"You are taking too long to decide; we have to decide by next week," chuckled Lal.

"I need to think." Kharak let out a deep sigh as he turned his head and looked above at the clock on the tower.

This decision would ultimately decide his direction in life and what fate would throw upon him. A direction that even he had never imagined or made plans for.

Mombasa
Eight Months Earlier: 30th May 1897

4

The long rainy season that runs from late March to May in East Africa was nearing an end, and this was evident in the clear cobalt-blue sky. Apart from a few small pools of stationary water on the cleared ground, there was hardly any evidence of the rain from the previous day.

The mid-morning sun in Mombasa accentuated the mugginess in the air. There were British railway officials and dignitaries, most of whom were dressed in white cotton shirts and suits and replica white Wolseley Pith helmets, seated on the wooden chairs that were set up in front of the flat, rocky outcrop overlooking the cleared ground. Their wives sat next to them, all dressed up and wearing hats to protect their faces and flaunt their status. Surprisingly, despite the insects and flies that were commonly found here, none of these hats were netted fascinator hats.

George Whitehouse, the chief engineer of the project,

was absent as he had another important engagement to go to. Everyone sitting had been hoping to hear a few words from him relating to this project.

A few palm trees overhanging from behind provided brief moments of shade to some of the people in the rear seats. Elsewhere, there was no reprieve from the direct sun as there was no shade; the only consolation was the brass band playing tunes that were familiar to the dignitaries.

White chalk-markings drawn around wooden pegs dug into the ground were visible on the cleared ground and these ran as two parallel lines. This was the 'laying of the first rails' ceremony to mark the start of the Mombasa-to-Uganda railway line, the self-important building project of the British in this part of Africa, striving against the Germans.

On the opposite side were a group of Indians, the majority of whom donned workers' gear and held pikes and shovels as they stood next to a pile of steel sleepers, ballast and Vignoles-pattern steel rails. The soil here at the coast was salty, therefore steel sleepers had to be used instead of pine sleepers.

These were the first of the nearly two thousand workers engaged from India by the British to help construct the railway line. More would be called upon.

Only a handful of them stood out as they were dressed in uniform – they were the supervisors. One of these was a Sikh named Ungan Singh, who was tall, brawny and had a thick beard.

His responsibility on this day was to oversee the initial breaking of ground and ensure that the laying of the first rails went smoothly and according to the requirements of the engineers. A lot of taxpayers' funds were at stake and the government had been under pressure over this mammoth project.

Fredrick O'Callaghan, who was the managing member of the Uganda Railways Committee, gave a brief speech instead of George Whitehouse, stating the importance of the project.

Though it was brief, the speech was inspiring to the British seated and they punctuated it with claps and vocal agreement.

"I officially declare this project started!" he shouted, pointing his hands towards the ground.

Claps and cheers from the crowd completed his speech as the workers and engineers began their operation.

MARIAKANI, BRITISH EAST AFRICA
JANUARY 1898

Mariakani is about twenty-three miles from the port town of Mombasa and still within range of the moisture-rich trade winds that blow from the Indian Ocean from March to May, giving rise to the long rainy season. This area around the Rabai Hills is rich green, with wooded forests consisting of a variety of species of trees like the Mvule, which are a solid hardwood trees; huge baobab trees and the impregnable thorn trees.

In the distance, between the two low valleys, angry grey clouds were beginning to form, yet the sun was shining on the railhead, making the steel rails gleam.

"I must admit that it is difficult working in these humid conditions," an Indian worker exclaimed to his colleague.

"These Mvule trees are annoying to work with and I have never come across such hard work," a third worker added in despair.

This was the most forward group of workers, five miles ahead of the tracks. Their work was to clear the land ahead in preparation for the platelaying work as the railway track moved forward. The work was slow; on average, 300 yards of path were cleared in a single day, which was sluggish.

Ungan Singh was the foreman of this group of workers for part of the day. A devoted worker compared to some of the others, who at times were indolent and would look for any reason to slow down.

"We are running behind schedule. The weather has not helped us in any way with all the rain," Ungan said as he gauged the work that had been completed since the morning.

"I cannot work any quicker. I only have two hands," said a voice from the back. The worker made sure that he was not seen, but only heard.

"Think of it this way: the sooner this project ends, the sooner we can go back home to our families and away from this uncomfortable situation," Ungan replied with conviction and truth in his voice, while gazing directly into the eyes of the workers.

Some of the workers understood what was being said, while others just smirked. One could understand their circumstances. In the last two months, the East African coast had received rainfall that had never been seen before in that region. This had altered the working environment totally and such a scenario had not been considered in the planning of this huge project.

All of a sudden, an Indian worker standing not very far from Ungan felt an uncontrolled spasm in his belly. Next, he sensed a deep, sharp pain and nausea, together with cold sweat overwhelming him. His instinct made him look around and on spotting the nearest dense scrub, he dashed off.

Another victim of the dreaded loose motions, Ungan thought to himself. "Make sure you cover your pit with soil completely. The rest of us do not want to join you in your condition!" he shouted at the Indian running behind the bush.

The poor man, clutching his white dhoti, the cloth tied around the waist by Hindus in the subcontinent, barely managed to reach the bush before his involuntary bowel movement gripped him. The environment was playing havoc with some workers' stomachs.

It was mid-afternoon and, after a brief rest without any further incident, Ungan Singh led the workers back to their task.

24

He, like the others, knew that the grey clouds forming were an ominous sign that a rainstorm was brewing.

"Looks like we are going to have another deluge of rain again this evening. I'm fed up of it," Chand remarked.

"On that point, I agree with you." Ungan turned his head to Chand as he put his palm on the trunk of a young Mvule tree.

"The ground is soggy due to the rain we have had over the past two months and yet they say this is the *short* rainy season," Chand said, unable to hide the scorn in his voice. "The working conditions are appalling. Look at my feet! All I see is mud and filth." There was a brief pause. "The ground is slippery and the bottom of my dhoti gets mucky with mud splashes."

"It's a bit like India during the monsoon, is it not?" the coolie next to Chand pronounced, trying to remind him that these conditions were not entirely alien to them, unlike their few British supervisors.

"You are right. Well, I've had my few minutes of moaning and I feel better." Chand forced a smile.

"Here comes the worker with diarrhoea out from the bush," said another labourer, laughing as he saw the rather relieved worker emerge, tying his dhoti and looking slightly better. This was his third visit to the bush.

"Turning to work, fellows, you must be aware that we have approached a 400-foot-wide ravine, which is just 200 yards ahead. That will slow us down, as we will have to wait for directions from John Allen and George Whitehouse," Ungan stated.

John Allen was the chief engineer at the railhead and a man with vast railway experience, having previously worked in India with the expansion of the railway network there. Although he had worked in the Indian subcontinent, he still had not mastered the language sufficiently to be able to understand it as well as give direction. This was a hindrance to effective communications with the Indian workers, and at times led to him fuming not at himself or the workers, but at the whole situation. He often wished that there could be some sort of translator to overcome this problem.

The angry grey clouds were now upon the Mariakani Hills. Thunder halted the muttering amongst the rail workers. It was the clouds' turn to be heard and feared. The distant low valleys that had been clearly visible earlier could not be seen; they were hidden by the convectional rain falling there.

"Time to call it a day," a concerned Ungan said, looking at the sky. He was well aware of the hazards in heading back to camp in the rain and increasing darkness. The tropical dusk approaches quickly and the rain has a synergistic effect on this.

It was four o' clock, and this afternoon felt different. There were no birds singing; the wind had picked up, causing the branches to sway wildly, and as it passed through the leaves, it created a howling effect. The rain could be seen moving towards them.

"Will we make it on time?" a worried Chand asked.

"Do not worry."

In a very short space of time, the tools were gathered and all the workers were walking hurriedly back through the clearing that had been forged by them in the past few days and heading towards their camp, which was a two-mile walk away.

The blue sky that had been visible earlier was now totally covered with the grey clouds, and the air felt cooler and moist on the skin. Ungan had made a count of all the workers before they began their trek back to make sure no one was left behind a bush.

"Men, listen." Ungan spoke to his colleagues in a wavering tone as he moved hastily. "I know I have mentioned it before, but if it does rain, nobody takes shelter under any tree. Is that understood?" His voice got sterner.

When he spoke, everyone in his group listened.

"If we get wet, we get wet. No hiding under trees." He knew the dangers of standing under a tree during a thunderstorm; he had heard stories of people dying and trees catching fire due to thunder and lightning.

"And let's all be careful while walking. Watch your footing and the thorns. We do not want any more infected wounds. There are already enough people unwell due to carelessness."

Chand began to exchange views with his workmate about the health of the others who were unwell and being treated for disparate conditions.

"There are over a hundred workers ill and being looked after at the medical camp further down the line." He paused to take a breath. He was not one of the fitter workers. "Some are suffering from illnesses that I have never come across."

"Damn these vicious thorns. Never get pricked by them," was the sound advice from his fellow worker. "They can turn severely septic and I've seen them get really bad," he added while grimacing.

"Are you aware that last month was really bad?" Chand lowered his voice as if he did not want anyone nearby hearing what he was saying; a bit fatuous considering that the baying wind would have made it impossible.

His companion lowered his head closer to Chand's face in order to hear clearly, while holding the strap of the canvas bag of tools that was hanging from his left shoulder, preventing it from slipping down.

It started drizzling.

"Last month was mournful. The dreaded malaria struck and there were nearly 500 of our mates down with it." Chand let out a deep breath. "There was a shortage of space in the hospital tent and they were leaking in the rain. I never want to be in that state!"

"Who falls ill next? One does not know, especially here in the jungle."

This was nature at its worst, from a human point of view. The short rains that had started three months ago were showing no signs of abating. Normally, they lasted up to the beginning of December, but it was now January and it was still raining. The ground was moisture-rich and sodden. Puddles of water collected at every opportunity, especially where the earth-moving workers had excavated. This became a fertile breeding ground for mosquitoes to multiply, causing the malaria epidemic to surface.

It was not only the wild animals and fierce tribes that were to be feared: these tiny insects that were often overlooked were ferocious in drawing blood. They could only be ignored at one's own peril.

The cracking sound of thunder jolted quite a few workers as they walked hurriedly.

This does not look good, Ungan thought. He knew that there was another mile to walk to their base camp and there was the smaller tributary of *Maji ya Chumvi* to cross. This was the native name of a stream, meaning 'salty water', that flowed through a chasm, but due to the rains, it was flowing more like a river now. There had been a temporary viaduct built to cross it as the main railway track had not yet reached there – a permanent one was going to be built as soon as the rains stopped.

"Come on," Ungan urged as he waved his hand with urgency.

The thunder cracked and the rain finally arrived. Tropical rain in Africa was a stunning sight. It started with a drizzle on the dry soil longing for rain. The aroma that rose due to the moisture and dry earth as they coalesced was one of the most alluring natural fragrances the weather had created.

Ungan Singh and his workers were in no mood to appreciate this. They had to get back.

A bolt of lightning blazed through the grey clouds as the rain increased in intensity and an unusual darkness swept the area. The raindrops were now huge and stung the faces of the workers as they broke into a run; it felt like needles touching the skin.

The heavens had virtually split open, the rain was falling very heavily, and even the leaves felt the pounding of it. The baobab trees were a strange grey as the rain had washed the dust away from their bark.

Puddles formed on the ground where it was flat and little streams of surface water flowed across the ground as gullies. Visibility was reduced to fifty feet.

Ungan knew that they all had to cross the *Maji ya Chumvi* chasm as soon as possible; the risk of flash floods was real as these were common with this kind of rain, especially as it had been raining in the surroundings hills.

Everyone was now hurrying in single file, with Ungan at the front constantly turning his head to make sure all were following. Not only were there splashes as the raindrops hit the ground, but also as running feet hit the puddles of water. Their cotton clothing was soaking wet, their footwear was squelching and rainwater was dripping from their faces. The storm had not lost any energy; it was pouring. It felt cold.

The ferocity of the rain was unyielding. The already-saturated soil could take no more and muddy brown water could be seen all around, either in puddles or gushing along the gradient.

As the chasm neared, the vegetation around it got denser and the slope got steeper. The approach to the temporary viaduct was naturally concealed behind the rocky ridge, which was now slippery in the wet; care had to be taken.

"Carefully now," Ungan shouted. "It is going to be slippery so watch your step."

As he moved round the ridge and approached the chasm, he saw what he had never expected to see. Or not see.

There was no viaduct!

It seemed to have been washed away. All that remained were wooden poles on either side of the chasm – between, the water, at an extremely high level, flowed in torrents.

Their camp was on the other side. The rain was still coming down and it took a while for it to sink in. They were stranded!

Lahore
February 1898

5

Kharak and Lal were in the Anarkali Bazaar, sitting at the rear of Lal's father's grocery stall, having a rare break from university. It was a basic brick building with the main structures made out of wood. The sloping roof was constructed with red clay tiles, which were laid in a haphazard manner; the finish was similar to the other stalls in the bazaar.

In the little shop, there was a raised earthen platform on which were hemp baskets filled with wheat, lentils, nuts, rice and spices. Behind this was the raised counter with just enough space for the trader to stand and be within reach of all items. On the wall facing the platform were baskets that were hung for sale, whereas at the bottom of the wall were three different mats rolled up and resting against it.

"I cannot wait to start work, now that I have decided what to do." Kharak smiled.

"That will be a laugh; you and I doing our final few weeks

of work together on the railways." Lal beamed with his toothy grin. "So, what made you decide on the railways rather than the irrigation engineering?"

It had not been an easy decision for Kharak to come to. The huge irrigation canals that crossed the farmland in Punjab, and their construction, had always intrigued him, and their ability to transport water for miles from the rivers to the wheat fields never ceased to amaze him. He enjoyed spending time on the banks of River Ravi, which flowed right along the edge of Lahore. It was on the banks that he often reflected on his life and took time out to be alone in contemplation.

"I cannot say exactly why."

"Your decision surprised me totally. I thought that you would have done irrigation engineering."

"Nearly did it." Kharak raised his eyebrows and let out a smile.

"And I thought I knew you pretty well."

"I think that railway work involves a lot more hands-on work in terms of skill required, and that's what I already have: masonry and woodwork and..." There was a pause.

"And what?"

"It felt right. I cannot explain but it was as if there was something drawing me to it."

"So it was gut instinct?"

"If that is what you wish to call it. Remember, though, that I also knew I would be working with you." Kharak winked.

The glass of lassi went down well after the midday meal; the light, yogurt-based drink with a peppery tinge was refreshing.

"That was satisfying. Your mother makes the best lassi in the bazaar."

"Another glass for you?"

"No thank you. I think we ought to make our way to the campus and get registered with the Punjab Railways officials. Also, we need to collect our new uniforms."

"Oh, nearly forgot about that. I don't want to be late and take our next step on the wrong foot and look like idiots." Lal stood up and took the empty glass from Kharak's hand.

Minutes later, they walked along the narrow, dusty path that encircled the stall and led to the front and onto the bustling Anarkali Street.

At the front of the stall, Lal's father was seated.

"Thank you for the lovely lunch, Mr Sena," Kharak said courteously.

"Do not mention the thank you, but do come again," Mr Sena replied, raising his hand and smiling, revealing the gap of his missing front tooth.

"You know to treat this like your own house and you are welcome at any time," Mrs Sena said warmly as she stood at the doorway that led into the tiny shop.

"Thank you, and I am aware of that, Mr and Mrs Sena."

"We are off to the campus now to collect our uniforms. I will see you in the evening," Lal interrupted.

Lal's parents were very fond of Kharak. Right from the first time they met him, they were glad that he and Lal were close friends, and it was reassuring to know that he was in good company. To them, he was like the second son they never had and they treated him as part of their family of three children: Lal and his two sisters.

"Do pass our warm regards to your parents from us, Kharak."

"I will."

Due to their friendship, both families had become close and frequently visited each other. Although the Sena family was Hindu and Kharak's were Sikh, they were all from the same community of Lahore.

Luckily for them, the midday spring sun was not as intense; the mid-year heat can be strength-sapping in the Anarkali Bazaar. The walk to the Punjab University from the bazaar was approximately two miles of narrow lanes with small shops and stalls on either side.

"I think that we will look immaculate in our new uniforms." Lal gleamed as he placed his hands in his pockets, trying to visualise how he might feel in it. "Just like the British we will look, wearing our trousers and shirts. Everyone will be staring at us."

"Yes, actually, that will be something new for us to look forward to, apart from hard work."

There were numerous bull carts and rickshaws along the road, moving in all directions, and everyone seemed busy with their own work.

The city of Lahore had thirteen gates; one of which was the Lohari Gate. To the south of this ran the Anarkali Bazaar, which led to the modern part of the city with its broad streets and sandstone buildings, which gave it a British feel. One could see a few white British people wearing their immaculate three-piece suits – noticeable in this part of Lahore as the various colonial governmental offices were established here.

The road that ran towards the west led to the Punjab University. It took them a good forty minutes to walk there. Upon reaching the campus building, they took the nearest flight of steps to room marked *2A*, which was at the end of the corridor on the first floor.

Kharak knocked on the door and there was an immediate reply – "Come in" – in a heavy British accent.

In the office, sat behind a wooden table, was a British man with a bushy brown moustache and round-rimmed spectacles that rested low on the bridge of his nose. There was a tweed coat with the initials *B.I.R.* embroidered on it hanging from the coat hanger behind the chair where the man sat. He was the British Indian Railway official attached to the university and was responsible for the work placement positions in the railway-engineering department.

"What can I do for you?"

"Good afternoon. I'm Kharak Singh and this is Lal Sena, and we are here to register for our work positions."

The man took off his spectacles and shifted his gaze towards them. "Let me have a look in the register and see if I can find your names listed," he said in a raspy voice.

A black hardback register was retrieved from the drawer under the table and placed on the table. *This is it*, Kharak thought. As the registrar flicked the pages over to find the appropriate page, Lal turned his head slightly towards Kharak and raised his eyebrows in anticipation. Kharak winked in acknowledgement.

"Ah, here we are." The man's finger moved down a list on a page. "Yes, I can see your names on the register." He then got up and walked towards the cupboard at the far corner of the room. Two paper-wrapped parcels were picked from the cupboard and placed on the table. "There you go, young men. This is your uniform."

There was a pause as he read out the name on each parcel.

"This is for you." He pointed at Kharak's parcel. "And this is for Lal Sena."

There was a sense of relief for both; the wait was over and it was finally sinking in that they were very soon entering the workforce.

The registrar handed them each an envelope. "This gives you all the details of your work, the times and whatever you will need to know. Report to work on Monday morning at nine o' clock at the engineers' yard, which is located in the western part of the main railway station."

"Thank you so much," Kharak and Lal said in unison.

"Before you leave, have a look at this poster about a well-paid employment opportunity that has come up." The man pointed to the poster on the wall beside him.

They both turned around and looked keenly at the poster. It stated that the British were hiring manual labourers as well as railway workers with an engineering background from India to work for them in East Africa. The pay on offer was very generous and all transport costs were paid for.

"This could be the way forward for you young gentlemen for a better future. This kind of opportunity seldom comes."

"Thank you for informing us; we shall think about it," Lal said hurriedly as he looked at Kharak for agreement.

"Good luck, young chaps, and do think about it seriously," the registrar said.

Without wasting any time, they were both out of Room *2A* and heading out of the campus, clutching their parcels firmly in their hands.

"Let's go back to Anarkali Bazaar and celebrate, as from Monday you know we will be very busy with work," Lal said excitedly. "What do you think?"

"I've got to go back home now and share the good news with my family; they will be waiting for me. I will probably see you over the weekend."

"That is fine. I will definitely see you the weekend before we start work and we can discuss it then."

"Do not forget to try on your uniform to see if it fits," Kharak laughed. "We don't want to look like idiots on Monday."

They laughed together, shook hands and went their separate ways, each wrapped in their own thoughts of exhilaration mixed with anticipation.

Home was where Kharak intended to go straight afterwards, but there was an inner urge to pass by the River Ravi, hence he decided to take the route home that ran partly by the edge of the river. The brisk walk took half an hour through the streets of Lahore, past the imaginary outer boundary of the European Quarter, which the majority of the Europeans, especially the British, frequented.

The narrow loose dirt track snaked over the grassy alluvial plain, leading to the edge of the river. A few yards off the track was the evergreen neem tree, with its shiny, serrated dark green leaves providing welcoming shade. This was his favourite place overlooking the river.

He sat under the tree, taking a deserved rest from his walk, gazing at the flowing river with a lone fisherman's boat bobbing on the opposite shore. Kharak felt an inner contentment with what he had achieved so far: his course was over now, work at the railways beckoned, at least in the immediate future, and he was proud of that.

"Next will be the issue of settling down and getting married," he thought aloud.

He was aware that his family would want him to get married very soon now that his course was completed. In India, everyone got married at an early age and he was surprised that his family had been fairly liberal when compared with others.

I will just have to wait and see what unfolds next, he thought as he threw a stone in the river and watched it skim the surface. He grinned as he picked up another stone; he enjoyed that.

Another five minutes were spent in this way before he decided to trek back home as the shadows were lengthening.

As he got up, he noticed a British couple walking in the distance holding hands. It made him raise his brow and he smiled.

Perhaps one day, he thought as he stared up at the distant sky.

Kharak's mother, Seva, was busy feeding their herd of cows with freshly cut native alfalfa grass in the early evening sun. In the cattle paddock, there were four young calves getting animated as they saw the adults grazing hungrily. The paddock did not cover a large area. It was located adjacent to the farmhouse and had a woodshed to provide a warm area for the animals during the cold season. Located at the edge of the enclosure was a collection pit for dung, which was then made into fuel bricks and these provided energy when burnt. Seva mainly had the duty for this, although everyone helped out whenever they could.

The stone farmhouse and the paddock were in the centre of a five-acre piece of land dotted with mango and pomegranate trees, with maize, melons and local vegetables, like spinach, growing.

Neina was busy handing over the grass to her mother as she fed the animals. Two red ribbons stood out in her plaited hair as if two flowers had been placed in the plaits. When she saw Kharak walking along the dusty track, she dropped the grass that she was carrying and ran towards him.

"Hello, Neina," he said as he walked towards her, leaned forward and lifted her.

"How was your day, son?"

"Very well, actually." He broke into a smile. "I got my registration completed and I was given my uniform." He showed his mother the parcel. "Work starts on Monday at the railway station."

"I'm happy that you succeeded in getting work there," she said with a forced smile, "but I hope that your time there finishes quickly."

"Why do you not want me to work there?"

"It's just the loud metal machines that move and whistle that I do not like. They scare me!"

"Oh, Mother, they are known as trains and you do not have to be afraid of them. I'm not going to hang and swing from them as they move." Kharak tried to ease his mother's anxiety. He reached out and opened his arms and gave her a big, warm hug.

"Lal will be working with me, hopefully at the same place, and we will be together. It has been our aim for a while; all those days and hours that we have put in was for this."

"I am proud of you, my son. Ignore my worries, as you know, at times, I worry unnecessarily." She squeezed his hand affectionately and the frowns on her forehead eased and disappeared slowly. He was still her baby son, despite his age.

Bath
February 1898

6

It was the night before they were due to travel to India. It was a typical winter's night outside; cold, but it had not snowed for a while.

"Have you packed your suitcases, Catherine?" Ethel asked as she walked through the bedroom door.

"Yes, Mother. This is the fourth time you have asked me tonight. You shouldn't worry."

"How can I not worry? As a mother, it is normal to be anxious."

"You know that's not true, Mother; you do tend to worry unnecessarily at times. I know you." She smiled.

Catherine found that getting prepared for travel to the British India was quite a task, as she had to make sensible choices when buying clothes. Her mother had told her over and over that clothing that was suitable for one part of India would not be suitable for another, which implied that clothes for humid

Madras, for example, would not be appropriate for the winter months in Punjab.

Catherine's father Gilbert was in Lahore and had kept in touch and written to them often, describing the weather and living conditions, and had advised them what to bring and what not to bring, as the local dressmakers in Bath had no such experience.

For women, the main items that were considered essential were flannel suits and Assam silk suits, as well as an evening dress coat, a frock coat and for informal occasions a dinner jacket. Another couple of unusual necessities were a tea basket and a small tin case, which was just large enough to carry sandwiches while travelling.

The leather suitcases were all packed and were resting under the stairs in the hallway, ready for the early morning departure.

"Goodnight and sleep well tonight. Get a full night's sleep. You shall need it."

"I shan't be long before I retire to bed. Goodnight and see you in the morning, Mother." She hugged her mother and kissed her cheek.

Ten minutes later, Catherine was tucked up comfortably in her cosy and warm feather-filled bedding and duvet. *I will most definitely miss this bed*, she thought. She was excited at the prospect of travelling to India and to be able to capture a new visual and cultural experience; maybe they would even manage a tiger expedition.

I wonder what it will be like and whom I will meet? That was her last thought before she drifted into sleep. She had had a tiring day.

Outside, the wind howled mercilessly in the dark night.

At eight o' clock the following morning, there was a knock on her door.

"Catherine."

It woke her up. Still groggy, she instantly recognised the maid's voice.

"It's eight o'clock in the morning and it is time to wake up. We cannot be late and miss our ship."

Filled with exhilaration, Catherine wasted no time in getting out of her warm bed and heading to the window. Drawing one of the curtains to take a look outside, it was still grey and, for the first time, she was glad that it had not snowed during the night. The room felt comfortable; the maid had got the fire going in the fireplace since the early morning.

Within thirty minutes, she was ready and seated at the kitchen table for breakfast. She picked up a slice of granary bread.

"Thinking about it, I will miss a lot of things from here."

"One thing: do not get too friendly with strangers," Ethel said sternly.

"I'm not like that." Catherine quickly cut her mother short. "You are exaggerating." She grinned.

"I wish I was. I know my own daughter," Ethel said, gazing directly at her while spreading strawberry conserve liberally on her slice of bread.

"Anything else?"

"Not that I can remember," Ethel replied as she relished the sweet flavour of the conserve on the crispy bread.

Breakfast was over in half an hour and all work in the kitchen was completed thereafter. Food that was left over in the larder was to be given to the Knightleys who lived next door and had promised to keep an eye on the Roses' residence while they were away.

The brougham carriage was waiting outside, ready to take them to the railway station.

"Good morning, ladies," their driver said in greeting. "I'll take your suitcase, madam. You don't have to pick it up."

"Thank you very much."

The driver secured the suitcases on the rails on the roof of the black carriage with great care.

Catherine felt the cold breeze pinch her cheeks as she sat inside. The winter sun was trying to break through the grey clouds on this winter's morning as they were about to embark to the railway station.

A quick flick of the leather reins and the horses broke into a trot on the cobbled surface and headed towards the end of the arc that was Royal Crescent and onto Brock Street.

Mrs Rose could not help turning her head to see the curve of the house fade into the background. "It feels unnatural knowing that we will be away for a while," she whispered, still conscious of the need to hide the fact from the driver.

They were now on Brock Street, which linked Royal Crescent to the Circus, two spectacular areas of urban creation. The Circus was another architectural masterpiece, with houses built around a circular street with three other streets approaching it and dividing it into three arcs. It was paved throughout without any interruptions and gave a sense of defined space, with plenty of light and fresh air in the urban development on the gentle hill.

The carriage turned right onto Gay Street, which was one of the three streets that started from the Circus. The railway station was a short ride away.

Within fifteen minutes, Catherine and Ethel were in the station and on the platform under the closed roof. The train to Bristol was embarking within the next half hour.

The journey to Bristol was uneventful apart from the Great Western Railway viaduct that was designed to carry the railway line over the Avon River. It was like the entrance to a university with its Gothic doorways. The train chugged through the vicinity of Salford, Kensham and finally into Bristol Station.

The train whistled slowly into the platform under the box-frame roof and cast-iron columns above the Tudor arches.

This was Temple Meads Station in Bristol, the oldest railway terminus with an elegant station building. Although the harbour was a walking distance away, they decided to take a carriage there as they had their accompanying suitcases.

"I'm cold," Catherine said as she adjusted her grey mantle cloak to cover as much of her as possible. "It will be a relief to be inside the ship."

"We are nearly there now. There – can you see the ship docked?" Ethel pointed her gloved hand in the direction of the ship, which could be seen, together with the P&O sign on its hull, docked in the harbour. There she was, the ship that was going to take them to the port of Southampton, first for a brief two-hour stopover before continuing the nearly four-week journey to Karachi in British India through the Suez Canal.

The porters were loading the suitcases into the hull as Catherine kept staring at the boarding passes in her hand, reaffirming that the trip was real.

"Come on," her mother said as she gestured towards the boarding gangplanks on her way into the ship.

Catherine took a small step towards the gangplanks, lowered her face and gazed at her feet. A pensive smile appeared on her face.

She was halfway along them when she turned her head to see how far she had walked. *I wonder what this journey will reveal*, she thought.

Thirty Miles From Lahore
March 1898

7

Beneath the hazy blue midday sky, the railway track went as far as the eye could see. It was a grand sight of two parallel metal lines that seemed to converge on the horizon. This was the Lahore-to-Jhelum line, which had been completed twenty years earlier. It was the gateway to Kashmir and Jhelum, a city founded by Alexander the Great and named Alexandria Bucephalous after his horse that died there in battle.

Kharak and Lal had been based in Jhelum for the past two weeks. Their work involved the repair and maintenance of the track that crossed the Jhelum River under the guidance of the local British engineer. They had a couple of days off from work before being posted for a while at the railway yards in Lahore Station to take part in repair work on the tracks.

The train clicked and clacked along at an increasing pace as the mountainous terrain changed to a flatter one.

"Lal, what do you think of the experience gained here over

the last two weeks?" Kharak asked, scratching an itch on his forearm as the breeze blew across the train carriage.

"It was just putting theory into practice," was the short reply. "Already, I am looking forward to the two-day break back home."

"I can see that you missed home."

"No. Definitely not." Lal cut him short. "Mother's cooking, I did miss."

"I must say, we do look very different from everyone in our village when we wear this uniform," Kharak exclaimed as he straightened his collar with a twinkle in his eye.

"The memsahibs better watch out! Two dashing young Indian men out," Lal chuckled in response.

Looking out of the moving train, Kharak's thoughts wandered off to what Lal had just mentioned. *It would be nice if that could be true, albeit just for a while.* He arched his right eyebrow and smiled as the green fields passed by.

Twenty miles from Lahore Station, there was a train from Multan. Only about fifty miles separated the two trains and with every minute that passed, the distance between them got shorter.

Seated in one of the first-class carriages were two British ladies.

"We are nearly there now," sighed Ethel as she adjusted herself on the leather seat.

"It has been a treasure for the eyes, Mother. So much to take in over the past four weeks – I have been astonished at the sights and different colours. That excitement kept my spirits up," Catherine said, adjusting her hat over her hair in preparation for their arrival. "I wonder if Father will be waiting for us at the station?"

"Of course he will be there."

A soft knock interrupted their conversation. It was the porter, who had to collect the teapot and china cups from their cabin.

It had been a gruelling journey. The newer train route was from the port of Karachi to Multan, from where they changed and boarded the train to Lahore.

Looking out from her cabin, Catherine saw the green wheat fields dotted randomly with vivid colours. Women were working in the fields and their traditional dresses stood out.

Feeling warm, Catherine unbuttoned the top of her blouse, hoping that it would ease the discomfort.

"You will have to get used to this climate. Here, take this, it will be of use." Ethel took out a fabric pocket fan and handed it to her.

"Thank God you remembered this." Without any hesitation, Catherine fanned air across her face, blowing her curls away from her forehead.

Forty minutes later, more rail tracks appeared, running along the main line. Minutes after, the train slowed and the rail sheds of Lahore Station were seen in the near distance. It had been a long and wearying journey and the thought of an end to it was a welcome relief.

Catherine grasped the leather handle of her suitcase and arranged the cases near the cabin door ready for the porter to pick them up. With her bag under her arm, Ethel scanned their cabin to make sure that nothing was left behind on the seats or in the baggage hold.

Glancing outside the window while seated impatiently, Catherine saw the train slowing down further.

At the approach to Lahore Station, there were two enormous arches that propped up the roof, which was constructed of corrugated metal sheets supported by grey-painted poles. Further inside the roofed station, the raised concrete platform extended from the red-brick railway building with arched doors and windows. The whole approach to the platform was shielded from the weather by corrugated sheets, which formed a majestic high ceiling arch very similar to those of the railway stations in England – a seamless blend of Indian and British architecture.

The whistle from the steam engine signalled the imminent stopping of the train.

"Have you managed to spot your father on the platform?"

"Not yet." Catherine scanned the platform, hoping to spot him. "I am sure he will be waiting for us."

The Indian porter responsible for the first-class passengers knocked on the cabin door, ready to pick up the Roses' baggage and hoping for a decent tip at the end of it. Ethel took the lead and instructed the porter as she slowly walked towards the exit at the end of the carriage.

"Make sure that the porter is ahead of you. Keep him in your sight until we are outside," she whispered.

Stepping onto the platform, despite it being the cool season, the still air felt uncomfortable to Catherine and Ethel. Catherine was glad of the fan in her hand, which brought a breeze to her face. The first thing she noticed was the distinctive aroma in the air and the busy noise of the people. She took a step closer to her mother. *More people than I thought there would be.*

Ethel glanced over the entire platform through the crowd in search of her husband.

"There is no sign of your father." She had a concerned look on her face. "I hope he hasn't forgotten us… although I did write to him informing him of our arrival date and the approximate time."

"Where take luggage?" the porter asked politely in broken English, attempting not to interrupt them. Carrying two leather suitcases on his head and a third in his hands, he wanted to know where to go.

"Here will be fine," Ethel replied. They were in the centre of the platform next to the only wooden bench. The porter promptly placed their luggage on it.

Searching in her brown embroidered bag, Ethel got out a few local coins that her husband had given to her on one of his previous trips back to England and handed them to the porter. Having got his tip, the porter made a quick exit to the outside of the station, looking for his next customer.

The loud whistle of the platform conductor startled them both. They saw their train moving ahead and away from the platform. Ethel looked across the two rail tracks to the platform on the opposite side, which was near enough a mirror image of the one they were standing on. Gilbert could not be seen there either. Of the people who were on either platform, there was no British person who resembled him.

"What should we do now?" Catherine asked with a little anxiety in her voice.

"Let's head for the exit, which is there on the left," Ethel pointed, "and wait just outside the station for your father, and hopefully away from the direct sun."

Lugging the suitcases from the centre of the platform, they followed the exit passage and headed through to the lounge.

"This is awkward, trying to carry this luggage," Catherine thought aloud, while trying to make sure that her embroidered blouse and skirt were not creasing. Ethel was out of breath by now.

"Why should we not rest here and wait instead of outside?" Catherine remarked as she realised that her mother was tired.

Looking around, the lounge was a small, rectangular room with a wooden bench running along one wall. There was only one space on the bench, with all other spaces taken by what seemed to be two Sikh families and one Hindu family.

"Take that seat, Mother," Catherine instructed.

Ethel gladly took the seat while Catherine stood next to her. Feeling exhausted, Catherine placed her right hand over her shoulder and massaged it to relieve the tension and stiffness that seemed to radiate from there.

Having other things on her mind, she did not hear the whistle of the other train approaching the station on the opposite platform.

8

The train was slowing and coming to a halt.

"Finally, we have arrived," Kharak said as he stood up from the wooden seat, picking up his military-green canvas bag that carried his belongings. "What are your plans for this evening, Lal?"

"My aunt and uncle are coming over for dinner, so I need to go home straight from here. What about you?"

"Nothing. Just spending the evening with family at home and hopefully enjoying a delicious supper."

With a jerk, the train came to a stop, followed by the customary sound of escaping steam from the outlet of the engine near the wheels.

"By the way, I have to go down to the engineer's office here at the station before I leave for home. Do you want to wait for me?" Kharak asked as he stepped onto the platform.

"Sorry, *yaar*, in a hurry today and cannot accompany you. I may see you tomorrow, though."

"Alright, I will see you soon. Give my regards to your family and leave some food for me for tomorrow." Kharak winked.

"Maybe," Lal laughed. "That is, if I don't have it all for myself."

Kharak smiled as they shook hands, ready to part ways.

Standing near the wooden door frame that led outside the station, Catherine peeked through the glass pane in the door, hoping to see her father outside. The red-brick archway, with roses as the backdrop, was all that she could see.

Opening the door, she picked up her skirt as she took a step outside; the temptation of seeing what was on the other side overcame her. Her mother was busy looking in her bag and never saw her step out.

Walking by himself across the footbridge that linked the two opposing platforms, Kharak adjusted his canvas bag over his shoulder and headed straight towards the head engineer's office, which was located at the end of the corridor that ran from the lounge in the main building.

Stepping into the lounge, he noticed a middle-aged European woman. *She must be British*, he thought as he saw her fiddling with her bag. *It seems odd to see her all by herself with her suitcases. I wonder whether she is coming or going?* But then he realised from her attire that she must have just arrived; her dress sense was not quite what the British woman living here would be wearing in this weather.

Sharply turning left, he started walking towards the engineer's office.

Just outside the station, there was one rickshaw, supposedly pulled by a single man.

"*Aap ko kahan jana heh?*" the man asked as he approached Catherine.

Bewildered, Catherine could not begin to think what to say.

"I beg your pardon," was her straight but polite reply. "I have not understood a word you have said and I am sorry that I am unable to speak your language. Can you speak English?"

"*Kya kaha apne?*"

This was tough going for her. Feeling vulnerable, she looked over the man, then her eyes wandered left and then right, hoping that she would see her father walking along the dirt road leading to the station. Still, there was no sign of him.

Nailed to the door was a small sign with the name *Richard Smith*: the engineer's office. Knocking on the door, there was no response. While waiting for a response, Kharak looked around the corridor to see if he could spot anyone; there was no one. He knocked again. Getting no response, he turned around ready to leave, knowing that he would soon have to make another trip back here to see Mr Smith.

Realising that there was no point in wasting time by waiting, he turned and walked purposefully towards the lounge with the thought of going home.

By now, there were three local men attempting to talk to Catherine in a language that she did not comprehend.

Nervousness was engulfing her and it was not only the heat that was making her palms sweaty. Instinct made her take a couple of steps back towards the door as the men carried on talking to her and making gestures – though unbeknown to her, they were harmless.

With exhaustion, heat and language issues holding a grip on her, she did not hear the door open behind her.

Walking through the lounge, Kharak saw the same middle-aged British woman still seated there, anxiously looking around. While gazing at her, he reached out with his left hand for the station door that led outside and pulled it ajar.

A slender young lady suddenly turned around without looking and took two steps back. Her shoulder bumped into Kharak's chest as he attempted to step aside.

Startled, her senses shocked, fear overcame Catherine as she bumped into the man and momentarily lost her balance. Her shoes did not help her. With heart racing, she was already preparing herself for a fall.

9

In an instant, there were warm, strong hands holding her upper arms and Catherine realised that her balance was restored.

On turning her head, instinctively she uttered, "Oops, I am sorry!"

"That is not a problem, erm… ma'am."

That took her by surprise totally. "You can speak English?" she asked, hoping for a yes as she regained her balance and faced him.

"Yes."

She let out a silent sigh of relief

"I'm sorry for not looking where I was going," she said with an embarrassed look. "I got worried—"

"Don't worry about it, it happens to the most careful ones," interrupted Kharak. "Are you going away or have you just arrived here?" he asked as they moved away from the door and a few feet into the lounge.

"We arrived about half an hour ago, but we're waiting for my father to pick us up and I cannot see him," Catherine said, trying hard to hide the disappointment in her voice. "I went out to see if he was there, but I was surrounded by locals and, in a panic, I took a step back without looking and bumped into you."

Kharak smiled genuinely; he wanted to laugh, but didn't. "They all want to help you, and are the owners of the public bull carts and rickshaws; the main means of transport here in Lahore."

"I got scared and I was going back to my mother." Catherine pointed at her, seated on the wooden bench.

He cocked his eyebrow. "Your mother? I did wonder who she was as I walked through the lounge on my way out."

"Since you are the only one here that I know can speak English or, should I say, the only person I know so far, my mother will be pleased to find that we might have a way out of our dilemma."

Kharak was taken by surprise. This was not something he was expecting. Most of the British he had met were quite reserved and kept to themselves.

Catherine stepped into the waiting room and held the door for him, indicating that she wanted him to follow her inside.

"Mother, this is… oh, I don't know your name." Her cheeks were turning red in embarrassment as she glanced at him.

"My name is Kharak."

"I am Mrs Ethel Rose," the older woman said as she got up, "Catherine's mother."

"And I'm Catherine," the younger added.

"Pleased to meet you both."

"I could not see Father anywhere. He must have forgotten that we were coming today."

"There must be a reason for him not being able to come. It is unlike him."

"Is there anything that I could help you with?" Kharak asked. He felt concerned for the two women, who were in a strange place and unfamiliar with the language. "Do you know where he lives or where you are meant to go?"

"I have it written down," Ethel said as she opened her bag. "But I do not know whether we should wait here for him."

She handed her fan to Catherine as she rummaged through her bag looking for the residential address, while thinking about the best course of action. She was in two minds. Should they make their way to the house or wait here for her husband? It was lucky that they had come across this man who could at least speak English and seemed genuine enough in his desire to help.

Catherine helped her make that decision.

"Mother, we would be better off if we were at home rather than waiting here. We are hot and tired after our long journey and it would be comforting to be in our own compound."

"The address is 18 Victoria Avenue, East Lahore," Ethel read out from her little diary as she looked directly at Kharak.

"I know where that is. It is not very far from the river; it will take you about twenty minutes by carriage," he replied. "If you wish, I could try to arrange a carriage that could take you both there," he added.

There was a pause.

"That would be really thoughtful of you, Kharak," Ethel said as she broke the brief silence.

"What I shall do, then, is go and speak to the men outside. I know some of them, and I will try and arrange transport for you."

It was a relief for the women, like a heavy load was being lifted from their shoulders, the tension across their foreheads dissipating.

"Thank you," Catherine said as she blinked slowly.

Kharak thought of Nandu, who had his own four-wheeled carriage and whom he had got to know during his frequent related visits to the station for work. This was his main route and he was the one whom Kharak hoped would be able to help him.

"I will be back soon; I just need to go out and speak to one of the carriage owners whom I know and he will be able to take you where you want to go."

He turned and walked out and both Catherine and Ethel gazed at him as he strode out of the lounge. The afternoon sun felt warm on his skin and the shadows started to extend as he went to search for Nandu.

"Our first experience of the locals of Lahore," Ethel whispered, slowly and with a comfortable smile. She had been worried about being in a foreign country with her daughter and in a situation where she didn't know what to do.

"I think he is employed by the local railway company." Catherine grinned.

"What makes you say that?" her mother asked, looking slightly surprised.

"I saw the motif of the railways on his canvas bag and his attire was a reflection of some kind of uniform."

"That was very observant of you."

"Also, he can speak good English and therefore he must have some sort of education." She was trying to impress her mother.

"Let us see how he can help us," Ethel commented. "It seemed that he wanted to help us and I just want to reach the house safely."

After speaking to a group of men outside the station, Kharak managed to track down Nandu, who was resting under the shade of a walnut tree about 300 yards away. His unusual horse-drawn carriage was not exactly a carriage of the sort that could be found in Britain. He had found it abandoned by a British family in a state of disrepair and he had worked to restore it, resulting in a kind of hybrid with characteristics of both the Anglo and Indian styles, the colourful Indian decorations adorning the outside of the English carriage.

Back in the lounge, Catherine held her mother's hand and squeezed it gently.

"It will be fine. Do not worry, I'm sure that there must be a good reason for Father not being able to come and meet us."

Seated right beside her mother, she rested her head on Ethel's upper arm while holding her hand. She felt better now, comfortable and secure, and for now, looking forward to her stay in Lahore. She kept on gazing at the little girl across the room who was about three years old, playing with the red ribbons in her dark, plaited hair and staring directly back at her with an innocent smile on her face.

I wonder what she will be doing and where she will be in the next twenty years? Catherine thought. *Life is interesting.*

10

The discussion took less than five minutes – whenever there was a chance to make a few extra rupees, Nandu was always eager. Kharak had briefed him about the situation, that he needed his help to ferry two British women to their destination in East Lahore.

"Not an issue. Let's go to the station and introduce me to them and I will take care of the rest." Nandu beamed in earnest. It was his good fortune to be able to get passengers at this time in the late afternoon.

"One thing," Kharak said as looked directly at him. "Do not overcharge them. Anyone else, you are free to charge as you please, but not them."

"All right, I will not... but why?"

"Just do not take advantage of them at this time of vulnerability. They are alone." There was sternness in his tone.

"You have my word. Now, let's not waste any unnecessary time; instead, let us hop into the carriage and go."

Considering the type and size of Nandu's carriage, the short 300-yard ride to the station seemed bumpy to Kharak. His afternoon was getting longer and longer; he had not anticipated this. A normal day was what he had been expecting on his return to Lahore.

"Wait here for me; I will get them," Kharak instructed; stepping down from the carriage as it stopped a few yards from the entrance of the railway station along the approach road.

"What were their names?" he mumbled to himself as he strode towards the entrance. *Nothing would be more embarrassing than that right now. Catherine was the daughter's name and Ethel was her mother's name*, he reassured himself.

With a hint of urgency, he pushed the wooden door that led into the lounge. Turning his head to his left, he immediately saw Catherine resting her head on her mother's shoulder. She seemed to be staring intently at the little girl playing by herself across the waiting room.

He walked purposefully towards them, ready to tell them what was to happen.

Catherine was the first to notice him.

"Is everything all right?" she asked, lifting her head from her mother's shoulder. Her light brown curls briefly came down across her face.

"All is fine. I have arranged a local carriage and Nandu, the driver, will take you to your destination."

"That is very kind of you," Mrs Rose replied as she stood up. "We will be glad to finally reach home after this long journey."

With slight hesitation, Kharak went to pick up the three suitcases. "May I take them to the carriage outside?" he asked, to the surprise of the two women.

They did not expect this act of courtesy in a foreign land far away from their home. Any little doubt they had about Kharak seemed to disappear from their minds with this act, especially for Catherine.

"Unfortunately, I don't have the strength to carry it any further." Ethel smiled. "I am sure Catherine can carry the smaller of the three bags."

With a suitcase in each hand, and his own bag over his shoulder, Kharak walked towards the exit where the little girl with ribbons in her hair looked inquisitively at the two foreign-looking women following him.

Once outside the station, whilst on the dusty stone pavement, a quick wave of Kharak's hand was all that Nandu needed for him to drive his carriage towards them.

"Unusual-looking carriage; looks familiar but colourful," Catherine commented as she saw it approach. "That is a very small and scrawny horse – never seen one like that before. I do feel sorry for it."

"He is a healthy horse – he might look tiny compared to the ones in England, but he can trot, and I have experienced that." Kharak grinned.

"We shall soon see whether that is so."

Nandu hopped off the carriage with agility and an eagerness to impress. Any energetic show was a good way to obtain a healthy tip and such chances did not come that often. He approached them.

"This is Nandu." Kharak lifted his hand towards him and at the same time looked at Catherine. She looked tired, yet held herself well. "I have spoken to him and he will take you to the address you intend to go to." He paused. "If it is all right, can I ask him to place your luggage in the holding area?"

"Can he be relied upon?" Mrs Rose asked with hesitation in her voice. There was slight anger within, too, towards her husband, who was meant to be here to meet them. She felt vulnerable, her maternal instincts resurfacing in this faraway land, all alone with her daughter and having to rely on a local whom she did not know but had decided to trust. She hoped everything would turn out fine.

"Mrs Rose, I have known him for a few years. You have my word that he is trustworthy and will take you there safely," reassured Kharak.

"Can he speak English?" she asked.

There was a pause before Kharak forced a reply.

"He has a good instinct of communication but he cannot speak English very well. He can speak broken English, but do not let that be a cause to worry."

"I am worried." Ethel cut him short. "The ghastliest circumstance we could find ourselves in is being lost and, at the same time, my husband looking for us all over Lahore. I am tempted to wait here, then leave when he arrives."

Kharak raised his eyebrows in surprise. It was understandable what she had said. He felt a slight apprehension, which he ignored; he was already going out of his way to assist them.

Nandu had a perplexed look on his face, not knowing what to do; whether to pick up the luggage and load it onto the carriage or not. All he saw was the three of them talking feverishly with no attempt being made to board his carriage.

"Why don't you accompany us, Kharak?" Catherine asked, glancing at him, then at her mother, as if looking for some sort of agreement. "It would be a huge help if you were with us, guiding him to our residence. We have a language problem and you can overcome that for us." She paused. "You have already assisted us a great deal up to now," she added genuinely.

Kharak adjusted the strap of his bag over his shoulder uncomfortably. The cool northern breeze was already attempting to subdue the just-warm afternoon air. He knew that his family would be getting worried if he did not turn up at his normal time.

"We would be ever so grateful if you could come with us." Ethel Rose agreed with her daughter and spoke without the worry that seemed to have been evident in her eyes earlier.

He didn't know what to say. Being in two minds and having already started to help them, he had to make a decision.

Noticing his thoughtful pause, Catherine's mother spoke. "I do not mind paying you for the time that it will take you to go back to your home after dropping us, including the fare for the carriage," she stated, interrupting his thoughts.

"No, Mrs Rose. That will not be necessary and it isn't an issue at all," he replied straightaway, letting them know that he had no intention of making some quick rupees from them and that if he were to help, then it would be for humanity's sake.

Kharak sensed their desperation from what Ethel had just said and that helped him make his mind up. He decided to follow up what he had started, which was to help them.

"All right then, I shall accompany you and take you home, but I am not taking any kind of reward for it as that has never been my intention."

A smile broke out across Catherine's tired face and the worry lifted from Ethel's as the frown lines on her forehead disappeared. It was as if an extremely heavy burden had been lifted from her shoulders.

"Thank you very much. I can breathe easily now that I know we shall reach home safely."

"Not to worry, Mrs Rose, but I think we should start moving now, otherwise it will get late for all of us. Now, let me take your luggage and put it on the carriage.

"Nandu! Take these suitcases and put them on the roof. Be careful with them and make sure they are held safely at the top. I do not want them to get damaged or topple onto the streets as you drive. These are important suitcases, probably expensive," Kharak instructed in Punjabi with urgency.

It took less than two minutes before the brown leather suitcases were safely stowed on the roof rack of the carriage, with a rope weaved out of cloth holding them in place.

Three feet from the carriage, the ladies stood still, to Kharak's puzzlement. He was expecting them to step into the carriage, but they seemed to be staring at the lower part of the door panel. Standing beside them, he wondered whether they had lost something or if they were waiting for instructions.

"I cannot step into the carriage." Catherine managed a slight giggle. "There does not seem to be a step to enable me to climb inside." Her gaze was still fixed on the carriage door.

This was the Punjab and, to Kharak, this seemed trivial. People who could afford to travel by this means were not perturbed by this inconvenience; hopping on board, albeit clumsily, was part of the normal routine of using one of these carriages for the locals. Was this being overly fussy?

He glanced at Nandu, hoping for an answer, but he was busy with the horse's bridle. Turning around, Kharak took a step towards Catherine, who was still thinking about how to get on board.

"Here you are. Take a step and you can get in." He leaned down next to the door of the carriage and cupped his hands together, creating a step for her to use.

Catherine did not know what to do. She hesitated only briefly before placing her foot delicately on his hand, while at the same time holding the door handle to hoist herself inside. *I hope I didn't hurt his hands*, she thought.

Mrs Rose had no trouble in getting up and into the carriage.

Kharak climbed into the carriage effortlessly and instructed Nandu to put his 'service' into motion.

He sat opposite Catherine, who was seated next to the window.

Gilbert's bushy eyebrows furrowed as he gazed above his circular metal-rimmed reading glasses to stare towards the door at whoever had the audacity to disturb him while he was completing his clinical paper.

"Dr Rose?"

"Yes?!" was the abrupt reply.

"Err, sorry to disturb you, but as you asked me, I have come in to remind you that you have to go to the railway station to meet your family, sir."

The discontentment on Gilbert's face was replaced by one of self-reproach. He glanced to his left at the bronze clock on the wooden book cabinet, hoping that his worst fears had not come true.

It was not to be.

Engrossed in his work, he had failed to remember that he had to fetch Ethel and Catherine from the station.

"Thank you for reminding me," he mumbled, trying not to show any sign of worry or guilt. "I shall leave soon," he added emphatically.

Dr Gilbert Rose was not fond of making mistakes or showing any signs of incompetence. Working within the British Empire, he had a sense of patriotic pride and, to him, any sign of weakness was not acceptable. He truly belonged to the stiff-upper-lip class and he was aware, and to some extent proud, of this.

His glassy stare and slightly slim physique for his age, together with a well-trimmed moustache that curled upwards at both ends, made him less approachable to people who did not know him.

"That will be it for now," Gilbert hinted to the clerk, "and thank you once again," he added, trying to be polite.

As soon as the clerk shut the door behind him, Dr Rose stood up instantly, cleared his dark wooden table of his papers, which he placed in his leather briefcase, and grabbed his beige linen jacket and hat from the hanger beside his desk.

He looked at the watch again.

"Damn! How could I have forgotten the time," he mumbled to himself as he left his room at the Lahore Medical College hurriedly.

He was silently furious.

11

With Lahore being an important city in the Punjab at this time, the British had planned it in a way to enable them to administer it with ease. Most of the British colonial houses were built in the eastern part of Lahore rather than randomly all over the city. Part of this was due to the River Ravi flowing along the western fringes of the city: any flooding that occurred during the monsoon rains would not affect the colonial masters' houses. This part of Lahore was known as the Eastern Colonial Quarter.

Number 18 Victoria Avenue, which was the Roses' residence in Lahore, was approximately four miles from the railway station and off the Grand Trunk Road.

Nandu was proudly controlling the reins of his horse and carriage as it rolled along the dusty, sloping road that led away from the railway station.

"I have observed that it is indeed very dusty here in comparison to England," Catherine said as she gazed out of the carriage, looking back at the main building of the railway station.

"It is difficult for me to agree or disagree with you, ma'am, as I have never travelled to your land," Kharak replied.

"Also, the weather is much colder back at home," she added. "How cold does it get here in Lahore?"

"During our cold season, which you have just missed, it can drop to around five degrees at night, whereas during the day, it is around ten degrees. In the hot season, which is in June, it does get quite hot – about thirty degrees!"

"Well, it never gets that warm in England."

Ethel sat silently with her hands clasped together next to Catherine and took no part in any of the conversation. Her thoughts were with her husband and where he was, and why he had not turned up at the station. She was exhausted as well.

"Goodness gracious me!" Catherine exclaimed as she was lifted slightly off her seat as the carriage went over a rut in the dirt road. "Ouch!" She let out a sigh as her elbow hit the wooden edge of the carriage window as the wheels hit a second rut.

"Are you all right?" Ethel broke her silence.

"Yes, I am. I was not expecting the sudden jolt and it surprised me," she said as she rubbed her right elbow.

"Nandu!" shouted Kharak as he leaned out of the window and faced him. "Drive carefully, *yaar*. Your passengers are not appreciating your rough handling of your carriage and you need to be careful of the luggage on the roof as well. It should not fall off or get damaged with your obtuse control!" Then, he added in Punjabi, "If you want that good tip you are thinking of, then drive carefully."

Kharak was not affected by this kind of bumpy travel, he was used to it, but it was the look of concern on Catherine's and her mother's faces that made him shout at Nandu.

"May I ask what you were saying to the driver?" Catherine asked inquisitively.

He smiled. "I just instructed him to ensure that the ride in his carriage is not uncomfortable or dangerous for you."

As the road leading from the railway station came to the first junction, it was evident that Nandu was heeding what Kharak had requested as he slowly guided the carriage to take the first left and onto Mayo Road, which followed a south-easterly direction.

"Look!" Catherine pointed her finger across the road. "There, I can see a pink church with its spire."

"That's one of many churches across the city, but the Lahore Cathedral, which is near the centre, is quite magnificent. It's relatively old – I think the building of the cathedral began around the 1880s, about fifteen years ago," Kharak said. "My grandfather was one of the carpenters who were commissioned to assemble the wooden benches of that church," he proudly added.

"We ought to try to visit it on a Sunday morning for prayers," Ethel interrupted; she was a keen churchgoer.

"I thought that Lahore would be a fairly small town, but to my surprise, it is bigger than I thought."

"It is quite vast, I think, ma'am."

"You can call me Catherine." She looked at Kharak as the wind blew her ash-brown hair across her forehead.

Kharak stole a glance at her. He never knew what to say or think about this. Everyone he knew called British women 'ma'am' and that was what he had learned and observed while growing up. But she did not want him to address her that way; it would take him a while to get accustomed to that.

Although the journey had been long and arduous, Catherine now felt relaxed, inspirited by the new sights of the place, the different way of life she was going to encounter and the unique scents of a foreign land in the air, from its dust to fragrant flowers.

"How far away do you live from here?"

"My village is just on the outskirts of Lahore, south-east from here. It takes me about an hour to walk from my home to the station."

"You cannot be serious! Do you really walk all that way to the station?"

"I do that quite often when I have to go to work at the railways. It is not really that far; one does get used to the walk."

"Mother, I was right when I said to you that Kharak's work is associated with the railways," she said as she glanced at Ethel.

"How did you know that?" Kharak asked in bewilderment.

Catherine smiled. "I saw that motif of the railways on your bag." She pointed at it.

"That was very observant of you."

Catherine took that as a compliment.

"Two months ago, I was posted by the railway company fifty miles from this city to be involved in routine maintenance of the tracks. That is over now and I have a couple of days' break. Thereafter, I will be working in the railway yards at Lahore Station," Kharak added.

"Back in England, in Bath, the town where I live, we often take a ride in a carriage, especially in the cold winters." Catherine smiled.

The carriage took a left turn and onto Victoria Road, which was a through road that joined the Grand Trunk Road.

"That's where the railway offices are." Kharak pointed towards the stone buildings with corrugated iron roofs behind the yellow-flowering Amaltas trees. "I often have to go there to meet my superior officers and that is where most of the administration of the railways around Lahore takes place."

Catherine did hear what Kharak had said, but the trees grabbed her attention. "Those trees have unfathomable beauty – it's like they have been set on fire!" she said, leaning forward to have a better view of the trees in bloom.

"These trees, being native, are found growing here, especially on the outskirts. The planners of this city over the decades have all had a liking for this tree and, as a result, they are found growing by the roadside as well.

"Those are the railway workshops further ahead." He pointed to the sprawling but low-rise building constructed out of corrugated iron sheets. "That's where they refurbish and repair all the steam engines and the passenger carriages."

"So all this surrounding area must still be part of the railways then," Catherine stated.

"Yes. The Indian Railways own it."

Kharak glanced at Ethel, who was nodding, her eyes heavy and periodically opening and closing. It had been a long journey and the side-to-side movement of the carriage in motion was inducing slumber. Yet at every bump, she would open her eyes. She had to be aware of what was happening around her, where they were going and whether her daughter was still there.

"Catherine," Kharak whispered. "Your mother is sleepy." He raised his eyebrows, rolled his eyes towards Ethel and smiled at the same time.

That was the first time Catherine recalled Kharak actually calling her by her name; it sounded different in his accent. She noticed that he had smiled for the first time as well. *Maybe he felt uncomfortable at having been put in this situation and now he is more at ease*, she thought.

"I think she is weary. She has not slept well in the past two days and now it is catching up to her," she whispered back.

"Are you not tired yourself?" he asked.

"In a way I am, but there is so much happening around me that my senses seem overwhelmed." She daintily hung her white-gloved hand outside the carriage, feeling the wind brush past it. "And I think I am too tired to nod off."

"Tonight, before you retire to sleep, you should have a warm glass of milk." He paused. "Then again, do not have milk tonight!

Since you have just got here, your stomach may not tolerate the milk from our cows," he realised.

Catherine, with a coy look, laughed quietly at the thought of what effects the milk might have on her.

The road started sloping upwards and straight ahead, the railway tracks could be seen cutting across the road. Nandu slowed down the carriage as they approached the railway crossing. There being no bridge, it was a level crossing and he had to stop to make sure that there was no train approaching before he crossed the railway line.

"We are crossing the railway tracks; just hold on as it may get slightly uncomfortable as the wheels cross the line," Kharak forewarned.

"I think we are getting used to all this jarring from one side to another in here." Catherine looked at her mother, hoping to get a nod of agreement. "Ah, bless her, she is still nodding," she laughed, covering her mouth with her hand.

There was a jerk as the carriage crossed the tracks. Ethel opened her eyes, rolled them and closed them again. The time her eyes were shut seemed to get longer and longer as her body relaxed.

Straight ahead, the road forked and joined a wider road, which was the Grand Trunk Road.

The Grand Trunk Road was built in the 16th century and started in Sonargaon, which was a town in Eastern India, and crossed right through the northern part of India up to Peshawar, a total distance of nearly 2,500 miles.

"We are now on the Grand Trunk Road and this should take us right to Victoria Garden Avenue, which leads outwards from it." He gestured with his hand.

"Is that so? That is most definitely a very long road, quite unbelievable." She paused. "I do notice that this road is wider and there are those trees. What are they called again?"

"Amaltas trees."

69

"Yes, those trees, growing on either side." She laughed. "They must be a relief to the weary traveller, like me, who can sit under their shade to break their journey, albeit briefly."

"Yes, a rest to all, apart from your mother who does not need the cool shade of the Amaltas tree to rest. The shaking carriage is good enough for her!" Kharak teased.

They both laughed.

Kharak had been reluctant to accompany them but he never anticipated that he would enjoy showing off his city. As the carriage travelled along the road, it was not only wider, but seemed smoother as the ride got less bumpy. The shadows of the trees fell across the road as the afternoon sun dipped lower in the Lahore sky and the rays just started to display an orange hue.

The rays of sunshine falling through the carriage window onto Catherine's face brought out the intense colour of the curls across her forehead as she gazed outside.

Kharak, seated opposite her, stared intently at her face in that brief moment, knowing that she would not be looking at him – her face was turned towards the glassless window and she was busy looking outside. It was a long glance. For the very first time, he noticed her fair and near-perfect complexion, which was framed by her wavy hair.

His timing was good. Before she could catch him glancing directly at her, he rolled his gaze towards her mother, who still seemed to be asleep, her mouth gaping.

"What is over there?" Catherine turned her head towards Kharak, pointing with her index finger towards a clump of trees in the distance.

"That's where the Shalimar Gardens are. You must visit that place while you are here in Lahore. To me, it is the most beautiful garden, not only in Lahore, but, as everyone says, possibly in India."

"I never thought there would be huge gardens here," she admitted.

"Catherine, I'm not just saying so because it's my city, but it is definitely worth your trip here," he insisted modestly. "There." His index finger pointed in the same direction. "Can you see the white stone arches?"

Catherine squinted her eyes to reduce the glare of the sun directly ahead as she focused where he was pointing.

"Oh yes, I can see them."

"That is where the main entrance to the gardens is. It is enclosed by the red sandstone wall, which has other smaller gates built in," he said, still pointing.

"That does seem like a vast garden," Catherine stated, the distance from the carriage growing smaller as it drew closer to the gardens.

The carriage eventually passed by the entrance and Catherine managed a quick glance through the arches and into the green space beyond them.

"Maybe you could show me around these gardens in the next couple of days." Catherine turned, tilted her head and looked directly at him.

That took him by surprise. His thoughts were muddled for an instant and his face went blank. In that moment, he asked himself whether he had heard correctly what she had said.

"I'm not quite sure what you mean," he managed to say after what seemed like a brief pause.

"I see that this is a foreign place to me and I know no one else here who knows the place like you do. It appears that you really do know a lot about your city and, more importantly, you can speak English and I can talk to you with ease." She paused and gestured with her hands. "It seems that you are of a similar age to me and that makes it unlikely that I will get bored in your company." She smiled nervously, hoping that this was true.

Kharak had never shown anyone around Lahore, let alone a woman. There was a very close-knit community in the city, and all of a sudden, he was apprehensive about the prying eyes of the local people who knew him and the subsequent irresponsible chatter that would rise throughout the community. At the same time, he knew that the British didn't usually mingle at all with the locals.

But there was an urge inside him to show off the splendours of his city to whomever he could; it was his heritage and he was proud of it. Part of him wanted to show her the Shalimar Gardens, yet part of him was unsure.

His thoughts were interrupted.

"Kharak, when did you last visit the gardens?" Catherine enquired.

"It must have been a while. I went with my family."

"There you are, then; another reason for you to take me there. You can visit them again," she exclaimed, her tone growing slightly excited at the thought of being able to see something unusual in this foreign city.

Kharak was aware that he was on two days' leave from work and time was not an issue. Still, he was about to decline the offer.

"I need to think about it," he blurted out.

"Alright," Catherine paused. "But I would like it if you could." She lowered her gaze.

The conversation was cut short as Ethel woke up.

"How far are we from our house?" she asked groggily.

The ride to the railway station was as quick as the horses could pull the carriage; it was very bumpy and the carriage left a trail of dust in the late-afternoon sun.

Gilbert Rose sat edgily in the carriage, holding on to the leather seat to ease his discomfort, his bushy eyebrows furrowed. At this moment, his comfort was the last thing on his mind; there was only apprehension and worry.

His regular driver slowed abruptly as they approached the railway station entrance, which nearly caused Gilbert to lose his seating on the shiny but slippery, faded red leather seat.

With a quick hop, he was out of the carriage. After adjusting his hat, Gilbert strutted towards the entrance door of the station, hoping to see his wife and daughter waiting. *No time for excuses, but an apology would have to be given*, he thought.

When he stepped into the waiting lounge, the young Sikh family with the little girl had left. Being late, with no trains arriving or leaving the station any time soon, there was no one to be seen. He walked briskly through the lounge towards the door leading to the platform. There, he looked left, then right and finally across the tracks to the opposite side.

He could not see them anywhere. There was no one on the wooden bench and, apart from a few locals further away at the end of the platform and a porter leaning on the iron pillar supporting the roof frame, there seemed to be no sign of Ethel and Catherine. His palms were getting sweaty and his shirt felt tighter at the neck.

Turning back, Gilbert decided to go and speak to anyone he could find at the ticket desk.

Back in the lounge, he followed the sign leading to the stationmaster's office, which was the first door along the corridor.

The door was ajar and seated behind the desk were two Indian men, one with a tiny frame and greasy black hair with a neatly combed parting.

"Good evening," Gilbert greeted him hastily. "Can you tell me whether the afternoon train from Multan arrived on time today?

"Yes, it did, sir," was the prompt and confident reply.

"My wife, Ethel Rose, and daughter, Catherine, were on it and I have come to pick them up, later than I should have, but I cannot see them."

"That train arrived fifty-five minutes ago," the stationmaster stated precisely.

"Did you see a British woman and her daughter get off that train?"

"No, I did not," replied the stationmaster.

The stationmaster's assistant, who was seated beside him, had paused in his task of counting a stack of papers and was intently listening to the conversation. He interrupted his superior timidly.

"I did see them. They were the only two British women who walked through the waiting room from the platform. One was older and seemed to be the mother of the younger woman."

"Where did they go?" Gilbert asked tautly.

"They took the horse carriage; I think they knew where they had to go."

"They could not have. They have never been here before," Gilbert replied with a concerned look.

"One of the employees from the railway was with them and I saw him being handed a piece of paper by the older woman."

This jogged Gilbert's memory. He remembered that he had indeed made sure that Ethel had the address of the house where he stayed in Lahore, for just such an eventuality as this.

"Thank you," was his short reply. He turned around, deep in thought, and walked out of the office.

12

The colonial house at 18 Victoria Avenue was not overly stately, but still had a presence. It was rectangular, had two storeys – with the upper built within the angled tiled roof – and was made of stone. There was a veranda supported by stone pillars that ran right from the front to either side of the house. The front glass-paned door was at the centre of the house and extended to occupy nearly a third of the veranda.

There was a garden bed of erupting roses just a step down from the veranda. An expansive lush green lawn stretched outwards from the earthen path that approached the house.

Nandu's carriage approached the dense cypress hedge, which enveloped the one-acre compound that surrounded the house. He stopped in front of the solid wooden gate that divided the hedge.

"Reach," he said in broken English.

Before anyone could reply, a pair of eyes peeked through the large peephole in the gate. There was a clanging of metal, a soft creaking and the wooden gate slowly opened.

Nandu could not resist the chance to take his carriage right into the compound and, without asking, guided the horses inside.

"Gosh! It is a marvellous house," Catherine said as she stared out of the carriage towards the house.

Kharak sat quiet, wide-eyed, and observed the place as the carriage trundled slowly along the path leading to the front of the house.

Ethel sighed as she adjusted her hat and the sleeves of her dress in anticipation of finally reaching home; an unexpressed relief.

As the carriage finally stopped, two Indians, whom Kharak rightly presumed were the Roses' servants, approached to open the door. Kharak was out first, hoping to be able to help the two ladies step out of the carriage. He hopped out effortlessly.

"I'm glad that our long journey has finally come to an end." Catherine beamed as she stood at the door of the carriage before taking a step.

Without hesitating, Kharak slowly offered his hand to her. He felt her white-cotton-gloved hand grasp his.

She felt his masculine hand, making sure that she secured her balance as she stepped down.

"Thank you." She exchanged looks with him.

"Get the memsahibs' suitcases and take them inside," one of the Indian servants, who wore a black suit and white gloves, instructed the other in Hindi, as he pointed his finger towards their luggage on the carriage roof. He was Vadu, the head butler in charge of supervising all the servants who worked there, including the gatekeeper, the cook, the gardener, two house servants and a lady's maid.

"Welcome to your home. Memsahib Rose, I presume?" Vadu said, bowing his head towards Ethel.

"Thank you. Where is Dr Rose?" she asked directly after getting out of the carriage with the help of Kharak.

"Dr Rose was going to collect you from the railway station this afternoon, memsahib."

"Well, he was not there and so we had to find our own transport here. Not what we had anticipated," was her short reply.

"I'm sorry, memsahib."

"It's not your fault. I hope Gilbert has not forgotten about receiving us this evening."

"I am sure that is not the case. We were expecting you this evening," Vadu replied as he folded his right hand behind his back respectfully.

The suitcases were shuttled carefully from the carriage and onto the veranda by the other two slim servants.

"Take them to the room that I told you about this morning." Vadu gestured to the servants.

The temperature had started to drop. It was getting significantly cooler and, the wind having picked up, the native rock buntings could be seen flying to their nests.

As Ethel saw their suitcases being taken into the house, she turned towards Kharak.

"Thank you, young man. How much do I owe you?"

"You owe me nothing. Having talked to Nandu earlier, his fare is one paisa," Kharak replied.

"I will pay your fare as well," she added.

"I do appreciate that, but no thank you. I have an arrangement with Nandu," Kharak lied.

"Kharak, thank you so much for helping us." Catherine gazed at him. "We were in a muddle, not knowing what to do, how to get home or what the journey would be like. You made it wonderful." She smiled.

Kharak smiled back.

Ethel handed five paisas to Nandu. "Keep the change," she added as she saw him fumbling with the coins jingling in his buttoned shirt pocket. She turned around and walked towards the three steps that led onto the veranda, gesturing to Catherine to do the same.

Nandu had leapt back onto his driver's seat. Kharak shifted and turned his back to climb into the carriage.

"When will you show me the Shalimar Gardens, Kharak?" Catherine asked sincerely.

It was an unexpected question, which surprised him. There was a pause.

"Soon," he replied absent-mindedly.

"I shall take your word. Goodbye, and..." Catherine hesitated. "See you soon, then." She waved gently.

He blinked, smiled, reciprocated the wave and boarded the carriage.

Gilbert had asked his driver to take him home as fast as he could. He was concerned about the whereabouts of his wife and daughter and was hoping that they had got home safely. The cooler breeze drifting through the carriage window provided no comfort to him as it crisscrossed through Lahore.

For the extra fare that he would get, the driver ensured that the journey to his passenger's home took ten minutes less than it normally did.

A huge weight of torment lifted off Gilbert's mind when, upon arrival, his gatekeeper gave him the news he had hoped for right from the time when he first walked out of the railway station. His family had arrived home safely.

The family reunion was filled with joy, yet Gilbert made sure that his affection was not overly expressed. He felt that as he was the head of his family, revealing too much of his emotions would be a sign of weakness and call into question his masculinity. Despite this, he did apologise for being late to arrive at the station.

The brief time leading up to an early dinner was filled with him proudly showing them around the house and its mix of Indian and British interior decor.

"How did you this manage to find this man to bring you home?" Gilbert asked as he rested his hands on the table on either side of his dinner plate.

"His name is Kharak," said Catherine immediately.

"We met him in the waiting room at the station, or I should say that he bumped into us," Ethel added.

"Actually, I bumped into him at the door," Catherine laughed as she corrected her mother.

"Did this Indian treat you well?" Gilbert asked churlishly.

"His name is Kharak, Father."

Gilbert picked up his fork and knife and resumed eating his roast chicken leg.

"He was respectful, spoke English quite well and did not even take up my offer to pay the cost of his trip," Ethel said.

"Really? He must have been the odd one here. Most Indians would have asked for payment." There was a hint of cynicism in Gilbert's tone. "I am glad that he brought you here safely," he added as he wiped his mouth with his napkin.

Vadu entered the dining room and Gilbert raised his finger, indicating the end of the meal.

"Would you like some ginger and cinnamon biscuits, memsahib?" Vadu asked Ethel politely.

"No, thank you. We shall be retiring to bed early tonight, as we are extremely tired after our long journey. We will certainly have those biscuits with tea tomorrow."

"I am exhausted, too, Father. You will have to excuse me as I need to retire to bed."

"See you tomorrow morning when you will feel refreshed after a good night's sleep and you will get a better feel of this place," he replied. "Have a restful day at home tomorrow and, perhaps, if you wish, you can travel with me into Lahore the day after, as I have to attend a brief meeting with a British engineer."

"I would like that, Father, but for now, goodnight," Catherine said as she groggily acknowledged her parents.

The servants picked up the fine china dinner plates carefully from the hardwood dinner table. They were glad that it would be an earlier-than-expected night for them too.

It would start raining two hours later, but by then, Catherine was snuggled in bed, already asleep.

13

Kharak's journey back home was uneventful and seemed short, as he was occupied with the realisation that his parents would be concerned he was late.

His father was not at home as he had gone to help repair the wooden wheel of their neighbour's cart. His mother was relieved to see him and quickly prepared supper, instinctively knowing that he was hungry.

There was a large iron pot on a wood-fired brick stove at the rear of the house, which had hot water ready for him to freshen up before supper. Twenty minutes later, he was seated at the dinner table, his tiredness soothed away by the hot water. He felt warm in the cool evening; the breeze had picked up, hinting that rain was on the way.

There was no fine china or silver cutlery set up on the table; just simple bronze plates and spoons. Supper consisted of chickpea stew and spinach with traditional bread, which had a hint of smoked woodchip flavour.

Kharak was halfway through his meal when his father joined him after returning from the neighbour's farm and another two places were set at the table; one for his mother and the other for his father. She had waited for her husband to get home before they had supper together.

"How was your day?" Mann Singh asked as he tore the final pieces of bread to dip in his stew.

"It was an intriguing one. I left work and travelled with Lal, thinking that I would have an early evening with you all before my two days off from work, but it was not what I was expecting."

He recounted the events of the late afternoon. To his surprise, his parents supported his decision to help the two British ladies who could have been stranded in a city that was unknown to them.

"It's not very common for the British living here to ask for help from a local. It's just how they are. They are well known for their stiff upper lip," Mann explained. "Perhaps it was because they had just arrived from England or maybe they were just unconventional," he added.

Kharak nodded as he stared through the window. It started raining.

The next hour was spent around the fireplace, talking about work and the opportunities that the railway had brought to Punjab and India.

"You need to settle down now and get married." Mann changed the subject.

"I do realise that."

"What are you waiting for, then?"

There was a brief moment of silence.

"You know perfectly well that you should get married," his mother added softly.

"Going to the Technical College is what you wanted and also what we wanted for you, and that has pushed your marriage forward at the same time." His father looked directly at him as he took a sip of warm milk laced with almonds.

"I know that and I'm really thankful."

"There is a lovely girl from the next village whom your uncle mentioned to us." Mann paused to take another sip. "Her family has a similar background to ours. The girl has three sisters and two brothers and she will be compatible with you."

"She is tall, fair skinned and beautiful," his mother went on, gleefully.

Kharak was gazing at the embers within the stone chimney as they faded. He knew what his parents were implying and, in a way, they were right. It was time to settle down.

"She could be a possibility," he remarked, still gazing at the chimney. "I need to think briefly about it," he blurted out. He did not intend to say this, but somehow it managed to surface from his subconscious.

"Think about what?" his father asked in an orotund tone.

"Just…" He paused to think. "About change in my life as it takes a new direction after marriage. A bit of apprehension, I suppose."

"Are you seriously saying that?" his father asked as he handed his empty glass to his wife.

"It's fine, Kharak, you can think about it." His mother put her arm around him.

"I shall see you in the morning." Mann stood up, sighed quietly and excused himself, taking one of the lanterns with him to the bedroom.

Kharak slouched further in his seat and rested both his arms behind his head without shifting his gaze from the chimney.

The room grew quiet again. His mother broke the silence.

"Your father is concerned about you, nothing else; he will be fine in the morning. You will understand this kind of worry and feeling only when you become a father."

"I know and I'm all right, Mother."

"It's getting late now. Go to bed, have a restful night and we will see you in the morning." She patted his back.

"I'll sit here for a short while and then I shall go to bed."

"All right then. Goodnight and don't stay up too late." She stood up slowly and left for the bedroom.

The light dimmed as Kharak lowered the wick of the only lantern left in the room. It was raining outside, with the pitter-patter of drops on the leaves the only sound interrupting the silence of the night.

He recalled the day and how it had unfolded unexpectedly; he thought back in time to when he was on the train, then reaching to open the door of the waiting room at the railway station, then Catherine's face with its worried expression. He remembered the wind blowing the curls over her eyes in the carriage, her cotton-gloved hand flicking them back across the forehead.

The image of the colonial house was clear and so was that of her mother walking towards its entrance as the servants looked on.

When will you show me Shalimar Gardens? He could still hear her elegant voice clearly; she had asked him a question. What struck him now was that he never gave her a precise answer. He wondered why.

His thoughts were interrupted by the bark of the neighbour's dog. He got up reluctantly to look out of the window. It was too dark to see anything; the rain clouds were covering the sky. All seemed fine.

He walked into his room silently and sat on the edge of his bed, noticing his uniform resting on the chair beside it. His eyes picked out the motif of the railways.

She saw this and concluded where I worked, he thought of Catherine.

Slowly, he picked up the shirt and hung it on the hook behind the door. With tiredness creeping in, he went to bed.

It was still raining.

On the eastern side of Lahore, the sky was also heavy and the lawn of the colonial house was being soaked with rain.

Catherine was snuggled in her warm cotton-stuffed blanket, deep in sleep, already dreaming about reaching her hand out and picking the yellow Amaltas flowers from the trees in her garden and filling her basket. She felt delighted.

14

The chirps of the native rock buntings were a poetic harmony to wake to. The golden rays of the morning sun trickled through the glass window and hit the bed. Catherine's eyes slowly adjusted to the bright morning sun as she gradually woke up. Her body felt weightless, relaxed, and her mind addled.

A knock on the door finally awakened her senses and she realised where she was.

"Come in," she answered, befuddled.

The door creaked open and Sana, the lady's maid, wearing a peach sari and holding a tray with a teapot and teacup on it, walked in.

"Good morning, memsahib," she said softly. "Your bed tea is here. I shall leave it by the bedside."

"That will be lovely, thank you," Catherine replied as she leaned up and backwards, resting on satiny cotton pillows in front of the cushioned headboard.

The aroma of the Darjeeling tea brewing in the teapot beside the bed was invigorating.

"Is there anything else you need, memsahib?"

"No, thank you."

The woman bowed and effortlessly walked backwards in her sari, closing the door behind her.

Without hesitating, Catherine made a cup of tea and took her first sip; it was different to the tea she was accustomed to. It had a refined taste that she immediately liked. She placed her cup on the tray, got up and walked towards the curved armchair next to her bed and collected her bath gown to wear over her nightdress.

Picking up her cup of tea, she walked towards the window and twisted the brass handle to open it. Lavender-flowered jacaranda trees intertwined with red-flowered sumbul trees greeted her eyes. The lawn was lush green and finely manicured. The air was filled with a fragrant scent that was appealing and fresh.

Seeing the garden reminded her of the dream she'd had the night before. She scanned the garden, looking for those yellow flowers she had plucked, but there were none. After all, it was a dream.

It then came to her where she had seen the yellow flowers and she remembered Kharak's face.

She smiled to herself as she sipped her tea.

Kharak woke with a jolt. His heart was pounding as beads of sweat rolled down his forehead. He was breathless and hollow. It took him a few seconds to realise where he was and it was the biggest relief he had ever had.

It was just a nightmare. Mighty soul-destroying and numbing though it was.

He should have held her hand; never let it go. Perhaps he should have stopped her before she ran across the wooden bridge.

It was disturbing to hear the cracking of the wooden planks and to see Catherine drop through the gap. He had held her hand, but it had slipped through his. She screamed as she fell into the raging, brackish water of the river and disappeared. He yelled for her.

That's when he had woken up. *It was just a bad dream*, he reassured himself, wiping the sweat from his forehead as he allowed his pulse to come back to its normal rhythm.

He sat up on the edge of his bed with his feet on the floor and his forehead resting between the palms of his hands, and gradually the images of his dream drifted into the background as his reality overcame his sleepy thoughts.

The warm sun streaming through the gap in the curtains soothed his face. He could hear the familiar voice of his mother talking to their neighbour outside, the clucking of the chickens and the intermittent mooing of the cows. Never had that sounded so pleasing. He was surprised by the random dream he had had.

Consciously, he recalled Catherine's face in the carriage from the previous day so as to eliminate her worrying appearance in his dream. It worked; the dream was over and he felt better.

There was work to be done that day. He had to help his father mend Dharm's cart, as well as the northern fence poles around his family farm, which were crumbling. As regular as the sun, he knew that his father had probably already begun his work.

An hour later, after freshening up and enjoying a hearty breakfast of potato-stuffed chapattis and a glass of milk, he was off next door.

His two days off from the railways were about to begin.

15

Catherine enjoyed the next three days at her new temporary home, allowing her body to get accustomed to the new Indian time and the warmer climate. Having numerous servants around her was a new experience and she was unsure of how to interact with them. It was difficult for her to speak to them as emotionlessly as her father and some of his associates did.

Whenever she could, Catherine spent most of her time out in the garden, gazing at the blue sky with its spontaneous dots created by birds flying. She already had a favourite spot, at the far end beneath the jacaranda tree.

The reclining chair was restful. Her eyes followed the gardener as he pruned the low-hanging cypress branches and dragged them to the heap of branches he had already cut. The fragrance of the cut cypress was distinct and strong.

From the corner of her eye, she saw the familiar figure of

her father walking towards her from the far end of the garden near the house.

"I see that you have found a favourite spot in the garden," he remarked as he approached her. "Feeling restful?"

"Ah, I'm enjoying the warmth and the green hue of the trees. Really pretty; one hardly sees this intensity of colour in the leaves back at home in England."

"It's been a glorious day," Gilbert added as he pulled up a garden chair to sit beside her.

"Is Mother having a nap in her room?"

"No, she is overseeing the servants cleaning up and reorganising our bedroom. You know her nature; she cannot help it." He paused. "I am travelling to Delhi tomorrow for a few days. It is related to my work, but I am also meeting Dr Freeman's son, Ivan."

"It's a familiar name, but I cannot remember who they are," Catherine replied.

"You know my friend from Bath, Dr Freeman, who helped me get this post?"

"Ah, yes."

"His son. He works for the British India Company and I hear that he is here, briefly, in Delhi to purchase two second-hand train engines to send them over to East Africa."

"I remember him now. We played lawn bowls at their house a few years ago during a summer garden party. We were both younger then," Catherine replied after thinking.

"Yes, that's him. I would like to meet up with him and to see what news he brings from England and Africa."

"When do you leave?" she asked.

"Tomorrow morning, by train."

"Can I drop you at the station?"

"I do not think it is a good idea," was his instant reply. "You are not only in a new town, but a new country. You may get lost and there is always a concern that something may happen to you."

"You shouldn't worry," was her flat reply. "How are you getting to the train station?"

"Vadu is arranging the carriage to take me there."

"Well, then, I could accompany you to the station, drop you there and return back home."

"I don't—"

"Vadu can come along and accompany us, and return home with me," Catherine interrupted with a smile. "It has been a few days that I have been resting at home; it will give me a chance to see the city. I'm sure that one of the reasons for Mother and I coming over is to take a look at this place."

Gilbert paused for thought.

"A bit of thought is required. I will let you know tonight." He got up, straightened his coat and started his walk towards the house.

Catherine grinned as she saw her father walk away. She knew that she had out-reasoned him.

16

There was a break in the unusually searing heat; it was still warm but not overbearing, and the clouds made it a muggy mid-morning. Catherine was glad that her new magnolia cotton dress was comfortable for this climate as she walked down the steps from the veranda.

The carriage was ready and Vadu had ensured that Gilbert's leather suitcases were all tucked away safely.

"I shall see you in a few days, Ethel." Gilbert kissed his wife on the cheek as he adjusted his hat.

"It's a shame that you cannot join us at the station, Mother."

"That's all right. You know that I have to oversee the preparation for lunch as our neighbour, Mrs Wittingham, will be joining us."

"See you at lunchtime. I will be back as soon as Vadu can bring me home, so don't worry." Catherine eased any apprehension her parents had.

Soon, they were on board and Vadu guided the carriage driver around the drive, which cut a crescent-shaped path from the front garden leading to the gate that exited the compound and headed onto the street. There was eagerness on Catherine's face as it was her first day out of the house since she had got to Lahore.

She saw that this part of Lahore, which was on the eastern fringes of the city, was affluent with relatively large, sprawling houses that had neatly manicured hedges. The majority of the people living here were British. There were gatekeepers manning the gates and she saw a few gardeners working methodically, beautifying the compounds, seemingly in competition amongst themselves.

There were very few carriages on the road, and most of those were owned by foreigners. She did, however, spot a tiny number of carriages that seemed to be owned by the few rich Indians, as they had every family member travelling in them.

The road came to an intersection and the driver veered towards the right-hand fork. The road opened up and she saw them and smiled.

"Those are the Amaltas trees." Catherine pointed at the tree-lined road.

"Really? And how do you know?" her father asked, rather surprised.

"I saw these beautiful yellow-flowering trees on the way home when we got here, the other day."

A courting pair of bulbuls flew off a branch on one side of the road and perched on another across the road. In that moment of pause, she recalled when Kharak, seated opposite her in the carriage a few days ago, had enlightened her about these beautiful trees. She had decided that the Amaltas would be her favourite type of tree from now.

"Kharak told me the name of these wonderful trees," she stated.

Her father had an unimpressed look as he rolled his eyes, but tried to hide it. "Oh." He paused. "I see."

After a further five minutes, the residential area came to an end, the dirt road became wider and more people from the city could be seen. They were all darker-skinned; the Sikh men wore coloured turbans whereas the Hindus draped dhotis, a fine cloth, around their waists.

There were moments of déjà vu for Catherine as she looked out from the carriage. All seemed much clearer now than when they had first travelled from the railway station to their house. She thought this could have been due to their tiredness after their long journey. There seemed to be more people out and about – some busy walking, others standing and staring at every carriage that went past.

With inquisitive eyes, she keenly absorbed the visual differences and delights of her briefly adopted city.

As they neared the denser part of the city, the sounds of nature were interrupted more often by the background noise of people doing their daily chores; metal hitting metal, as well as the trotting of horses. This area was known as Naulakha.

"We are not very far from the station. There is the railway track." Her father pointed ahead.

A few minutes later, the carriage crossed the bumpy railway crossing and turned left.

"If we went straight ahead here, we would come to the Delhi Gate, which is one of the gates of Old Lahore. There, between the trees, in the background, you can see the outline of the gate." He pointed in the right direction.

At first, she could not see what her father was trying to show her, but as the carriage moved further along the road, there in the background in the gap between the trees, she saw the gate.

"I saw the gate, just for a brief moment."

Ahead in the distance, Catherine could see the fort-like

outline of the turrets of the railway station; a sight that was familiar to her. With its sprawling tin-sheeted sheds, the area encompassing the railway station was fairly large.

At the busy junction, the left turn led to the dirt road that went towards the railway station. Catherine thought that there were more people milling around than on the day she had arrived the previous week.

There were numerous colourful carriages on this road and she strained to see if she could get a glimpse of the one they had used a few days ago. She remembered Kharak; his hand gestures as he had calmly organised the carriage for them.

"We are nearly there." Her father interrupted her thoughts.

Their carriage trundled to a halt under the stone archway just before the front entrance. What impressed Catherine was that the horses pulling the carriages here were all well trained despite looking scrawny.

"My train departs in half an hour." Gilbert adjusted his hat. "Vadu will take you back to the house."

"I would like to spend the half-hour with you here at the station and see you off, Father. Vadu can wait for me outside by the carriage."

Gilbert looked at his daughter. "All right then. Keep the porter in sight," he instructed Vadu.

He helped her off the carriage whilst Vadu called for a porter to carry Gilbert's luggage into the station and onto the platform. There was a throng of people going in and out of the station; after all, it was the busiest time of the day.

As they passed the entrance and headed towards the main door, Catherine recalled the panic she had got into that nearly led her to fall through the door of the waiting room. She felt glad that she did not – what an embarrassment that would have been.

Beyond the door, the waiting room was the same, just a lot busier and noisier. The tiny girl with the red ribbons was not there, but there were other children clinging on to their parents with curious eyes. Two of them had runny noses.

Kharak could be working here. It suddenly occurred to her. She tried to remember that conversation they had had. *He did say that he was going to be working here for a few days. I'm sure he did.*

17

"We have to go to Platform 2," Catherine heard her father say. "There is a walkway that goes over the tracks and onto the platform."

Gathering her thoughts, she walked beside her father to the end of the passageway that led onto the platforms. From there she could see, on the far left, the freshly repainted cast-iron walkaway. The platform area was quite majestic, with the stone Mughal-inspired arches at the edge of the platform supporting the whole roof structure.

At the same time, scanning around, she spotted what she was looking for. It was the sign indicating the stationmaster's office and she decided to memorise its location, for she would need to speak to the stationmaster on the way out.

A loud hoot gave her a fright. It was a train slowly backing along Platform 2.

"That's the train I have to catch to Delhi. We timed that very well," Gilbert stated, whilst keeping an eye on the porter ahead, who was carrying his luggage.

The approach of the train for boarding caused a rush of activity on the platform, with people ready to jostle.

"It does not concern me whatsoever, all this hive of activity; I am travelling first class after all," Gilbert stated with an air of importance. "And those carriages will be at the rear of the train, there." He pointed.

Catherine kept on observing the people around them and how they carried themselves with a carefree manner, jostling, talking loudly and rushing to jump on board the train.

One of the most unusual habits she discovered was how people carried their luggage on their heads; even the porter carrying her father's suitcase was resting it on his head. It did make it easy to keep track of their porter.

Vadu was not far ahead; he had joined the porter as they walked up the metal steps of the walkway. A young, excited Indian child with a beaming smile ran through the crowd, his mother shouting behind for him to slow down.

The first-class carriage was denoted by a sign just outside the door leading into it; not that anyone would miss it, as all the passengers inside were British. The porter at the door was a tall Sikh man wearing a grand red turban with a matching coat that had golden embroidery on the collar and cuffs. He looked quite impressive.

"Welcome on board." He bowed, as trained. "May I take your luggage to your cabin?"

There was a nod and the porters exchanged the suitcases.

"Do hop on board with me, Catherine, and you can marvel at this train's first class." Gilbert encouraged her to follow him.

The interior was quite grand. Although the cabin was tiny, it was wood-panelled and the edges of the two bunk beds were upholstered in maroon velvet. At the corner was a small ceramic sink.

"It is very cosy, much better than the train we arrived on," Catherine judged as she felt the velvet with the palm of her hand.

"It shall do me fine," Gilbert stated as he removed his hat and got comfortable on the lower bunk.

Vadu waited patiently outside on the platform for Memsahib Catherine.

The next twenty minutes in the cabin went by quickly as Catherine got engrossed in her father's conversation about what great things the British were doing in India. They were interrupted by a loud whistle from the front of the train.

"Well, dear, I shall see you and your mother in a few days' time. Do take care of yourself here." Gilbert hugged her.

"Look after yourself as well, Father."

"I will." He kissed her on the forehead.

Gilbert helped Catherine to get off the carriage and onto the platform. Inside, he was a little anxious about leaving her by herself. Perhaps he should not have agreed to her coming along and she would have been better off at home. It eased off somewhat when he saw Vadu; he knew that he was dependable and a trustworthy butler.

A few minutes later, the platform supervisor blew his whistle as he raised the green flag, which was followed by a hoot from the engine as the train started to slowly chug away from the covered platform. There was a lifting of waving hands in unison from the people on the platform. Catherine was no exception.

The train slowly became a moving dot on the horizon where the tracks seemed to merge. At the same time, the people on the platform began dispersing as quickly as they had converged.

For a brief moment, Catherine felt lonely.

"Memsahib, just follow me to our stationed carriage that is awaiting you outside the station." Vadu offered guidance.

Catherine nodded and started walking towards the walkway.

"I need to briefly talk to the stationmaster in his office."

Vadu did not reply, but walked a couple of yards behind her.

She walked purposefully as she did not have to ask anyone where the office was; she had memorised its location when she had got to the station half an hour ago.

The office was located along the corridor that ran off the platform; it was the second door on the right. She knocked faintly. There was no reply. She knocked her gloved knuckles harder on the wooden door.

"Yes."

The door creaked as she pushed it open and entered. She saw a tiny-framed Indian man with a moustache and a greasy parting of black hair, who was busy sifting through some papers that rested on his desk.

"Can I help you?" he asked without looking up.

"I'm looking for someone," she said. Her British accent made the man pause and look up.

Gazing at the admirable young British woman made him nervous, as this was an unusual occurrence. He stood up.

"I believe that a Mr Kharak is working here at the station; he works as an engineer for the railways," she said. "Could you please tell me where he is working?"

The stationmaster, bewildered, paused for thought while he shifted through his memory.

"I'm sorry, memsahib, I do not know of a Mr Kharak who works here."

"Are you sure?"

"Yes, I am," he answered reluctantly.

Seated beside the desk was a slim, dark-skinned man wearing a blue turban, who was listening keenly to the ongoing conversation despite filing paperwork.

"I believe that I may know the person you are looking for," he interrupted.

Catherine and the stationmaster both turned their heads towards the assistant.

"Do you?" the stationmaster asked, trying to maintain his authority.

"He does not work here in the station." The man paused in his task. "He is working outside the railway yards; he is involved in carrying out engineering work."

"Could you please show me where the yards are? I hope to see him." Catherine paused. "He is a friend."

The assistant glanced at his superior, hoping to get a nod of agreement.

"My assistant here," the stationmaster pointed, "will take you to where your friend may be working. It is a few minutes' walk from here."

"Thank you very much for your help, it is much appreciated," Catherine acknowledged.

The papers were set to one side of the desk to be completed later and, with a feeling of importance, the assistant got up and walked towards the tiny cupboard.

Catherine looked on as he took a set of keys out from the cupboard.

"Do follow me," he instructed politely as he started walking out of the office.

In the passage outside, Vadu, who stood waiting, was bemused to see Catherine following the slim, turbaned man through the corridor.

Genuinely concerned, he asked her as they approached, "Is everything all right, memsahib?"

"Everything is fine. I am hoping that this gentleman here will take me to see Kharak." She paused. "I thought of thanking him personally for helping us the other day." She resumed her walk towards the end of the passageway, following the station officer, who had not changed his pace either.

Vadu nodded and followed her a few paces behind. He did not have to think about walking behind her.

18

Turning right at the end of the corridor led them towards the platform, the same way Catherine had walked after seeing her father off. On approaching the platform, the officer turned right and walked lazily towards the end of it where the white-painted support arches came to an end, marking the abrupt end of the covered platform. It was a seventy-yard walk.

With slight apprehension, she carried on walking.

"And how do you know Mr Kharak?" the station officer asked as he jingled the set of keys in his hand.

"Oh, he helped my mother and me a few days ago, when we arrived in Lahore. He escorted us to our home."

"He should be working on the other side of the railway sheds." The assistant pointed.

Catherine noticed the huge wooden sheds through the gaps between the slats of the fence in the distance.

"You will have to take extra care while walking across the

102

railway tracks and the ballast; the ground is very uneven," he stated in his thick accent.

Away from the shade of the station roof, the sun felt intense on Catherine's forearms. She adjusted her sun bonnet to cover as much of her face as she could. In the sun, the railway tracks shone as they seemed to converge and disappear on the horizon.

It seemed quieter the further away they walked from the clamour of the platform, lowering almost to a background hum. The buzzing of the insects seemed more pronounced as they approached the shrub near the gate in the fence.

To the assistant's annoyance, as he reached out with the keys, he noticed that the gate in the fence had not been locked. Being an area that was out of bounds to the public, this should not have happened. He thought of reporting this to his superior.

The wooden gate creaked when he pushed it open.

Walking through, Catherine observed that there were four rail tracks that had to be crossed in order to get to the near side of the shed.

She was glad that she had chosen to wear her lace-up boots, as the tough leather would prevent her from twisting her ankle and offer protection against grazing by the ballast.

She walked gingerly, whilst lifting her long magnolia shirtwaist dress ever so slightly with her gloved fingers to enable her to keep the hems from sweeping the stony ground, and herself from tripping.

Vadu was not far behind.

The sound of track ballast being shovelled grew louder and so did the clangour as they approached the shed. She could hear the faint mummer of people, who seemed to be on the other side of the shed.

Catherine got a little nervous; the same nervousness that she had had when she had arrived in Lahore for the first time. Not knowing what to make of it, she carried on walking.

Going around the shed on the uneven, dusty ground, she

saw a group of men working on the tracks that led into the huge sheds thirty yards away.

A man holding some papers in one hand was talking to a group of three other men. He kept on pointing to the tracks, then to the papers, then to the tracks again.

From the distance, without the need to second-guess, Catherine saw *him*.

19

Kharak was engaged in illustrating to the workers the correct layout of the junction gap and its construction between the tracks. So far, the extension of the sheds that would be used to maintain the train carriages had been on schedule; however, there had been issues with the junction gaps and the men working on them could not grasp the technical know-how.

He was startled to be interrupted by a distant voice.

"Kharak, oh, Kharak," the railway officer bellowed whilst raising his hand.

Kharak paused, turned his head and looked up towards the voice. So did the other three men he was talking to, as well as the manual labourers shovelling the track ballast. Work stopped.

From thirty yards, he recognised the railway officer immediately, but could not recall the other man a few steps behind.

It took him a couple of blinks to recognise her.

Oh my, it surely mustn't be. I cannot believe this, was what went through Kharak's mind. *It is Catherine!*

He turned around fully, facing the three walking towards him. Down went his hand holding the papers. Even if he'd tried, he would not have been able to hide his smile.

"There is this memsahib who wants to meet you," the officer shouted in Punjabi. "I don't know what she wants," he added, as he approached. "Do you know her?"

"Yes," Kharak stated out loud.

The officer then motioned his head towards Catherine as he stopped walking. "That's Kharak, there." He pointed. "The person you wanted to see."

"Thank you very much for your help, it is much appreciated," she replied genuinely as she clasped her gloved hands together.

"I'm going back to the station, so I shall leave her here for you to handle," the officer stated to Kharak in Punjabi.

He turned around and walked back to his cooler office that awaited him at the station, leaving Catherine and Kharak with a distance of twenty metres between them.

Vadu stopped walking, but kept his eye on Kharak.

Leaving the workers staring at him, Kharak started walking towards Catherine.

She gingerly took a few steps forward as she tried to fix her gaze on him and the uneven ground simultaneously.

"Hello, Kharak." She smiled broadly as she took off her right cotton glove and reached her hand forward.

Taken by surprise, he hastily folded his papers, tucked them in his rear trouser pocket and wiped his hands clean on his trousers.

"How are you, Catherine?" He shook her hand gently, feeling the smooth, soft skin, hoping that his hands were not soiled. He let out a nervous sigh.

I have often been told that British women never remove their gloves when greeting people, he thought to himself. *That has not happened here. But how did she manage to find me?*

"I am truly well and savouring the splendid warm weather in your city." She felt his rugged hand.

He is gentle with his handshake, she thought.

"It is a surprise seeing you here. What brings you here?"

"My father left for Delhi a short while ago and I came to drop him to the station. As I have been resting at home since I got here, I had an urge to go outside the house to explore. Hence I decided to accompany my father to the station."

"All by yourself?" he asked

She smiled. "Not quite. Vadu, our butler, has been with us." She nodded in his direction.

Kharak shifted his gaze towards Vadu, who was standing a few feet away and acknowledged Kharak with a nod.

"I am mighty impressed and intrigued by your ability to find me working here."

"Well, it wasn't too hard." She smiled again, with a hint of pride. "I remembered our conversation in the carriage the other day and I recalled you saying that you were working here at the station for a few days, so I thought I would look for someone who knew you." Her eyes gleamed. "And I still remember the motif of the railways on your shirt and bag." She lightly touched the embroidered motif on the upper arm of his khaki shirt.

He looked at her soft white hand and wrist as he pretended to glance at the motif. After the nightmare he had had a few days ago, he was pleased to see that she was fine.

A brief pause followed as she clasped her hands in front of her.

"I also wanted to thank you, once again, for assisting and accompanying us home the other day," she said, raising her eyebrows in gratitude.

"You are most welcome, Catherine. I presume that you managed to uncover why no one came to pick you up from the station?"

"Oh yes. My father did not quite forget us, he just got the time wrong. I suppose he got too engrossed in his work at the Medical College." She laughed, which eased the tiny apprehension she had.

Her laughter revealed the subtle dimples in her cheeks and, together with the curls of hair that descended from her bonnet, enhanced her allure. That was what he realised at that moment.

"Is he a doctor?"

"Yes and no. He is a medical doctor, but, at present, he is appointed here by the British government to teach medicine at the Medical College." She delicately brushed a few curls across her right temple.

"The Medical College is not very far from the Engineering College where I studied."

"And that led you to work for the railways here?"

"Yes."

"Whilst walking here, I observed that you were busy giving direction to your colleagues." She looked over his shoulder at the workers, who had stopped working and were staring at them.

As Kharak turned his head around, some of them resumed their work bashfully.

"We have a schedule to meet; let's not waste time." He raised his voice in Punjabi to a few who were still staring.

All of them got their heads down and got busy. The noise of work restarted.

"It seems that you are involved in an important project," she remarked.

"There is a timescale that we have to adhere to and I have to ensure that it is fulfilled, as a lot of work is happening at the station."

"Really?"

"Let me show you," Kharak offered. "Of course, that is if you have the time now," he added, not wanting to be pushy.

"I'd like to see what is happening here." She smiled.

"Those there," he pointed, as he started walking, "are the new sheds."

Catherine followed him as he led her onto a flatter dirt path between the rail tracks, which had no ballast strewn over it.

I wonder whether he deliberately chose this easier path for my sake? Nice of him to be considerate, she thought.

"Oh my, the sheds do look huge; even more so as you approach them. Will the engines be stored here?" she asked.

"Not for long. Once completed, these will be the maintenance sheds where the steam engines and carriages that need repair will be housed and worked on."

The closer they came to the four sheds, the more their true scale became apparent. Their frames were constructed of steel, with bricks forming the walls, which had windows throughout the entire length of the sheds, and corrugated iron sheets forming their gable roofs.

As they turned around to the main side, the entrance to the sheds came into view. Railway tracks led into them.

Walking inside, all that Catherine saw was a dark space. It took her eyes a few minutes to adjust to the light.

"It is a mammoth structure." Her voice echoed and the echoes interrupted her in mid-sentence. She tilted her head towards the roof, noticing the large glass windows throughout its entire length.

"Kharak... hello, Kharak," she called out mischievously, just to hear the echo resounding in the large, enclosed space.

He let out a surprised laugh.

"I have never been in a building as large as this, not even back in England."

Kharak walked further inside the shed.

"That is where the railway tracks will be on raised pillars, but the ground around and beneath the tracks will be dug up so that when the trains are parked, the engineers can work beneath them as well." He gestured.

They walked and spent a few minutes there, and Catherine visualised how it would be when up and running with the steam engines as Kharak explained the work that would be done.

Around fifteen metres was the distance that Vadu had been keeping from Catherine and Kharak. She was the memsahib and he had been taught by his previous British families to keep his distance and never to overhear the conversations of his masters. That was not supposed to be his duty, nor was it his concern.

The midday brightness was intense as they came out of the dark shed and Catherine had to squint to adjust to the light. The open, sprawling land on this side of the city was dotted with jacaranda trees in the background, which was bisected by the railway tracks.

"What is that huge, circular ditch up there?" she asked as she walked towards it.

"That is where the railway turntable will be constructed."

"And what might that be?" She paused. "Mr Engineer," she added with a grin.

Her laughing jade-green eyes are something that I have never seen before, he thought.

"It is a revolving railway track platform that the engine compartment gets parked on and is then manually revolved to turn it in the direction that is needed."

"Ingenious. I have always wondered how they turned the trains around."

An unnatural silence followed the pause in the conversation. She broke the silence.

"So, Kharak, when will you show me the Shalimar Gardens, as you promised?" she asked with a slightly lowered voice. *Please say when. I am eager to discover Lahore, see its colours and smell the fragrance of its earth. Staying within a walled garden is not the reason I travelled thousands of miles. How can I tell you that I want you to lift the veil of my enclosure so that I can take a breath of Lahore?* she thought.

For a moment, he stood simpering, not knowing what to say.

"I am not working tomorrow." He paused. "Is that a suitable day for you?"

"I'll be delighted." Her eyes widened as she flicked her curls across her forehead. "How will I get there?"

"I think it will be better if I meet you at your house in the morning and then I'll take you to Shalimar Gardens from there."

"Ten o' clock suits me fine," she replied eagerly.

That was earlier than he wanted.

"That'll be fine with me," he lied reluctantly.

"Had I not asked you about this, would you have remembered to show me the place?"

"Of course I would have," he replied.

"That's reassuring." She smiled again, breaking eye contact.

A few of the workers occasionally paused their work to peek at them before resuming. Not all of their pauses were due to the heat of the midday sun or exhaustion; some were due to sheer curiosity.

As Catherine glanced around the huge yard again, one of the junior engineers who was being instructed by Kharak earlier took the opportunity to interrupt politely.

He briskly walked towards him. "Kharak, *mistry*, it is not for me to say, but it is nearly lunchtime and we are going on our break. We will be waiting for you," he said with his head slightly bowed.

"Go ahead and I will meet you afterwards to go over what we were discussing."

In acknowledgement, the junior engineer hurriedly walked away to start his lunch break.

"I'm sorry, Kharak, to keep you from your work. I will have to return home as well; my mother will be waiting for me."

"How is Mrs Rose?" he asked.

"She is luxuriating in having all the servants and butlers around in a large house," she laughed. "But really, she is enjoying her stay and has already made a few friends, one of whom is coming over for lunch. Which reminds me, I promised to join them," she realised.

"Do *you* have any friends here?" Kharak asked.

She paused and then met his gaze.

"Yes, I have. You are my friend here, Kharak," she said in her silvery voice as she raised her right hand to hold on to her hat as a sudden breeze blew across the yard. She maintained her gaze at him.

He was not expecting this answer.

Here is this elegant young Englishwoman, whom I would have thought to be elitist and have many friends from her own background, but that is not so. To her, I'm her friend, he thought.

"I'm privileged," he stated clearly.

"I'm looking forward to seeing you tomorrow morning then, Kharak."

"See you tomorrow morning, Catherine."

She turned around and started walking back along the path she had taken. Vadu was a few paces behind her.

She is lovely. Kharak saw her walk away towards the gate in the fence that led her back to the path to the platform. *I wonder whether she will turn around and glance back at me as she walks away.*

In a few quick and large paces, Vadu got in front of her to unlatch the gate and open it for her.

Taking a few steps towards the gate, Catherine paused, turned around and glanced over her shoulder towards Kharak, smiled and waved.

20

Dusk was still an hour away but the clouds were already reflecting its orange hue, and the buildings in the distance seen from the veranda at Lal's home got greyer.

"That is terrific news, Lal." Kharak leaned forward from his chair to pat Lal's shoulder.

The after-dinner glass of cardamom milk was worth the walk after work to Lal's place as Mrs Sena, Lal's mother, made one of the most delicious milk drinks in Lahore.

"When do you leave for Mombasa?"

"Next month. It is all confirmed and I have the letter from the Indian Railways detailing my post there," Lal said. "You should have applied as well and we could both work there for a short while. The salary for that post is twice what we are getting here."

Kharak tilted his head and stared at the thin wooden beams of the veranda roof. "I cannot accompany you."

"That must be the charms of your new-found memsahib talking." Lal winked and smiled.

"Come on, that is not true and you know it."

"She likes you – she even said so."

"No, she did not; she just said that I was her friend."

"Kharak, one can only be someone's friend if they like the person."

"You have a point. There is something about her that I like, Lal, and I can't explain it. When she came to see me this afternoon, not only was it a nice surprise, but I felt at ease around her."

"You must be looking forward to seeing her tomorrow."

Kharak paused for thought and took a sip from his glass. "I am. It's not something you do often; show someone your city."

"Especially if it's a young British lady who has asked you to show her around," Lal added with mischief. "How will you take her there?"

"I have not thought about it yet. Perhaps we'll take the rickshaw."

Lal interrupted, "Take the newer cycle rickshaw! Nandu has just got hold of a second-hand cycle rickshaw. They are compact and look great."

"I may see him tomorrow morning, then."

That evening, every time Lal's father walked onto the veranda, the conversation about Catherine was swiftly changed. The wood-fire stove provided warmth on the open veranda as it got cooler with the setting sun.

The conversation turned to Lal's trip to Mombasa and how although his parents were apprehensive about him leaving and working abroad, they had reluctantly accepted with the thought that, after six months, he could come back. Also, the salary was much higher. They knew that he would be away from all of them and they would miss him dearly, but they accepted on the basis that it was a temporary move.

"How will you travel there?"

"I will travel by ship, either from the port of Karachi or from Bombay to Mombasa via Aden."

"That will be a new experience for you," Kharak said.

"I have always wanted to travel and now I have the chance not only to travel, but to work and earn good wages at the same time."

"I will miss you while you are away," Kharak said.

"When I return to Lahore, you will probably be married," Lal remarked with a laugh.

"Who knows?" Kharak replied rhetorically.

21

On the other side of Lahore, dinner was finished and the servants were all busy cleaning the dining room and replacing the cutlery in the cabinets.

In the lounge room, Mrs Rose was seated with a gin and tonic in hand. Not that the tonic was a requirement for preventing malaria in these cooler months; it was her preferred occasional evening tipple.

Catherine was lying on the velvet couch with a blanket to warm her in the cool evening. Over the course of dinner, she had told her mother that she was going to visit the Shalimar Gardens the following day and that Kharak was going to be her guide.

There was maternal worry and, at first, Ethel was not keen on it.

"I would not have wanted you to go by yourself to the town centre. Having met Kharak a few days ago, and with him having assisted us, I find it a little easier to let you go with him as a guide as long as Sana, your maid accompanies you." Ethel took a slow sip of her gin.

"Thank you. It is an opportunity for me to see things that are new to me, Mother. I am an explorer at heart and staying within our lovely compound is enclosing at times."

"At least you will be able to see the class divide."

"What exactly would that be?"

"It's how we live compared to the Indians; we are more affluent, better educated and more sophisticated." Ethel raised her eyebrows.

"Really?"

"It's obvious. You will discover it."

Catherine remained silent, playing with her necklace while staring at the ceiling.

"What would Father have said about tomorrow?" Catherine turned her head to face her mother.

"Knowing him, he would not have been pleased for you to be shown around the town by a local. He would probably have arranged one of his British friends' sons to show you around."

"I believe that."

Catherine did not know what to think about all this. It seemed that while in England, all the British acted honourably towards their fellow citizens, but when abroad, in the British Empire, they changed their attitude towards others whom they were living amongst.

Is this how things are supposed to be? Is it because this is my first trip abroad and this feels unusual to me? she thought. *But I still feel that Kharak is different.* She carried on staring at the ceiling.

The air outside was crisp when Kharak reached home. His father was already in bed after another busy day repairing the wooden wall panels at the British Punjab Club in Lahore.

In the lounge room, Kharak's mother was busy threading the bed sheet beside the lit oil lamp.

"Has everyone gone to bed?" he asked.

"It is quite late and everyone is tucked away in bed. How was your day?"

"Long and fairly tiring," he said as he sat down on the chair opposite.

"How are the Sena family?"

"They are fine. "Lal has taken a temporary post in Mombasa."

"Where is that?"

"Along the coast of East Africa, about three weeks by ship."

She looked up at him. "Really?"

"The salary is very good and he wants to do it," Kharak said as he untied his shoelace. "He leaves next month."

"So, you will not be working together then? I know that you will miss him."

For a while, no one spoke. Kharak folded his arms as he got comfortable in the lounge chair while his mother carried on threading the sheet.

Kharak broke the silence. "Mother, remember the family I told you about, the mother and daughter whom I helped at the railway station?"

"Yes."

"Well, the daughter, Catherine, came to drop her father off at the station today and she managed to find me. She wanted to thank me for helping them out the other day."

"That's thoughtful of her."

He hesitated, with a hint of nervousness. "She asked me to show her our city."

"And…?" Seva stopped threading and gazed directly at him.

"She wants to see the Shalimar Gardens." He paused. "So I am showing them to her tomorrow."

Kharak could see that his mother was thinking. She rested the sheet with the needle on her lap and let out a long breath.

"She is our guest, a guest of Lahore and Punjab, and we take that responsibility with respect. Look after our guest tomorrow."

"I will," he said, with hidden elation.

British East Africa, Tsavo
March 1898

22

It was a relief for the workers building the railway when its construction had gone past the worst part of the Taru Desert. The desert extends for over 200 miles and its southern part is about thirty miles from the East African coast. It is not a typical sandy desert with dunes, but its surface consists of semi-arid acacia thorn shrubs and patchy savannah grass.

The landscape is unique; the Yatta Plateau, as it is known geologically, was formed by the ancient lava flow from the Ol Donyo Sabuk Mountain.

The stillness of the vast wilderness was constantly broken by the resonance of metal hitting metal and the humming of people. In this part of the world, this was not normal.

These Indian workers were fulfilling the ambition of the late Sir William Mackinnon, who had spent the latter part of his life trying to achieve the end of slavery and to exploit this unexplored land.

He had died on 22nd June 1893 in London and would not live to see how this civil project of building the railway from Mombasa to Uganda, backed by the British government, would change the entire region forever.

The place that the railway track had passed three months ago had been named Mackinnon Road Station in honour of the great man.

Although there was no platform as such, or any resemblance to a railway station, it was aptly named as a station as it had formerly been a slave-trade stopping point. When laying the rail tracks, the engineers had followed the dirt track that Mackinnon had often used from the port of Mombasa to the interior. The Arabs, who were the main traders of slaves, used this path to ferry native slaves caught from the interior to the port town of Mombasa, where they were sold at the slave markets.

William Mackinnon was himself greatly opposed to the slave trade and was instrumental in putting pressure on the British government to abolish this barbaric and inhumane trade of people.

Under the scorching sun, hundreds of men were busy doing their respective tasks. Their foreheads shone with streaming sweat, their skin even browner than before. The soil was dry and baking hot, the metal rails too hot to handle, and to make matters worse, there was no local supply of water. It had to be obtained and transported from the port town of Mombasa to their current location.

"This is hard work, especially under these conditions," Ungan Singh sighed, wiping the sweat from his brow and straightening his back to ease the stiffness due to constant bending while working with the clips on the railway track. "Never had I imagined that it would be this difficult," he added.

"It has been nine months since we began this work." His colleague Chand looked up at him from his squatting position, a rail clip in his dirty hand.

"I thought that it only got this hot in India, but this place is as bad, if not worse," Ungan said as he adjusted his turban under the afternoon sun.

"Chand, when we started the initial laying of the tracks in Mombasa, the area was pleasant, green with the occasional sea breeze, but here, it has changed completely. It's harsh." Ungan sighed before adding, "I am just mentioning the differences, but I don't mind the loneliness in the wilderness. It helps me to understand why I'm here."

"We were very lucky at the Mariakani Hills a few weeks back during the stormy weather. I never imagined that the weather would be that horrendous, but it was ordained to be that way."

"Your deep philosophical talk, I can never understand," Chand remarked as he stood up and faced Ungan.

"You will not comprehend the smaller things in life," Ungan chuckled as he pointed the spanner at his friend.

All the workers in his head group were extremely lucky, having spent a night out in the Mariakani Hills, caught out by the ferocity of the storm. Having been stranded across the chasm due to flash floods, they survived thanks to food and necessities passed on to them by rope by their colleagues on the camp side of the railway track. They would not forget that episode in a hurry. Life was precious.

Ungan Singh was a tall, muscular man; he was only thirty-two years of age, but very fine lines and furrows on his forehead emphasised long hours spent working in the sun.

Born in Lucknow in Punjab, Ungan was a father of two young boys, ten and six years of age. Living in an extended family, his children and wife did not feel alone but they did miss him very much. There was a simple reason for undertaking this work: to earn some extra income in a relatively short period of time. Bettering his family's lives was what he had in mind and whenever he yearned for them, the thought of improving their lives gave him the strength to carry on.

He knew that there was a chance that he could be away for up to five years if he stayed for the duration of the project.

The thicket of low acacia bushes that were about one hundred yards from Ungan and Chand shook unexpectedly. They could not help but turn their heads instinctively towards the movement.

"Look!"

Out popped the head of a zebra, followed by the neck. It stood gazing intensely at the two surprised men.

"Indian donkey with stripes," Ungan stated.

"Or a horse with big teeth and stripes," Chand added, trying to be humorous but with very little effect.

Out came another head from the bush, a bigger one this time. A few seconds later, another one, and soon there was a herd of ten zebras. They huddled close together at first, their legs reddish-brown as a result of the dry, ferric soil that was found in this area. Slowly, they started grazing at the dry, patchy savannah grass, but they were still watchful.

"This is the raw beauty of this place. No one knows what the next moment holds. It is different from the village in Punjab, yet some bits remind me of my village," Ungan thought out loud as he stared at the zebras.

This area was called Ndii, and it was more wooded than the patchy and harsher area they had traversed over the past few months.

A high-pitched whistle broke the moment. The zebras were startled and trotted off, disappearing into the grass just as they had appeared, much to the disappointment of Ungan and Chand. They had provided a break in the monotony.

It was the whistle of a goods wagon that took supplies to the camp. In the distance, they saw the Indian driver extend his charcoal-grey hand out of the train and wave, while the worker beside the rail track with a red-and-green flag guided the goods wagon to a stop.

As it came to a halt, the swirling steam from the railway engine formed brief clouds against the backdrop of the jagged edges of the Ndungu Escarpment, which rose in the distant background in the midst of miles of untamed savannah beauty.

Unknown was the peril that lurked ahead in this harsh paradise, and that would resonate for a hundred years and beyond.

23

Lahore

"We shall see you in the evening, my son. I did mention to your father that you would be away today, on the other side of town, showing your guest around," Kharak's mother said as she hugged him.

"Did Father say anything?"

"He did not say much, but it's all fine."

Kharak stood in brief silence. "All right then, I'd better leave now. I don't want to be late as I have to walk to the station to get the rickshaw."

Kharak's walk to the station was brisk. Luckily, the morning sun was not severe, whereas Lahore in the afternoon sun could get uncomfortable.

At the railway station, Kharak had to wait fifteen long minutes for Nandu, who was ferrying a passenger, before he saw him and his cycle rickshaw that Lal had told him about the night before.

Although it was small and compact compared to the human rickshaw, he was impressed with it. *It is going to be a bit confined. I hope Catherine will not mind*, he thought.

Instead of having to find another rickshaw later in the day, Kharak negotiated with Nandu a fare for his service for the whole day, which pleased him. With Kharak having used his transport services over a period of time, Nandu had got to know him well.

It was just after half past nine when they left for Catherine's house and, like anyone involved in transport, Nandu did not have to ask too many questions about where to go. He could still remember where he had dropped them the last time he had picked them up from the railway station. It was the memsahib's house they were going to.

Catherine wore her long-sleeved white rainy daisy dress, which had a pastel blue waist ribbon and a raised hemline. Not knowing exactly what she would be doing or how her day would turn out, she picked her attire to be as comfortable as possible. It was going to be a warm day and she was pleased that the matching straw hat would shelter her face from the biting sun.

Not only was she excited about the day ahead, but she was also pleased with her dress as she had spent a lot longer in front of the mirror that morning. To Ethel's dismay, their carriage was undergoing repairs to its axel and, as a result, the only available mode of transport that morning was their cycle rickshaw.

It was quarter to ten in the morning and Catherine was already seated in the front room, waiting in anticipation for ten o' clock. Looking out of the window, she could see the gardener squatting, busy trimming the edges of the lawn. He stopped his work and turned his head, facing the gate. Catherine glanced through the window towards the gate to see the gatekeeper, Balu, opening it.

She recognised Kharak seated in the cycle rickshaw and she stood up.

"Mother, I am leaving."

She walked out of the house and onto the veranda, where her mother joined her as the rickshaw approached and came to a halt. Sana was a few steps behind.

If ever there was someone in Lahore who stood out at this very moment, it has to be Catherine. I had never thought, but my, she looks wondrous today, Kharak thought as he saw her smiling face.

"Good morning, Mrs Rose," he said, choosing to acknowledge her first.

She nodded. "Good morning."

Catherine was already down the steps and ready to step into the rickshaw.

"Hello, Catherine."

"I am excited and glad to see you, Kharak," she said.

"It is the first time out in Lahore by yourself, do take care. Sana will be there, if you need anything," Ethel said to Catherine while looking at Kharak. She was apprehensive at seeing Catherine about to get into the wrong rickshaw. *She should have sat in our rickshaw with Sana.*

"Not to worry, Mrs Rose. I am sure that she will look after herself," Kharak said as he helped Catherine get onto the rickshaw.

Moments later, after a hurried goodbye wave from Catherine, Nandu was pedalling the rickshaw along the dirt driveway that led to the gate, followed by the rickshaw in which Sana sat. Ethel looked on in trepidation.

Shalimar Gardens were on the same, eastern side of Lahore as the European Quarter and Kharak knew that it would not take more than fifteen minutes from Victoria Avenue.

He sat pushing himself as close to the left-hand side of the rickshaw as he could, whereas Catherine seemed comfortable within the confined space and was busy looking at the splendours of greater Lahore.

A mile later, as Nandu pedalled leisurely, she spotted a woman wearing a faded magenta sari walking on the side of the dirt road with one hand holding the firewood balancing on top of her head.

"How does she do that?" She gasped in amazement.

"She has probably been doing this all her life," he replied.

"Oh. That must be difficult."

"And that's not the end of her work. She will also be cooking, looking after the family and even perhaps helping her husband out in the fields."

"Really?" She rolled her jade-green eyes in amazement. He liked that.

As the rickshaw pedalled past the woman, Catherine turned her head and kept observing her as she walked along the dirt path away from the road. Then, Catherine waved. The woman stopped walking and stood, startled.

Catherine smiled. She was outside in Lahore and not enclosed in her pretty house, and had this different sense of freedom. Yet she felt safe knowing that, with Kharak around, there wouldn't be any language barrier or uncertainty in this new place.

The rickshaw came to a junction and on the right side were Dina Nath's Gardens.

"This is a small garden, which now honours Dina Nath," Kharak said.

"Who was he?"

"He was part of Maharaja Ranjit Singh's government. He was head of the Civil and Finance Office. Some say that he was too close to the British during the Anglo-Sikh Wars and that all the wealth he had was bestowed by them."

"Is that so?"

"This is one of the few gardens that he built here."

"He must have been a lover of beautiful gardens."

"The British did give him the title of Raja." Kharak shrugged his shoulders.

Nandu took a swift left turn and pedalled hard, causing Kharak to slide slightly towards Catherine, nudging her shoulder. The rickshaw that followed them did the same.

"I'm sorry." He adjusted himself.

She looked at him and slowly blinked. "It's all right, Kharak."

In the breeze, she took a deep breath and shut her eyes, letting her other senses take over. *He is a true gentleman, simple and not pompous*, she thought.

For a few moments, neither uttered a word and the occasional ringing of the bicycle bell by Nandu became more obvious.

Kharak broke the silence. "There, ahead, is the area known as Baghbanpura. The surrounding land here, you see, was given as a gift by the Mughal Emperor Shah Jahan to a man called Mian, who had given his private village land to the emperor to build the Shalimar Gardens."

"That is a fascinating story."

"You will see that the area is lush with very many green gardens enclosed by gates that have arches of Mughal architecture." He paused abruptly. "There." He pointed in the distance to a brick gate with an archway. "One of the many small gardens."

"It's beautiful to see the different trees here – some bearing fruit while others have these vibrant flowers, which are a joy," she said.

I like his genuine enthusiasm for sharing with me what he knows about this place. His unusual accent of English suits him, she thought.

The road passed through this exuberant area and came to a fork joining the Great Trunk Road, which approached it from the right side.

On the left, beyond the dirt road, was a sprawling space enclosed by a high terracotta red-brick wall that was nearly half a mile long.

"Catherine, that is the boundary of the Shalimar Gardens."

24

The arched wooden door to the entrance was nearly twelve feet high. It was made of hardwood held together by six metal slats, which gave it a sturdy look. The spandrel did not cover the entire fifteen-metre-tall wall that formed the entrance, but fell short. The top ends of the entrance wall had circular domes, completing its symmetrical design.

On either side of the entrance, the wall was covered in deep blue-and-yellow mosaic patterns and indented arches.

"That is a magnificent entrance. I have seen grand entrances to castles in England, but the intricate and delicate patterns add beauty to it," Catherine said as she stood and observed it.

Kharak had just ended his conversation with Nandu, reminding him to stay around. "It encloses a beautiful garden," he replied. "Let's walk in." He led her towards the wooden gate. Sana followed them, walking ten feet behind.

"Oh, that's splendid!" Catherine exclaimed as they walked

into the enclosed passage room. The floor was marbled with red star shapes intertwined with beige droplet designs.

But it was the sight beyond the passageway that was breathtaking. The waves of architraves bordering the arched exit of the passageway formed a frame, with the clear blue sky at top and a water canal as far as she could see. The marble canal was the width of the arched entry and had fountains at the centre, which ran the entire length of the canal.

"This is beautiful." She beamed. "I now realise why you told me to visit this place the day we arrived here." Her eyes sparkled with joy.

They stepped onto the tiled area surrounding the canal. In excitement, she put her hand on his upper arm, pulled and squeezed it. She turned around, looking at the pristine green grass and trees.

"That pavilion you see, the white marble structure in the distance where the canal seems to end, is not the end of the garden. It gives an illusion that it is, but it isn't the end of the canal either," he said.

She let go of his arm. "Is that so?"

"Come on, let's walk and admire this." He smiled.

"You are a genius. You knew precisely where to take me and what to show me. How did you know that I enjoy nature?" She gazed directly at him.

"I didn't, but I'm glad that you appreciate this tiny part of my city. The Mughal Emperor Shah Jahan, who enjoyed being surrounded by opulence, built this. He instructed his best architects and engineers to build this grand garden."

They kept walking along the shallow water canal and towards the triple-arched white pavilion known as the Aiwan.

"It is very peaceful here. I'm trying to imagine how it must have been during the emperor's reign. I wonder if he ever spent meaningful time in this tranquil place," she said.

An English couple, startled at seeing the two, walked past

them. The man acknowledged Catherine by removing his hat. He did not make an effort to make eye contact with Kharak.

The gardens were not bustling with people as the majority of the affluent locals visited in the afternoon, at the peak of the afternoon heat. A young Sikh couple were seated beneath a walnut tree. Their children were running around after one another under the close supervision of their hawk-eyed maid.

"How often do you visit this place?"

"Not that often. My friend Lal – he works with me at the railways – we come here together and chat the afternoon away, especially in the middle of summer."

They passed another straight canal that was perpendicular to the one they were following and that crossed their path. They approached the Aiwan.

"Oh my, the next section of the garden is a few metres lower than we are!" Catherine realised as she entered the Aiwan and walked towards the half-metre safety wall at the edge and saw the ground level changing ahead.

"This level of the garden is called the Bestower of Pleasure. The next level that you see down there," he pointed at the large, square pool of water, "is the Bestower of Goodness. And the final level, which is further away, is known as the Bestower of Life."

She paused for a while in thought, taking in everything.

"Not only is it beautiful, it has this poetic meaning to it that just adds to its grandeur."

What a romantic place; it mesmerises me, she thought. *I like him, too.* She stole a gaze at Kharak.

The Aiwan had the same mosaic-patterned marble floor as the entrance they had passed through.

After a few minutes observing the view, Kharak spoke. "Let's walk down to the next level, to the Bestower of Goodness." He led her to a flight of steps that were on the side of the Aiwan, which seemed to go under it and out onto the middle terrace.

Catherine took two brisk steps to catch up with Kharak, and a third step just to be very close to him.

The entrance to the middle terrace opened up to an immense square pool, with more fountains shooting water in unison.

"I am lost for words at its beauty." Catherine turned around and levelled her palms at the cascade of water flowing from the upper level to the square pool over a slide of wedges. "Look, it's like sparkling diamonds falling. I cannot imagine how they built this waterfall."

She wanted to touch the flowing water, but it was out of reach.

Kharak walked to the raised marble throne platform at the edge of the pool. "The emperor and his empress often used to sit here and marvel at all this."

Catherine walked towards him and examined it. "Should I stand on it?"

"You can't manage that."

"Are you daring me?" she teased.

"You wouldn't."

"Watch me."

Holding on to the short marble balustrade on the platform, she placed her foot on the support and, in two steps, she was standing on the throne platform. Sana, who was further back, watched her with a worried look.

"I told you I could do it." She placed her hands on her hips.

"You surprise me."

Raising her arms to the sky and tilting her head upwards, she declared, "I am Queen of Lahore."

"Really?" he laughed.

"Of course. Right now I am." She paused. "Just for these ten metres," she laughed, unable to keep a straight face. "What's that?" She pointed to the terracotta pavilion on the other side of the pool.

"It's the pavilion the emperor used to use to rest and take a nap during the summer afternoons."

"Let's see it." Catherine extended her right hand, palm down, towards him, wanting him to help her step down from the throne. She felt his warm hand gently supporting hers.

She isn't wearing her gloves, yet her hands are silky. She squeezed my hand, he thought.

The breeze drifting across the pool eased the intensity of the midday sun, providing cooling relief. Tiny speckles of sunlight dotted Catherine's face as it seeped through the narrow spaces in her straw hat.

The two terracotta pavilions faced each other from opposite ends of the pool. It was cool under the shade of the pavilion roof as it was designed to allow the breeze to blow through it. The trickling sound of the water as it flowed from the fountain and into the pool of water added to the tranquillity of the pavilion.

Catherine walked to the edge of the pavilion bordering the pool. The sweet fragrance of the open red fruits still hanging on the pomegranate trees that surrounded the pavilion wafted in the air.

She paused before flexing her knee to raise her heel and, with feminine deftness, unlaced and removed her boots.

"I'm dipping my feet in the cool water." She sat down on the edge and let her feet dangle into the sparkling water. "Ouch!" she shrieked as the cool water lapped her warm feet.

Kharak grinned. "Cooled you instantly."

"Join me."

"I'm not too sure."

"I dare you, Kharak," she said, with impish delight.

Slowly, he took off his boots and socks. "How dare you dare me?" he laughed.

He sat down a comfortable distance away on the edge of the pavilion's mosaic-marbled floor and lowered his feet into the pool.

The tingling in my feet does feel remarkably good, he thought.

"Cold?" she asked.

"Not quite. It does feel nice, though."

Making circles in the water with her feet, Catherine observed the gardens around her from her current position. Parakeets flew from one tree to another, dancing on the branches, chirping in glory. There was a British couple at the opposite end of the pool, standing and staring at them. She had thought that there would be more people here.

She gaped at the top half of the small white single-storey building on the top section they had come from. It had a closed wooden door with two wooden shutters covering what looked like windows.

"What's that?"

"An addition by the Sikh emperor Maharaja Ranjit Singh. It was a rest house and it housed an earlier British traveller through Lahore there." He paused. "Talking about the British, during their fight against the Sikhs in the Anglo-Sikh War, they bribed a few Sikhs to betray us. And that is how they won the war."

"That's unfair. Do you resent the British?"

"Not quite."

"I am British – do you think of me like them? Do you resent me?" she asked genuinely, leaning closer to him and nudging his shoulder with hers.

"Of course not." He looked directly into her eyes. "You have nothing to do with what happened fifty years ago. I feel everyone is unique and I look at them individually."

"I'm glad."

"It doesn't feel right to blame you. You are a good friend and I like you," Kharak said, still holding his deep, lingering gaze.

With the sunlight hitting the surface of the pool, the ripples of water that were formed were reflected as shiny semi-crescent arcs on his face.

It was in that moment that she knew, and felt, that, to her, Kharak had become more than just a friend.

25

The midday rays of sunlight permeated the canopy of walnut trees, sprinkling the walkway that they lined in the lowest section of the garden.

Catherine and Kharak walked under this leafy cover, having spent an hour sitting under the restful shade of a mulberry tree conversing on the history of Lahore and the tapestry of its culture, which fascinated her.

Realising the time, Kharak asked her, "It's nearly lunchtime. Are you hungry?"

"A little. I seem to be eating more often here than in Bath."

"I admit, I didn't think about what to do for lunch."

"Is there somewhere here?"

"Not that I know of." Kharak brushed his hand lightly across his chin as he thought about what to do. "If you want, we could go to the centre of Lahore."

"I'd like that. It's not as if I'm in any hurry," she said without hesitation.

"My friend, Lal, his family run a small shop with a cafe and the food is very good, and they can always cook something not too spicy."

"That seems acceptable, as I am keen on trying the local food." She paused. "Should I worry about getting ill after trying some?" she asked, with a slight apprehensive rising of the eyebrow.

He smiled. "I'll make sure that they prepare something fairly light."

"Let's go, then."

Railway Road ran away from the station, with the old walled city of Lahore a further block on the right. Nandu pedalled vigorously in the midday heat with sweat dripping down his forehead. He was used to this and he was earning more that day than he would on a normal day; a satisfying day at work. The other rickshaw, in which Sana sat, followed them, always a few yards behind.

To Catherine and Kharak's amusement, the pacey return journey was bumpy with a lot of shoulder-nudging, which led to random laughter.

At the junction, a right turn along Nisbet Road led them into the furthest end of the bustling Anarkali area.

Catherine observed that the buildings were densely positioned, with few open spaces between them compared to the outskirts of the city. The buildings that lined both sides of Anarkali Street were architecturally very similar to buildings back home, with top storeys, but the main difference being the curved arches of the windows that came from the Mughal influence. This area had no trees lining the street.

The Senas' store was towards the near end, which was the wider part of Anarkali Street.

"I didn't think it would be this built-up. All these shops selling various things, with a throng of people around, it feels like a busy city," Catherine said as she raised her left hand to hold her hat.

"In this bazaar, one can buy anything that is made in the northern part of India."

"That's surprising."

As the rickshaw trundled along the street, an odd sight was an Englishman standing on the left-hand pavement holding an umbrella. At first, he was surprised to see them both in the rickshaw and, upon passing, he gave Catherine a reluctant wave and she reciprocated.

Ahead on the right side of the street was the Senas' store. Like most stores along the street, the front of the shop had flexible canvas awnings to protect it from the sun and the rain.

Nandu stopped the rickshaw and Kharak hopped off first to help Catherine. He offered his hand in support and Catherine held on to it as she carefully stepped down. To his surprise, he realised that, this time, she held his hand tightly and, despite being off the rickshaw, was still holding on to it.

I tremble every time she does that, Kharak thought.

Noticing the momentary frozen expression on his face, and feeling embarrassed, she let go of his hand and changed the conversation.

"There is a fine aroma of fragrant spices in the air."

"This is only one aspect of Anarkali Bazaar. Further down, it is like a maze of alleys that get narrower, which are daunting for someone who is new to the area," he said.

Some of the traders and shoppers observed Catherine – the British woman who seemed out of place with a Sikh man.

"Let's walk into this store." Kharak took a few steps and opened the glazed door, ushering her in. They both walked inside.

There were randomly placed stools on the uneven wooden floor. In front of the counter were open hemp baskets of ground red chillies, cinnamon bark, salt, sugar and dried turmeric root. The shelves on the rear wall were sparse, holding a few rectangular silver containers with lids.

138

What was unusual was that there were cotton sheets as well as hemp baskets for sale, hanging on one side of the room.

Behind the counter was a tiny middle-aged man with a moustache and a balding head.

"How are you, my boy?"

"Fine, thank you, Mr Sena. This is Catherine, my guest from England. I'm showing her around."

"Hello and welcome," Mr Sena said in Hindi, smiling.

Kharak translated for Catherine.

"Nice to meet you," she replied.

Mr Sena looked at Kharak. "Lal is upstairs; you go ahead out the back and I shall call him for you." He rolled his head and waved his arm, directing them further into the store. "Lal! Lal!" he shouted in his high-pitched voice, startling Catherine.

She followed Kharak, who led her through a narrow corridor to the rear of the store and finally out to the rear veranda in the courtyard, where they sat around an informal table. Sana sat alone on a chair at the far corner of the courtyard.

It did not take long for Lal to join them at the usual small family table. Catherine was sitting on the chair next to Kharak.

"Catherine, this is Lal. We grew up together and he is more of a brother to me than a friend. Lal, this is—"

"She must be Catherine," Lal interrupted.

"How do you know my name?"

"Kharak told me about you." He glanced at him deliberately.

"Did he really?" Catherine asked with a glint in her eye.

Trying to avoid any meaningful blushing, Kharak quickly avoided the conversation. "We are hungry, Lal, let's have lunch."

Lunch consisted of Mrs Sena's delicious green lentil stew with rice, and Catherine was in awe at its aroma and intense flavour. She had never tasted food like this and what she was accustomed to seemed bland in comparison.

The talk over lunch was delightfully light-hearted, with Kharak and Lal reminiscing about the fun they had had while growing up in Lahore. Catherine sensed a great bond between the two that reminded her of her friendship with her close friend Florence in Bath, whom she missed talking to.

It was noticeable to Lal that Catherine often stared dreamily at Kharak.

"I'm a bit sad that he is leaving me to go and work in East Africa," Kharak said, sipping a glass of lassi.

"Really? That sounds exciting." Catherine clasped her hands in her lap. "What will you be doing?" She shifted her gaze to Lal.

"The same thing: I will be working for the British, building the railway line from Mombasa."

"How long will you be away?"

"At least six months, maybe a year, depending on how working and living there turns out. I've never been abroad so don't know what to expect."

"That is still exciting, I think," Catherine said.

"I will still miss Lal."

"No, you won't; you will probably find a new friend to spend time with." Lal winked.

"Is that jealousy?" Kharak elbowed him.

"Your happiness comes first, *yaar*." Lal put an arm around Kharak's shoulders.

Catherine looked at the two friends sharing the table.

It's incredible to see that people are the same, wherever they may live, whatever their background and culture. Everyone has the same emotions and feelings that bond one to another, she thought.

The time after lunch passed pleasantly and Lal's mother often appeared with more food or to collect the utensils.

Catherine appreciated how welcome she was made to feel by her hosts, who did not even know her. Her earlier 'uninvited guest' feeling had evaporated within the first few minutes and she was glad Kharak had brought her here to experience a homely lunch in Lahore.

Standing at the door leading out onto the street from the Senas' shop entrance, Catherine was ready to step out.

"Nice to have met you and your family, Lal. Thank you for lunch and let your mother know that it was truly delicious."

"You are welcome. Kharak's friend is our friend. See you soon," Mr Sena said aloud in Hindi from behind the counter, which was translated by Lal.

Catherine waved her goodbyes to Lal and his family and stepped out with Kharak onto Anarkali Street, ready to go back home. Their rickshaw was on the other side of the street, but Nandu was not around.

26

They crossed Anarkali Street, including Sana, who always kept her distance. While waiting, Catherine peeked through the window of a tiny shop and spotted what looked like wooden boxes of various sizes.

"While we wait for Nandu, I'm just entering this shop to have a look."

"All right." Kharak nodded as he strained his eyes to catch sight of Nandu.

Catherine opened the flimsy, creaking door and walked into a cramped room, which had carved dark wooden trunks of various sizes stacked on the floor. Facing the door was a three-foot-high pine shelf cabinet that had miniature trunks.

As she stepped to take a closer look, a head popped out through the beaded string curtain that hung from the door at the rear of the room.

"*Kya chahte ho?*" the dark-complexioned, bearded man said.

"I am looking at these wonderful storage boxes."

"*Kya?*" he said, with a confused expression.

"Do you speak English?"

"*Na...*" He shook his head.

He picked up a couple of wooden jewellery boxes, opened them and exhibited them to her. One of them was four inches by three inches, with delicate, symmetrical carvings of interlocking patterns of leaves and flowers, and a brass inlay on its lid.

Catherine could not resist taking it from his hands to admire it intimately. The front side, which had a small latch, had equal numbers of wooden panels inlayed with brass. The wood was smooth with an elaborate grain and a waxed finish. The more she observed the box in her hand, the more she was astounded by its beauty.

Her concentration was interrupted by the sound of the creaking door opening. "Catherine, Nandu is here."

"Kharak," she turned around to face him, "this jewellery box is magnificent. I'm amazed at the craftsmanship."

Kharak walked towards her to see what she was admiring. By now, she had opened the box, revealing a deep blue silk inlay that covered the entire interior.

"Do you like it?"

"It's pretty, dainty and unique. I do like it."

"Should I ask him how much it is?"

She paused, looking at it again. "No, not today. Perhaps I shall get it another day – it will be an excuse for you to bring me here again." She grinned.

"Thank you very much," she said to the vendor. "Perhaps I will buy it next week," she added, handing it back to him as Kharak translated the message.

"*Jeete raho,*" he said with a toothy smile.

143

The mid-afternoon sun had slanted towards the west. There was less congestion of buildings as their rickshaw passed along Upper Mall Road, which bisected Donald Town, a south-eastern part of Lahore.

Catherine sat quietly in the rickshaw, thinking about the day. *If I had never encountered Kharak at the railway station when I arrived here, I would have never known him and I would not have had this wonderful day with him. What is it about him that I find so enchanting? Now that I'm going back home, why do I have an urge to see him again?*

"Kharak?"

He faced her.

"Thank you for a delightful day. It has been even better than I thought it would be." Her eyelashes fluttered slowly. "How can I thank you for taking me around and allowing me to experience real local food?"

"No need to thank me. I had a good day, as it's not often I do this. I probably won't get the chance to do it again… not for a long time." He paused for effect. "Maybe never."

"I was thinking, I want to thank you for today. So, how about a bit of English cuisine for you to experience in Lahore?" Her eyes widened.

"You cook for me?" he laughed. "You have all the servants to do that for you."

"That's true." She hesitated while thinking. "I would help prepare a picnic lunch for us and you could take me to another beautiful spot where we can enjoy it."

He took a deep breath. "I don't know."

"You don't know another beautiful spot here in Lahore? I disagree," she teased. Without giving him too much time to mull it over, she asked, "How about tomorrow, lunch?"

"Erm… I can't do tomorrow." He lowered his gaze.

"When will you be free, then?" Her tone lowered in disappointment.

"How about the day after tomorrow?

Catherine was glad that he had a specific day in mind. She controlled her excitement. "Perfect."

"Say, eleven o'clock in the morning and, like today, I will come over with Nandu to pick you up."

"Where will we go for our picnic?"

"I won't tell you," he replied with a glint in his eyes.

Balu, the broad-shouldered gatekeeper with a bushy beard, was present as ever at the gate when a tired Nandu pedalled his rickshaw to a halt. He got a brief chance to pause and take a breath before riding in towards Catherine's house.

"How much do I owe Nandu for his fare?" she asked.

"Nothing. I will sort it out with him."

"But surely..." Catherine could not finish her sentence.

"As my guest... and friend... I will not accept you paying for all or any part of the fare. That does not happen around me, Catherine. And with the arrangement I have with him, I will clear his payments at the end of the week."

"That's very kind of you."

There was one thought that had been lingering in Catherine's mind as the day had progressed: whether Kharak liked her as she liked him. This had eased when he had agreed to spend another day with her. *He says that I'm his friend. But how close?* she asked herself. She sat in brief quietude.

Being the late afternoon, the sunlight had an orange tinge but didn't feel very warm. Watering can in hand, the gardener was busy watering the new flowerbeds at the distant end of the garden. Sana, who was in the other carriage, felt that she had had a day that was different from her normal routine. Rarely had she been driven around Lahore in a rickshaw; she liked it.

Nandu brought the rickshaw to a rusty stop in front of the veranda steps. Stepping out first, Kharak helped Catherine off the rickshaw.

145

"Thank you for a glorious day, Kharak. I truly enjoyed it."

"It has been my pleasure."

Catherine took two steps towards him, glanced around to ensure that no one was looking, raised her heels to elevate herself and then pecked him on his cheek. "Thank you." She raced off up the steps and onto the veranda.

Despite his heart racing in bewilderment at what had just happened, Kharak sat back in the rickshaw without making it obvious. No one had ever done this to him before and he felt strange. It felt good.

As the rickshaw moved away slowly, Catherine waved goodbye, revealing her comforting smile. For Kharak, it was in that moment that he felt she was more than a friend.

Part 2

27

Tsavo, British Kenya

Around 3,400 miles away from Lahore, the Indian workers were returning to their camp after another blistering day under the simmering East African sun laying the railway tracks.

The white thorns of the acacia bushes gave them an ominous grey tone in the dry season. These bushes grew effortlessly in this harsh place where the dusty soil was red and so fine that it penetrated the toughest boots.

Time and time again, acacia thorns lacerated the unprotected legs of some of the workers, causing infection in their weeping wounds. The only remedy they had was iodine solution, which not only discoloured the skin, but also had an overpowering smell.

A fast-flowing stream, which was shallow during the dry season, had slowed the construction of the railway line across it due to the complications of bridge construction over a wide gully. In order to press on, it was decided that while the construction of a bridge across the Tsavo River progressed, the laying of the tracks would carry on over the other side.

Sandy patches sprinkled the banks of the river, which also contained palm trees, that mingled with the yellow-barked fever trees, producing cream scented flowers. The river's edge provided soothing relief from the dreariness of the thorny bushes.

After passing through the arid Taru Desert, this campsite seemed an ideal spot, and a few days earlier, one of the first things Ungan and Chand did after pitching their tent was to have an invigorating dip in the cool water of the flowing river.

The sleeping tents for the workers were split into two camps, one on each side of the river: one for the workers laying the new track and the other for the workers constructing the bridge.

Ungan's tent was on the opposite bank to the railhead and he was eagerly anticipating resting his head on his pillow. It had been a long day. The hissing sound of the insects became more pronounced as the evening approached.

Walking beside him was his friend, Chand, who always kept abreast of all the gossip that emanated from the group of workers.

"I heard that one of the coolies has been missing for a day now. No one knows where he's gone." Chand lowered his voice.

"That's news to me. What happened?" Ungan asked as he patted the dust off his sleeve.

"Rumour has it that there may be a gang of thieves amongst us here and they may have robbed him of his savings, murdered him and buried his body." Chand's eyes widened with fear. "What have Sahib Colonel Patterson and Sahib Allen said about these thieves?"

"I don't think they have said anything about this incident."

What Ungan and Chand never knew was that even the old caravan leaders disliked this place as a stopping post. It was often noted that porters seem to desert their caravans here. The local Akamba people had named this river Tsavo, meaning 'slaughter'.

The crossing of the river was a concern for the colonial authorities as it was causing a delay and that was something to be avoided. It needed a capable engineer with the right experience in such situations. Colonel John Patterson was the chief engineer commissioned by the Uganda Railway Committee to oversee the building of the bridge across the Tsavo River in earnest.

At five foot eleven inches, he was slim with broad shoulders. Although he bore a moustache, his symmetrical face and low cheekbones softened his robust features. Being a compulsive perfectionist, a man with a British military background and experience of constructing railway bridges in India, he was the ideal appointment and guaranteed patriotic vigour.

Since the arrival of Colonel Patterson, Ungan had been given the increased responsibility of supervising his four personal assistants, whose work included cooking and cleaning.

This was one of the last few days that he would work in the afternoon, as his hours on the building section were to reduce on the orders of Colonel Patterson.

"It's all very hush-hush. No one talks openly about it, but something is definitely going on," Chand said.

"Keep yourself low and don't talk too much about it to other workers whom you are not too sure about," Ungan suggested.

"But where do you hide your saved money?"

"Chand," Ungan sighed, "I know you are naive in certain things, but don't ask anyone that and don't expect them to tell you about it."

"I hide it in the folded seam of my tent," Chand whispered.

"Look, I'm not interested in knowing. And I said, don't tell anyone."

Having passed the first group of workers' tents, they trekked along the declining, dusty path leading to the temporary wooden walkway across the stream. Their tents were on the other bank of the river.

Walking carefully and avoiding the gaps between the planks of Mvule hardwood on the walkway, Chand glanced to his left side at the sprouting stone piers that would support the railway bridge above the burbling stream beneath.

The rocks used to build the piers were discovered by chance when Patterson, while searching the area, stumbled upon a ravine made up of the perfect stone a few miles away in the bush.

"Narain has done fine masonry work around the piers of the bridge. I know he works less there and more under you now," he said, pointing his finger at the incomplete piers.

"He has, but Patterson wants him to be one of his personal assistants, doing all his personal work for him."

"He must favour him."

"Are you a touch jealous, Chand? Maybe I could put in a word for you and you could be the cleaner."

"No thanks," was his prompt sniggered reply.

Narain was a multitalented Sikh and a former soldier of the British East India Company with excellent skill in stonework and an affable personality. Everyone got on with him. Despite being an ex-soldier, he was softly spoken and it was this that Colonel Patterson admired and had made him choose Narain to be one of his personal assistants.

Ungan crossed the walkway and looked wearily at the ascending path, which had rutted gullies created by the running rainwater during the previous rainy season. He thought of his wife and her glowing smile, and his two young boys running around the farm he intended to build.

He reassured himself that the money he earned here would enable him to buy a larger plot of land on which he would build his house and still have ample land to start a farm and be self-sufficient. The temporary detachment would be worth it.

Life will be better. It's another year of hard labour, he thought.

28

Lahore

Rays of early-morning sun were falling onto the wooden worktop in the kitchen through the French windows. The intermittent tapping of the knife blade on the wooden chopping board as it sliced through a cucumber interrupted the silence.

Catherine stood there, still in her night gown, busy working in the kitchen. Today, she could not allow her cooking skills to fail her. Preparation of the picnic lunch was underway and she felt the need to keep true to herself by not asking the house cook to help her.

The cook had already prepared the sourdough bread for the family the previous night, which was a bonus for Catherine, as she did not have to bake it. With the help of the cook, she had baked the sponge cake following her grandmother's recipe the previous afternoon, and now only the cucumber sandwiches and chicken sandwiches needed to be prepared.

She walked into the pantry, aiming for the large clay pot that was fitted on a special raised metal stand in the corner. The pot contained water, and in this water were bottles of Hockheimer wine and a few bottles of C. Butcher's freshly brewed root ginger beer. The clay pot kept the drinks cool by losing internal heat from its surface, thereby cooling the water. It was an effective method of cooling drinks, especially in the hot and humid summer before the monsoon.

Catherine took the lid off the pot and dipped her hand in. The drinks were cool and she decided to leave them in there until the very last moment before she left.

Catherine heard the kitchen door open.

"You are up early this morning," her mother said, walking in.

"You startled me." She turned, looking at Ethel. "I'm getting lunch ready, hopefully with plenty of time left."

Walking casually towards the kitchen cabinet, past Catherine, Ethel opened the lower cabinet, removed the wicker picnic basket and placed it on the worktop.

"You seem excited."

"Why do you say this?"

"It's obvious: waking up early this morning, doing all the cooking by yourself, coupled with the toing and froing in the house since yesterday." Ethel gazed at Catherine above her spectacles.

"I am looking forward to a nice picnic today."

"Don't get carried away, my dear."

"And what would that mean?"

There was a reluctant pause. "You can use this basket as your hamper."

"Mother, you are avoiding my question. What do you mean by not getting carried away?"

"Not getting too close to him." She directed her gaze at Catherine.

"I don't know what you mean exactly." Catherine let out a sigh. Deliberately not wanting to think about her mother's assertion, she changed the direction of the conversation.

"Where is the red-and-white checked groundsheet? I need that too."

Without any further awkward talk, Ethel helped Catherine to complete the preparation of the sandwiches, which were wrapped in thin paper and arranged neatly in the basket together with the sponge cake. In went the napkins, glasses and plates. Part of her was glad to see that Catherine was enjoying her stay in Lahore, as this had been a significant concern for her in Bath, not knowing how her daughter would accept the change. But another part of her dreaded the friendship that was developing between her daughter and Kharak. *This will be the last time I'll allow her to go and Sana will accompany her again.*

At ten minutes to eleven, Catherine had nearly finished dressing up. With her urge to be noticed, she had taken much longer than normal. Seated at her Indian oak dressing table, she lifted her silver pendant earrings, slanted her neck and deftly put them on her perfectly shaped earlobes. She opened the top of her bottle of Floris, her favourite fragrance, and rubbed a few dashes behind her ears and around her neck.

She felt enlivened.

It was fifteen minutes past eleven when her warm anticipation started drifting into uneasiness. Kharak had not arrived yet and she did not want to entertain the thought that he may have forgotten about the picnic.

Has he forgotten about today? I hope not, she thought. *I'm sure there will be a reason why he is late, but he will turn up. I know he will*, she reassured herself, while seated in the drawing room, looking out of the window at the gate in anticipation.

It was twenty minutes past eleven when her fixated eyes saw the gatekeeper slowly open the gate to reveal the now-recognisable Nandu and his pedal-rickshaw. She was more interested in his passenger.

155

Seated there was the unmistakeable figure of Kharak.

Catherine was delighted and, without wasting another moment, she was through the passageway and in the kitchen, asking Sana to pick up the picnic basket and the drinks from the pantry.

"See you in the afternoon, Mother," she said as she approached the door leading out to the veranda. She was oblivious to her mother's reply as she was keen to be out of the house.

Approaching the house, Kharak saw Catherine standing on top of the steps with her arms in front of her, holding the picnic basket. She was wearing a light grey summer dress that had a fitted waist belt and white lace neck and sleeves; it complimented her figure. The straw hat framed her natural wavy hair.

She looks beautiful.

Catherine smiled as she watched the rickshaw come to a halt.

"I'm sorry, Catherine, I'm late. I got delayed running an errand." He lowered his eyebrows apologetically as he got off.

"It's alright, I knew you would come." The delay no longer mattered to her. He was here now and that was what mattered.

Kharak took the hamper off her and, as he helped place the hamper securely on the little rack in front of the footrest next to a tiny brown-paper package, Ethel walked onto the veranda, dismayed at seeing Catherine not sitting in Sana's rickshaw.

"Hello, Kharak. It seems like it's becoming a habit, us meeting," she said, with a wry smile.

"It so happens, ma'am." He laughed it off.

"Don't be late. Mrs Wittingham is joining us again later in the afternoon; she's bringing her daughter as well." Ethel looked directly at Catherine.

"I won't, Mother," she replied as she sat on the back seat of the rickshaw, not paying too much attention to her mother's remark.

Kharak pinched his upper thigh to lift his khaki trousers as he climbed in to sit beside Catherine. For the first time since they had arrived in Lahore, Ethel felt uneasy to see him sitting beside her daughter and riding off, yet she knew that Catherine felt at ease.

29

The breeze had a cooling effect as Catherine and Kharak travelled across the European Quarter towards the centre of Lahore. This was a relief as it took the edge off the sultry day.

The surroundings had a familiar feel as they passed the same railway crossing, with the train station towards the road leading to the left and the Railway Road straight ahead that led towards Anarkali Bazaar.

It seemed that each day in the city was the same, yet different. Catherine noticed the local people, men in their bright turbans and women in their colourful saris, talking and shouting; the drama seemed the same but with a different frame around it. There were genuine smiles on the faces of the locals.

Nandu was right there, being part of the drama with his rickshaw, winding around and avoiding the bullock carts, pull-rickshaws and even the lazy long-horned cows sitting in the middle of the road. Never did he shy away from using his bell on the handle to warn everyone around him, sweat trickling down his face and arms.

"Where are we heading to?"

"There is a lovely spot by the Ravi River. I occasionally go there when I need a bit of solitude. I think it will be a good place for our picnic."

"Perhaps. I shall be the judge. I'm looking forward to seeing the place." Catherine had that playful look again. The last few days had elevated her feelings and she had not missed home.

Every time the rickshaw swerved, it allowed Kharak to get closer to Catherine, albeit momentarily. He occasionally caught the refreshing whiff of the patchouli-and-musk Floris fragrance that she had on. It was intriguing.

At the junction of Lower Mall Road, Nandu took a left turn going southwards. Straight ahead was the sprawling white building of the Governor of Punjab with its manicured rich green lawn dotted with scarlet flowers in bloom.

From a distance, Catherine could see the horse guards in their immaculate blue kaftans manning the road at the entrance.

"I'm surprised to see the soldiers on camels. Never have I seen camels used in place of horses."

"It's very common here in Lahore. Some people even use them as part of their wedding processions," Kharak said, eyeing the governor's residence.

"I can see the resemblance to British architecture mixed with the Mughal arches."

This part of the city was spread out, with ample open spaces. It seemed obvious that the road they were on was a boundary of sorts, with the east side containing buildings whereas to the west, the ground was flat with open pastures.

A few minutes down the road, Nandu took a right turn into a much narrower and more uneven road that went towards the east.

"We are heading towards the river. It isn't very far from here."

"Oh gosh, the road is rather bumpy here." Catherine held her straw hat with her left hand.

There were ruts on the road that seemed invisible on the sandy surface. The road was raised in the middle and sloped towards the edge, with the Dab grass forming the boundary. Numerous Kikar acacia trees, with their spindly branches and leaves, broke up the flat grassland. Inhabiting these trees were purple sunbirds with their long beaks, dancing necks and intense glossy blue and purple feathers.

Beyond the mulberry trees and walnut trees, Catherine spotted a silvery sheet. "Is that the river?" She turned to face Kharak with her dazzling, excited eyes.

"Yes. We will travel along the road and you can see it curves to the left and seems to disappear beyond those shrubs between the trees." He pointed.

The road inclined gradually as it drew nearer to the river. Nandu was sweating profusely by now, having to pedal even harder.

At the top of the incline, the view of the river was clearer. It was nearly half a kilometre wide during the rainy season, but at present it was half that, with the blue-green water flowing gently. The bank with the floodplain was silted, with fine green grass sprouting.

"Stop there, near the path," Kharak instructed Nandu in Punjabi, pointing ahead.

The rickshaw eventually came to a halt at the precise spot where a trodden path led to a neem tree that was above the alluvial floodplain, yet still on the bank of the river. It provided shade over a perfect patch of grass with uninterrupted views across the flowing river for miles.

Kharak helped Catherine out of the rickshaw before getting the hamper from the rack, together with the tiny paper bag that he had placed there before reaching her house.

"I managed to get these foldable wooden stools to sit on."

He walked to the rear of the rickshaw and lifted the little cover of the storage space and removed two wooden stools.

"Please allow me to help you carry something." Catherine leaned forward with her hands open.

"You don't have to."

"Kharak, I should help you. No need for formalities between us." She blinked slowly.

"You could carry this bag, then." He handed her the tiny paper bag.

Kharak instructed Nandu to pick them up at three o' clock and, until then, he was free to carry on with his work elsewhere. Walking over to Sana's rickshaw, he shrugged his shoulders and told the driver that he could wait or come back at three o' clock. Sana got out of the rickshaw and the driver decided to wait.

Carrying the stools in one hand and the hamper in the other, Kharak led Catherine along the trodden grass path towards his favourite spot.

"I will help carry the stools," Sana offered.

"Today, we won't need a lot of your assistance." Catherine smiled.

Sana acknowledged Catherine's meaning and kept her distance.

Minutes later, Catherine and Kharak laid the checked red-and-white sheet on the grass, placing the wicker hamper in the middle and the two short stools side by side overlooking the river. Twenty metres further back, after unrolling her cotton sheet, Sana sat down in the sun.

Catherine gazed across the bank of the river, taking in the splendour of the place. It was away from the sounds and clatter that dominated the built-up area of the city. There was serenity in this remarkable place. She turned around, facing Kharak, who momentarily shifted his gaze from her. Feeling relaxed, she removed her straw hat and fluffed her hair as she ran her fingers through it.

"You look pretty today," he blurted out. "I mean, err... the colour, as well as the dress, suits you," he added, feeling embarrassed.

"Thank you. I bought this from a boutique just off Milsom Street in Bath. It was being fitted on a mannequin in the window when I saw it, so I just walked in and bought it. Although I had to have it altered to fit my frame," she said as she sat down on the stool beside Kharak.

The clear sky across the river above the treeline was broken by puffy clouds. In front of this backdrop, a black kite drifted in the thermals, looking down below for suitable prey. The small pier that went a few metres into the river was empty and there were no boats roped to it.

"I'm quite amazed when I think that I never knew what to expect here in Lahore and what it would be like. I was totally wrong to assume that my time here would be full of boredom," she said, as she stared blankly at the flying kite. "Meeting you has really made this time wonderful indeed." She paused. "I really mean it, Kharak." She looked towards him with sincerity in her eyes.

It was true that the past few days together had been memorable, yet he found his fondness for her inexplicable and that frustrated him.

"What do you intend to do when you go back?" he asked her.

"I have been lucky to have completed my general education at Queen's College, London and obtained my certificates of knowledge. In time, I hope to teach, but my parents want me to get married soon and that would mean the end of me being able to teach. But eventually, as desired by society, I will get married and start a family."

"Has your family got anyone in mind?" he asked.

"I don't know about their thoughts, but I have not found anyone there yet. What about you?"

"About what?"

162

"About you finding a suitable person to get married to?"

Kharak paused. "No one, but my family keep pushing me, just like your family." He took a deep breath and sighed internally.

It could have been the lingering fragrance of the fresh grass coupled with the river water in the air that encouraged them to open the hamper. Catherine carefully unwrapped the sandwiches, got the napkins out and decorated the plate with food before passing it to Kharak.

Taking a bite, he was actually impressed with the freshness and taste of the sandwiches. "This is delicious. Surely you couldn't make this." He winked at her.

"Mr Kharak, this is all my work." Catherine lifted the empty glasses. "What would you like to drink? Ginger beer or Hockheimer white wine?"

Unsure, and never having tasted the wine, he passed that decision to her. "Pour me whatever you think will be right with the food."

I like this simplicity about him. There is no pretentiousness and I feel at ease whenever I'm around him, Catherine thought.

She poured half a glass of white wine for him and one for herself.

Lunch went by watching the Indian pond herons gingerly wading through the shallow pools of water, searching for trapped fish at the edge of the river. Half a mile upriver, a few of the locals could be seen walking across the floating path that was built across the river. It was constructed of wooden planks with railings on floating wooden canoes, which enabled it to float up and down with the water level. Nearer to them, the iridescent butterflies fluttered from one wild flower to another.

After finishing lunch, Kharak looked at the skyline across the river. "There is a rainstorm brewing."

"How do you know?"

"The puffy clouds have grown upwards and the edges are getting greyer and flatter." He pointed at them.

Catherine flicked her curls of silky hair behind her ear as she observed the clouds.

"How long do you think before it starts raining?"

"Cannot say. Depends on the wind speed and direction."

"It doesn't bother me if it rains. It shan't ruin my afternoon." She raised her glass, taking a sip.

She is pretty.

The next instant, she lowered her head reflexively as a white-breasted kingfisher with a toad trapped in its huge bill flew to rest on the branch of the neem tree beneath which they marvelled at the scenery.

Kharak could not help but giggle.

Catherine gaped at him and started laughing. The next moment, they were both chuckling, and every time they looked at each other, the laughter just increased. Soon, Catherine had tears trickling down her cheeks and her sides were hurting with joy.

Still laughing, Kharak leant forward to pick up the napkin lying in the hamper for Catherine to wipe her tears. The stool pivoted on its front leg, which slipped on the ground cloth, and the next moment he lost his balance and ended up on his knees.

Another uncontrollable fit of laughter erupted. Catherine had her left hand holding her aching stomach and her right hand went forward, grabbing his hand that held the napkin.

He felt her warm palm glide over his hand and eventually take the napkin from his fingers.

They eventually managed to control their laughter, but it needed both to stand up to ease the stitches in the sides of their bellies.

Unknown to her, the last invisible barrier that was forbidding her to get close to him had just faded away in that moment of tittering joy.

A rumble of thunder in the distance interrupted the moment.

"You were right, Kharak. Looks like it is raining over there." She patted her lower eyelids dry.

"The signs were there. Hopefully we will reach home before the rain."

Raising his eyebrows, Kharak remembered the little package. He turned his torso, bent down and picked it up from the side of his stool.

"Catherine, I have got something for you." He reached for his bag. "I hope you like it." He handed her the package wrapped in brown paper.

This took her by complete surprise and she did not know what to say or do. "Whatever this is," she hesitated, "you shouldn't have got it," she said as she accepted it.

Intrigued, Catherine undid the knot of the jute string before proceeding to unwrap it carefully. Her eyes widened when she saw the wooden jewellery box; the exact one she had seen in the shop in Anarkali Bazaar!

"Oh! Kharak, you should not have bought this for me."

"You liked it and I wanted you to remember your time in Lahore when you go back to England," he said softly. "So I got it for you."

"Thank you so much." Catherine took a step towards him, leaned forwards and gave him a soft kiss on the cheek. "It will always remind me of you."

Gosh, she will remember me, and she admitted it, Kharak thought with an inner smile.

"There is something else to it. Let me show you."

She handed over the jewellery box to him. Holding it with his left hand, he opened it.

"Right here." Kharak lifted the blue silk padding from the inside right corner, revealing a minute wooden protrusion. "You press that tiny lever, like this." He showed her how.

At the same time, on the outside of the jewellery box, a small, flat drawer slid out.

"A secret drawer!" Catherine cried in excitement.

"Yes."

"It is astonishing craftsmanship to create a concealed compartment in something as beautiful as this." She carried on admiring its beauty.

After a couple of attempts, Catherine could activate the opening of the secret compartment flawlessly. She ran her right palm over the brass inlay on the cover, feeling its finish.

"It's beautiful."

30

The next half-hour was spent talking about the artisans of Lahore, including how Kharak's grandfather and father were apt at woodwork and the work they had carried out for the British.

The wind picked up, the temperature dropped and the grey clouds now blanketed an even larger part of the blue sky. The clap of thunder was much nearer this time.

"Nandu should be here soon. We should pack up before it starts raining," Kharak stated as they started to stroll towards their neem tree from the river's edge.

As three o' clock approached, the picnic hamper, which was lighter now, had been repacked. Kharak picked up the stools and the hamper and they ambled upwards along the path that led towards the dirt track where they were to be picked up. Sana waited for them to walk past her before she followed them.

The radiance of the sunlight diminished as the sky became overcast. The smell of rain was in the air as the grey clouds were now overhead.

Walking along the dirt track, random dark dots soon appeared on the ground, accompanied by a subtle thrumming. It had started to rain. What was evident to Catherine for the very first time was the fragrance of the first raindrops coupling with the soil – the most unique essence of nature. She inhaled deeply.

As they reached the dirt road, they saw Nandu furiously pedalling towards them in the distance. The rain was now showering the leaves on the trees in a melodious harmony of pitter-pattering.

"We are in for an extremely wet journey back. I didn't remember to carry an umbrella." Kharak glanced at Catherine, whose hat provided some cover from the rain.

"It never occurred to me either."

The intense rain could be seen hovering over the river as a misty shroud and moving towards them.

Coming to a halt, Nandu jumped off his seat and swiftly helped stow the basket and stools. He then ran to the rear of his rickshaw and attempted to raise the lightweight canvas roof to cover the passenger seat. To his dismay, it only went halfway up, with the final panel stuck and unable to slide open.

"I'm sorry," he said to Kharak, still trying to heave it without damaging it further.

"Do you want to sit in the other rickshaw?" Kharak asked her.

"No. I will sit with you," Catherine said without hesitation.

The clouds finally let go and it started raining.

Kharak and Catherine hastily sat on the damp seat.

They saw Sana striding towards them. "Here, I have an umbrella for the memsahib." She drew out a black umbrella she was holding and handed it to Kharak, before running back to her rickshaw. As soon as Sana sat on the seat, the driver turned around and started pedalling. By the time Nandu started pedalling, the other rickshaw was far ahead of them.

Kharak opened the umbrella with care as one of the spokes

was bent. "Catherine, here you are. Take the umbrella." He offered it to her.

"What about you?"

"I'll be fine here."

"I cannot let that happen." Her eyes glistened as she took the umbrella from his hand.

Holding the open umbrella between them and away from her face, she edged closer towards him until her left shoulder met his right shoulder and her outer thigh pressed lightly against his.

There was instant warmth in this closeness, which was soothing in the falling rain. Her right hand held the umbrella for both of them, although she made sure that more of it sheltered him rather than her. It was just how she felt in that moment.

Her inner beauty mesmerises me. She has moved so close to me; she surely must like me – or is it more than that? Whatever she feels, damn, I adore her!

In their haste, the ride was bumpy, but neither Kharak nor Catherine realised this. A sudden gust of wind brushed across the rickshaw, catching the umbrella and plucking it out of her hand. It danced in the air and floated slowly behind them.

"Oops!" She cupped her hands over her mouth, laughing. "Sorry," she added, raising her shoulders in innocence.

"Stop! Nandu!" Kharak yelled in Punjabi.

He scampered out of the rickshaw and spotted the umbrella thirty feet behind, caught between the tall, golden blades of grass along the edge of the road with its handle resting in a muddy rut. He capered towards it. The driver of the other rickshaw kept pedalling ahead, oblivious to what was happening.

At the same time, Catherine got out of the rickshaw and took a few steps away, leaving the rickshaw behind.

Standing in the rain, she opened the palms of her hands and felt the warm raindrops. Every drop on her palm seemed to instil in her a consciousness of joy and liberation. She took off her straw hat and hurled it onto the seat.

Looking up towards the sky, Catherine closed her eyes and stretched out her arms. The raindrops caressed her face as they rolled down.

As Kharak retrieved the umbrella and turned around, he stood still, spellbound. There, in the rain, he saw Catherine, face up towards the heavens, twirling in utter enchantment.

For a few moments, he stood in awe of her grace and beauty, still holding the umbrella by his side, having forgotten to use it.

He took a few gentle steps towards the rickshaw and stopped, still observing her.

Catherine opened her eyes and met his gaze. She stopped twirling and smiled, revealing her dimples. Pearls of water trickled down her ash-brown curls, pausing briefly at the tips before dripping to the ground. She pranced towards Kharak, stopping abruptly an arm's length away.

For both, there was silence. The only sound that they heard was the sprinkling of rain on the grass. Still holding each other's gaze, neither realised that they were both standing in a puddle of water.

In silence, Kharak saw her laughing velvet-green eyes through her moistened eyelashes.

The hypnotic attraction was unbearable for Catherine. She went on her toes and leaned forward towards him. He first felt her warm breath amongst the raindrops, followed by her tender, warm lips on his. In that moment, their eyes closed.

They were oblivious to everything around them apart from each other's lips and the tightness in their stomachs.

After their lips unlocked, Catherine wrapped her arms around Kharak's neck, embracing him. He felt her wet hair against his cheek and smelled the patchouli overtones of her Floris perfume, together with the scent of rain. It felt mystical.

His lips were still tingling as he let go of the umbrella, leaving it to fall to the road, and folded his arms around her and held her tightly. He felt a warmth emanate through her sopping dress.

For a while, in that embrace, life seemed to come to a pause all around them – a beautiful pause.

I hope he hears my trembling heart. A mind of its own, it has, and only listens to itself. It seldom listens to me. I am as helpless as a slave to a master, Catherine thought, still holding him in her tight embrace.

As quickly as it happened, the embrace loosened and opposite arms brushed together in search of the other's hand as they still looked fixedly at each other. With their fingers intertwined, Kharak broke his gaze to pick up the umbrella from the road with his free hand and gently led Catherine towards the rickshaw. It was still raining.

Catherine climbed in the rickshaw wearing a beguiling smile. Kharak withdrew the checked ground cloth from the hamper before sitting beside her and using it to blanket their legs from the rain.

Sitting close together, Catherine snuggled up to him and rested her head below his shoulder, just above his chest. He wrapped his right arm around her shoulders, holding her near, while his left arm held the sheltering umbrella.

Their warmth was comforting and soothing. Not a word was uttered between them, yet, in the silence, it was the unspoken word that was the loudest. It was like they both heard what was unsaid. Their eyes flickered in admission. It did not matter that they were soaked in rain, because being present in that moment next to each other was inspiriting.

31

It had stopped raining and, through the gaps between the woolly clouds, rays of late-afternoon sun shone through the wet canopy of glistening leaves on the Amaltas trees, dispersing the light like a mosaic window.

Catherine by now was familiar with the streets in the vicinity of her residence. She felt a rising swell of delight tinged with sadness, knowing that her afternoon with Kharak was coming to an end.

Nandu was astounded at having witnessed Kharak and Catherine kiss. His mind wandered as he took the right turn onto Victoria Avenue and pedalled further towards the middle of the avenue to their intended destination.

Catherine spoke first. "Kharak, please tell Nandu to be at my house every morning at eleven o'clock."

"That's a surprising request."

"I would like to meet you during your break from your work."

She had that rosy look. "Albeit briefly. And…" She paused. "I can wait for you by that fence enclosing the railway yards where you work."

"You stole my thought!"

The grinding of the brakes brought the rickshaw to a halt outside the imposing gate, followed by the ringing of the bell on the handlebar.

"Nandu, would you like regular business for a while?"

"Of course I would, sahib," he replied.

Kharak leaned forward. "I want you to be here every morning at eleven o' clock for the memsahib. You will take her wherever she wishes. Remember… you look after her! One more thing… what happened there between me and memsahib stays with you only." His furrowed eyebrows underlined his intent.

"I will, sahib, I will." Nandu rolled his head sideways.

As Balu opened the gate to let the two rickshaws in, Kharak let go of Catherine's shoulder and, at the same time, she subtly lifted her head from his shoulder, giving rise to a pretend distance between them.

Clasping her hands beneath the groundsheet, she pressed her palms together as he moved to uncover his legs from the shared sheet, taking the warmth out with him. To an outsider, she had had the checked sheet all for herself.

A forceful salute given by the gatekeeper ushered the rickshaw towards the colonial house. There was no one in sight; even the gardener had allowed the heavens to water his garden. Under the overcast sky, with diminished light, it seemed much later in the day than it was. From the outside, the rooms of the top floor already appeared well lit with lamps, which was unusual.

Vadu opened the impressive front door of the house and strode towards the rickshaw, eager to carry any items that needed to be unloaded.

As Kharak and Catherine stood facing each other, she placed her hand above the damp chest pocket of his linen shirt and caressed him sideways towards his shirt button. She pinched the placket and tugged it gently.

"Thank you for an unforgettable day."

"The pleasure is mine." He blinked slowly.

She let go of his shirt, her eyes momentarily holding the gaze, before turning and nipping off towards the steps leading to the door, only briefly looking over her shoulder at Kharak. She then went inside, holding the small canvas bag containing her gifted jewellery box.

Moments later, Kharak was outside the compound seated in the rickshaw, his world a warm, indistinct place.

As Catherine stood on the polished oak floor in the hallway, the familiar voice of her mother sounded from the front room.

"Catherine, is that you?"

"Yes, Mother."

"I'm glad, dear. I was worried about you in this stormy weather," she said as Catherine heard her soft, padding footsteps approaching the hallway.

"I'm perfectly well."

"Oh my Lord!" Ethel cupped her hands, covering her mouth as she walked out from the front room. "You are drenched!" She felt the sleeve of Catherine's dress.

"We got caught briefly in the storm." Catherine could not help but smile.

"You'll catch a cold, so better change out of these damp clothes. Luckily, I told the houseboy to get the wood heater going as it's raining. Sana will get your hot bath ready."

"That is what I really need now: a hot, relaxing bath," Catherine said as she bent down to remove her damp boots.

"I almost forgot, how was your picnic?"

For a brief moment, Catherine glanced up towards the corner of the ceiling. "Beautiful." Her tone was low and distant.

"How about the company?"

"His name is Kharak, Mother. You seem never to say his name." She pushed her boots near the skirting with the side of her foot.

"Yes, him." Ethel let out a sigh.

"He was a gentleman, as always. We had our lunch by the bank of the Ravi River." She paused in thought. "I like him. He is a charming person."

Ethel narrowed her eyes. That utterance was a jolt to her. In England, if Catherine had said the same, it would not have mattered to her, but it mattered now. It was like a splinter beneath the nail; very uncomfortable.

Ethel changed the subject. "Freshen up and get out of those wet clothes." She turned and left, walking towards the kitchen.

The half-hour Catherine spent in the hot bath surrounded by floating rose petals, diffusing their scent into the air, was soothing. Most of that time was spent staring aimlessly at the ceiling with images of that moment in the rain running through her mind. As she drifted in and out of her own little dreamy world, she realised that she had been smiling all along.

This absent-mindedness remained as she brushed her hair in front of her duchesse dressing-table mirror after her bath. Tucked away with care in one of the small drawers of the dressing table was her new jewellery box.

Voices from the lower floor of the house startled her out of her world. The chatter was loud, tinged with surprise, and it seemed like there was more than one person talking in English accents. *Must be Mrs Wittingham*, she thought.

Despite Sana's help, Catherine took her time to dress. There was no need to hurry. Kharak wasn't going to be waiting for her; he had long gone. She felt empty at that thought.

Eventually, she put on her delicate off-white cotton sateen, lined in linen, and slippers before setting off downstairs to meet the guests, her hair still slightly damp.

Halfway down the stairs, the voices were more audible now and coming from the living area.

When she recognised one of them, she could not believe it. She scampered down the last steps, turning to the living room on her right.

"Hello, Father!" she called out as she pushed open the door.

"Hello, my dear," he said in his usual laconic voice.

Catherine walked towards her father, who was seated in the green leather Dunelm wing armchair that was in direct view. He stood up to greet her, which was normal for him. That was his way of showing affection, especially when there was an outsider around.

"I would like you to meet Ivan Freeman." He pointed to the opposite side of the room.

As Catherine walked towards her father, part of the room that had been out of her visual field and partly obscured by the opened door came into view, and there, seated cross-legged in the other armchair, revealing his Church's crafted brown Derby boots, was a tall, slim man with a ginger triangle broom moustache.

The man stood up, staring at her with his gunmetal eyes, which were framed by arched eyebrows.

"Hello, Mr Freeman." Catherine extended her hand.

He took it, gently raising it before leaning forward to kiss the back of it.

"The pleasure is mine, Catherine." He did not blink. "And call me Ivan. We have met before, although that was a few years ago," he said, still holding her hand.

Gilbert interrupted. "He will be staying with us as our guest for a few days before he travels to East Africa. As he had completed his work in Delhi, I invited him to spend some time here in Lahore with us."

Feeling slightly unsure at this surprising news, Catherine subtly withdrew her hand, forcing Ivan to let go. "It'll be nice to have a guest." She smiled.

"I am looking forward to a few splendid days." He gestured with his hand.

"If you could excuse me, I need to help Mother."

Accepting the excuse, Ivan bowed slightly, still maintaining eye contact. She turned and walked out of the room while he watched her.

What is someone like her doing in a place like this? Just like a rare flowering orchid in the desert. A delicate butterfly flaunting her vibrant feathery display and she does not realise the spell she has already cast on me. Saying she is attractive would be an injustice to her, as she possesses a rare beauty that I have not seen in all the other ladies I have known. Not only do I love pretty things, but I must have them at all costs! Ivan thought as he rolled his right thumb over the ring on his pinkie.

32

Sitting in the corner of the kitchen, Kharak's younger sister Neina was busy playing with a stitched doll on the cotton sheet covering the floor. She would talk to her doll, then give intermittent glances at him. He adored her.

His mother was wiping the copper pots and pans dry and stacking them on the shelf, ready for the next day. The aromas of lentil stew and charcoal still lingered in the air. Kharak had slouched in the chair next to the kitchen door.

Earlier, while having dinner together, Seva, as a mother, had noticed that he had been chirpier than usual, but at the same time strangely detached from his normal self. Also, he had less to eat than usual.

"Has freshening up with hot water helped you relax and feel comfortable? You were soaking wet when you arrived."

"Yes, I feel warm."

"If you want, I could prepare you a glass of warm milk. It will help you sleep."

"No, thank you. I've had too much to eat already." Kharak toyed with the orange in his hand.

A brief silence prevailed, which was punctuated by Neina chattering away to her doll.

"How was your day with your English... guest?" Seva adjusted the cotton scarf around her neck.

"She enjoyed the views across the river. The lunch she prepared was delicious, but different."

"Really? She cooked lunch? Now, that is a surprise."

"Surprise?"

"Obviously – why does she have to cook when there are cooks and servants to help her?" Seva gave a faint smile as she stacked the last pan and turned to face him.

"She obviously likes cooking." Kharak paused to gather his confidence. "And she wants to see and experience how we live here in our community, away from the city," he half-lied.

"And...?" Seva folded her arms.

"I was wondering if it would be all right for her to attend one of Amol's evening wedding celebrations?"

Amol was the neighbour's daughter and at, the age of seventeen, she was getting married to an arranged suitor from the neighbouring village. It was a time of celebration and support for the whole close-knit community and lasted for a week, particularly given that the bride was from their village.

"I will talk to your father when he returns from his meeting with the elders tonight." She paused. "If you do invite her, you should invite her whole family and not just her, otherwise everyone will talk about why she is here alone."

"Ah, the village people again." Kharak shrugged his shoulders. "All right, then."

She is right, but the only person I will invite will be Catherine. At least I know she will appreciate this new experience; the whole drama of the wedding celebration. I don't think that would be the case for her mother or father. I sense their indifference, he thought as he walked out of the kitchen.

That evening, dinner was an event for Catherine, allowing her to see her father after a few days apart. Not surprisingly, Ivan took the lead in most of the conversation over dinner, being quite the self-seeker regarding his achievements and career.

With her keen eye, Catherine did notice that the black-and-silver ring on his pinkie bore what looked like two inverted Vs with the letter G in the middle. It was very similar to the ring that her father wore, the only difference being that his was golden. She recalled that she had asked her father about his ring a few years ago when she was younger, but he had ignored her.

"One of my keen interests is the sport of polo." Ivan gestured with his palm facing downwards. "I'm a committee member of the Hurlingham Polo Association in England." He raised his eyebrow and narrowed his eyes in pride.

Seated opposite him was Gilbert, who wiped his mouth with his cotton napkin. "You should visit the Polo Club of Lahore. It has a marvellous clubhouse and is located at the racecourse. Perhaps you could have a day joining our fellow Englishmen jostling on horseback."

"I'll make a point to do that. Perhaps Catherine could accompany me and we could make it a day out?" He glanced sideways at her seated beside him. "That would take both of us out of the house," he added.

She remained silent.

"Catherine would enjoy that." Her father smiled broadly. "Wouldn't you?"

"I've never been keen on horses—"

"You'll have a wonderful time," Gilbert interrupted her.

"I suppose so," she lied.

Born with a silver spoon in his mouth, Ivan had studied at Eton College, where he had excelled in horse riding and had been captain of the rifle club. It was instilled in him there to never accept the ordinary, but to strive to achieve the impossible.

At Oxford University, he had completed his engineering degree. Not many people outside Oxford were aware of his spell as one of the leading members of the university's Bullingdon Club, where he was responsible for the infamous initiation sessions for new members. He was one of the members who, four years earlier, had smashed all of the windows of Christ Church in Peckwater Quad.

Although Ivan had obtained his degree, it was his personality that had really changed by the end of his formal education. It had been drummed into him that he could achieve whatever goal he aimed for and his ego expected ruthlessness to be the path to this achievement.

Being ambitious, Ivan had used his familial connections, as well as his secret liaisons with women, to get into the British East India Company. His quick mind allowed him to become aware that vast tracts of land within East Africa would be carved up and granted to the colonists. He was hungry for power and this accumulation of land and its resources was his chosen route to achieve it.

In a short time, he was procuring steam engines from the colonies for his company and now he was where he wanted to be: amongst the people running the Uganda Railways Committee.

After dinner, Ethel joined the conversation in the comfort of the lounge room, where Ivan's stories carried on. Catherine's parents were intrigued by his charm and achievements at such a young age.

"And what have you been doing over the past few days, Catherine?" Gilbert took a sip of his port.

"She, accompanied by Sana, has been seeing Lahore, believe it or not," Ethel replied before Catherine could.

"Mother is right. Kharak showed me the marvellous Shalimar Gardens, the busy city and the River Ravi."

"Did he now? I'm not keen on him," was her father's short reply. "He must have another motive, I am sure of that."

"Who is he?" Ivan could not help his prying nature.

"He is a Sikh engineer who works here with the Indian Railways and he seems to be spending rather a lot of time with Catherine. I got their arrival time wrong and he helped them get home from the station." Gilbert took a larger sip of his port.

"I asked him to show me this city – it was not him who offered." Catherine glanced at her mother, hoping she would defend her word.

Ivan broke the brief silence that followed. "If Mr and Mrs Rose don't mind" – he looked directly at them – "I'm sure we could see Lahore together as we are both new to it. We don't have to rely on any local." He grinned.

"I think we would be comfortable with that, wouldn't we, Ethel?" Gilbert turned his head towards his wife.

In the corner of the room, Catherine pretended to be engrossed in reading *The Yellow Wallpaper*, the novel that she had in her hand. It was a perfect strategy she had picked up from her college days to avoid involvement in conversations that she did not want to be part of.

Luckily for her, Ivan started talking about the steam engines he had purchased that were to be shipped to Mombasa, where they would be part of the fleet of railway engines used for the building of the Mombasa-to-Uganda railway.

"By the way, Ethel and I are holding a garden tea party on Saturday afternoon." Gilbert rolled his palm over his armrest, looking at Ivan.

Ethel stared at her husband in surprise.

"Yes, we are; Ivan is here and it will be wonderful for getting to know our friends in Lahore. So, my darling wife, you can arrange it how you would like it to be and instruct Vadu to get it organised," Gilbert said in a slightly tipsy tone. "He has done it before."

"That will be nice, dear."

"I know you can organise anything and at any time." Gilbert winked at his wife.

"The Wittingham's will definitely want to come. She was here for a short while this afternoon and, I remember, she kept on talking about the marvellous Lahore garden parties."

Catherine looked over her book in silence.

Their talk wandered towards whom to invite, what to have for tea and how glittering they wanted the event to be. Ivan sat there giving his suggestions now and then, but at every opportunity, he ogled Catherine when he thought he could get away with it.

Damn! She gets prettier every time I look at her. Wavy, silky hair, perfect complexion and voluptuous figure – I'm becoming besotted by her. Of all my triumphs, she has to be the sparkling pearl and I will have her by my side, he thought.

Earlier than her usual bedtime, Catherine excused herself and went to her room after what seemed to her a long evening. Physically, she was weary, but in her mind she was not; she was in a state of soft bliss.

There was a surreal stillness in the night air. It was past eleven o' clock. The faint light of the oil lamp flickered on the pillar of the gate as the night moth hovered around it in search of his lover in a deadly game of life and death.

Across the murram driveway, there was a dim light in the bedroom. Although there was a slight chill in the air, the window was ajar.

Inside, all alone, Catherine rested on her cosy bed, holding and admiring the jewellery box she had received earlier in the day from Kharak.

She paused halfway while placing her pearl earrings in it and glanced outside her window at the silvery, moonlit sky, not knowing what made her do it. The next thing, she placed the jewellery box beside her on the bed, lifted her cotton blanket, stepped out and walked barefoot towards the window in anticipation.

As she peeked out of her bedroom window, her eyes gradually adjusted to the darkness.

There was nothing to see.

Catherine sighed. What had she been anticipating?

A sudden movement in front of the sumbul tree caught her eye and she strained her eyes to see clearly. It was only the cat! He was the famous and gorgeous neighbourhood cat that lived further up the street. Obviously, he was on the prowl, trying to mark his territory.

Catherine grinned and thought about Kharak.

The sky was darkening; a storm was brewing from the west. In an instant, a flash of lightning cut a jagged ribbon through the inky sky, momentarily illuminating the place. Visions of the earlier afternoon events replayed in her mind. She longed to see him again.

She turned and stared at her gift on the bed. It seemed like it had a captivating ability to draw her towards it. There was something about it. She could not figure out what made it so enchanting, apart from its beauty.

She closed her window as the raindrops started hitting the glass pane and a final glance outside revealed that the cat had disappeared. So had the moth.

Walking towards her bed, Catherine still had her eyes fixed on Kharak's gift and was eager to carry on putting her favourite pieces of jewellery into it.

After she was done, she made herself comfortable in her blanket, hoping to sleep. Then, she looked up and saw herself in the mirror beside her bed and smiled; there was a glint in her velvety eyes.

In that moment, she was not scared, nor did she feel lonely. Catherine had decided to see Kharak the next day.

33

It was a difficult task for Kharak to wake up the following morning after a night of tossing and turning. He did not sleep well. It was not due to the thunder, the neighbour's dog nor the wind; it was Catherine. His thoughts of her, as well as the memory of their tingling kiss, had kept him awake.

It will be a long and tiring day at work today... but it's a consequence I'm willing to accept in exchange for just thinking of her – and it's not as if I have command over them. She is getting into a habit of sneaking into my thoughts and nudging me awake, he thought.

There was no sign of the previous day's storm as the sun was bright and the sky was clear, which helped him get out of bed and get ready for work.

After breakfast was over, as he walked by the kitchen door on his way out, carrying his satchel, his mother spoke.

"Your father has gone out early." Seva paused. "He said that you can invite Catherine and her family to the Thursday evening get-together," she added as she spread diced green chillies on the wooded tray to dry.

"All right. That's nice, I'll let her – I mean, them – know." Kharak tried to hide his jubilation behind the excuse that he was running late. "See you in the evening, Mother." He strode towards his bicycle before hopping onto it.

In the kitchen, Seva sensed that her son wanted Catherine to see the way of life of the Lahore people. He would not discover that his mother had managed, with patience, to influence her husband into thinking that it would be good for the whole community if someone from the outside could come into their little locale to experience and share part of someone's joyful moment in life. They would be held in high esteem.

As she took a step out into the courtyard to place the tray of chillies to dry in the sun, her concern was whether Catherine's parents would be present that evening or whether they would allow her to be there.

They will feel it is beneath them to be seen here amongst us and I really hope this does not upset Kharak. Her maternal instincts spoke to her.

That morning, Catherine had not been upfront with her mother. Leaving the house at eleven o' clock, she managed to tell Ethel in haste that she was going to return Kharak's coat to him, which she had used the previous day to keep warm in the rain. She had no coat to show, so she picked up one towel and rolled it into a bundle before tucking it in her bag just in case she had to show it. Before her mother had the chance to tell her that Vadu could return Kharak's coat, she was out of the house.

She timed the moment perfectly by walking unannounced to the gate at eleven o' clock. Upon Nandu's arrival, she signalled to him to wait, which he did as instructed, before she hurried on to the veranda to pick up her bag. Then, with her heart racing, she ran out of the gate.

The late-morning sun was shining off the railway tracks running across Lahore Station. The morning rush had dissipated – as the two main trains that departed from and arrived there were early in the morning and late in the afternoon.

It was a lot easier at the railway station now that she knew exactly where she was going. Despite this, Catherine had a nervous twinge in her stomach as she walked through the entrance. As she strode past the ticket office, she recognised the tall officer who had escorted her to where Kharak was working a few days ago, busy counting tickets.

The platform was quiet apart from the peanut vendor standing on the opposite platform. However, Catherine's heart was anything but quiet; her palms were getting slightly sweaty with pleasant nervousness.

Step out of this nervousness now. You know one another, she told her inner self as she walked beyond the end of the platform and towards the gate in the fence.

On the other side of the gate, Kharak was supervising his understudy near the ballast heap. His prediction about having a difficult day was an understatement, as he was having a torrid time concentrating. It just wasn't the shortness of sleep, but every so often, he drifted to Catherine's presence in his mind, where her soft eyes, her hypnotic voice and that kiss tortured him.

It was in one of those drifty moments when his understudy poked him in the arm with his dusty hand. "Sir, there is a memsahib waving at you by the fence."

Snapping out of his hazy state, Kharak turned, facing the distant fence. The sight of the familiar figure with its mesmerising smile forced him to blink a few times to ensure that his mind was not creating distractions. That worry was lifted when he saw her neck tilting and hand waving.

Catherine!

All the paperwork on his board, along with his leather measuring tape, was promptly dropped to the ground before he cantered towards her, beaming. His heart was jumping in his ribcage.

At the fence, Kharak paused in silence for a fleeting moment, savouring her aura before he opened the gate.

"Hello, Kharak." Her eyes glinted.

"Catherine, nice to see you here." He took a step forward.

"I promised to meet you here every day."

Conscious of his work-soiled hands, he wiped them on his trousers. As he was about to repeat the action, Catherine extended her hand and grasped his.

"Sorry my hands are dirty."

"It doesn't matter to me." She squeezed his hand, feeling the contours of his palms.

That relaxed him, and in the next moment, their fingers were entwined. Her soft, feminine hands felt like the petals of a lotus flower. Again, there was an emptiness in his stomach, a beautiful feeling.

Catherine let out a sigh. Even that seemed graceful to Kharak.

He turned around and glanced over his shoulder, and saw his colleagues staring at them.

"Let's walk to the bench," he said.

As if in unison, they let go of each other's hand, but still maintained their closeness.

"I have a few minutes. We could sit there." He pointed to the bench at the end of the platform as they walked from the gate and towards the platform.

"I can't remember that bench." Catherine thought aloud. "It's the only bench that is outside the covered platform. I must have missed it when we had just arrived in Lahore. Mind you, it was heaving with people that day."

They walked together towards it. She looked at the wooden slats that formed the seat of the bench to make sure that it was clean before she sat down. Lifting her slate-beige dress ever so slightly to ensure that the hem did not get dirty with the dust on the platform, Catherine sat down right in the middle of the bench, knowing that he would have to sit very close to her.

"It's wonderful today. From the unannounced storm of yesterday to the cloudless sky today," she said.

"It's a near-perfect day today."

"Yesterday was perfect for me," she interrupted him, fluttering her eyelashes.

"I'm glad you had a great day."

"Put it this way: I have not thought about my home back in Bath so far. That must be a good sign."

"So I gather that you do like Lahore?"

"It's different – very vibrant, full of life, simple and with very accepting people. Yes, I like Lahore and its people... like you."

He smiled, but inside he was overcome with an unbelievable feeling that he could not explain; a knowing that the person sitting next to him not only found him to be unique, but liked this uniqueness and had allowed him to get closer to her.

"I remember you told me you would like to know more about the people of Lahore. Could you be persuaded to spend a colourful and festive evening with me in my village?" Kharak asked her. "Catherine," he carried on, not wanting to hear her reply yet, just in case it was not possible, "if I may say so..." He took a long breath. "Who knows where life will take me or where life will take you, but I truly hope that life unfolds its riches generously for you, more so than you could ever expect."

Kharak gazed in her eyes. They were mesmerising, as ever. He knew that he had to overcome the urge to break eye contact at this moment.

"It is said that one's life is a journey from one mysterious place to another. My thinking is that life is like a train travelling from one initial destination to the final destination, stopping at every station – where people step out and move on to their next train, which will take them to their respective, preordained destinations." He paused for his words to sink in. "And it is at these various stops that people meet other people they have never met before, and encounter experiences that relate to the events one goes through in life at any time… some happy, some sad." He subconsciously shifted his posture ever so slightly towards Catherine on the wooden bench.

"Right now, in my life, I see myself sitting on a bench on one of these platforms, waiting for my train, and sitting on the same bench waiting for another train is a person whom I had never met before." There was another pause. "And this stranger sitting by my side is no one else but you."

It seemed that his heartbeat had never been this loud until now. He was surprisingly nervous; after all, he never thought he would have been able to share this thought with her.

Catherine lowered her gaze coyly.

Kharak thought of saying something to soften the effect of what he had said. "This brief moment on the bench, here in Lahore, while waiting for my destined train, I'd rather spend conversing with you and making the wait pleasant and hoping that, as we carry on with our respective journeys through life, in years to come, I can look back and feel that my stop at the junction of Lahore was enchanting."

He did not have to be worried about Catherine interrupting him; she was left in a bewildered philosophical haze by what he had said.

In the awkward silence that followed, she slowly moved her hand, placed it on his own warm hand, which was resting on his knee, and caressed it.

"You put that so marvellously. I certainly believe that no one will ever put the analogy of life to me as beautifully as you have." Catherine's smile twinkled as she tilted her head towards him.

"I cannot say no to you, Kharak. I accept your invitation and I promise to spend the evening with you as you show me even more splendours of your lovely city."

In that moment, the colours within life seemed to brighten. Each and every trivial scene around them was imbued with a sense of magic and beauty, and this feeling was felt by both of them, yet they never knew how mutual it was.

"The event is on Thursday evening."

"Event? What will there be for me to see?"

"Oh, I got carried away and forgot to mention that our neighbour, who is very close to us, his daughter is getting married. On that evening, there is a gathering to bestow best wishes upon the family."

"Now, that should be exciting." She nudged his shoulder. "Especially getting there."

"I could pick you up in the evening on Thursday, using Nandu." He smiled.

"That would be lovely."

Kharak leaned towards her and pulled a piece of roughed-up blank paper from his hind pocket. Getting a pencil out from his front pocket, he drew a map with directions as clearly as he could.

"That's a map to my house with written directions… in case you ever have need of it. The rickshawallas, including Nandu, would be able to get you there without any difficulty."

"That's amusing to read – *Kharak* with an arrow pointing to a square on the map," she laughed.

"That's my home."

Catherine took it from his hand and put it in her bag. "Thursday evening it shall be, then."

Across the boundary of the railway station, behind the low-lying sheds, were two paper kites flying in the air with their owners hidden from view. Sitting on the platform, Catherine and Kharak watched the kites glide and soar in the air. As their owners each attempted to take down the other kite, it was like the kites came to life as they danced one after the other in the Lahore sky.

"My supervisor will be here soon... I'd better get back to work otherwise I will be doing Nandu's job!" Kharak chuckled as he stood up.

"Shame about that, I wish we could have spent a bit more time here... but you have got to go and I wouldn't want you to be dismissed." Catherine lowered her shoulders in acceptance.

She looked around and saw a group of people further along the platform, staring at them. She knew that, this time, giving Kharak a kiss would not be possible. Instead, she held his hand in both of hers.

"I'll walk you to your rickshaw. Is it Nandu who got you here?"

"Yes. He was right on time this morning. He's a good find, Mr Kharak." Catherine gave him that playful smile as she let go of his hand.

Tsavo

34

The construction at the railhead had progressed rapidly and now there were two areas where there was a hive of activity: at the railhead where the hundred-gauge railway track was being laid and at the construction of the Tsavo Bridge.

It was a concern that another worker had gone missing the previous night. All that was known was that at around midnight, he had wandered out from his tent to relieve himself at the pit latrine, and in the morning, he was nowhere to be seen. His belongings were still intact in the tent and nothing seemed to be missing. The only unusual observation was that the bushes near the latrine were somewhat ruffled.

Later in the day, Colonel Patterson ordered a surprise inspection of the tents. In the afternoon heat, Ungan and Narain searched in and around every tent as ordered, looking for suspicious goods, valuables or weapons. Blankets were turned over, trunks opened and even the two latrines were examined for hidden cavities.

The disappearances were a mystery, with no suspicious person pinpointed. The only observation was animal paw prints around the campsite, which was normal as they were in the middle of a vast natural wilderness inhabited by diverse wildlife.

That night, seated around the reassuring campfire in their wooden chairs after dinner, were Colonel Patterson and John Allen. Every weekend, they would meet up and catch up on the progress that was being made. As the railhead was progressing, it was now difficult for John to camp daily at the bridge campsite due to the increasing distance. Their canvas sleeping tents were erected a few feet away and each had a wooden post pitched outside, from which hung a lit kerosene lamp. Beyond the tent line was pitch-darkness.

"This matter of labourers disappearing is troubling me," Patterson said, swirling his whisky in his glass. "It just shouldn't be happening."

"Yes, but we have checked their tents this afternoon and haven't found anything yet." John scratched an itch on his left forearm.

"Having thought about it, the only conclusion I have come up with is that there must be one or more scoundrels amongst them."

A gust of wind howled, causing the flames to flicker nervously, yet the embers glowed intensely. Using rocks as stools, Narain and Ungan sat ten metres away around their own campfire, far enough away to allow Patterson and Allen privacy, but still near enough to heed the call of their commanders.

"How long are you taking in compassionate leave?" Patterson asked.

"At least three months, in England."

"I hope your wife gets better and…" He paused. "I'm sorry about her state of health."

"The timing has been awkward, but that cannot be predicted. The amusing thing is that she was the one who was concerned about me coming to East Africa and falling ill with a horrendous disease, yet it is her who has taken ill in England." John smirked.

"David Livingstone's death all those years ago, and it being on the front page of the *Daily Telegraph & Courier*, does not give people resounding confidence in the safety of Africa." Patterson took a sip of his malt whisky.

"Yes, that's true."

In the brief silence, the muffled voices of Ungan and Narain were audible as they waited for their kettle of tea to boil over the fire.

"Will Ivan be capable of handling this huge project while you are away?" Patterson wiped the rim of his tumbler with his left index finger.

"From what I gather, George Whitehouse particularly believes that he would be skilful enough to handle the work while I am away."

"When is he arriving?"

John Allen rolled his eyes in thought. "I believe next month, when the boilers for the steam engines arrive from India at the port in Mombasa. At present, I am told that he is in India purchasing them."

"Only time will tell whether he lives up to his reputation. This is Africa and it isn't as easy as milking the cows in Wiltshire. Here, the animals bite back," Patterson said as he stared directly at Allen, taking the last sip of his whisky before placing his empty tumbler on the arm of the chair.

"I have been reliably informed that Ivan Freeman is an extremely shrewd person." John raised his eyebrows.

35

Lahore

Despite it being morning, the sun was already warm as it shone across Catherine's smiling face. She had spent another night wide awake; her body weary, but her mind restless, wondering if Kharak was awake like her. It was a beautiful thought, realising that it wasn't about missing someone, but knowing that he was missing her too.

That morning, breakfast was being served in the open courtyard at the rear of the house, which had access through the kitchen and rear lounge area. The resident bulbuls were chirping away busily in the branches. The table was set with a crisp white cotton tablecloth and blue-and-white linen napkins. Wafting in the fresh garden air was the smell of fried eggs, bacon and pan-roasted bread.

Ivan took the opportunity to sit opposite Catherine at the hardwood table; he wanted to catch her eye and it was easier to do that sitting directly opposite her. Gilbert and Ethel took the other seats.

Putting some homemade marmalade on her toast, Catherine decided to tell them about Thursday evening.

"Father, I have been invited to a cultural function on Thursday evening."

"And what might that cultural function be?" Gilbert avoided eye contact as he cut a strip of bacon.

"It is an evening get-together before a wedding."

"What wedding?" He cut her short.

"Not mine, obviously." She tried to make a joke of it, which did not amuse her father. "It's taking place on Thursday evening—"

Gilbert interrupted her again. "As I asked, what wedding, whose wedding and, more importantly, who has invited you?" He looked at her directly.

"Kharak has invited me to his family friend's wedding." She did not hesitate in her reply.

"I should have known that it would be him. Why is he always swooning around you?

"That's not true."

"Not true? You must be ignorant, Catherine." Gilbert raised his voice. "You will not be allowed to accept that dark Indian man's invitation. You are above that – remember that, always!" Her father pointed his knife towards her.

"That's very unfair and unwarranted." Catherine's nostrils flared as she controlled her inner revulsion.

"No, it's not. I don't want my daughter to be associating with classless and inferior people here, and you'd better get used to that." His bushy eyebrows rose.

Catherine had the urge to walk away from the breakfast table, but she managed to retain control. There was a guest at the table. If defending the absent Kharak was what was required, she was going to do that.

How hurtful it is to hear such ghastly things about Kharak. Father does not know him and has not met him for long enough to judge his character… and here I am ready to defend him to the hilt. It feels awful, she thought, with a lump in her throat.

The tension blanketing the silence around the dining table was evident. Ethel carried on with her breakfast, albeit slowly and with her head down. No one paid attention to the chirping birds or the still air that was making it the perfect morning to be seated outdoors. Only the silver cutlery clinking against the china plates punctured the edgy quiet.

Ivan felt smug, his mind ticking rapidly, taking in all that was happening around him as he wiped his lips with his napkin.

"If I may say something…?" He broke the silence.

"Yes, you can," Ethel said, hoping for a change in the conversation.

"It may not be my matter to be involved in, but allow me to propose a solution," Ivan paused for effect. "I'm more than willing to accompany Catherine. It will also give me the opportunity to see the people of Lahore." He lowered his eyelids slightly to hide his motive. *I couldn't care less about the natives, but to be closer to you, Catherine, I will do anything,* he thought.

Catherine sat in silence, resting her hands on her lap. After hearing what her father had said, her appetite had left her.

Ethel finally spoke. "That is a sensible idea. What do you think, Gilbert?" She gazed at her husband, who had his head down, busy eating. "The two of them could keep each other company." She glanced with leniency at her daughter.

"It would be lovely to spend the evening there with you, Catherine." Ivan stared at her.

That is the most opportunistic sentence I have ever heard, she thought whilst maintaining a straight face. *But if in order to meet Kharak, I have to accept you accompanying me, then so be it.*

"Oh, you could see the occasion, too. It's a wonderful idea." She forced a smile, hoping her father would come around.

Ivan's smugness grew. He had managed to set a plan in motion that he was confident would lead Catherine to him with Kharak set aside. "Thank you, Catherine." His eyes gleamed. "I'm sure it will be a remarkable evening."

Gilbert gestured and clicked his fingers at Vadu, who prompted another servant to pour the freshly brewed tea from the china pot.

"Ivan, I accept you accompanying Catherine that evening. If you aren't free to go with her, then I'm afraid she will not be allowed to go." He tilted his head towards Ivan as he stirred the silver spoon in his cup.

"I appreciate your condition." Ivan bowed his head slightly towards Gilbert in acceptance. "I will look after her."

He is a fine young man, respectful of my authority and willing to compromise. Very few young men like him nowadays, Gilbert thought.

Ivan adjusted his tie. *It feels powerful to be able to compel someone to do what I want, yet make him think that it was his decision. But all along, I am in control,* he thought.

Seated opposite Ivan, Catherine was still filled with distress at her father's comments about Kharak and it surprised her how intensely they had hurt her. *This isn't how I hoped to see Kharak, but I have managed to find a way to go and visit him. Although it was Ivan who offered a route, I have ended up doing what I wanted to.*

Ethel sighed. *Someone sitting around this table is going to get their feelings hurt!* she thought.

36

Cycling through Donald Town, the south-eastern part of Lahore, Kharak pedalled along Montgomery Road and passed the Queen Victoria statue before taking the left and on to Cooper Road. It was surprisingly busy, with carriages to avoid as well as pedestrians, including the revered cows straggling along the road.

A new type of happiness glowed from within that he hadn't experienced before. All it required was a thought of Catherine and every issue seemed to fade away in irrelevance.

He was on his way to work that morning and was meeting up with Lal outside the Cecil Hotel, from where they were going to cycle together to the railway yards.

Looking ahead for possible hazards, his eye caught a rickshaw travelling towards him. He could not believe it when he saw Catherine seated in the back wearing a beige hat. He slowed down and came to a halt, with the bicycle tilted and supported by his right leg.

He was about to yell out her name when he realised, as the rickshaw got closer, that the woman was not Catherine at all!

His racing heart slowed. Lately, it seemed that everywhere he turned, visions of her sneaked up on him like a rising wave in the ocean and they were always enchanting. As the rickshaw passed, he chuckled to himself, knowing that Catherine was more stunningly beautiful than the woman he had seen. *That would have been embarrassment of the highest order*, he thought.

The Cecil Hotel was at the junction between Beadon Road and Copper Road, and had pretty lavender plants hanging from the wooden pillars that supported the arched roof of the walkway at the entrance to the hotel.

Waiting there, straddling his bicycle, was Lal.

"You've been very smiley lately, Kharak." He winked.

Kharak, grinning, winked back. "Life is beautiful."

"That is obvious, with your new-found friend."

"Come on, let's set off for the yards, otherwise there will be a lecture to listen to." Kharak slowly pedalled away.

They pedalled leisurely, side by side, past the cathedral.

Lal spoke. "Catherine seems like a wonderful person. There are not many like her who are willing to accept and get to know us, the local people. After what you told me, it seems like she more than likes you, Kharak. "How do you feel?"

Looking towards Lal, he said, "I've started reading poetry."

"Ha ha!" Lal nearly lost his balance. "You are done, my friend, done."

Kharak carried on smiling and pedalling. "*In her light, I learn how to love. In her beauty, I learn how to recite poems. She dances inside my chest where no one sees her, but sometimes, I do, and that feeling, my friend, is what Heaven must feel like,*" he recited in utter contemplation.

"Wow!" Lal's mouth widened. "I am amazed. She has that effect on you, hey?"

"I wonder whether she gets into the same confused yet blissful state as I do at times."

"Don't doubt yourself, I know she does. That day when you were both around having lunch, I saw her stare at you at every possible moment, and every time she did that, her eyes shimmered with affection for you." Lal hesitated. "But… what if she adores you more than you adore her, what then?"

Kharak's pedalling slowed down as, for a few moments, he was lost in thought. Lal got ahead of him.

"I don't know what I would do," he mumbled.

Lal slowed down to allow him to catch up.

"Guess what?"

"Go on."

"I've invited her to Amol's *jago* celebration evening."

"You what?" Lal's eyes widened.

"I have."

"You're audacious."

"I can't help it." Kharak shrugged his shoulders. "Anything to see her."

"My eyes will be on both of you that evening and I will see whose eyes dance more for the other." Lal gave a broad smile.

"That is why you are very close to me and I trust you." Kharak rang the bell on his bicycle handle to warn a group of men carrying bundles of cloth on their heads by the roadside.

"I need to say something."

"Say it."

"I worry."

"About what?"

Lal hesitated to gather his words. "If what is happening between you and Catherine gets past the point where there is no turning back… what happens then?"

There was silence between them and, apart from the voices of the traders on the footpath, the other sounds were their bicycle chains revolving and the clatter of the bullock carts.

Lal carried on. "She lives in England, which I'm sure is completely different to Lahore. Her family will have colonial traditions and you know that we will be looked down upon. However, I know that she is different from them all. She is special."

Having been given the chance to be honest, Lal wanted to lay bare the leap of faith that Kharak and Catherine would possibly have to make.

"What about your family? Could you see her family associating with them?" He sighed. "It's the pain of heartbreak that worries me."

Deep in thought, Kharak still managed to swerve past a stray cow that had wandered onto the dusty road. He was appreciative that he had someone like Lal who had thought about the torment he was going through and was able to comment on it as a person standing outside and looking in.

With the morning sun beating down, they came to the crossroads between McLeod Road and Railway Road, where Kharak stopped at the junction with the railway station not far ahead. He turned his head towards Lal.

"Lal, these thoughts have crossed my mind. I feel that whatever happens between Catherine and myself is like taking a thousand-mile journey in the dark with just an oil lamp. It provides light for only a few yards ahead, but as we take steps forward, the next few yards are illuminated and this eventually helps the thousand miles to be covered using just an oil lamp. It is not necessary for them all to be lit up at once."

Lal furrowed his eyebrows in awe.

"I am here for you all the way, brother, by your side and that's a promise." He extended his hand to clasp Kharak's in an arm-wrestle grip.

37

Ivan stood in front of the oak-framed mirror in the guest room, finely adjusting the side parting of his hair. He even used the comb to brush through his arched eyebrows and triangle broom moustache to satisfy his compulsion for perfection. He turned his head right, then left; his assessing eyes staring at his reflection in the mirror. *Impressive*, he thought.

The evening had finally arrived when he had the chance to spend some personal time with Catherine. His attempts to explore Lahore with her over the past couple of days had not succeeded, as she always seemed to have the perfect excuse.

When he thought back to his first day with the Roses, he confessed that he was wrong about how he felt about her. Having stayed a few days and observed her liveliness, his desire for her had grown obsessively. Whenever she passed him, her perfume would trigger his impulse to leer at her. In every conversation, he would overly compliment her. His mind kept ruminating about his move to win her over.

He glanced at his Dreyfuss & Co. watch. *Plenty of time left*, he thought. If it were not for Catherine, he would not have wasted his time at some ragtag evening celebration.

Looking at the hat rack, his black top hat was there. At first, he had not intended to wear it that evening, but now he thought it would enhance his superiority and authority by making his presence felt.

Further down the corridor, Catherine was seated on her dressing-table stool fastening the tiny clasps of her pearl earrings behind her ears with a smile on her face. Her ivory evening dress laced with gold netted hems and cuffs was pretty and complemented her looks perfectly.

The fading golden hue of the early-evening sun streaked through the window, giving the room a warming feel. Glancing at the top of the dressing table in front of her, she beheld her new jewellery box. She picked up the map that Kharak had drawn to his home from inside the box. Looking at his handwritten words that explained the map, together with his drawing, she felt his presence. Again, she felt the same feeling that she got in her stomach every time she thought of him.

Closing the jewellery box, she had a final look at her hair in the oval mirror on her dressing table. It was tied back in a bun with curls hanging on either side of her forehead. She was happy.

Upon Ivan's direct instructions, Vadu had organised a showy carriage to take them that evening. For Ivan, status could never be compromised.

Standing in the lounge, Ivan stared blankly at the large framed batik that adorned the wall, as he waited in anticipation for Catherine to come downstairs.

After what seemed like an eternity, he heard faint footsteps trailing down the stairway. He brushed the lapel of his jacket and straightened his shirt collar again before walking into the hallway. There, he saw Catherine, as he had never done before. *She is stunning beyond anything,* he thought, as he twitchingly felt the ring on his little finger with his thumb.

"You look beautiful!" he said out loud.

"Thank you."

"The carriage awaits us." He gestured with a smile.

Catherine walked towards the door, making sure for the third time that she held Kharak's map folded in her hand. Stopping in front of Vadu, who was standing by the carriage, she gave him the map to show to the driver. As the conversation between Vadu and the driver progressed, she stood patiently.

"The driver is aware of where he has to take both of you. Kharak does not live very far from there," Vadu assured her.

"As he knows where to go, I would like my map back, please," she requested.

"Yes, memsahib." Vadu bowed.

After a brief conversation in Punjabi, the driver handed the map back to Vadu, who, in turn, returned it to Catherine.

"Thank you," she replied as she slipped it into her bag.

Ivan, taking two steps forward, offered his hand to Catherine to help her step into the carriage. For a moment, he drifted in thought, imagining how her fingers would feel ungloved. He let out a sigh.

Realising that his sigh was very evident, he let out a short fake cough, hoping to drown it. Stepping into the carriage, he was in two minds as to whether to sit opposite her or beside her. He decided to sit opposite her. *At least I will be able to see and admire her tremendous beauty,* he thought.

Catherine peered out of the plush carriage as it smoothly moved off. *I cannot wait.*

Across the streets of Lahore, not only were people dispersing, but the bulbuls seemed to be in a flying rush against the golden-orange backdrop of the sky. Even they were aware of the approaching evening.

"I'm surprised you took that map back," Ivan stated, with his hands resting above his crossed knees.

"It was important to have it back."

"What importance would a hand-drawn map on a piece of raggedy paper that is of no use have?" He smirked.

"It is of significance, to me, anyway." Catherine smiled.

"I would not have thought." Ivan brushed his hand on his knee. "Anyway, you look beautiful this evening." He gazed directly at her.

She briefly met his gaze. "Thank you." She shifted her look to the outside. The unexpected comment made her uneasy.

"I have seen that Lahore is very noisy and not a well-developed city... yet you keep talking about it. What is it about the place?"

"It's the people I admire here, Ivan. They are simple yet enduring, and very welcoming." Catherine crossed her hands whilst holding her bag on her lap.

"Have you missed England?"

She looked out of the carriage window again. "No, I have not missed it yet."

"Surely you must have. Perhaps you are missing your friends there, if nothing else?"

It was her close friend Florence whom she missed the most. They were childhood friends – they had gone to the same school, and, as children, had tried to dress alike. They were inseparable and people who didn't know them thought they were sisters. Florence's gregarious nature hid her rational nature and Catherine yearned to talk to her about Kharak and all that had been happening in Lahore.

Still, she decided not to mention Florence. "No, I don't miss anyone at present."

This reply pleased Ivan. *She isn't involved with anyone... though even if she is, it really does not matter*, he thought.

There were a few moments of silence when the only sound was the clattering of the revolving wooden wheels of the carriage on the surface of the dirt road.

Ivan interrupted the silence. "If I may ask." He paused on purpose. "Have you been spoken for?" His penetrating eyes fawned over her.

It took Catherine a few breaths for his question to sink in. "I beg your pardon? I don't understand what you are asking." She led him on.

"Well, I mean… you are young and beautiful, and perhaps you or your parents have already chosen a suitor for you. That is what I'm asking." He lowered his voice.

No one had been handpicked as her suitor by her parents, although there had been a few men who had been introduced to her over the past year. For some reason or another, she never felt at ease or drawn to any of them as her life partner.

"I haven't been spoken for…"

Despite trying to conceal his excitement upon hearing her reply, Ivan's eyes widened. As Catherine altered her gaze across the carriage to look outside through the other window, she noticed him rolling his little finger over his ring again. She then glimpsed an unsettling smile across his face.

"… that I am aware of," she added.

"Do you have anyone in mind?" Ivan took a subtle deep breath to broaden his chest.

She remained silent. The conversation was heading in an awkward direction.

"That's a very personal question and I do not wish to answer."

"I understand."

It is the chase that matters and it seems that she will be my greatest quest, he thought.

Their carriage passed the entrance of the Lahore Racecourse where horse trainers were busy taking part in evening training sessions with their lean horses. Their owners, who were English by majority, were keenly observing their respective jockeys riding the horses.

As they passed close to a group of white men with binoculars around their necks, Ivan raised his arm and waved to them. Upon realisation that he was like them, they reciprocated.

"Africa is the next frontier that we, the British, are colonising. It is inspiring to see our citizens taking their leisure pursuits wherever they settle."

Catherine did not seem to have heard him. She was thinking of Kharak. Not knowing how the evening would unfold and the anticipation of being part of a different culture had a certain delight about it. The evening breeze drifted through the carriage and gently stroked her flawless curls. She felt happy.

Ivan felt smug at the thought that Catherine's parents had accepted him to accompany her for the evening. Thinking of the conversations he had had with her father over the previous days, he was certain that Gilbert Rose was impressed by his achievements and status. *Mrs Rose likes me as well*, he thought. *It's now.* He cleared his throat mutedly.

"If I may ask…?"

Catherine looked at him. "Yes, you may." She pursed her lips.

Gazing directly at her with his fixed stare, Ivan spoke. "What if some British gentleman here asked you to be his beloved?" He disguised himself.

She raised her eyebrows in disbelief as her jaw nearly dropped. Her heart started beating rapidly as the reality of his question sunk in.

Is he talking about himself? Perhaps I'm overthinking, she thought as she settled herself.

She lowered her gaze. "I don't think that would be a good idea. Err… I'm not comfortable getting involved with anyone right now, especially given that I'm away from home," she lied.

"You and I both know that eventually you shall be back in England, so what if that someone was hoping to start getting to know you in earnest?" He raised his right eyebrow.

"Let's take our case." Unknowingly, she chose the wrong example. "We only met a few times when we were growing up, but I don't remember much about you, so with all due respect, I really don't know you. So, if a stranger were to ask me to be his beloved, it would be so much harder."

This hit Ivan like a thunderbolt. *How could she not remember me? She says that she doesn't know me; that's not possible. I have been living for a few days under the same roof!* His hand tightened its grip on his knee as he thought. Catherine did not notice it.

The carriage turned left onto Ferozepur Road, which led out from the southern fringes of Lahore. It was a fairly straight road crossed the Bari Doab Canal that took water to the farming areas.

After a further mile, the driver took a right turn onto a much smaller and bumpier road. Recalling the map from memory, Catherine knew that this should lead them to Rahmanpur. She started casually straightening her sleeves and brushed her hand over her hair.

The carriage passed a bull cart driven by a turbaned Sikh hauling hay back to his cows. This was a farming area, with young wheat and maize crops enveloping the landscape with dotted farmhouses. At this time, the evening breeze was comfortingly fresh with the fragrance of night-blooming jasmine beginning to permeate the air.

It was half past six in the evening when the carriage slowed, approaching a cluster of walnut trees on one side of the road and low-fruiting mango trees on the other. There were numerous houses built closely together on opposite sides of the road.

The carriage came to a halt and the driver was heard talking to someone. *This must be Rahmanpur,* Catherine thought.

38

Catherine shifted her position closer to the edge of the seat to peer outside. A face suddenly appeared in front of her, startling her. It took her an instant to recognise that familiar, affable smile that was now so soothing to her inner self.

"Oh, Kharak, you made me jump," she laughed, revealing her perfect smile as she stood up and moved closer to the carriage door.

"I didn't mean to."

She carried on beaming with delight. He was wearing a white kaftan with sky-blue embroidery running along the neck. It matched his sky-blue linen trousers.

"I like your outfit. You look very elegant."

"Thank you." He liked her comment. "Welcome to my home town, Rahmanpur."

"Where are we heading to?" she asked.

"The function is at a house a few hundred metres ahead. We could either walk—"

"Let's take the carriage, Kharak. Hop in and we'll go together."

All this time, Ivan sat with keen eyes observing Catherine's demeanour and how it seemed to have changed in an instant upon Kharak's arrival; more engaging, less apprehensive and her smile appeared to be permanent. It disturbed him.

"Oh, I forgot to mention – Kharak, this is Ivan, a family friend who is with us for a few days," she said.

"Good evening, sir." Kharak extended his hand to shake Ivan's. He was surprised to see a new face.

"Evening, young man." Ivan straightened his jacket. He ignored Kharak's hand. "You can sit there and get comfortable," he said with a hint of sarcasm as he pointed to where he had been sitting. Without hesitation, Ivan sat opposite him and beside Catherine. He wasn't going to allow Kharak to sit next to her on his watch.

During the entire two-minute journey, Ivan sat in silence but his mind was darting, observing Kharak. He subtly rolled his eyes towards Catherine and saw that she was still smiling. *So, he is the one whom Catherine has spent the most time with here. Unbelievable! What does she see in him… the face of Lahore?*

"Are you comfortable, dear?" Ivan asked her.

She nodded, missing his intonation as she was too enthralled at the prospect of spending the evening with Kharak.

Amol's farmhouse was much smaller and more compact than Catherine's house in Lahore, yet it was larger than the neighbouring houses. It had a flat roof with iron-framed windows that lacked intricate metalwork, but were decorated with festive beads of crimson carnation flowers. With the drive to the entrance dusty, it was evident that the dust was visible on the external walls of the farmhouse.

Noisy children had gathered at the side entrance, pointing fingers at the carriage. Soon, the message had got to everyone that the white guests had arrived. This was the biggest attendance that had ever been in the village and, soon, more inquisitive eyes, young and grown-up, peered at them.

Kharak disembarked first from the carriage, then helped Catherine down by holding her hand. The surrounding children started clapping and yelling. For the first time in her life, she felt like royalty, not only because of all the jovial faces absorbed in her presence, but also the number of lit lanterns and oil lamps that sparkled, making the arrival of dusk a magical moment.

In contrast, Ivan felt annoyed by the commotion and being surrounded by people whom he thought to be backward, dirty and inferior. What pierced him more than anything was seeing Catherine at complete ease with Kharak. *This is utter madness*, he thought.

The rectangular courtyard was at the rear of the house and enclosed by walls. At the far end was a mango tree that had lanterns hanging from its branches. Chairs were arranged on two sides of the courtyard, with the women seated separately from the men. In the central part, there was a large rectangular canvas covering the floor where the women were seated. There was a woman supporting her flexed knee on a dholak, a small two-headed hand drum, as she played it. The other women around her were clapping in rhythm and singing traditional Punjabi wedding songs.

At the nearside of the courtyard, there were two Belter-style armchairs that had been hastily arranged for the two British guests, overlooking the singing women.

A few minutes after taking her seat, Catherine saw a middle-aged woman wearing a traditional indigo *salwar kameez* approach them. She looked familiar and had striking soft hazel eyes and years of sun-browned complexion.

"*Jee aya nu!*" she said to Catherine and Ivan in Punjabi.

Standing between the woman and Catherine, Kharak spoke. "This is my mother." He wrapped his arm around her shoulder. "She says welcome," he translated.

213

Catherine stood up, removed her white glove and shook her hand. "Very pleased to meet you and thank you all for inviting us here this evening."

With the singing in the background, Seva's reply was not heard by Catherine. All she saw was Kharak grinning.

"What did your mother say?"

Kharak lowered his mouth closer to her ear. "My mother said that she hopes your husband Ivan has a good time."

Catherine covered her mouth as she burst out laughing, revealing the faint devilry in her eyes.

Ivan could not hear their conversation. All he noticed was Kharak whispering in Catherine's ear and the two laughing thereafter. There was a rage swelling within him and he could not control his envy. It was a relief when Kharak was tugged away by an older, chubby man to help him carry some cushions from inside the house.

The joyful commotion came to a brief lull as a woman strutted into the courtyard holding on her head a clay pot decorated with beads. It had lit oil candles at the top. This was the *jago*. The woman started dancing and swivelling her hips to the tune of the folk songs.

This encouraged everyone to clap harder as, one by one, the clay pot was passed on to the next woman to do the same. Laughter accompanied everyone's beaming faces.

Soon, the women dragged the male family members to the middle of the courtyard to join in and, within a short period of time, there were only a few people seated. Kharak was nowhere to be seen.

Kharak's mother, having had her turn at carrying the *jago*, twirled with the bride-to-be towards Catherine. Before she knew what was happening, Catherine was being pulled to join in. It wasn't just politeness towards her hosts; she genuinely couldn't resist the invitation to take part.

Catherine started clapping as she capered around Amol, the

bride, who was now carrying the *jago*. In a little while, she got so captivated by it all and let her inhibitions go – was when she felt like part of the 'tribe'.

Seeing Catherine enthralled by it all, in a surprising gesture, Amol lowered the *jago* in her hands and handed it to her. Despite being caught unaware, this did not faze Catherine. Her nervous smile appeared as she nodded in acceptance. Gingerly, she placed it above her head, still holding it with both hands. As she found her balance, she danced slowly as all the women clapped, swivelled and sang around her.

Through the group of dancing women, Kharak spotted Catherine. *I'm surprised she is carrying the jago. I would never have imagined that I would see her inner beauty shine so soon*, he thought.

Without any second thoughts, he joined in where the men were dancing and made his way towards his mother first, who was close to Catherine. When she saw Kharak, Catherine's smile broadened. With her twinkling eyes widening, she showed off her ability to carry the *jago* to him. She lowered it from her head and offered it to Kharak to carry and twirl next.

As he was about to get hold of the *jago*, it was as if they both knew what would follow. Their fingers touched and caressed purposely as the exchange took place. For that brief moment, their stare was locked. He subtly winked at her and, with impish eyes, she winked back.

In the midst of these happy people, no one who was dancing in celebration noticed this.

Across the courtyard, with his hawk-like eyes, Ivan did not fail to see what had just happened. His nostrils flared and his fingers folded into a tight fist. His facial muscles twitched as he clenched his jaw together. *How dare he do that? She is my Catherine... this will never happen again, not under my eyes.*

The singing and dancing came to an end with the serving of dinner, which was simply lentils and spinach with traditional bread. Ivan did not have it and gave an excuse of an ache in his stomach. Gladly for him, the evening soon came to an end. It had been mentally draining for him, having torrid thoughts of possibly losing Catherine to Kharak.

Just like their arrival, their departure was curious and filled with pomp as they boarded the carriage surrounded by ladies, who sang songs they did not understand. All Catherine saw was humbleness and contentment on their faces, whereas what Ivan saw was backwardness.

Kharak shuffled his way through the women to the front. He had to see Catherine.

"Thank you for coming this evening and I hope you had a wonderful time."

"The privilege is mine and I had such a lovely time. A pity it had to come to an end." Catherine's eyes narrowed in despair at leaving.

I so want to hug you and wish you goodbye right now, but I cannot. What a torment, she thought.

Gently, she lifted her right hand and waved him goodbye. Kharak wanted to hold her hand, but he knew he couldn't. He just responded with a low wave. *I miss her already and she hasn't even left.*

She placed her left hand on the ledge of the carriage window, holding her white cotton glove. Just as the carriage was about to move, she let go of her glove deliberately with her eyes fixed in his gaze, clearly stating her dismay at leaving. The glove landed softly on Kharak's hand. He carefully hid it in his palm as the carriage moved off.

As the carriage trundled away, the clamour and waves of goodbyes were displaced by the quietness of the early night. Hovering in the air was the scent of evening blossom twinned with the settling dust.

Hiding his smirk, Ivan broke the silence. "It seemed that you didn't hesitate to join in the merrymaking tonight."

"It was a wonderful evening and I enjoyed it,"

I know why you had a wonderful time... I know exactly why, Ivan thought.

It was the only time Ivan spoke throughout the entire journey back to the house, but in his mind, resentful thoughts were pounding relentlessly.

On reaching the house, Ivan said goodnight and excused himself to Gilbert and Ethel, stating that he was tired and needed an early night.

He got to his room and gently shut the door. Then, in a fit of rage, he removed his jacket and threw it across the room. He slumped at the edge of the bed and held his lowered head in his hands.

After a while, he walked to the washstand in the corner of the room and splashed cold water over his face. He stood still in front of the bowl, holding its edges with straight arms, staring into the depths of the mirror above. His icy eyes watched the drops of water trickling down his face from the ends of his bushy eyebrows.

He wiped his face dry with the face cloth hanging on the rail and flung that into the corner of the room as well. Hastily, he arranged the pillows in front of the headboard of the bed and, without changing his clothes, lowered himself and lay upright in bed, his Derby boots still on.

As he twiddled his thumbs slowly, deep in thought, a plan started formulating in his mind.

39

The next morning, Ivan had a hurried breakfast with the Roses, apart from Catherine, who was still upstairs getting dressed.

"I do apologise for leaving hurriedly this morning. With only a few days left in India, some urgent matters have come up that need addressing," he stated.

"Oh, I was looking forward to taking you to the Polo Club today." Gilbert wiped his mouth with his cotton napkin.

"I am sorry about that."

"Is there anything we can do?" Ethel asked.

"Actually, could you tell Vadu to organise a carriage for me? I shall be covering a lot of Lahore today as there are a few people to meet."

Gilbert raised his eyebrow. *Striving for success even here in Lahore. He has a terrific future... I must bear in mind that he may be suitable for Catherine*, he thought.

As Ivan excused himself from the breakfast table, Vadu was

promptly instructed to cater to his needs for the day. Within a quarter of an hour, Ivan was in the carriage going towards the Indian Railways head office.

TSAVO

Despite the search, the mystery of the coolie's disappearance from the camp remained unsolved. This led to rumours and superstitions rising about what had happened to him.

It was not long before whispers surfaced that Karim, who was a coolie working amongst the workers, may have had something to do with it.

Karim was a brawny man with jet-black hair and shifty eyes. He seemed to be the natural leader of a group of coolies, who had a reputation not only for being lazy, but deceitful, even faking injuries to avoid work.

Karim was a troublemaker even in the city of Karachi, where he had been an informal revenue collector for the local gang leader. As the bubonic plague of 1897 had spread through the city, he was forced out and discovered that the British were paying workers very well to travel and build the railway line in East Africa.

Two days earlier, Karim had not reported to work in the morning and was summoned by Patterson to see him. To his surprise, Karim made an appearance at midday outside Patterson's tent on a charpoy carried by four of his close associates.

"Now, what happened to you?" Patterson asked in a gruff voice.

"Ah, my whole body aches and I cannot move. I'm dying and nearly got killed in a theological debate," he whined sarcastically.

After removing his blanket and examining him, Patterson knew that Karim was making it up, as always. *Today, I shall make an example of him*, Patterson thought.

"I shall go and get some medicine for you."

Walking into Narain's tent, Patterson collected some tinder and wood shavings, placed them underneath the charpoy and set fire to them. In a jiffy, Karim jumped up, to the amusement and laughter of the other workers around him, including his associates.

This embarrassment triggered his vindictive nature and he wanted to get even.

Two days passed and Ungan went searching for Patterson at the river's edge. In the blistering midday sun, he saw the colonel supervising the arrival of stones that had been cut from the ravine and transported to the construction site in rail wagons along the temporary track.

"Patterson Sahib, could I speak to you in private? I have some knowledge that is of importance to you."

"Yes, Ungan." Patterson walked away from the group of workers he was supervising.

"Sahib, you should not go for your daily walk towards the ravine today."

"Why?"

"I have been made aware that a plan has been hatched by some unscrupulous coolies to cause harm to you today. It will happen along the narrow path that runs along the side of the ravine."

Patterson pursed his lips in thought. "Is Karim one of them?"

"Perhaps. I cannot say for sure if he is the ringleader or not."

"Thank you, Ungan, for letting me know. I will ensure that their intentions do not come to fruition." Patterson tapped his shoulder.

With that, Ungan turned back and Patterson carried on with ensuring that the stones were stacked correctly at the bank of the river. He glanced at the foundations being laid and the progress being made. The last thing he wanted was someone planning to hurt him. It was worrying.

In the late afternoon, Patterson went for his usual walk. Upon reaching the narrowest part of the path, a group of coolies came out from the thorny acacia bushes, wanting to challenge him.

He did the most unconventional thing by getting his notebook and pencil out and writing down the names of the coolies, while calling out the names of the ones he knew.

As one of them, after hesitation, rushed towards him, Patterson jumped out of his way, causing him to fall embarrassingly.

"Your names have been passed on to the British police, as I was aware of your plan. You will be dealt with severely by the British sepoys." His voice thundered, echoing around the ravine.

For impact, he stayed silent for a moment. "Now, if anyone wants to carry on working, he is more than welcome."

In the minutes that followed, all the coolies present turned ashamedly and walked towards the Tsavo campsite. The lone figure of Karim was left behind, casting a lengthy shadow onto a large boulder, unsure of whether to go back with his colleagues or stay here. Eventually, he too decided that the sensible thing to do was to swallow his bruised ego and walk back.

Tsavo continued to be enshrouded by the perils of the unknown, as believed by the local Akamba people. Missing people, conspiracies to cause harm, brutal weather and mishaps at the construction site seemed to add weight to the meaning of Tsavo's name: *A place of slaughter.*

Lahore

40

The purple-orange colour of the western sky across Lahore could be watched from the courtyard in the rear garden. The male crickets were just beginning their nightly ritual of chirping to attract the females.

Catherine sat in the lounge chair with her shawl wrapped around her shoulders, gazing at the bright Evening Star, Venus. Her mother had been quietly observing her for a while.

"It's been a few days now that you've seemed a bit distant and busy in your own little world, Catherine. Are you all right?"

Turning her head, Catherine had a contented smile. "Everything is... beautiful, Mother."

It is strange that when one thinks of someone who is dear, one loses all sense of time. I may look idle, but thousands of his thoughts keep my mind busy. You are but a few miles away, Kharak, yet I sense you here. Why do I feel this way? Catherine thought.

A few miles away, opposite the racecourse, was the Punjab Club of Lahore with its majestic white Tuscan columns forming the impressive facade.

Inside the dining room, the majority of the members were dining after a long day in Lahore. Some were horse owners who had walked from the racecourse after watching their horses train, while others were tied to the government ministry.

The hardwood parquet floor extended outward to the gallery. It was there that Ivan and Gilbert sat in their tufted club chairs, relaxing, having finished their meal. Above them, hung on the wall, the English fusee wall clock ticked.

"Unusual to see you away the whole day. Hope you got everything done." Gilbert clicked his fingers at the Indian waiter.

"I managed to meet with most people I needed to see and it ended up a good day, overall." Ivan adjusted his collar. *I've got to tell him now*, he thought.

"Get me a gin with tonic water." Gilbert looked at the waiter, followed by a glance at Ivan. "What will you have?"

"The same."

"Make that two." He pointed at the waiter.

As the waiter left, Ivan felt an uneasy silence that was just in his mind. He cleared his throat.

"Dr Rose," he paused, "what do you think of Kharak?"

Gilbert raised his eyebrow. "You know that I dislike him... and that grows every time Catherine mentions him."

"Well, that's another thing we share: a distaste for Kharak." Ivan leant on his elbow to get closer to Gilbert. "I wish not to be the bearer of bad news, sir, but Catherine and Kharak are quite close." He lowered his tone.

"What do you mean?" Gilbert's eyes widened as he rose from his slumped position.

Now I know I have your full attention, Ivan thought.

"Last night, they were dancing together... very closely together... with their eyes locked onto one another. There was a lot of flirting going on, Dr Rose. And I saw them wink at each other as well."

Gilbert furrowed his eyebrows in displeasure. "I knew this Kharak could not be trusted and now he seems to have my daughter fluttering like a hummingbird around him... Kharak this and Kharak that!" He tried to control the anger in his tone.

Ivan maintained silence to ensure that the gravity of the matter sank into Gilbert's mind. "To confirm this, I propose that we invite Kharak to our garden party and you can observe this actually happening—"

"I don't feel like inviting him," Gilbert interrupted abruptly.

"I feel the same as you do, sir, and the last thing I want is to see Catherine with him. She deserves someone of British stature and heritage." Ivan lowered his gaze on purpose to show submissiveness.

"I admire your honesty, Ivan. I hope that Catherine can see it."

"You need to see this before we can ensure that what we foresee can be averted."

"Should Catherine know about this?"

"No."

"Then how do we invite Kharak?"

Ivan had already thought of this in his calculating mind. It was just the beginning and, so far, it pleased him to see that it was going according to plan.

"I spoke to Vadu and he confirmed that she met him at the station, where he'd been working." Ivan took a deep breath. "We instruct Vadu to go and meet Kharak and pass her invitation to him."

"Does Vadu know where to find him?"

"Yes, he does, at the railway yards."

"You never fail to surprise me, Ivan." Gilbert's fingers tapped the leather armrest.

Ivan smiled. *It's all for Catherine*, he thought.

"Well, if this is what is happening in my daughter's life, I need to see it with my own eyes."

Ivan eased gently into his club chair.

"The first thing I do tomorrow morning will be to send Vadu to give Kharak the invitation on behalf of Catherine."

At that moment, the waiter walked towards them with a tray in hand. This was one drink that Gilbert could not wait for. His nerves needed calming.

41

Being employed by the Indian Railways, every Saturday was a working day for Kharak; however, on this particular Saturday, he had taken the day off. He could not bear the thought of going to work. Catherine had invited him to her garden party and it would be the first English social event he had attended.

He was nervous, but was not sure whether it was because he was going to meet Catherine, or because he didn't know what to expect or do. It was the thought of her that spurred him on.

With a sense of importance, he decided not to use his bicycle but instead ask Nandu to take him there. Also, the afternoon heat would have made him feel hot and flustered, and he wanted to give a good impression to everyone there.

Wearing his only smart linen jacket with trousers, he hoped that he was not overly dressed, but, deep down, he felt dapper.

Stepping off the carriage in front of Catherine's house, he brushed his lapels with the palms of his hands and adjusted the rear of his jacket. His palms were slightly sweaty. A quick wave of goodbye and Nandu was off, having not charged him; after all, his business had been good of late and all because of Kharak.

Balu had been made aware and he promptly opened the gate to allow Kharak in. As he ambled towards the gate, the first thing he noticed was the humming of people. As the view became clear upon entering, he saw the front garden teeming with guests.

Erected on two sides of the garden were plain marquees, providing shade from the intense sun. Seated there were mainly women wearing fancy hats, fans in hand, making themselves comfortable.

In the central part of the garden, men were busy in conversation, trying to gloat over their achievements. Kharak felt a little uneasy and out of place as the 'odd one'.

Soon, this uneasiness grew as faces around the garden started staring at him. It started with one face, but in a short time, nearly everyone was staring at him.

He scanned the grounds for Catherine, but did not see her. He managed to recognise Ivan in the distance, talking to a middle-aged man.

Ivan leant forward and whispered into Gilbert's ear. "There's Kharak."

"I thought so. He had the urge to see Catherine." Gilbert stared at Kharak in the distance. "Let him wander aimlessly for a while," he added.

Still searching for Catherine, Kharak felt out of place and it seemed that he was the centre of attention. He spotted Vadu standing at the steps leading onto the porch, the place where he had, in the past, dropped Catherine on previous occasions. Vadu half-bowed to acknowledge him before turning his head to face the door into the house.

At that point, the door swung open and Catherine walked

out. Kharak was the first to notice her. Even at this distance, wearing a flawless light cream dress, she was staggeringly beautiful. His heart fluttered and he smiled.

Vadu spoke a few words to her, after which she turned and looked towards Kharak. She lurched down the steps towards him, her hands pinching her dress, raising it a few inches above the ground. She wore the most bewitching smile.

With her hands close together and forwards, Catherine approached him and held his warm hands. He felt her squeeze them with affection.

From the centre of the garden, Gilbert saw this. He glared as his hand clenched around his Kilmarnock whisky tumbler. There was a rage building up inside him, and the more he thought about what Ivan had told him, the worse it got.

Yet if only Gilbert could have sensed what Ivan was feeling at that moment, even he would have been surprised at his overwhelming hatred for Kharak. Ivan was being viciously torn apart by the sight of Catherine holding Kharak's hands. The only thing that calmed his outward appearance was thinking about the plan.

"You were right, Ivan. This has to be stopped before it gets any worse." Gilbert took a step forward.

Ivan gently held his arm. "Sir, let's not make it too obvious what is happening. There are guests here who don't need to know all this."

Gilbert huffed. "You are right."

"Let's take this afternoon calmly as it unravels. Status is important." Ivan gently tapped his shoulder.

They both kept watching Catherine and Kharak.

"I'm so pleased to see you." Catherine tried to contain her joy. "I wasn't expecting you."

"Really?"

"It's a wonderful surprise."

"I thought you invited me." Kharak had a bemused look. "Vadu came over to the station to pass on your message yesterday."

Catherine turned and glanced at Vadu, who was still standing at the porch, and gestured to him to come over. After a brief conversation with him, she learned that it was her father who had instructed him to send an invitation to Kharak on her behalf.

"That was a pleasant surprise." She cast an eye around the garden to spot him. "Ah, there he is." She waved. "Let me introduce him to you." She led Kharak towards her father and Ivan.

Gilbert had his gaze firmly fixed on both of them when he saw them stroll towards him. "Why is she bringing him here?"

He shifted his gaze to Ivan, hoping that this would somehow make Catherine avoid them. It was a useless attempt.

"Hello, Father. This is Kharak."

"How do you do, sir?" Kharak offered a handshake.

"Fine, I suppose," Gilbert mumbled in a gruff tone. He refused to shake his hand.

Kharak felt awkward and drew his hand back. Catherine raised her eyebrows in embarrassment.

Turning, she continued, "You must remember Ivan, from the other night?"

"I remember him. How are you, Ivan?" Kharak reluctantly offered a handshake.

"Very well indeed," Ivan said in a penetrating tone. He gripped and squeezed Kharak's hand hard. It caught Kharak unexpectedly, causing discomfort until he firmed his grip in response.

"Enjoy your afternoon here," Ivan smiled wryly.

"You should count yourself lucky to be here, as you are the odd one out. Every guest here is white and British." Gilbert paused. "Apart from Vadu, who obviously is our servant." He gave a sardonic smile.

Oh dear, my future father-in-law! That was flawless, but it was not the most appropriate moment to state that! Ivan thought.

Visibly disgusted at her father's comment, Catherine tactfully decided to take Kharak away.

"Let me show you the drinks and food marquee," she said as she pulled his arm.

As they sauntered across the garden, all eyes were on them, but Catherine did not care at all. She was beside Kharak in this moment and that was all that mattered. Similarly, he was engrossed in her presence, drowning in the indescribable bliss he felt when he was with her.

Despite being mid-afternoon, the majority of the men had a pale ale in hand – even in this part of the British Empire, the staple followed these intrepid colonists.

Just outside the marquee, there were white circular tables with chairs. Catherine went towards a couple who had just got up, leaving behind a vacant table that had two chairs.

"I'm so sorry for how my father behaved towards you just then." She put her hand on Kharak's arm as they sat down.

"He doesn't like me."

"My father can be like that. At times, he can be abrupt and avoids showing me any affection."

"Where is your mother? I haven't seen her."

"She is around. Busy with her new best friend, Mrs Wittingham, and her friends – and with us staying here for a while, she has got to know other English housewives."

"Don't you know them as well?"

"Not really." She looked at him. Her thoughts required careful expression. "You are the most important person to me here, so I haven't had time for anyone else… and I am so pleased to see you." Her eyes shimmered. "I missed you, Kharak."

These were the most beautiful words Kharak had ever heard.

"You only saw me the other day."

"I know, but I can't help it."

"Catherine, I do like spending time with you." He smiled. "I never imagined that I would be so close to someone like you."

Across the garden, hawk-eyed Ivan kept watch on both of them. With every moment of observation, his anger grew. *I should be there, not him.*

His way of gloating at social events to further his ambitions went haywire that afternoon. His focus was on Catherine and Kharak, and the mental pain he was going through was like someone tightening a vice around his thumb every time they smiled at each other.

And now he saw that she had even brought a slice of orange sponge cake for him to try with a pot of Earl Grey.

A while later, to his relief, he saw Ethel walking towards them. *Now, don't just talk to them, sit with them!* he uttered under his breath.

"It's a surprise to see you here." Ethel crossed her arms.

"Hello, Mrs Rose," Kharak replied politely.

"Catherine, dear, you did not tell me that you were inviting him."

"I didn't invite Kharak, Father did, but I wish that I had invited him instead." Catherine spoke out.

"Your father didn't tell me that."

"Does it matter, Mother?"

"Oh… not at all," Ethel lied. "And by the way, Mrs Wittingham wants to see you, so don't keep her waiting too long."

"Yes, I will do that."

A wave from a lady across the garden interrupted Ethel and, without saying another word, she walked off towards her.

"I'll be all right, you can go and meet Mrs Wittingham," Kharak said as he took a sip of Earl Grey tea.

"That's not important. I'd rather be here with you… I can see her tomorrow."

The hired brass band had just started playing under the gazebo on the opposite side of the garden, and all the murmuring of the guests was drowned out. Soon, the central area of the garden became unoccupied as people trickled away to the edges.

It wasn't long before the glasses were down on the tables and most men with the urge to show off were in the centre with their partners.

The intermittent feathery clouds offered relief from the lowering sun as the afternoon progressed. The fragrance of freshly cut grass from the morning still lingered in the air. With the band playing, a numinous ambience enveloped the garden reception.

"I want to have a twirl with you." Catherine's face tingled as she took a deep breath.

"Phew! Do you really want to be the attraction today?" Kharak gave a nervous smile.

Catherine lowered her gaze. "I feel like a dance with you."

"Do you think it will be all right…" he paused, "with your parents?"

"I'm sure they will not mind; Father invited you and, if they do, it will be too late." She felt daring.

With a sudden surge of boldness, they both nodded, winked at each other and that became their cue to stand.

They timed their walk to the boundary of the dancing space perfectly, as there were more people dancing and occupying it, which favoured their attempt to be inconspicuous.

"I've just realised that I don't know how to dance in this style." Kharak's breath quickened.

"Don't worry. Just follow my feet and replicate what I do," she whispered in his ear as she extended her arm around his neck, ready for the waltz.

Their fingers clasped together and they felt each other's touch. Naturally, he found his other hand embracing her lower back and, slowly, as her feet moved in rhythm, he followed.

Gilbert's jaw dropped and he nearly lost his pipe when he saw, through the crowd, Catherine and Kharak having a dance.

Standing beside him, Ivan's face turned scarlet and his eyes bulged with jealousy and rage. He had to turn around to force himself to regain some composure.

Looking around, he saw quite a few of the guests staring in earnest at the two dancing and this ruffled him even more than it did Catherine's father. He felt his reputation bleeding away right in front of his eyes.

42

The few minutes of dancing together were the most memorable for both Catherine and Kharak. Their initial apprehension and nervousness were overcome, in time, by sheer joy and fulfilment.

Soon, just as they had blended onto the dancing space, they blended out quietly.

"I loved that dance," Catherine admitted. "You were amazing."

"I'm glad you think so. I thought that I was very average."

They walked back towards the table where they had been seated, only to discover that someone else had already taken it.

"Looking at it now, your front garden is bigger than it seems."

"It's a decent size. Looks very different today with everything set up." Catherine daintily flicked her curls from her forehead.

"It's a lovely place, though."

"Oh! You haven't seen my house properly. Come on, I'll show you."

They walked towards the paved path that meandered away from the front garden and towards the dirt driveway from where steps led onto the veranda. It was a place where, so often, Kharak had dropped Catherine, having said the dreaded goodbye. Never had he passed that invisible boundary that led into the world where Catherine lived and daydreamed.

As almost everybody was outside, the house was empty apart from the servant in the front lounge room and Vadu, who frequently walked in from outside to oversee the servants.

Kharak was fascinated by the grandeur of the house, especially when he compared it to where he lived. Catherine showed him the study, with its impressive bookcase along the rear wall. There was a whiff of tobacco in the air and he thought that this must be where her father spent most of his free time.

"Let me show you the layout of the house."

They walked along the corridor towards the staircase, where another servant saluted them just as Vadu walked in again.

"Do you need anything, memsahib?" He bowed.

"No, thank you. I'm showing Kharak the house."

Vadu took a step back, his head still bowed, as they walked past him, going up the stairs. Kharak noticed the head of a blackbuck mounted on the wall facing the intermediate landing. Further up a few steps, Catherine stopped to show him four black-and-white paintings of a hunting party adorning the wall.

"Your father is a keen hunter."

"Yes. But I don't admire it." She took a step closer to him. "When I was twelve years old, he took me fox hunting in Somerset and I found it traumatising seeing the hunt – ever since, I find it cruel."

At that moment, Catherine's hand purposely swayed towards his, touching it. She held his hand and their fingers slid together. She blinked, her velvet eyes gazing at him with affection. He responded to her touch.

Clutching his hand, she led him to the upper floor towards

the window at the end of the corridor. From there, they had a view of the garden from above. The sound of the band was distant from here, but couples were still dancing in the middle, whilst some of the men congregated in groups, chatting and enjoying their late-afternoon tipple.

Catherine pointed at Mrs Wittingham and the women who were standing next to her. They were her mother's acquaintances here in Lahore. With a keen eye, Kharak tried to spot her father and Ivan, but they could not be seen.

With her hand in his, he felt a constant ebullience that grew every time she looked at him. He was the happiest he had ever been in her presence. Every time he uttered her name under his breath, he felt whole. *If only she knew*, he thought.

Muffled voices were heard coming from the bottom of the stairs.

"That must be Vadu, stamping his authority on the other servants," she said. "My parents' room is further down the corridor on the right." She half-turned her neck.

She twisted the latch and opened the window, which let the breeze in to blow her wavey hair across her face. With that, the sound of the brass band got louder.

"That's my room." She pointed at the door nearest to the window.

"So that's where your hidden world is?" he asked with a chuckle.

Catherine fell silent, let out a sigh and took a deep breath. "You are my world."

Her words sent warm waves through him. It dawned on him that it was not only him who felt this way about her, but she felt the same about him. It was insanely difficult when his thoughts remained as unspoken words on his lips, unable to describe to her what he felt.

In silence, they stared into each other's eyes, still holding hands, unaware of what was happening around them.

Catherine took a step closer.

A thundering voice interrupted them.

"How dare you come up here!" her father's voice boomed from the centre of the hallway where the stairs were.

Turning towards the voice, Kharak and Catherine saw Gilbert's red face, bulging wide eyes and chest puffed up. A few steps behind him, Ivan carried a smirk on his face.

"What are you up to? You menial brown man!"

"Nothing, sir," Kharak replied, distancing himself from Catherine.

Catherine was incensed at that derogatory remark. "Father, that was very rude of you to speak to my friend in that manner."

"Don't tell me what I can say and what I cannot. My eyes don't lie to me; I saw how close he was to you." He pointed his finger at them.

"I was showing him the house and the view from up here—"

"I don't want to hear another word," her father interrupted her.

"Sir, she is telling the truth." Kharak maintained a low tone.

"Leave my house immediately. I don't like cadgers."

"With all due respect, I was invited here, if not by Catherine, then by yourself." Kharak stood up for himself.

"That was a huge mistake on my part." Gilbert paused. "But I've seen all I needed to." He lowered his eyebrows and squinted his eyes.

In the tense and hostile mood that lingered, with one hand in his waistcoat pocket and the other busy fidgeting with his ring, Ivan took a few forward steps and stood beside Gilbert. *This is unravelling better than I hoped. I must take this chance to look sympathetic to both Catherine and her father. Be ice above the fire*, he thought.

Ivan carefully rested his hand on Gilbert's shoulder for support. As his head turned towards him, Ivan narrowed his eyes and nodded to suggest keeping calm.

237

"It's all right, Kharak. Tempers are fraying right now and to unruffle things it may be a good idea to call it a day." Ivan twisted his lips with half a smile. *I am great.*

"Don't leave, Kharak." Catherine leaned forward with hunched shoulders and tugged at his arm.

Gilbert wanted to say so much to both of them, but, with difficulty, refrained from it. All he wanted at this moment was for Kharak to leave his house.

Muddled with anger and disappointment, Kharak held his breath, gazed into Catherine's eyes and reassuringly felt her hand on his arm.

"I think it's best I leave for now."

In his voice, Catherine heard the sadness that his eyes confirmed. With a fleeting frozen stare at her father and Ivan, Kharak walked towards the stairs and past them.

"I'm so sorry, Kharak, so sorry," she uttered despondently as she followed him downstairs.

Ivan was not only satisfied at what was happening; his ego spurred him on. He felt like a chess grandmaster with all his pieces positioned perfectly and an actor with the ability to mask his true self.

Ivan and Gilbert followed the two downstairs as they walked out onto the porch. Vadu was standing on the dirt driveway just off the veranda.

It was painful for Catherine to see Kharak leave in this manner; it felt so wrong watching him take steps down the veranda to the drive. She darted towards him.

Grabbing his arm, she turned him around. "I'm sorry for the hurt my father has caused you." Tears formed in her eyes.

"I feel fine, Catherine. Don't be too concerned." Kharak fixed his gaze on her and wiped her tears with his fingers.

"I promise to come to you and see you again." She squeezed his arm.

Behind them, a thundering shout came from her father,

"Get that bloody Indian out of my house!"

All guests in the garden stared with intrigue at the drama occurring on the driveway. They exchanged looks before murmuring started amongst them.

Vadu hurried towards Balu in response to his master.

Never had Kharak felt this hurt before, but his pain was tinged with exasperation as he walked towards the gate. It was the frustration of not knowing what to do.

He turned around one last time to catch a final glimpse of Catherine. She stood alone with drooping shoulders, her arms wrapped around herself and her eyes puffy and red.

43

Night had fallen in Lahore and the plumes of afternoon clouds had closed in, forming a low-lying blanket that covered the sky and hid the stars – and this darkened the night.

The servants had managed to complete the clearing up of the marquees and the litter of the tea party just before darkness had set in. The hissing of the night beetles could be heard in the now serene garden.

In the house, everyone was seated at the dining table, apart from Catherine, who was seated alone on a stool in the kitchen, trying to have her dinner. At this time, she could not bring herself to sit amongst her family after the incident earlier in the afternoon. Resting her head on her supporting left hand, all she had done so far was toy with the food on her plate, as hunger had deserted her.

She decided that she could not eat anything, so she pushed her plate aside and decided to walk back up to her room.

With trepidation, she walked into the dining room to pass through.

"Why could you not sit with us for dinner? That is rude." Her mother broke the silence.

"I did not want to. And rude is what Father said and how he acted towards Kharak today."

What followed was a definite thump of Gilbert's fist on the table, causing the cutlery to rattle on the fine china.

"You, young woman, are crossing your boundaries. Have you forgotten how to speak? Is that how we have brought you up?" He raised his voice.

"No, you haven't." She paused. "Because that is why I don't see him as different to us."

Ivan's eyebrows furrowed in displeasure, but he maintained silence.

"If this is your thinking, you should not have come here," her father said. "You have made me a laughing stock with this afternoon's antics."

Without replying, Catherine walked out of the dining room with tears in her eyes and went up the stairs to her room.

In Rahmanpur, Kharak positioned Lal's bike, which he had borrowed, by the wall at the door to his house. He had got back after seeing him. After all that had happened that afternoon, he had needed to talk to him and share his thoughts, and now there was a slight lifting of his emotional burden. He missed Catherine, though.

Aside from Lal, he kept the events of the evening to himself, not wanting to say much to his family. He was keen to wander in his thoughts. In spite of his mother having cooked his favourite chickpea dish, he had no appetite.

Seated in the back room with his toolbox open, his quietness was noticed by his mother. She noticed him staring blankly at his tools.

Walking into the room, she sat beside him and placed her comforting hand on his lap. "Is everything all right, son?"

"Of course, Mother." He picked up the saw from his toolbox.

"You seem distant."

"I have a heavy head today."

"How was Catherine's party?"

This caught him by surprise. "It was nice," he replied and quickly changed the conversation. "I will have a glass of warm milk tonight. I need to go to bed early."

"An early start at work tomorrow?"

"No, I have a couple of days off."

Her maternal instincts knew that something was bothering him, yet she walked away, allowing him to choose when to talk if he wanted to. She didn't want to pester him.

Ivan exhaled perfectly formed rings of smoke as he took pleasure in the cigar while leaning on the armchair in the study. He wanted to rest his legs on the side table, but could not as Gilbert was standing across the study, gazing out of the window and into the dark Lahore night, occasionally taking a puff from his pipe to relieve his tension.

Now would be a perfect moment to tell him of my proposition, Ivan thought.

"Dr Rose, I understand the concerns you are having regarding Catherine." He paused for effect. "I may have a solution to your worry."

Gilbert turned around and took his pipe from his mouth. "What worry?"

"*Kharak!*" Ivan's eyes narrowed.

"Catherine's actions are unsettling me," Gilbert admitted.

"She is kind, but a little naive, and she cannot see what is happening. She just needs to be away from that Indian leech."

Gilbert pointed his pipe at him. "I'm not surprised that you feel the same about him as I do."

"It's just that I don't want any harm coming to Catherine... and I feel strongly about that." Ivan let out an intentional sigh. "I am on your side, sir."

For the first time that evening, Catherine's father smiled. *I knew there was something wonderful about this young man*, he thought.

"What have you in mind, my boy?" He took a satisfying puff from his pipe as he sat down behind his oak desk. "I'm listening."

Over the next half hour, Ivan described in detail what his plan was and how he intended to set it in motion. Gilbert sat starry-eyed at what was said and was in complete awe at his canny plan. *This young man is driven and he cares about her.*

"I wanted your approval before I initiated this. That is why I had to speak to you first," he lied to impress.

"And you are sure that what you have suggested has already been agreed?"

Ivan placed his cigar casually between his lips, then reached into his inner pocket and retrieved an envelope. He pulled a letter from the envelope and slid it towards Gilbert across the desk.

"This confirms it in writing."

Despite not doubting Ivan at all, Gilbert still put his reading glasses on to read the letter that was in his hand. It took him a minute to go through it to confirm what Ivan had said.

"How did you manage all this?" His eyes widened with surprise.

Ivan always relished when people were impressed by his abilities. His ego soared. "I have contacts here through work." He smirked. "And this always helps me." He showed Gilbert his elaborate ring with the compass motif on his little finger.

"This is great news! What's next?"

"On Monday, we go and arrange the momentous meeting at the railways headquarters for Tuesday... and that will give us enough time before I leave Lahore two days later." He exhaled cigar smoke. "In a few months, I shall meet you all back in England when my contract comes to an end."

"Splendid." Gilbert reached for the tumblers in the tray. "This calls for a double of Walker's Kilmarnock whisky." He uncorked the silver flask.

Part 3

44

Catherine lay in her bed between the soft blanket and fine cotton sheet, staring blankly at the white ceiling. It was eleven o' clock and this was late for her to still be in bed. The sun was out and the chirping birds could be heard through the window. She paid no attention to either the birds or the mid-morning sun. Her thoughts were elsewhere.

With visions of the past two days going round in her mind like a merry-go-round, she had not slept well, intermittently waking and nodding off.

The previous morning, she had realised that her father and Ivan were not at home. Nandu had been outside as per the arrangement he had with her and Kharak – that if she ever needed to travel within Lahore, she could use his rickshaw.

Accompanied by Sana, Catherine had gone to see Kharak at the rail yard to apologise for her father's behaviour the other day. Also, she had been missing him, but, to her disappointment, he had not been at work. Despondently, she had returned without seeing him.

Now, as she lay on her side, Catherine gazed at the map on her bedside table. It upset her to see Kharak's handwriting; it was perfect to her. She picked up the map. *I should have gone to see him at home yesterday. Why was I too nervous to do that?*

She remembered his eyes and, as much as he had tried to hide it, she had seen the dejection on his face as he walked out of the gate of her house. *How must he have felt at the insult?* She felt at fault for Kharak's agony and a tear rolled onto her pillow.

"I'm sorry," she whispered.

While Catherine lay in bed holding the map in her hand, a few miles away at the railway yard, a newly recruited messenger carrying a letter plodded across the work site looking for Kharak. After asking around, he was directed to where Kharak was presiding over a section of track adjustment.

"Kharak?"

"That's me. How can I be of help?"

"There is an urgent letter for you… and you are summoned at this very moment to the head office." The man handed Kharak an envelope before walking away.

Kharak scanned the envelope and saw the logo of the Indian Railways. He opened it and removed the handwritten note from James Witt, who was head of recruitment. All he had stated was, *Come and see me immediately in my office.*

What would he want me for? What have I done wrong? He thought of the worst.

He downed his spanner, dusted off his work trousers and washed his hands in a bucket of water before setting off to the head office. He felt unsettled.

The head office was located in the adjoining building to the railway station, which was connected by a series of corridors. On that day, the walk there seemed never-ending to Kharak.

Turning the corner in the final corridor, Kharak slowed his walk as he approached the door with James Witt's name on the plaque. He stopped to straighten his collar and have a final glance at his appearance before knocking.

"Yes," was the high-pitched reply.

Kharak walked in and saw a slim Indian man with oily, jet-black hair seated at the desk.

"My name is Kharak and I have come to see James Witt."

The Indian man looked up from his papers. "He is busy in a meeting."

"He is expecting me." Kharak got the note out from his shirt pocket and handed it to him.

After reading it, the man got up and casually walked towards the door that led to the adjoining room before knocking on it. He walked in and was in the room briefly before walking out.

"Take a seat. He will see you soon."

Kharak sat down to wait, nervous, as he had never been summoned here before. The wait was only five minutes long, but seemed like an hour before the Indian secretary spoke.

"You may go in." He pointed to the door.

Kharak knocked on the sturdy door before turning the doorknob to enter the room. As he opened the door slowly, the space in the office that came into view suggested that the high ceiling was a highlight. Tobacco smoke lingered in the air, magnified as the sun's rays made the air hazy near the window. Above the half-panelled wooden cabinets, there were shelves with files neatly stacked.

As he stepped in, he turned to face the opposite side of the room where Mr Witt's desk was.

To his surprise, he saw two additional faces he was not expecting; faces he had seen before. Ivan and Gilbert sat on either side of Mr Witt behind his desk.

A single chair had been placed in the middle of the room, a few feet from the desk.

"Kharak, I presume?" Mr Witt spoke first.

"Yes, sir."

"Take a seat."

Kharak sat on the chair, feeling uncomfortable, not knowing whether to look directly at them or not. This was the first time he had met Mr Witt, who was a thin-lipped, middle-aged man with deep-set eyes that were accentuated by the reading glasses he wore.

After an intentional hesitation, Mr Witt spoke, "Mr Singh, I am led to believe that you have been doing a good job here at the railways over the past months."

"Thank you."

"As a result, you are to be transferred to work in the British East Africa colony." Mr Witt paused before adding, "With immediate effect."

There was silence in the room.

"Sorry, I don't understand," a bemused Kharak replied.

Mr Witt removed his spectacles. "To be direct, you are being transferred to work for six months under Mr Freeman in East Africa, helping the British build the railway from Mombasa to Kampala."

"Erm…" Kharak raised his eyebrows in disbelief as words failed to roll off his tongue. "How can that be possible?"

Ivan spoke for the first time. "If I may, James." He reached into the pocket of his jacket and removed folded sheets of paper. "These are your tickets for the sea voyage, which leaves in three days from the port of Bombay."

Kharak felt nauseated. His palms were sweaty. "I don't know—"

Mr Witt interrupted him. "You will be well remunerated, up to twenty rupees a month, which is ten rupees more than what your equivalent will get there."

Kharak realised that this would be twice his current salary. "Money is not everything," he replied.

Ivan was losing his patience and the tension in his neck was evident. His eyes glared. He had a menacing look. He leaned forward.

"You have no option but to go." There was firmness in his voice.

Catherine's father observed the conversation in silence as he took another puff from his pipe.

"If you don't do as you are told, I will ensure that your family's livelihood will be destroyed." Ivan pointed his finger threateningly.

Kharak froze for a moment with wide eyes. His mouth went dry and his pulse quickened. "What do you mean?"

From the papers in his hand, Ivan retrieved the one that was at the bottom.

"This is a letter from Sir Henry Lawrence, one of the Board of Commissioners who is responsible for the administration of Punjab. We both know that it was through him that your grandfather and your father were able to get work and contracts respectively." He calmly walked towards Kharak. "This letter states that if you do not accept this contract, your father's work will stop. Your family's land will be confiscated and Mr Witt can confirm that you will lose your job here at the railways." Ivan gave a malicious smile as he handed the letter to Kharak.

Kharak's confidence dropped and tiny droplets of sweat formed on his forehead. He forced himself to read the letter. It had the official heading at the top and, as he read it carefully, it stated exactly what Ivan had said. At the bottom, it had the Punjab Governor's seal and stamp.

With all the statements thrown at him, Kharak's head was disoriented with all sorts of thoughts going around in circles with no end in sight.

Ivan lit a cigar as he observed Kharak reading the letter. "You sign this contract and your earnings will double and your family's livelihood will be secured." He paused as he took a puff.

"Everyone's future is in your hands: your family's, your own... as well as Catherine's future."

Kharak hesitantly spoke. "I would like to discuss this with my family."

"I'm afraid you cannot; you need to sign this now... however, I will give you a couple of minutes to let all this sink in." Ivan walked over to the other side of the room.

A better salary was the last thing on Kharak's mind. He knew how hard his father worked to earn a living, but it was the threat of losing the family land that disturbed him. That was his ancestral land and he had a future responsibility to it. Then, there was Catherine. He would never see her again and that thought pierced him. He felt his palpitations rising.

Through the internal turmoil, it was the statement that Ivan had made about Catherine's future that gave him some clarity. The more his mind wondered over what had happened in the last few days, the more sense things made.

He wants me away from Catherine! And he wants this so badly that he is willing to send me away from here! What do I do? I'm torn. Kharak's heart sank.

Mr Witt, who had been seated behind his desk, spoke, "It is a very good opportunity to earn over a years' wage in the space of six months and, better still, you will be working with your good friend Lal."

In this unexpected situation he had been thrown into, Kharak had forgotten about Lal. Of course, he would be with Lal for six months.

The next couple of minutes felt like two breaths. Where was time when he needed it? With three faces staring at him, masking their own hidden agendas, it was suffocating.

Ivan walked across to the desk from the window. His boots tapped on the wooden floor with each step he took. He picked up a pen that was on the desk and walked towards Kharak. *All he has to do is sign and that will be the end of the episode.*

252

"You need to sign there on the two copies." Ivan handed him the paper and pen.

With the burden of the decision, Kharak felt a tightness in his chest and a sick feeling in his stomach. The tobacco smoke in the air did not help.

What will my family feel and say when I tell them that I will be away for six months? Will I ever see Catherine again? I realise that my decision affects others and I hope they all understand my dilemma. Kharak's thoughts pinched him.

He nervously took the pen from Ivan's hand and signed the contract.

Ivan's face wore an odious smile he couldn't hide as he took back a copy of the signed contract as well as the letter. Behind the office table, Catherine's father adjusted his blazer as he leaned back comfortably in his chair with his pipe in his mouth.

From the inner pocket on the other side of his jacket, Ivan took out a brown envelope. "In here is your train ticket to Bombay, as well as your ticket for your ship from there to Mombasa, together with details of the trip. I will be travelling at the same time as you, but the only difference is that you are travelling in standard class whereas I will be residing in the first-class cabins," he gloated.

"I am pleased, Kharak, that you signed and I can assure you that your higher wages will be paid starting from today. You can leave here now to prepare for the new position that awaits you," Mr Witt remarked.

Kharak sat slouched, a lonely figure with clammy hands clasped together.

"You may leave now," Ivan reiterated as he flicked the end of his cigar above the ashtray.

In despair, and with his head held lower, Kharak slowly got up, feeling the narrowing in his throat as he walked out with the contract in his hand. He felt sick to the stomach.

As he opened the door, Catherine's father broke his silence

253

for the first time. "One more thing." He paused. "Do not attempt to see Catherine again, otherwise what you read in the letter will happen." His bushy eyebrows furrowed.

"And I can second that. Do not see Catherine." Ivan's icy stare was prominent.

Kharak walked out without looking back.

A few minutes had passed since Kharak had left the room. All the self-congratulating handshakes were done and the three men sat relaxed in their armchairs with a satisfied feeling.

"I'm curious as to how you managed to get Sir Henry Lawrence to sign the letter?" Mr Witt asked Ivan.

"Same here. How did you do that?" Gilbert asked.

Puffing out rings of cigar smoke and with wickedness in his eyes, Ivan replied, "I had it forged!"

45

Lal's mother brought a freshly brewed cup of spiced ginger tea out onto the porch. Mid-afternoon tea was a British tradition that the Indians had developed a liking for.

On any other day, it would have been a delightful afternoon, but on this day, the mood that enveloped Kharak and Lal was sombre.

Being too busy with the front of the shop, Lal's mother did not notice the absence of laughter and playfulness between them as she placed the wooden tray on the table before going back to her chores inside.

Lal felt unsettled when Kharak revealed to him in detail the events that had unfolded earlier in the day.

"I feel for you, Kharak. This is terrible."

"I know."

"What about Catherine?"

Kharak took a deep breath. "I'm already missing her." He

stared blankly at the cup of tea. "It's only now I can admit that my feelings for her are immense."

Lal pushed his chair closer and put his arms around Kharak's shoulders. "I'm here for you and I shall be there for you."

"Thank you."

"The way they have blackmailed you into working away is so cruel—"

"It's to punish me for liking Catherine," Kharak interrupted.

"You are very brave to give up your dreams for the sake of all." Lal tapped his shoulders.

Kharak remained silent.

"It's bizarre that you will be reaching East Africa before I do, yet you weren't meant to be going," Lal said.

"That's very true, but I will be glad you'll be there a week later to join me."

"Lucky for me that I will leave from the port of Karachi, otherwise it would have been over a fortnight later."

Lal poured the ginger tea into their cups, hoping it would be soothing for them both, as he kept an eye on the stray tabby cat who had just jumped through the fence and into his backyard.

He knew that Kharak was experiencing great anguish. He looked pale that afternoon, didn't talk a lot and was not his usual jovial self. Although he sipped his tea, his gaze was blank and aimed towards the fluttering clothes drying on the line.

"I need to go home now and tell everyone." Kharak stood up. "I will see you tomorrow, perhaps later in the day."

Lal embraced his shoulders, comforting him. As he left, Kharak passed through the front of the shop to thank Mr and Mrs Sena for their hospitality, as always.

It was late in the afternoon and Catherine sat by herself, beneath the gazebo in her favourite spot in the garden. If she had thought it would help her, it was having little effect. She still felt hopeless.

Busy in her thoughts, she failed to notice Vadu walking towards her.

"Memsahib, would you like a pot of tea?"

"Not yet, Vadu."

He nodded and turned around to walk away.

"Vadu?"

"Yes, memsahib?" He stopped and turned around.

"What do you think of Kharak?"

Vadu hesitated in surprise. After a few moments of thinking, he chose his words carefully. "I feel he is a good man, an honourable man," he replied as he bowed his head.

"Thank you for that." She smiled. "And I've changed my mind, I'll have that pot of tea."

At the same time, a few miles away, beneath the neem tree on the bank of the River Ravi, Kharak sat with his arms wrapped around his knees, watching the herons wading at the water's edge. Cycling back home from visiting Lal, he had decided to stop at his favourite place to reflect on the whirlwind that was sweeping through his life. He was going to be away for a while and he wanted to see this place again before he went.

Everything around him seemed faded. The trees, the river, the sky, all seemed washed out. What was vivid in his memory at that moment was the day he had spent with Catherine at this very spot. Her warm smile, her fragrance and her presence were clear in his mind.

The memories of that day flooded back. His spirit yearned to see her, yet he knew he could not. It was dawning upon him that he would never see her again. In anguish, and despite trying not to, tears formed at the corners of his eyes until he could not hold them back. He was glad that no one was there to see them roll down his cheeks.

46

The orange-purple tint permeated the evening sky over Rahmanpur village. At this time of the day, the alleys and paths that ran within the village had begun emptying of people.

Inside Kharak's house, the mood was sober. He had told his family of his new short-term work contract and what had transpired that morning. Purposely, he missed out the part about how he was threatened with the consequences of not signing. The family had been in discussion for over an hour.

His mother was in tears as she slumped on the couch, while his father, with his burly frame, stood in silence with his hands behind his back.

"The wage is excellent and the manager at the railways advised me to take up the offer as I was the only capable person around," Kharak half-lied. "When I return in six months with my earnings, I will be well settled."

"I don't want you to go," his teary-eyed mother stated.

"Lal will be with me, Mother." He sat down beside her and put his arm around her.

Kharak tried his best to be poker-faced, putting forward a more positive argument for going.

"You don't seem overly happy with it." His mother's instinct niggled with doubt.

"Is your mother right?" Kharak's father asked.

Kharak paused to give himself time to think. "Of course I am happy. It's normal to feel this way as I only have two days before I leave."

Mann Singh paced to the other side of the room and sat heavily in his favourite armchair. "This delays your marriage." His voice was forthright.

Kharak's head dropped in thought. Catherine's face resurfaced in his mind as his heart fluttered. He slowly spoke. "When I return, I will marry the girl whom you have in mind, the one you told me about." He felt a bulge in his throat.

"Is going to East Africa what you truly want?" his father asked with a straight gaze.

"Yes."

"Then go, my son, fulfil your dream and make us proud. You have our blessing." He shifted his gaze to his wife to reassure her.

Later that night, the shadowy light of the oil lamp flickered around the room. It was past midnight and one of the green canvas bags on the floor was packed with clothes, its buckles only just managing to close.

In an attempt to keep his mind from wandering, Kharak had decided to wear himself out by packing his bag. It had failed. As he sat on the old, creaky chair beside his wooden desk, he felt physically exhausted, but his mind was overrun with hundreds of 'what if?' situations playing over and over again, each ending with thoughts of Catherine. Not being able to say goodbye to her before he left hurt him.

He glanced at the to-do list on a sheet of paper crumpled at the centre of his desk. At the bottom of it, he saw the name *Catherine*.

Quietly, he opened the side drawer of the desk, got his notebook out and placed it on the desk. He uncapped his blue fountain pen and started to think as he looked blankly at the darkness outside the window. The village dogs were barking at the stray cats in the distance, not that he paid attention to them.

He was about to write his final words of goodbye to the person who had raised his inner happiness to a higher level, just like a butterfly flying for the first time, unshackled from its cocoon.

I must not be sad that I will never see her again; I should be glad that I had the chance to spend time with her. Joyous I should be that we met and enlightened knowing that she chose me to be close to... I'll live with that, but will still miss her.

With that thought, he started writing a note to her.

After completing the note, he folded it and left it on the desk, still observing it.

It was a full ten minutes later when he opened the drawer again and took out a smaller piece of paper. He paused before he began writing on it. A minute later, he was done writing and folded the much smaller second note.

On the bookshelf that rested on the desk, he managed to find a small envelope, into which he placed the smaller note before sealing it tight with paper glue. He ran his finger firmly around the edges, making sure that it was sealed.

After a few minutes, he wrote across the sealed flap of the envelope:

Only open in the future, when life throws at you seemingly dark days or moments.

Next, he fumbled amongst the papers in the other drawer and managed to find a slightly larger envelope.

Into this envelope, he placed the first folded note, together with the smaller envelope. He sealed it and wrote *Catherine* on the envelope before placing it in the inner pocket of his jacket, which was hanging over the chair. His hand trembled slightly.

He walked over to his bed and lay there with his heart twitching at the thought of her opening and reading his note.

It was well into the night when Kharak finally fell asleep, missing a glimpse of the moon's glow through the clouds.

Gazing at the moon through the floating net curtains as a gentle breeze flowed through her room, Catherine lay awake on her side, thinking of Kharak.

47

In the day and a half that followed, apart from getting together his things for the next six months away, Kharak spent time briefly visiting his close relatives and friends nearby, saying his goodbyes.

Within half a day, the whole of Rahmanpur knew that he was travelling abroad to work in the wild land where the people were thought to be strange. No one from his village had been on a ship before and that made Kharak a celebrity, in a funny way.

The unexpected turn of events had not given him time for the enormity of what was happening to sink in. The number of tasks that he had to fit into a very short space of time intermittently took his mind off the anxiety of going away to a place he had never been before and the threat that Ivan had made, but Catherine was always at the back of his mind.

That evening, the last person he had to meet before he left the following morning was Lal.

Catherine had noticed over the previous two days that Ivan and her father had been spending more time together than before, and they seemed unusually close. More apparent was a look of haughty smugness that seemed to emanate from Ivan. His demeanour had changed; he smoked more and he seemed to enjoy barking orders at the servants more often. It was his permanent smirk that Catherine started to dislike.

To make matters worse, earlier that morning, she had planned to go to the rail yard again, hoping to meet Kharak, but was disheartened to see that Ivan and her father had decided to stay at home to play a game of bridge.

It had come as a relief the previous day when her mother made her aware that Ivan was leaving Lahore the following morning. She was glad that she would now be able to enjoy the comfort of her home in a more relaxed manner without having a guest. She felt that he had been around for too long.

As the fresh air of dusk with its lingering floral scent spread in the garden, Catherine rolled the stem of a yellow Amaltas flower between her thumb and index finger as she sat alone on the bench at the edge of the rear terrace, overlooking the lawn. The bulbuls were silent, settled in their nests for the day.

It was the whiff of cigar smoke that gave his presence away.

"Ah, I have been looking for you."

It was Ivan, but Catherine didn't pay him any attention.

"I'm leaving tomorrow for East Africa for a few months, before going back to England."

"Yes, my mother told me." She refused to make eye contact as she kept on rolling the flower in her hand.

"As it's my last night here, I was about to leave for the Punjab Club with your father for the evening." He paused. "And noticing that you retire to bed rather early of late, I came to say goodbye."

Catherine stood up to face him. "I hope you enjoyed your time here."

"It has been splendid. You have been the perfect host." Ivan inclined his head.

There was a brief uncomfortable silence.

"I shall see you back in England in a few months and spend some meaningful time with you."

Catherine chose to ignore his last comment. "Do have a safe journey."

"Thank you." He leaned forward to kiss her.

Taken by surprise, she managed in time to turn her head to the side. His kiss landed on her cheek.

Damn! he thought.

A moment later, Catherine took a small step back. "It has got rather chilly now. I'd better fetch my shawl." She started walking.

Ivan walked by her side as she strode towards the rear porch door.

Lal's room was much smaller than Kharak's. There was a tiny table in front of the window, upon which rested three large glass jars of lemon pickles that his mother had prepared to sell. He picked up his shirt, which was lying on his bed, and hung it on the door handle before pulling out a chair for Kharak to sit.

Lal got comfortable as he sat on the edge of his bed. "Tomorrow is the day."

"Yes."

"How is your family taking it, now that you are leaving?"

"My father seems fine, but not my mother. She tries to hide her worry."

"It's only for a few months and, before you know it, you will be back in Lahore."

Kharak nodded and pursed his lips. "Lal, can you run an errand for me?"

"Of course, brother."

Kharak leaned to his left, placed his hand in his shirt pocket and retrieved the envelope.

"I want you to give this envelope to Catherine."

Lal raised his eyebrow as he took the envelope with *Catherine* written on it.

"My train leaves tomorrow morning at eight o'clock. Please give her the envelope around eleven o' clock in the morning. Ensure that she receives it long after I have left Lahore."

Lal heard the sadness in his tone.

They both went silent for a while.

"I feel for you. It shouldn't be happening like this."

Not feeling emotionally strong enough at that moment to talk about it, Kharak decided that it was time to say goodbye for now. He sighed and stood up. Lal followed him.

"Thanks for everything."

They shook hands and engaged in a manly hug before walking out of the room. On the way out through the back door, Kharak said his goodbyes to Lal's parents, who were busy hosting their relatives.

The western sky was still light as the sun set, yet at the same time, the stars were becoming visible in the darker eastern sky. Kharak went to get his bicycle, which was resting against the wooden back gate.

"One more thing." He turned around. "Make sure that, even after I have gone, Nandu goes to Catherine's house every morning at eleven o' clock. I have arranged his transport for her, if she ever needs it."

Lal acknowledged this in silence with a smile and by raising his hand to his forehead in a salute.

Kharak got on his bicycle. "See you soon."

He pedalled off along the road and was a silhouette within moments as Lal watched him pass from sight.

48

There was an unseasonal chill in the morning air at Lahore Station. The sunlight had not yet dispersed the pockets of mist that overhung the city.

Walking through the entrance of the station, Kharak saw the door that led to the waiting room and it triggered vivid memories of the day he had met Catherine for the very first time at that very spot.

There she had been, with a worried look drawn on her face, which had enhanced her grace; her falling silky hair setting off her mesmerising soft eyes and pretty face. He felt hollow at that thought.

He turned his head, glancing sideways towards that door as he passed it.

Kharak's train carriage was at the rear of the train. He had envisaged seeing more workers like him undertaking the same journey, but there was only one other person whom he recognised from the Indian Railways.

Having already boarded the carriage to see his seat, he now stood on the platform with his two canvas bags. One was half-full of dry food that his mother had prepared for his gruelling and uncertain journey.

Beside him stood his younger sister, Neina, with blue ribbons in her plaits, holding their mother's hand. Their father put a reassuring arm around Saran, Kharak's younger brother, who stood with a nervous look. He, too, had come to see his brother off.

The platform started to clear as the passengers slowly got on board after the first whistle was blown by the conductor, which indicated that departure would be within the next ten minutes.

Kharak spotted Ivan strutting in their direction, together with Gilbert. He turned his face, hoping that they would avoid him. To his disappointment, they walked towards him.

Ivan stopped as he reached Kharak.

"I was about to check your carriage to make sure that you were on board. Good to see that you made it – after all, you are an intelligent man," he scoffed.

Gilbert had a satisfied look.

"I'm about to board the train," Kharak said.

"See you in Bombay," Ivan remarked.

With that, he and Gilbert carried on strutting towards the front of the train where the first-class carriages were.

"Are they your superiors?" Kharak's father asked.

"Kind of."

Kharak knelt down before Neina and kissed her forehead. "Don't be too mischievous, and when I see you next, I hope to see you this tall." He pointed well above her head. She gave him a toothy smile.

"And you." He got up and took a step towards his brother. "Take care of Mother and help Father out. You will be the older one now." He hugged Saran.

He then gave a hearty hug to his mother, who had tear-filled eyes and used her shawl to wipe them away.

"See you soon, my boy." His father folded him in a tight hug.

Kharak was emotional and could not say a word. He held himself together, not showing his feelings to his family whom he was leaving behind.

He trod carefully on the steps and climbed into the carriage, pausing to turn around to see his family all huddled together waving at him. He waved back.

His seat was a few feet down the carriage. As he sat, the final whistle blew and the door was slammed shut. The hoot of the train was heard as he glanced outside through the steel bars that went across the window.

The train slowly started to move and, through the spaces between the bars, he watched his family drift away as the platform seemingly started to disappear. He poked his hand out and waved furiously.

"I will be fine. See you soon… and goodbye!" he shouted.

Slowly, they turned into tiny specks on the horizon before vanishing in the clearing mist.

Only then did Kharak let go and allow his suppressed tears to trickle from his eyes.

49

That morning, Lal decided to use Nandu to take him to Catherine's house at eleven o' clock as arranged.

The sun had failed to burn through the faint wisps of mist, which still hovered over the treeline along the dirt road that led to her house.

He was not completely certain where Catherine lived, but Nandu was familiar with her address.

The rickshaw came to a halt outside a large wooden gate.

"This is the memsahib's house." Nandu pointed at the gate.

Lal got off the rickshaw and paced towards the gate, hoping to see the gatekeeper nearby. Any worry that he might have had about how to ask for Catherine was dispelled when the Balu approached the gate, having peeked through the wooden slats.

"Are you looking for Memsahib Catherine?"

"Yes, I am."

"She is expecting Nandu today and she instructed me to tell

him to wait for her. Are you with him?" The gatekeeper tilted his head.

"In a way, yes. Tell her that Lal has a message for her." He did not blink while staring at Balu directly.

Without hesitation, the gatekeeper walked off towards the house.

Earlier, after another night of broken sleep, Catherine had made her mind up to go and see Kharak at the rail yard that morning – and if he was not there, she was going to his house in Rahmanpur. She had the urge to meet him after what had happened at the garden party; it was the not knowing how he was that was causing her anxiety.

Having finished breakfast by herself, she walked out of the kitchen and into the hallway. She had taken two steps up the stairs when she heard Vadu.

"Memsahib?" He bowed in apology for interrupting. "Balu says that there is an Indian man called Lal outside the gate, who claims that he has a message for you. Do you know him?"

Catherine raised her eyebrows. She turned around, skipped a step and strode towards Vadu.

"Yes, I know him." Her eyes widened.

Kharak must want to meet me and that's probably the message that Lal brings. I must somehow discreetly find out when Father isn't around, like he is today, so that I can meet him!

Catherine pranced down the steps of the porch and loped towards the gate, both her hands raising her dress off the ground.

As she approached the gate, through the slats, she recognised that it truly was Lal from his features.

"Good to see you, Lal." She waved as Balu opened the gate.

"Hello, Catherine… I hope I'm not barging in to meet you unannounced?"

"Not at all." She smiled.

270

Lal went silent, not knowing what to say and how to reveal the circumstances to her. His hand went up, brushing his brow, then rubbing his temple.

"Could I have a moment alone with you? I have a message for you." He lowered his voice, not wanting Balu to overhear.

"Yes. Come on in."

They took a few steps away from the gate and onto the edge of the front lawn. The grass was still moist with dew.

"How is Kharak?"

Crossing his hands in front of him, Lal pinched his palm with his fingers in angst.

"He… has been transferred from Lahore."

"What do you mean?"

"His train left this morning for Bombay."

"Really?" She paused. "Is he working in Bombay?" Her brow wrinkled in dismay.

"No. He will take the ship from Bombay to Mombasa. That is where he has been transferred to."

Catherine's face crumpled and her shoulders slumped.

"That cannot be true. I'm certain he would have told me that he was leaving and… he would have met me before he left."

"Sorry, Catherine, it is true."

Catherine's heart sank. There was a sudden hollowness in her stomach and she felt nauseated. She sensed a bulge in her throat.

I should have gone to see him at his house the other day after missing him at the rail yard, she thought. All of a sudden, a void seemed to engulf her; an emptiness at the thought of not seeing him again.

Lal noticed tears pooling at the corners of her soft green eyes.

"When will he be back?" She tried to maintain her composure.

"At least six months… maybe more."

Those words were like a trapdoor shutting her in a cellar surrounded by nothing but dark emptiness. Her tears were too many to be held in her eyes, which had longed to see him again. One after another, they rolled down her cheeks.

"Why did he have to go?" She shook her head.

It was upsetting for Lal to see the true affection she had for Kharak and he realised then that Kharak never knew how deep those feelings were. Now, at this moment, Lal was the only person aware of some of Kharak's inner thoughts and that came with huge responsibilities.

"Catherine, Kharak feels the same way as you."

She looked up at him. "Then why did he have to go like this?"

In silence, Lal looked away, feeling helpless. *Forgive me, Kharak; after all, you didn't instruct me not to tell her*, he thought as he tried to justify what he was about to say.

"He was forced to go away... It was not his choice."

Catherine wiped her tears across her red cheeks. "By whom?"

In the minutes that followed, Lal revealed to her what had happened to Kharak at the head office of the Indian Railways on that fateful day and who was present when he was forced to sign the contract. Whatever he had told Lal about that day, Lal made it known to her.

Catherine's jaw dropped in shock. The weight of the sky seemed to have collapsed on her. Her fingers trembled as she cupped her face and soon her tears ran over her fingers and down the sides of her palms.

"How could my father do that?" Her voice was muffled by her hands.

"I feel sorry..." Lal paused. "For you and for Kharak."

"I'm shocked that he asked Ivan to help him do all this. I looked up to him and, with what he has done, my respect for him has gone. I feel totally lost."

In a daze, her teary eyes gazed blankly to the side without blinking. "All this pain, Kharak. You don't deserve it," she whispered.

Although the sun attempted to peek through the mist, she felt everything around her was cloudy, dark and oppressive.

Lal put his hand in his shirt pocket and retrieved the envelope that Kharak had given him.

"He gave me this to give to you."

Catherine looked straight at his hand holding the envelope. There, written in Kharak's unmistaken handwriting on the envelope, was her name, *Catherine*. Never had her name looked so beautiful to her as it did in his handwriting that day.

She took the envelope and stared at it.

"I will leave now," Lal said.

"Thank you so much for this," she said in her teary voice.

Lal had turned around and taken a few steps before he stopped. "Kharak has made sure that Nandu will always come by at eleven o' clock in the morning if you ever need to travel."

Damn you, Kharak! She forced a wry smile.

"And remember that he asked me to help you if ever you need anything."

"Thank you." She bit her inner lip.

Catherine watched Lal walk out of the gate and towards the rickshaw, the same rickshaw where she and Kharak had huddled together in the rain.

Inside, she walked straight through the hallway, up the stairs and into her room with quick steps. It wasn't that she did not want her mother seeing her in this state, but the anticipation of opening the envelope.

Entering her room, she shut the door and turned the key. She walked to the edge of the bed that faced the window and sat down. Carefully, she lifted the seal of the envelope without tearing it.

She saw the white, folded piece of paper inside. As she opened out the seal further, she spotted the small envelope tucked at the front of the note. Using her thumb and index finger, she removed them. The folded note came out first. She unfolded it and started reading it.

Dear Catherine,

I never thought that I would encounter someone like you, who would have travelled thousands of miles and become my favourite hello and hardest goodbye!

I care about you deeply, Catherine, I always have. But the funny thing is, I don't know why. I have asked myself that question often, but have never found the answer… and I probably never will.

As I leave, it is with deep sorrow, knowing that I could not change the circumstances that led me away. Sorry.

Will we meet again? I don't know if we ever will.

I wish you well. Always.

Goodbye and farewell.

Kharak

Her stomach fell and she felt hollow. With trembling hands, she reread the note. Her eyes welled up and tears rolled down her cheeks and over her quivering lip.

It was in that moment of fractured emptiness that she realised she had already fallen in love with him.

As she refolded the note, she saw the small sealed envelope with his message written on it:

Only open in the future, when life throws at you seemingly dark days or moments.

The temptation to open the envelope was strong; not knowing what was inside was mind-numbing. It was the thought of Kharak and the instruction he had written to her that held her back. It was the respect and depth of feeling she had for him that made her not open the small envelope.

There was a knock on the door.

"Catherine? Is everything all right?" Her mother's voice came from behind the door.

She wiped her tears away. "Yes, I'm fine."

"Mrs Wittingham is here and she would like to see you."

"I'll be down soon."

She heard Ethel's steps fade as she walked away. Catherine got up, walked towards her dressing table and opened the drawer where the jewellery box was. Setting it on the table, she unfastened it and placed the note under her jewellery.

Using her index finger, she probed the corner of the jewellery box and pressed the tiny latch. From the side protruded the little secret compartment, into which she placed the tiny unopened envelope. It fitted in the space perfectly. She pushed the compartment back until she heard the click of the lock.

The jewellery box went back into the drawer before she walked to the washstand to splash water over her face. The tears might have been washed away, but her inner turmoil had just taken a turn for the worse.

50

Tsavo

In Tsavo, the wind had picked up, sending whirls of fine red dust across the railway tracks that had been laid. All the workers were walking back to their tents within the campsite after another hard day of work in the wilderness. The shadows had stretched and one thing everyone working there realised was that in East Africa, the sun went down very quickly, making dusk a brief event.

On any given day, the workers would see a variety of wild animals. However, on this day, it seemed different. Absent were the grazing herd of zebras and the ungainly ostriches hopping across the tracks. The noises and sounds of the bush were also less prominent.

The current news was that another coolie had gone missing a few days ago and had not been seen since, and this had increased the tension within the camp.

Ungan Singh, having been promoted to one of Patterson's personal assistants, had his tent moved from the railhead campsite closer to the main campsite, to the dismay of the other coolies. Having been given his choice of tent companions, he had chosen to share his tent with his friends, Chand and Narain.

As night fell, the night beetles and crickets were out chirping in search of their mates. Having heated water over the fire for Patterson to freshen up after another dusty day at the bridge, Ungan heated up water for himself. These were some of the perks of being an assistant, but it was because he was trustworthy and a diligent worker that Patterson admired him.

For supper, Narain had prepared a slow-cooked lentil stew with traditional bread for the three of them. For Patterson and Allen, he had an additional course of roast goat meat.

That night, Chand, Narain and Ungan sat around their crackling fire a few metres from their tent, enjoying their meal and making fun of Chand, as always. They had good comradeship and their conversation often broke into laughter.

As the routine went, Patterson and Allen would have their dinner and sit near the fire sipping their whisky. Before retiring, Patterson always went for a stroll around the campsite with Ungan to ensure that the workers weren't staying up late. Now, with three workers going missing over the past two weeks, this night walk became important.

"All right, Colonel, I'm off to sleep now and hopefully will see you in the morning before I leave for Mombasa," Allen said with heavy eyes.

"Goodnight. I feel like retiring as well. I'd better tell Ungan to get ready for the walk."

Allen stood up from his chair and started walking towards his tent. "Go for a short walk instead, Colonel," he mumbled.

Patterson lumbered into his tent to pick up his .303 rifle, which he took with him every night before heading towards Ungan's tent.

Ungan was shifting red soil into the firepit to put out the fire when Patterson approached him. The others had already gone to sleep.

"Are you ready, Ungan?"

"Yes, sir."

Ungan went for the two hurricane lanterns that were hanging on the cast-iron hook attached to the wooden pole in the clearing near the firepit. He handed Patterson one lantern and held the other in his hand as he picked up his wooden stick.

"I'm ready."

The night was clear and the stars twinkled, providing faint light that was masked by the yellow glow of the lanterns. At night, the camp was a very different place. There was no murmuring of the workers or rattle of labour at the construction site; instead, the swishing of the Tsavo River was more pronounced, together with its occasional shimmering surface beneath the stars.

"It's an exceptionally quiet night, eerily quiet," said Patterson as they circumnavigated half the campsite.

"I agree with you, sahib."

In the faint light, the two tall wooden poles came into view on the eastern edge of the site. Patterson stood still for a moment, observing them.

"These poles look bare; they need the British flag flying high above them. We may have some blue and red cloth here; ensure tomorrow that the stitching of the British flag is started so that these poles have our flags on them."

"I will do that, sahib." Ungan nodded.

As they were tired and it was later than usual, they took a shorter route than normal. Twenty minutes later, they were back at their end of the site.

After a brief goodnight, and as Patterson went into his tent, Ungan took nine minutes to walk to his own. Before entering, he lowered the brightness of his lantern, knowing that Chand and Narain would be fast asleep. He lifted the folding canvas covering the entrance and saw the outline of them fast asleep.

With stealth, he tiptoed to the cotton-filled blanket that he used as his mattress. As he was always the last to sleep at night due to his patrol, he had chosen to sleep nearer the entrance so that he did not disturb his tent-mates.

The crickets and beetles had also quietened down in the still air and an uneasy silence hovered over this part of Tsavo.

Ungan pulled the canvas down and tied its strap to the supporting pole in the middle of the entrance before turning the lantern off. It was eleven o' clock at night when he snuggled under his light cotton sheet and, within a few minutes, fell asleep.

At three o' clock the next morning, Narain was awakened by a faint shuffling noise coming from his head side of the tent. It came from outside. As he drew himself up and rested on his elbows to hear it properly, it stopped as suddenly as it had started. He blinked his eyes for clarity. There was a sudden odour of musky, drying leather that made him crinkle his nose as he struggled to make sense of what it was. He heard the shuffling again; this time, it was louder and came from near the entrance of the tent. His heart started to pound nervously.

He thought of waking Ungan, who was near the entrance, and extended his arm to reach him.

In an instant, he spotted two huge, piercing eyes through the opening. Paralysed with fear, his body did not respond. He wanted to shout, but the words caught at the back of his throat. Before Narain could take another breath, the large feline head with a muscular neck pushed in through the flimsy canvas. The beast's jaw opened, revealing the largest canine teeth he had ever seen, with saliva drooling from them. With a quick snarl, the lion grabbed Ungan by the neck.

In the furore, Narain saw Ungan's arms flailing all over the place, trying desperately to loosen the grip around his throat.

"Let go... let go of me!" were the only words that were heard.

There was a short cracking sound and, in the next instant Ungan, despite being burly and heavyset, was dragged out of the tent in one swift motion.

Narain and Chand, who had sat upright in shock, heard the rustling of him being dragged along the dusty ground. They were transfixed with fear and could do nothing at all to help their friend.

Moments later, they managed to yell for help. "*Bachao! Bachao!*"

As the chaos spread, hurricane lamps were lit and dazed and confused people woke up, shouting. The eerie silence of the night disappeared and was replaced by horror.

An hour later, a shocked, hysterical Narain spoke to Colonel Patterson to explain the dreadful event. Picking up his rifle, together with a hastily lit lamp, Patterson strode towards their tent, not knowing what to expect.

The coolies had fled a distance away from Ungan's tent; it seemed as if they were scared to approach it, fearing that the same fate may fall upon them.

As Patterson approached them, they dispersed in the middle, leaving space for him to walk towards the tent. He asked Narain to hold the lamp.

"Follow me. I need light."

Approaching the tent carefully, he observed the ground near the entrance of the tent. There, he spotted paw prints and a puddle of fresh blood that was soaking into the ground. Leading from the puddle was a trail of blood that could be seen under the light of the lamp.

The eastern sky had a faint light that signified dawn was about to break.

"Soon, dawn will break fully. I need a few men to come with me as I follow the blood trail." Patterson expressed his seriousness with furrowed eyebrows. "I need five or six men."

After some hesitation, six men raised their hands, of which one was Narain. Despite his closest mate having gone missing, Chand was too traumatised to go.

The discussions of what had happened and what the outcome could be went on. So did inspections of the surrounding tents for the next hour.

As dawn broke and the sky brightened, the search party took off, led by the colonel. The trail of blood went across the rail tracks, over the gravel and into the bush.

Everyone in the search party was silent. The situation was tense, fraught with the dread of the unknown and concern at the prospect of being attacked by the beast.

Bloodstains were seen on the tall stalks of the golden-brown savannah grass amongst the low-growing acacia trees. It was easy to follow the trail of bloodstained pugmarks where the grass had been flattened as the lion passed through, dragging Ungan.

Half a mile later, there was a clearing where the grass was shorter. What they encountered there was a ghastly sight. Blood splatters were all around the grass. Lying there in the centre of the clearing was part of the lifeless body of Ungan; its torso torn open and surrounded by the splintered bones that remained of his limbs. Part of the skin on his face had peeled where the lions had licked it off. The worst part for all present was the sight of his eyes, wide open in terror.

Two of the coolies retched. The other three initially turned their faces for a while before gathering their courage to look at the body. Only Narain, who was devastated, stood by Patterson, examining what had happened.

"Get some rocks and cover what is left of the body," Patterson instructed as he briefly removed his hat as a mark of respect. "Then, Narain, you need to go back to the camp and get a sheet to cover it, and some sort of stretcher to take the body to the medical officer."

Getting closer to the body, Patterson crouched, examining the ground. He let out a sigh. "This is typical of a man-eating lion." He paused. "This is what they do. They lick the skin off to get fresh blood."

Patterson did not fully reveal to the coolies what he had deduced.

It's better that they don't know that from these pugmarks, I can see that it's not one, but two man-eating lions who did this! he thought as he pressed his lips together.

51

Lahore

Catherine's moist eyes adjusted to the darkness in her room as she tossed in her bed, unable to sleep.

All that went through her mind, over and over again, was the time she had spent with Kharak in Lahore. Visions of his face, with the reflections of the crescent-shaped ripples of the water fountain in Shalimar Gardens falling across it, were as vivid now as they had been that day.

Throughout the day, she had reread his note over and over, and each time she read it, she sank deeper and deeper into his pool of affection. There was the ecstasy of knowing that his feelings for her were as intense as hers for him, yet too there was the intolerable pain of realising that he was far away, with little hope of meeting him again.

It had been difficult during the day to hide her emotions from her mother, and it was only in her room that she found refuge and could sit on the edge of the bed. It was her place to cry.

Simmering under all this was the anger she felt at how her father had forced Kharak away from her, not knowing that Ivan had been the true mastermind of this plan.

Not wanting to have to answer all her parents' inquisitive questions, she pretended to be ill, spending time alone in her favourite spot in the garden or in her room. She was glad that Ivan had gone, otherwise there would have been another person's questions to avoid.

Nandu was there at the gate as always at eleven o' clock, and it was upsetting for her to walk to the gate and wave him away in his rickshaw, the same rickshaw where she remembered cuddling up to Kharak in the rain. Even Balu now knew the routine and he made less fuss than he had done during the first couple of days.

Catherine was glad that Mrs Wittingham came to visit her mother again in the afternoon, this time bringing her pomegranate jam. It meant that she would get at least a couple of hours without Ethel prying and asking how she was feeling.

At dinner, it was just Catherine and her mother at the table as her father was out at the Punjab Club. She sat down, playing with her fork while resting her forehead on the palm of her hand. Since it became known to her that Kharak was no longer in Lahore, her stomach was knotted and she wasn't hungry.

"Catherine, my dear, you don't look well. We should get your father to have a look at you."

She did not reply immediately.

"I don't want him having a look at me. I'm fine... however I feel," she snapped eventually.

"Catherine..."

He is the cause of my pain, she thought.

"I'm off to bed early. I need to rest." Catherine excused herself, having barely eaten her dinner.

Back in her room, deprived of any hope, she slumped in the armchair in the corner and began to cry.

After a while, she got her jewellery box and took out Kharak's note and read it again, just to feel his presence.

This had been Catherine's daily routine for the past two days.

That night, in the room further down the corridor, Gilbert was undoing his tie. Ethel was sitting on her dressing-table stool removing her earrings and getting ready for bed.

"Something is not right with Catherine. I can't recall seeing her like this before – as she has been for the past couple of days." Ethel turned around to hold her husband's gaze.

Gilbert loosened the top button of his shirt collar. "She will be fine. Have you spoken to her?"

"She does not want to have a meaningful conversation… I have tried." Ethel paused. "I'm getting concerned about her."

"Let's give her a couple of days and if she is still the same, I'll talk to her."

A few minutes later, Ethel was adjusting her pillows to her preferred sleeping position and Gilbert was leaning against the headboard in the dim light of the lamp, reading his work notes.

"You haven't mentioned lately when you are to be posted to Africa," she said.

This caught him by surprise. There was a long pause. "I have changed my mind. I'm not keen on going to Africa, so, instead, when my posting comes to an end here, I will be heading back to England."

Ethel's eyes widened. "I wasn't expecting that."

"I feel that I've been away from England for too long… and my family."

"Wasn't going to East Africa one of your ambitions?"

"It was a few months back, but things have changed and now I don't have the same desire to go there as I did."

"Well, I am pleased that you shan't be going there."

With a wry smile, he carried on reading. He had not found it necessary to mention to her how Ivan had managed to send Kharak away from Lahore, and, more importantly, Catherine.

Ethel blew out the lamp that was resting on the French bedside table and snuggled close to him.

"Goodnight."

At three o' clock in the morning, Catherine woke and sat bolt upright, sweating, for the third night in a row. On this night, it was due to the spilling over of anger that had been rising inside her since the day Lal had told her that her father wanted Kharak away from her.

The dull headache was like a heavy load pushing down on her. Another night when she would stay awake till the early hours before eventually getting some sleep. She let out a sigh.

Thoughts of regret started to manifest in her mind. What had happened to Kharak was not just. She felt guilty and needed to share what he was going through – all the agony of being away from his home and the people he loved. It wasn't just his fault; she was equally responsible.

She rested her head on her pillow, gazing at the dim moonlight seeping through the window between the gap in the curtains, casting a silvery blanket onto the wooden floorboards below the windowsill.

I wonder whether he is asleep and safe at this moment? How will the wilds of East Africa twist his fate and mine? At least he will have Lal there with him soon, she thought.

Immediately, her eyes widened, and she sat up and rested on the headboard. It came to her. Boldness was what was required of her if she didn't want to lose her love. All the despair seemed to have floated off above her shoulders, replaced by unflinching courage.

Her heart was thumping and her mind was racing. A plan began to form.

It will be audacious, but I have no other way. I must believe.

52

The following day, Catherine did not remain asleep until the late hours of the morning like she normally would have. Her mind had been racing since three o' clock that morning, tossing and turning. As a result, a heavy, dull headache persisted.

With a vigour that she had lacked over the previous days, she managed to have some toast with marmalade and a cup of tea.

Upstairs in her room, Ethel had heard the sounds coming from Catherine's room and then the kitchen downstairs. She glanced at her husband, but his snoring indicated that he was still asleep. *Catherine is up early this morning*, she thought.

After her breakfast, Catherine walked into the front lounge room, moved the rocking chair beside the window and sat down facing the front garden and gate, waiting. It was only eight o' clock.

She was oblivious to her mother and father walking past

her later that morning. The three days of poor sleep had taken their toll and, with the gentle rocking of the chair, she had fallen asleep.

At half past ten in the morning, Catherine woke up with a jolt. *No! I shouldn't have fallen asleep.* She looked at the longcase clock on the opposite wall as she sat upright in her chair. An immediate relief was felt as her breathing came back to normal. Her eyes were now fixed on the gate outside.

Just before eleven o' clock, she got up and walked out of the front door and along the drive towards the gate. Prompt as ever, Nandu arrived, as he had been doing daily for a while.

"Memsahib, will you be travelling today?" he asked. It had been quite some time since she had actually used his services and that question had become routine for him.

She took a few steps out of the gate. "I want you to pass a message to Lal. Could you do that for me?"

"Yes, memsahib." He saluted her.

"I want you to tell him that I need to see him urgently. It is very important." She fixed her gaze on Nandu, stressing the importance of what she had said.

"Right away, memsahib." He rolled his head a few times.

"Make sure he gets the message."

Nandu rolled his head again, then stood upright on the pedal and forced it down, causing his rickshaw to move forward. Soon, he was down the street, watched by Catherine, squinting her eyes in the bright Lahore sun.

In her mind, she already knew what she was going to propose to Lal. Lahore felt empty to her right now, with no heartbeat of life. Kharak was what had made it alive, unforgettable, and his absence made her realise how much she wanted to be with him.

Inside the house, Ethel was busy directing the servants in a thorough clean of the kitchen and pantry. She saw Catherine walk into the kitchen and was glad that she seemed better than before.

"How are you, my dear?"

"I'm fine." Catherine hesitated, wanting to keep her conversation to a minimum. It then dawned on her that the next few days would be critical and that she needed to appear to be her usual self, however difficult that might be. "I'm feeling much better, Mother." She forced a smile.

"I was worried about your health, but I'm glad you are better. Would you like a cup of tea?"

"No, thank you. I will be resting in the back garden." She slowly walked through the rear kitchen door that led to the courtyard.

There, Catherine went towards the wooden bench swing. After arranging the cushions for utmost comfort, she slumped onto the swing and drifted again into her own realm of anguish and nervousness. *I am doing the right thing.*

She skipped lunch as her appetite had vanished, but forced herself to join her mother at the table.

"I will be going to meet your father at the Punjab University at three o' clock. Would you like to accompany me?" Ethel asked.

"No, thank you. Rest is what I need."

"Vadu and Sana are always here if you need anything."

The plates and cutlery were picked up by the servant and replaced by fine china cups in preparation for the tea that Catherine had decided to have with her mother.

Afterwards, she excused herself and went to her room. She realised that she needed to go through her wardrobe to see what she had, and thereafter make a list of anything else she might require.

At about three o' clock in the afternoon, the house became quiet. Ethel had already left to meet her husband, while the servants were taking a break in their quarters that were tucked at the rear corner of the compound.

In her room, Catherine stood looking down at the same

part of the enclosed garden she had viewed on the first morning she had woken up in Lahore. Now, it seemed dull and lacking the same spirit as it had possessed that day. Even the chirping bulbul flying from one tree to another did not captivate her in the warm, serene afternoon sun.

She spotted Vadu at the front gate having a relaxed, jovial chat with Balu. They had known one another before being employed here and they met up at any available opportunity.

Their talk was interrupted by someone at the gate, making Balu stick his head out of the gate momentarily before gesturing to Vadu to join in with the conversation.

A few moments later, she saw Vadu walking purposefully towards the house. She thought nothing of it and went back to staring at the tan-coloured Malabar squirrel hopping on the branch of the Amaltas tree.

Moments later, her thoughts were interrupted by a knock on the door of her room. She turned away from the window and walked towards the door.

"Memsahib?" It was Vadu.

"Yes?" She opened the door.

"There is someone outside the gate called Lal. He claims that you sent for him and that you are expecting him."

Her eyes lit up. "Yes, I am expecting him." She rushed past Vadu, along the corridor and down the stairs.

Lal turning up on the same day that she had passed the message was unexpected, but she was pleased about it.

Outside the gate, she saw that he was wearing the same work uniform that Kharak wore and, for a brief moment, her spirit soared.

"You wanted to see me. Is everything all right?" he asked.

"Come on in, I'll show you the garden."

Catherine knew that her parents weren't at home and she wanted to speak to him in private without being overheard by anyone, including Vadu and the other servants.

They walked along the stone-paved path that bordered the lawn.

Catherine took a deep breath and squeezed her palms together in front of her. "There is something I want you to do for me." She paused, making sure that they were far enough away to keep them from being overheard. "I want you to get me a ticket to Mombasa on the same ship that you are travelling on."

For a moment, it was as if Lal had misheard her. "I beg your pardon?" His jaw dropped.

"Yes, I will be going to meet Kharak with you!" she stated clearly.

"But, Catherine, how can you go there alone?"

"On the journey, I will be with you, and when I get there, I will be with Kharak."

"Have your parents agreed to this?"

Catherine hesitated a bit. "I'm not telling them." She lowered her tone. "I need to see him, even just for a few days, and then I shall return, hopefully with matters clearer between us."

"Surely that can't be right."

"It is right in my eyes. After the way they forced Kharak to go away from me and his family, I shall do the same to them. But I shall be away for about two months in total."

This conversation was unexpected and the implications for everyone were far-reaching. Lal took a deep breath as he tried to calm himself.

"I can't do that. They'll accuse me of kidnapping you."

"I've made the decision of my own free will. No one is kidnapping me. Also, no one needs to know. And right now, only you and I know about this – no one else does."

"But—"

Catherine interrupted. "You did promise Kharak that you would be there for me and him, if ever the need arose." The corners of her eyes crinkled.

Lal hesitated to gather his thoughts, his fingers brushing across his eyebrows.

"Wait here a minute, I shan't be long." Catherine turned around and scurried towards the house.

"Think, Lal! Quick, think of all the possible consequences!" he mumbled to himself as his mind raced. He remembered Kharak's face when he had said goodbye; the anguish was there, but hidden. In all the years Lal had known him, it was the first time he had had a glimpse of his emotional side. He had seen through the false curtain of well-being that Kharak had hung to hide his true feelings.

Catherine dashed back out of the house, clutching her purse. By the time she got to him, she was out of breath.

She fumbled in opening her purse. "Here…" She got out a handful of rupees coins. "That's for whatever expenses you may incur for the ticket and the journey." She held her palms forward.

"I can't take that."

"You have to take the money to cover my costs." She paused. "I'm paying for it… and besides, no one can say that you kidnapped me if I do." She grinned.

"That's too much."

"Take what you need and some extra… just in case."

Lal understood that she had a point, so with further hesitation he took the right amount of money to buy her ticket.

"When do we set sail?" she asked him.

"My ship disembarks from the port of Karachi early in the morning on Sunday. But I must say to you that I don't promise anything as I don't know if I will manage to get a ticket for you."

"I believe you will – it is destined to be… Destiny can't be that cruel to me, allowing me to meet Kharak and then cruelly torment me with his going away." Her voice stuttered.

"How will you manage to leave the house?"

"That is my problem, Lal. I will think of something, but I will need to know what the exact plan will be."

Lal took a deep breath and thought about the long and probably arduous journey. *Here is a woman who is willing to make such a journey, not knowing what to expect, and all that drives her is the unshakeable hope of seeing Kharak. Is this what love does to you? She must love him dearly.*

"My train departs at seven o' clock on Saturday evening for Karachi and arrives the following day. That same evening, the ship leaves for Mombasa via the port of Aden."

Catherine was listening keenly. "I thought I heard that the ship leaves from Bombay?"

"That is the more popular route, with ships leaving for East Africa once a week, whereas they leave Karachi every ten days."

"Timing is important," she mumbled under her breath.

"I will try to get the same tickets for you as I have. Tomorrow, I will send a written message with Nandu informing you whether I managed to get them or not."

The paleness across her face seemed to lift. "Thank you, Lal."

He bowed his head. "Don't mention it. I'd better leave now as there is a lot to do."

They walked back towards the gate. Vadu had, by now, left Balu and was in the house as Lal walked outside the compound and sat in the rickshaw.

"Take me to the railway station," he directed.

53

It had been another night of lurching into disjointed sleep. Anxiety about the journey had begun creeping into Catherine's mind, despite her going over and over what she had to do in the next three days.

Not wanting to prompt any awkward questions from her parents, she decided to lie in bed till after her father had left home instead of waking up early. She wanted to force herself back into her old routine.

"You seem more like yourself," Ethel said as they were finishing breakfast.

"Whatever it was, I fought it off."

"I'm glad."

"Mother, as I'm feeling better, I want to go to John Brown's clothing store to get a few items. I feel like adding a few new clothes to my wardrobe." Before her mother could reply, she added, "Vadu can take me there and wait for me. I shan't be too long."

Ethel hesitated, but with Catherine's persistence, and knowing that she had just overcome her illness, she agreed.

Vadu arranged a small horse-drawn carriage to travel to Brown's store, which was on the Upper Mall Road near the British Punjabi Governor's office.

It felt strange to be travelling to the centre of Lahore knowing that Kharak was not there. He was absent, but she felt his presence in every street that she recognised. Vivid memories flooded back, tightening her stomach.

Brown's was the only store in Lahore that retailed British outfits for the colonial residents. The majority of their clothing was imported from England, with a few outfits stitched in local cloth with subtle changes.

In the shop, an English woman, Mrs Brown, served Catherine. She asked for three pairs of skirt suits with matching blouses. As these were not too common, the woman stared at her.

"I'm going on a horse-riding trip," Catherine lied.

The woman smiled, then took her measurements. A few minutes later, Catherine had picked the ones she liked.

Looking around, she spotted a light magnolia dress. "Now, I would like that dress and that one there." She pointed.

A few minutes later, she was in a small cubicle at the rear of the store trying on the clothes, assisted by the shop girl. Luckily, the skirt fitted quite well but the blouse was slightly loose, though that did not matter to her.

Mrs Brown asked her if she wanted the dresses to be altered for a proper fit, but Catherine declined politely.

"Could you please pack them in two separate packages: one with the skirt suits and the other with the dresses?" she asked.

"Certainly," Mrs Brown replied abruptly.

It had taken Catherine forty minutes to complete her shopping. As she walked out of the store with Sana carrying her two packages, she glanced at the clock above the facade of the governor's office. It was half past ten. *I will just be in time for Nandu*, she thought.

Vadu helped Sana to stow her packages and ensured that she climbed safely inside the carriage. It was frustrating when he told her that the cook had asked him to pass by the grocers to get some yeast for baking the bread as they were out of it.

This diversion added fifteen minutes to the journey home, which concerned her. *What if Nandu leaves when he realises that I'm not at home? That will be a dilemma.*

By the time they reached home, it was ten minutes past eleven o' clock. As their carriage approached the house, Catherine spotted the familiar rickshaw parked opposite the gate. *Phew… he is waiting.*

Not only was Nandu there, but Lal was seated on the rickshaw as well. The carriage stopped at the gate.

"Vadu, I will get out here. Kharak's friend is here to see me."

"Yes, memsahib."

"Take this package into the house for me." She handed him the one with the magnolia dress. "I'll bring this one with me."

Vadu nodded without questioning and walked away with Sana. Catherine then hopped off the carriage and walked towards the rickshaw as Lal got off.

"Good to see you, Lal."

"Likewise, Catherine."

"Let's take a walk in the garden." She gestured, raising her eyebrows. He understood.

Lal spoke first. "There were arrangement issues, but I managed to get first-class tickets for you from here on the train and the ship. Not many people travel first class so there were tickets."

"That's great news." She gave a nervous smile.

"The train departs at quarter past seven in the evening, so you need to be there by seven o' clock."

"I would like you to keep hold of the tickets for me, Lal, until I get to the station."

Having thought about it, the main hurdle for her was getting past Balu without him knowing that she had left the house, as he would eventually mention this to her parents. She needed to get at least an overnight head start in case they came after her. Once on the ship, it would not matter.

"The thing is that I need to get past the gatekeeper on Saturday evening and that seems to be a hurdle."

Lal's eyes darted from right to left in thought. He realised that she needed a strategy to fulfil her ambition of leaving the house and getting to the railway station without being caught.

"I have an idea. On Saturday evening, at exactly quarter to seven, I shall ask Nandu to get one of his colleagues to bring his carriage to stop just past the gate and then to get the gatekeeper away from the gate to distract him. At this precise time, you will need to sneak out." He pursed his lips.

Without blinking, Catherine listened intently to what he was saying.

"Once outside the gate, walk quickly to the turning to the next block, George Street; that is a hundred yards away. Further along that street, Nandu and myself will be there in his carriage."

"What about my suitcase?"

He paused. "Have it ready tomorrow at eleven o' clock in the morning and give it to Nandu when he makes his daily visit to your house. If anyone asks, just say that it contains old shoes and items of clothing that you are giving away."

"In that case," she turned around to make sure no one was looking, "take this package with you. These are some of the clothes I will need to take to Africa." She quickly shoved it into his hand.

"How will you get away from your parents without raising suspicion?" he asked as he took the package.

"I have an idea, but that will be a problem for me to solve.

As things are, you have already helped me tremendously, and I thank you."

Knowing that spending too much time on the Roses' property would raise questions, Lal did not stay any longer and was brief in saying his goodbye and wishing her luck for Saturday.

It now dawned upon Catherine that her desire to see Kharak again had been set in motion. Tucked away in all the nervousness that resided in her at this very moment was a spark of elation.

Stepping inside the house, she saw that Vadu had placed the package in the hallway. Picking it up, she went into the lounge, sat down and deliberately started opening it. Just as she had envisioned, her mother walked through the door.

"How was your trip to Brown's? Let's see and compare your new dresses to those we get in Bath." She rubbed her palms together.

"I love this one." Catherine lifted the dress with both hands and tilted it towards the sunlight pouring through the window, highlighting the coloured fabric.

This was the exact reason that she had separated the clothes she had bought into two packages, as it would have been exasperating trying to convince Ethel of her reasons for purchasing the skirt suit.

For the first time in a few days, at lunch, she ate a normal portion, not knowing what kind of food she would get in the days ahead.

After lunch, she headed straight to her room and opened her wardrobe. From the bottom shelf, she retrieved one of her leather suitcases that she had travelled with from Bath. It would now accompany her to another continent.

She gathered clothing, boots, her sun hat and personal items she thought she would need and placed them swiftly in her suitcase before fastening it and placing it behind the door.

Despite her haste, this had taken her an hour. Now seated on the corner of her bed, her mind went over had the items she packed, hoping that she had not missed anything.

At the same time as Catherine was packing her clothes in Lahore, across the ocean in Tsavo, during the mid-morning of that fateful day that Ungan's body was discovered, the remains were taken to the medical officer responsible for the well-being of everyone constructing the railway line. There was no need to confirm the cause of his death, as it was quite evident what had occurred.

Being close to Ungan, Chand was affected the most by his horrific death. He felt that he had lost the one person he could openly talk to. All the coolies closed ranks and stood by to support one another.

By the afternoon, wood for the pyre to cremate Ungan's body had been collected. The three-foot-high pyre was built on the bank of the river half a mile from the bridge.

The cremation was carried out late in the afternoon and work came to a temporary halt so that any worker who wanted to pay his last respects could do so.

That night, fear set in within the camp, with large fires lit at every concentration of tents. Groups of coolies squatted around them, constantly murmuring amongst themselves in dread. The reflected orange glow of the flames hit Chand and Narain's faces as they sat around the fire. No one had a good appetite that evening and a lot of the food was stored away for the next day.

Patterson felt that there was a chance that the lion would make another visit to the campsite. He therefore decided to climb a tree near Ungan's tent and spend a considerable time there in the hope that he would be able to shoot and kill the lion.

Narain was the first to tell Chand what Patterson's plan was for the night.

"I don't know about you, but I will be up that tree as well," Chand replied, with fear scrolled across his face. "Ungan was like my elder brother and I miss him."

Narain put an arm around his shoulder. "It's not only you who is affected by this, it's me as well. I'm here for you… and I hope you are here for me too."

Chand remained quiet and numb.

An hour passed by and no one felt like leaving the comfort and the false sense of safety of being around the crackling fires. They didn't want to walk into their tents to sleep.

At around nine o' clock, they noticed Colonel Patterson with his .303 rifle slung over his shoulder, climbing up a baobab tree.

"I'm going up that tree as well, next to Patterson Sahib," Chand said.

A few minutes later, he scampered across to the tree and, without any hesitation, clambered up it. Seeing what he had done, one by one, the nine workers climbed the two trees that overlooked their tents.

Patterson had not anticipated that all the workers who had their tents in this vicinity would also decide to climb the trees for safety. He did not stop them, though, as it was the first night after the horrific event.

There was no wind and an odd stillness appeared around the tents, which was sensed from their high vantage points up the trees. Apart from the flickering, red-orange flames of the fire that shaped moving shadows nearby, it was dark beyond fifty yards from the firepit. There were no sounds of animals apart from the night beetles humming.

Despite the wide branches of the baobab tree, it was uncomfortable and difficult to nod off. Coupled with the fear of falling if they fell asleep, Chand and Narain felt chained by mental anguish.

They knew that, just like them, Patterson had been listening for any unusual rustling sounds and looking out for any odd movement around the shadowy bushes that may forewarn them of the lion returning.

Two restless hours passed and there had been no sign of any animals below them. The flames had died down to embers as no one had dared to add more firewood.

Then, it started.

Over half a mile away, across the river, where one of the railhead camps was located, distant shouts and frightful screams broke the still night. Chand, Narain and the rest of the workers were in panic and reluctant to climb down from the trees. They clutched the branches tightly.

"Patterson Sahib is very brave," Chand whispered nervously to Narain as he saw him climb down the tree with his rifle.

"We need to help them. Who will accompany me?" Patterson looked up at the tree.

No one spoke and many looked away. A few moments later, it was Narain who spoke.

"I will come and walk with you, sahib."

After carefully clambering down, being unarmed, Narain was given a two-foot-long machete by the colonel. In a hurry, he lit a hurricane lamp, which he carried with his other hand. Minutes later, they prowled towards the campsite where the commotion was.

With his heart thumping against his ribcage and the rifle pointed ahead, the thorny bushes around them seemed sinister and every shadow felt as if it wanted to pounce at them. With eyes focused and ears pricked, they moved as fast as their visibility allowed towards the dim light in the distance from the lamps that were now being lit by the workers at the affected campsite.

The shouts and wails of anguish got louder as they approached the campsite. Some of the workers had climbed the only baobab tree in the vicinity. Others huddled together with sticks and shovels for protection.

As they approached, a brief sense of relief could be seen on their faces. Without any hesitation, they all pointed towards a partly collapsed tent that was pitched at the far end of a semicircle.

"*Sher! Sher!*" they shouted.

Beads of sweat formed on Patterson's forehead as he trod carefully towards the tent. The whole tent would have crumpled if it wasn't for the two front poles that supported it.

Pointing his rifle at the tent, using the dim light of Narain's lamp, he observed that the rear part of the canvas was ripped open. As had happened the night before, a trail of blood streaked the bed sheets and disappeared into the collapsed part of the tent. They edged quietly around the outside of the tent and the bloodied trail was seen heading into the tall savannah grass. Drag marks were present between huge pugmarks, which clearly indicated the direction the lion had hauled the victim through the bush.

This was worrying. What had happened to Ungan the night before seemed to have occurred again here, but this time, the victim was chosen from a different part of the site. And that was most uncanny.

The next morning, Sana brought Catherine's tea to her room. Leaning on the headboard with her pillows providing comfort, Catherine held the cup in both hands, sipped the Darjeeling tea and thought of Kharak, where he was and how he was doing. She had never missed anyone as much as she missed him right now. *Not long now*, she thought. *Tomorrow I shall leave and in three weeks, I shall see you. But I need to figure out how to leave the house unseen.*

Her morning routine was the same: she got dressed, she had breakfast, then spent some time by herself on the swing in the back garden.

But on this day, Catherine left the swing earlier than usual and headed straight upstairs to her room. She pulled the dressing-table chair closer to the windowsill and left the net curtains ajar to give her an uninterrupted view of the gate. Seated on the chair, she glanced once again at her packed leather suitcase that was positioned behind the door. The room was silent apart from the gentle ticking of the wall clock, which made her look at it. *Not long now.*

At precisely eleven o' clock, Balu was seen lumbering outside the gate. She knew that it would be Nandu outside. Waiting for a moment, she caught a glimpse of his rickshaw through the gate. She jumped out of the chair and picked up her suitcase, which was a little heavy, and lugged it towards the stairs.

She looked along the corridor and downstairs for her mother, but she was nowhere to be seen. With some difficultly, she managed to carry the case downstairs.

"May I help you, memsahib?" Vadu asked as he walked from the lounge room. It made her jump.

"Take this to the gate," she instructed in haste.

"Certainly." Vadu took the suitcase and effortlessly walked towards the gate.

Outside, he waited for Catherine to catch up. Being courteous, she greeted Nandu before asking Vadu to place her suitcase into his rickshaw. She did not say much and kept the conversation brief. Within a couple of minutes, she watched the rickshaw leave. *There is no turning back now.*

She turned and walked through the gate and towards the house. As she stepped onto the veranda, Ethel walked out of the door.

"Ah, there you are. Is everything all right?" She raised her eyebrows.

"Yes, Mother, all is well."

"I saw Vadu carry the suitcase—"

"Yes, of course, I forgot to mention it to you," she interrupted. "I gave some of my old, unwanted clothes to Nandu's family as I didn't feel like throwing them away. I'm sure his wife can adjust them to suit her needs."

"You gave away your durable suitcase as well?"

Catherine quickly thought of an answer. "Oh no… he will be returning the suitcase tomorrow."

"Oh, I see. Talking of tomorrow, we have been invited to attend the annual British ball at the Punjab Club at six o' clock in the evening. Do you feel well enough to attend?"

Catherine thought fast. "Although I feel much better, I still need to rest, Mother. In fact, a few early nights are what I need to fully recover."

"That's a shame, but we understand. Let me get you some peppermint tea." Ethel led her into the house and towards the kitchen.

Catherine knew that her worry about leaving the house unseen had just been eased.

55

Saturday was an intense day for Catherine, as her anxiety was compounded by an eagerness that led to a feeling of constant tightness in her stomach. The sunshine through the cloudless sky was soothing on her face as she walked in the garden along the boundary of her home.

She paused briefly, admiring the effect of the sunshine on the house surrounded by its plush green lawn, trees and scrub. It looked stately. Knowing that it would be at least two months before she would return to it, she took in this sight for as long as she could.

As always, her father was hardly ever at home – and after what had happened with Kharak, she was not keen on being around him anyway. Her emotions were still raw.

A considerable part of the afternoon was taken up by helping her mother direct the ayahs to rearrange some of the furnishings in the lounge. The display cabinet was moved to the opposite corner and replaced by the worn-out leather armchair. Some of the pictures that hung on the walls were repositioned to alter the focal point of the room. Having completed the task, the room had a different feel and look about it as the late-afternoon sun shone through the window.

At teatime, Catherine saw her father walk through the hallway and into the dining room. There was a brief conversation about her health before they were seated around the dining table.

As dinner was being served, Gilbert chose to speak. "As you feel better, I will be taking a few days off from work and your mother and I have decided that the three of us should spend some time in Delhi as a family." He adjusted his napkin and looked directly at Catherine.

"It will be lovely for us to see the splendours of Delhi." Ethel glanced at Catherine as the servants dished out the potatoes.

We could all go, but I won't be here, Catherine thought.

"That will be wonderful and I look forward to seeing Delhi," she lied. "When do we leave?"

"Before next weekend, probably Friday," her father replied.

"Lovely." She forced a smile.

Dinner was uneventful, with her parents talking a lot about the ball they were attending that evening, as well as the Delhi trip. The only part of the conversation that Catherine listened to closely was about the ball. She was curious about the time they would leave, which would allow her to plan her escape.

After dinner, as the cutlery and dishes were being picked up, Catherine uttered the words that she had rehearsed over and over in her mind over the last few days.

"I'm feeling rather tired tonight, so I will retire early to bed. Please tell Vadu not to disturb me and please also inform Sana not to bring my morning tea as I plan to have a lie-in," Catherine stated as she massaged her temples with her fingers.

"Ah, you poor thing. Helping me today must have worn

you out. Not to worry, dear, I shall make sure that you won't be disturbed." Ethel placed her hand on Catherine's arm.

Forty minutes later, her parents went straight upstairs, as they had to get dressed for the ball.

In her room, Catherine sat at her dressing table, got a piece of blank paper from the drawer, picked up her pen, ensuring that it was inked, and started writing. This was the letter that she would leave behind on her bed for her parents to read, hopefully the following morning.

It didn't take her long to complete writing it, as she had rehearsed it already in her mind. She folded it and placed it back in the drawer to be retrieved later, in case her parents walked into the room before leaving.

At fifteen minutes past six o' clock, there was a knock on her door.

"We are about to leave, Catherine."

"Just wait a minute. I'm coming downstairs."

Catherine took a deep breath and held it for a few seconds. Only then did she walk out of her room. Her mother was already walking down the stairs.

Her father was ready, standing in the hallway adjusting his charcoal coat sleeves. Catherine walked over to her mother and gave her a hug.

"Do have a lovely evening at the ball."

"We will, my dear. You go and have a rest; we will see you in the morning." Ethel kissed Catherine on her forehead.

She stared at her mother, hoping to hold on to this image of her.

The clatter of the carriage being brought over by Vadu made Catherine's pulse quicken. She did not move as they climbed into the carriage and Vadu shut the door.

Ethel turned, facing her, reached her hand out of the carriage, smiled and waved as the carriage began to move.

Catherine waved back as she saw the carriage move down the driveway and out of the gate as dusk fell. She felt anxious.

The greying sky had overcome the diminishing orange light of the setting sun. The night beetles started their buzzing as the fragrance of night-blooming flowers wafted in the air, as it did most nights.

Catherine walked into the house alone. Vadu had gone with the carriage and the servants were in their quarters after another long day, as she had told them that she wished not to be disturbed that evening. She dimmed the lamps in the lounge room and the hallway before walking into the kitchen, where she put out the lamp there. She carefully walked up to her room, drew the curtains and glanced at the clock on her dressing table. She had half an hour.

Outside her room, along the corridor, was the bedding cabinet. She opened it and got three pillows out and took them to her room. Pulling back her blanket, she placed the pillows along the mattress and covered them. She adjusted the pillows and took a few steps back, and was pleased that it looked like she was asleep. Next, she opened her dressing-table drawer and got the letter she had written earlier and placed it on the bedside table with the words *To Mother and Father* easily visible.

Next, she took her purse from her wardrobe and went through it again. She confirmed the Indian rupees and British pounds were still there. She then placed her purse in the buttoned inside pocket of her bag. All her other personal items that she thought she might require were in the bag.

Before closing her wardrobe, she removed her charcoal-grey shawl and her soft-soled Derby boots and put the boots on. Now completely ready, she glanced at her clock; there were ten minutes left. She sat on the edge of her bed for a few moments to compose herself. Her heart was racing.

Exactly five minutes later, she got up, picked up her bag and shawl, extinguished her lamp and walked out of her room.

As she had dimmed most of the lamps, apart from the one in the hallway, it was fairly dark inside the house. She walked into the kitchen and stood by the window that had the angled view of the gate. Her gaze shifted between the gate and the wall clock.

Outside, the remnants of the evening light were just enough to outline and give a picture of the gate. At precisely fifteen minutes to seven o' clock, Catherine observed Balu walking towards the gate. He opened it and took a couple of hesitant steps outside.

I've got to go now!

She opened the rear door that led outside into the courtyard and stepped out, silently closing it. As she scanned around, she wrapped the long grey shawl around herself, including her head, leaving only her eyes visible. Clutching her bag underneath her shawl, she skulked towards the gate, approaching it from the side.

Voices could be heard from the other side of the gate. She stopped and inclined her neck to peek from behind it. Balu was about fifty yards down the street where a craggy rickshaw stood, deep in conversation with two men. It seemed that he knew them, from the cordial talk and laughter. Catherine paused, waiting for the right moment. Her heart was thumping against her ribs.

As Balu walked, examining the rickshaw, one of the men put his arm around him and took him to the front of the rickshaw, so that he faced away from the gate. At that moment, with stealth, Catherine stepped outside the gate, took a right turn and sneaked away. She took hurried steps without turning around to look until she reached the next junction of the adjoining street, where she took the right turn.

A few feet down the road, she could make out a carriage. There, Lal was waiting with Nandu as planned. She was glad to see them.

"You made it, Catherine Memsahib," Lal whispered, as she got close.

"Yes. Feeling nervous."

"Don't worry," he reassured her.

Within a minute, she was on board and the carriage headed for the railway station.

The journey to the station was short for Catherine, as her nervous mind had been wandering. The only thing that grounded her amidst her fear and anxiety about the unknown was the thought of Kharak, and somewhere within her, for an unknown reason, she felt that she owed him this journey.

By the time they reached the station, the night sky was setting in. The oil lamps were lit throughout the station and it was easy for Catherine to follow Lal and the porter who carried their luggage.

At Platform 2, Lal's family were present. After a brief introduction to Catherine, Lal directed the porter to the first-class carriage that was ahead.

"This is your cabin." He handed her the ticket. "I will be in the next carriage, which is standard class… so don't worry." He pointed at it.

"Thank you, Lal, for all this. I appreciate it."

"Don't mention it. Now, if you excuse me, I have to say my goodbyes to my family… I shan't be long." He left her boarding the train.

Looking at the ticket, she entered her first-class cabin followed by the porter, who stowed away her luggage. It reminded her of the journey she had taken with her mother to Lahore.

At precisely quarter past seven, the hoot sounded and the train started to move. She slumped on the bunk bed and held her head in her hands. Her eyes filled up.

There was a knock on the cabin door. She quickly wiped her tears away with her hands.

"Yes?"

"It's only me. Don't worry, I'm in the next carriage," said the reassuring voice of Lal.

At least there is one person I can rely on.

Part 4

Mombasa   # 56

There was one thing that Kharak discovered about himself over the three-week journey and that was that he suffered from seasickness. It was the nights that were terrible: long bouts of nausea and the uncomfortable bedding, coupled with a lack of sleep, made the journey one to forget. Daytime was what he looked forward to, as he was able to get on deck in the sea breeze and gaze at the horizon, which helped to alleviate this problem.

Prior to this journey, he had never seen the sea lapping on a sandy shore. The sight of green palm trees on the distant shoreline against the aqua-blue sea was his finest moment. As land approached, a huge, chalky grey fort on a ledge bordering the sea stood out against the palm trees. It was unlike the forts of Lahore, which were intricate. This was sturdy, somewhat smaller, with no domes, signifying its European origins, having been built by the Portuguese in the 15th century.

The *SS Karanja* ship navigated past the fort, which was

surrounded by weathered stone buildings with Arabic curved architecture intertwined with newer wooden buildings. He found it strange, seeing for the first time the dark-skinned African natives observing their ship from the shore.

Mombasa was a modest island separated from the mainland by a small body of water. Slowly, the ship passed the fort that was on the right side and approached the opening to a body of seawater, which was the entrance of a natural harbour. There, in the distance, the port of Mombasa, known as Kilindini Harbour, came into view, which was the new harbour that was constructed the previous year by the British to replace the centuries-old harbour on the opposite side of the island. They needed a harbour that would be suitable to handle the vast cargo of construction material and steam engines that would be passing through it.

The ship eventually docked at the port and the gangplank was lowered to the dock.

After half an hour of heaving, shoving and organised commotion, they had disembarked the ship with their baggage and were instructed to wait outside, where the entrance to the port was. A track of railway lines originated from a station that could be seen fifty yards ahead. This was where the railway headquarters were.

A slim, uniformed British man took control and barked instructions at them, herding them towards one corner of the open garden at the front of the port entrance.

Kharak scanned around, but could not see Ivan anywhere. It took another half hour in the hot afternoon sun before the same British man started the roll call from a list, to divide the workers into those who were going to be based in Mombasa and those who would be going inland to work on the construction of the railway line. The transition from the breezy deck of the ship to the still, oppressive heat on land was uncomfortable. The hot and humid afternoon was unlike anything Kharak had experienced in Lahore, where the days were perfect.

An hour later, the two groups were led away in separate directions to their temporary accommodation. Their walk, which was a detour, took twenty minutes through the main street, known as Vasco da Gama Street. It was a narrow street with white Arabic-influenced buildings adorned with overhanging balconies on either side. There was a lazy, timeless feel about it. Running right in the middle of the street were tracks for a tram and also located here was one of the few freshwater wells. Everyone was asked to fill up their bottles before they left for Tsavo the following morning.

It was a relief for Kharak to be able to stretch his legs after days on board the ship. As they arrived at their sleeping quarters, they observed that the building, nestling amongst tall palm trees, was fully constructed of corrugated iron sheets with tiny wooden-framed windows that broke the grey, metallic monotony. Inside, it felt like a furnace, with the sun heating up the iron sheets. There were rows of low-lying wooden beds with mattresses made of cotton balls stuffed in sewn fabric, and a cotton sheet was all the bedding there was. It was going to be a tough first night.

After washing, which involved using a bucket of cold water in an outdoor bathing area, Kharak felt a sense of relief. As the evening approached, the direction of the breeze changed. The sea breeze blowing through the whispering palms that lined the town was refreshing.

That evening, not a single worker left their quarters to visit the town. It wasn't the tiredness, but the apprehension of an unknown, new place, and seeing people who looked completely different to them and who couldn't speak their language. Instead, they gathered together in small groups and talked about India and how different their work would be here. By eight o' clock, they had all retired to their rickety beds.

For Kharak, it was a struggle to get to sleep in the clammy air that hung in the sleeping hall. If he covered himself with the cotton sheet, it was too warm for comfort; if he slipped out from under it, the ferocious mosquitos with their high-pitched buzzing bit him awake. He tossed and turned, and was quite astounded by the ability of some of the men to be fast asleep, snoring.

He turned onto his stomach with his face down and dangled his arm beside his bed. In the dark, he groped around until he felt the side pocket of his smaller canvas bag. After a few attempts, he managed to unbutton the pocket with one hand and slid into it to retrieve the white cotton glove.

Clutching it in his hand, he placed it beside his face on the pillow. The fragrance of Catherine still lingered, drifting his thoughts away. He closed his eyes and he could see her, just there, holding his hand. The times with her were the greatest moments that life had gifted him. He missed her terribly. With thoughts of her, he drifted off to sleep.

The ominous dark clouds clustered over and the same brackish water flowed in torrents beneath the bridge.

With terror in her eyes, she kept crying out, "Kharak! Help, my hands are slipping!"

"I won't let go of you, I promise. Hold on," he yelled back, his hand gripping hers as she dangled over the footbridge. This time, it was raining. In horror, he felt her hand slip gradually from his. He tried to adjust and firm his grip; the pain in his shoulder was piercing and his arm was numb.

It happened in a blink of an eye. She let go of his hand and plunged into the forbidding torrent of the river.

In a jolt, Kharak sat upright, drenched in sweat, with his pulse racing. With trembling hands, he wiped the sweat from his brow. It was the same dream he had had a few weeks back. He hated it. As his breath came back to normal and his pulse eased, his anguish eased. He remembered her glove and searched for it, and was glad when he found it under his pillow. He felt it again, kissed it and placed it carefully back into the pocket of his bag where it had been.

It wasn't long before the cockerels could be heard crowing. Despite them breaking the silence that pervaded, it was reassuring to know that dawn was not far away. The heat of the night had faded to be replaced by the fresh, soothing air of dawn.

Within half an hour, what had been a quiet space was resonating with voices as nearly everyone was awake. The three-week journey across the Indian Ocean had gradually adjusted everyone's body to the different time zone of the East African coast, but the effect still persisted. Everyone felt chirpier after a night's rest.

With baggage packed and a simple breakfast of coarse bread and warm milk, they were all ready for the journey. Like the previous day, the thin British supervisor came at eight o' clock and took a roll call before leading the walk to the temporary wooden platform at the railway station they had seen the day before.

While walking with his folded blanket under one arm and his luggage in the other hand, Kharak noticed the smell of burning wood that tinged the fresh morning breeze in pockets amongst the mango and coconut trees. A number of unclothed, dark-skinned children stood watching them with their toothy grins. A woman with beaded necklaces adorning her neck and a wrapped red cloth around her hips walked along, perfectly balancing a clay pot on her head. Two young, naked children accompanied her.

An hour later, at the station, the paperwork was signed and stamped at the management office. Waiting at the platform with the rest of his colleagues, Kharak saw the UR35 train slowly chugging and whistling as it came to a halt at the platform. This was the only regular train service to a place called Voi, which was the main depot for the rail yards, 110 miles inland from Mombasa – the final stop for the train service. To go further into

Tsavo and to the construction site at the railhead, the labourers had to change to the construction wagon from there onwards.

As he was about to board the allocated third-class carriage, Kharak noticed Ivan, who was further down the platform wearing khaki trousers, a white linen shirt and knee-high boots, just about to step into the first-class carriage with the porters carrying his tremendous amount of luggage. With a tightening of his stomach, Kharak felt an aversion towards him that was greater than ever before. He knew the man ahead was responsible for sending him away from his family and Catherine. He maintained his glare, not taking his eyes off Ivan as he entered the carriage. Ivan did not see him.

57

Lahore

"Catherine must have had a good night's rest. She seems to have slept early and throughout the night. She's still asleep," Ethel said to her husband as they were getting ready in their room for the Sunday-morning church service.

"You are right dear," Gilbert mumbled as he buttoned his shirt.

Half an hour later, as they sat at the table for breakfast, Ethel spoke. "Vadu, is Catherine awake?"

Vadu, who was standing at the door between the kitchen and the dining table, took a quick glance at one of the maids who was in the kitchen.

"No, memsahib – one of the maids went upstairs to her room, but she is still fast asleep."

"That's odd, I hope she is well. I'd better go and see to her myself." Ethel's brow rose with concern.

Ethel got up and directed Vadu to pick up her plate, signifying that her breakfast was over, before she walked out of the dining room and towards the stairs.

Upstairs, outside Catherine's room, she knocked on the door and waited for a response. A few moments later, she knocked again.

"Catherine? Are you awake, dear?"

There was no response. She carefully twisted the brass doorknob, opened the door and gently popped her head in. *Oh dear, she must be really tired*, she thought as she saw the outline of Catherine lying in bed with the curtains still drawn. Ethel took a step inside the room and stood still as her eyes swept the room. *Very tidy*, she thought.

Being a mother, she could not help but call out her name again. "Catherine, are you all right?"

She waited for a response, to no avail. Slightly worried, she focused on Catherine's torso. "Catherine?" she called again, looking for the raising and lowering of her breath.

As there was no noticeable movement, in a panic, she walked towards the bed, still focusing on Catherine's breathing.

"Catherine!" she cried again as she reached for the blanket that completely covered her daughter's face. She lifted it.

Down in the dining room, Gilbert had just placed his napkin on the table when he heard a hysterical scream from the room above.

With dread, he jumped to his feet and dashed up the stairs towards Ethel's frightened cry, which came from Catherine's room. As he walked into the room, he saw Ethel's hands on her cheeks, her face white with her eyes wide open. She stood staring at the empty bed with pillows under the blanket. Beads of cold sweat suddenly appeared on Gilbert's forehead as the thought of what had unfolded became clear.

"She's been kidnapped!" Ethel blurted out between sobs.

Gilbert had a quick look around the bed and spotted the

letter on the bedside table. He picked it up, unfolded it and began to read.

His jaw dropped, his face reddened, his nostrils flared and he bit his lip as he dropped the letter on the bed. In the anger that followed, he grabbed the book that was lying on the bedside table and flung it across the room.

"How dare she do that?"

"What's happened?" Ethel wiped her tears away.

Gilbert did not reply. Ethel stepped towards the bed and picked up the letter.

Dear Father and Mother,

I am sorry for putting you through this, but I have to do it. I came to know that due to Father's hatred of my closeness to Kharak, he forced him to leave his family, his home... and me.

Just as you sent him to Mombasa, I have followed him there, so that you and I can go through the same pain that you forced upon him.

Do not be concerned, as I will be looked after along the journey from Bombay and I shall return here within three months.

Catherine

The words shook Ethel's world. As she felt the room enclose her, she sat down on the bed, drained emotionally. There was a moment of silence.

After gathering her thoughts, she plucked up the courage to ask, "Is there truth in what she has written?"

With hesitation came Gilbert's gruff response. "Yes."

There followed a nervous silence in the room.

"What do we do now?" Ethel tried to calm her breathing, with little success.

"I will attempt to send a telegraphic message to Ivan to tell him to look out for her at the port in Mombasa, in case she has left." He paused to take a breath. "I will take the next train to Bombay and look for her at the port there."

"It's worrying." Ethel's arched eyebrows twitched as she tried to control her crying. "All by herself, right across the seas, in a land full of savages. I don't want to lose her." Her tears rolled down her cheeks.

"Right under our noses, she managed to do this; it's either bravery or stupidity." Gilbert turned to stamp out of the room, trying to ignore his worry for Catherine. First, he was going to have a keen word with Vadu and Balu.

Ethel stood alone with teary eyes, the note held in her dangling hand, her world enclosed in darkness.

That evening, Gilbert walked into the house after a weary day. Things hadn't worked according to plan. The telegraphic message had failed to go through, which, according to the operator, could have been due to a problem at the Zanzibar telegraphic station, which could not forward the message to Mombasa.

He would have to catch the train to Bombay and try to resend it from there if needed. *Damn you two!*

58

Tsavo

Watching the largest, most incredible bird he had ever seen, hopping beside the train, was fascinating for Kharak. Yet he still felt a sense of trepidation.

The woody vegetation around Mombasa and the Rabai Hills had given way to the beginnings of the flatter, drier Nyika Plateau. The wildlife was abundant, as zebras and gazelles dotted the savannah grassland. Towering giraffes made an ungainly run as the blaring, unnatural sound of the steam horn caused a panic.

The heat from the glaring sun was much drier as the humidity dropped the further away from the coast one went. At Voi, the changeover to the wagon train took less an hour, which gave all the coolies time to stretch their legs. For the next fifteen miles to Tsavo Station, the seats in the wagon were plain wooden benches nailed together. What made it doubly uncomfortable was the fine red dust from the surrounding soil.

The rail wagon slowed as it snaked around the bend in the tracks. Kharak saw the newly painted signboard of Tsavo Station before the red clay tiled gablet roof of the tiny, corrugated house-like building with a veranda running around it. A lonely palm tree that seemed out of place grew beside it, and a few metres further was the towering metal water tank. Low, thorny acacia trees grew amongst the golden green savannah and low-lying rocky outcrops. The grey ballast and the railway tracks broke the continuous view of the surrounding thorny shrubs that swathed the underlying red soil. Kharak had arrived at the recently established Tsavo Station.

After ten minutes, all the coolies, including Kharak, had disembarked from the wagon with their belongings and stood in the intense midday sun, participating in another roll call that was taken by a scrawny junior British administrator. Standing two feet behind with his hands in his pockets was Ivan, looking smug.

The camp was 400 metres from Tsavo Station, through a trodden path with acacia bushes and blades of savannah grass on either side. By the time Kharak reached the campsite, not only were his boots and trousers covered in the red dust, but also the fine dust had penetrated his socks. He noticed that the tents had been re-pitched closer together, their previous positions still visible as rectangular patches of dirt further apart. A further hundred metres from the campsite towards the left, sounds of stone being cut, wood being sawn and metal hitting metal could be heard. He realised that it was there that the bridge over the river was undergoing construction. The railway track was on the left of the camp.

Narain, who was in the administration tent providing the list of supplies required, spotted Kharak amongst the coolies waiting outside the tent. He stood out from the others; he didn't have the demeanour of an unskilled labourer. His aura was warm and affable. Narain smiled at him as he walked out.

It took less than half an hour for the tents to be provided for pitching. Ivan, who kept a close distance to the newly arrived, could not help but bark orders.

"You all need to pitch your tents further out." He pointed. "I will not have you crowding the campsite. Do you understand that? Make sure that I do not have to repeat myself."

Having said that, Ivan walked away, leading the porters carrying his belongings.

It was not long after that that Kharak started walking to pitch his tent. Narain had been standing at a distance, observing what Ivan had said. As Kharak walked past him, Narain spoke.

"I wouldn't pitch my tent where he wants you to. It's not safe." He gave a friendly smile.

Kharak stopped walking.

"Hello. My name is Narain." He extended his hand. They shook hands.

"I'm Kharak."

"I'm Colonel Patterson's personal assistant and a stone artisan working on the bridge." He paused. "Come on, I'll show you where to pitch your tent."

Kharak was not expecting to see so many workers from his country there in the wilderness and it was somewhat reassuring. His thoughts went to Lahore, to his family... and to Catherine. It is always in the wilderness, separated by distance, that one misses one's loved ones the most.

Kharak followed Narain to the site he was talking about, which was further into the middle of the campsite. It would be later at night when Kharak would realise that his tent was adjacent to Narain and his mate Chand's tent. It took him an hour and a half to pitch his tent and get it as comfortable as he could, after which he contemplated whether to rest and have a nap or wander around the campsite to get a feel of the surroundings. He decided to have a nap; wandering could wait.

By nightfall, as the flickering stars came out around the shimmering half-moon, the night insects were already buzzing. Kharak was glad that his new-found acquaintances, Narain and Chand, had invited him to share the evening meal with them around the fire. Throughout the evening, he noticed that, of the two, Chand was quieter and had a nervousness about him.

"Earlier today, if you hadn't asked me to pitch my tent here, I would have pitched it on the outer side where the other newly arrived labourers are," Kharak said as he sipped his warm milk.

Chand furrowed his eyebrows and fixed his gaze on Narain, and Narain did the same back. They maintained their silence.

"There is something about nature… look at this place, it's dry with its unusual red soil, untamed—"

"My friend," Narain interrupted, "this place possesses unforgiving, savage beauty."

"Never walk alone here, especially in the evening and at night," Chand remarked as he stared at the glistening embers of the fire.

This pricked Kharak's ears. "Really?"

A hesitant silence followed. "A marauding lion prowls the area… already, two coolies have been killed and another three are missing." Chand lowered his voice.

Kharak stopped taking his sip of milk midway, and his forehead crinkled.

Chand carried on. "My closest friend, Ungan, was mauled to death last week…" He paused to regain his composure. "I hate this place."

Kharak felt uneasy. In silence, he observed the dimming flames of the fire as it turned to embers. His milk seemed to have lost its warmth as he took his last sip. He remembered the winter evenings in Lahore sitting with his family around the fire, roasting groundnuts, laughing and lazily awaiting the night. *Very different to the quiet, uneasy loneliness I feel here in Tsavo*, he thought.

Narain and Chand were the only people he knew here, but he remembered that Lal would be here in about a week. That thought settled his mind. He stood up to retire for the night.

"Thank you for today. It was good to meet you."

"Any day, brother."

With a friendly salute, Kharak walked towards his tent.

Despite the afternoon nap, it wasn't too long before Kharak was asleep, dreaming that he was teaching his sister Neina how to ride a bicycle in the narrow alley in Rahmanpur.

Outside, the temperature had dropped, which provided a bearable relief in contrast to the daytime heat.

It had been only three hours since he fell asleep when the discomfort of the hard bedding on the floor of his tent woke Kharak. Groggily, his hands touched the side canvas and, with half-open eyes, he saw the dark outline of the inner tent and realised where he was. He took a deep sigh and turned onto his side as the crickets hummed relentlessly. Apart from the insects, it was silent, with no sound of human activity. It was two o' clock in the morning.

He had nearly dozed off again when it happened.

The bloodcurdling screams cut the dark silence. For a few moments, Kharak was in shock, dazed and confused until he realised that they were human screams. What was more frightening was that he had heard women scream, not men. His heart felt battered from pounding against his ribcage.

It wasn't long before footsteps and voices could be heard. Poking his head out of the tent, he saw hurricane lamps being lit and the campfire being stoked up. There was total commotion. Heads with petrified eyes poked out of the other tents. The screams came from the other edge of the campsite. As the campfire blazed, men slowly came out of their tents and walked towards it, some carrying sticks. With unease, Kharak joined them around the fire. As the yellow-red light of the fire fell on their faces, he realised that, like his, their faces reflected fear.

He scanned around to look for Narain and Chand. They were nowhere to be seen.

An agonising ten minutes later, they got to know from a group of men who had just walked from the other side of the campsite that the lion had attacked again a few moments ago. Kharak spotted Narain standing at the back of the group who had just returned.

Not wanting to move away, the group of fifteen men all sat in a circle around the fire, alert, facing outwards, looking beyond the tents with eyes fixed on the dark, eerie distance.

Narain walked over to where Kharak was sitting and sat beside him.

"There were two attacks at the same time tonight, at different parts of the campsite." Narain's voice quivered as he whispered.

Kharak's face had a blank look.

"And you were lucky. One attack happened right in the area where you were going to pitch your tent tonight."

With a sudden cold sweat and a dry mouth, Kharak uttered, "I cannot thank you enough for your advice, Narain. Where is Chand?"

"He is probably huddled under his blanket in his tent," Narain replied. "I'll go and check on him."

59

The next morning was forgiving. With the endless, cloudless steel-blue sky merging into the dusky green horizon, one could easily forget the brutality that had been occurring over the past few weeks. At the back of everyone's minds, the past events lingered, but as every new day dawned, the sunny morning took the edge off the residing fear.

That morning, Ivan stood with one hand holding his cigar and the other pocketed in a pose of authority as he observed the labourers getting ready for the day ahead. His hawk-like eyes spotted Kharak going in and out of what looked like his tent.

"That man had the nerve to disobey me. You pitched your tent where you felt like it," Ivan muttered under his breath as he exhaled quick puffs from his cigar. *I may have sent you away from Catherine, but I haven't forgotten that you nearly took her away from me... You just keep rankling me.* He clenched his teeth together.

Ivan realised that with Colonel Patterson present and responsible for the bridge construction, he could not do what he pleased and get away with it that easily. He would need to be covert.

Later that afternoon, Ivan discovered the hidden path that would allow him to quench his vindictive thirst: Karim Bux.

With his chest puffed out, Karim was grasping and twisting the collar of a fellow coolie in a vice-like grip. Eyes bulging out, he was intimidating. At a distance of a hundred yards, it was not clear to Ivan what the argument was about. With his gaze still fixed on him, Ivan took a couple of steps towards the foreman overseeing the filling of ballast between the rails.

"Who is that man there?"

"Karim Bux, sir." The foreman rolled his head. "Trouble always follows him."

And without any acknowledgment, Ivan walked away, his mind busy.

Despite Kharak's engineering abilities, he discovered to his disappointment that he had been assigned the role of a manual labourer and allocated the task of transporting the rail plates. What he never realised was that it was Ivan who had completed all the paperwork for his application.

As the day drew to a close, he felt frustrated at not being able to apply his skills to the work he was doing. The knowledge he had acquired was more than just towing ballast and rail plates.

That evening, as he sat around the fire, he had never felt this exhausted. Even holding his metal mug of warm milk with blistered hands was a task; his lower back ached and his arms felt sore.

Two hundred yards from him, Ivan sat in his tent with a cigar in his hand. A message had been sent and he awaited the reply. A few moments later, a cough was heard outside his tent.

"He is here, sir," Chand uttered.

"He can walk in," Ivan replied.

Ivan, being the new supervisor, was not aware of the little groups of friendship that had formed within the camp and he had ended up instructing Chand, who had been working nearby, to summon Karim to see him.

The tent opening parted and the burly Karim stepped in. His rough stubble and the scar on his left cheekbone, together with the incident Ivan had observed earlier in the day, confirmed the type of person he was.

Ivan maintained silence to enhance his authority as he studied the man who stood in front of him. He finally spoke.

"I saw you holding a coolie by the scruff of his neck earlier. Why did you do that?"

Karim hesitated uneasily. "He had promised me a few things."

"Like what?"

"Mmm… food rations."

"Food?" Ivan sniggered. He sensed that Karim was lying.

"I had to teach him a lesson… for… err… breaking his promise," he stuttered faintly.

"For that, I could reprimand you severely." Ivan raised his voice for impact.

"All I can say is that I apologise and will ensure it does not happen again," Karim replied with a hint of insincerity.

Ivan stubbed out his cigar in the ashtray that rested on the small and flimsy wooden side table, and fixed his gaze on Karim.

"There is one thing you can do for me." Ivan narrowed his eyes.

"Yes, sir?"

"There is a worker newly arrived from Lahore; his name is Kharak. He needs roughing up a bit."

It was not what Karim had expected Ivan to say. "I don't understand what you would like me to do."

Ivan stood up and took a step towards him and stared directly in his eyes. "He needs to be taught a lesson and I think you can do that for me... otherwise I can have you reprimanded for what you did earlier today."

Karim did not have to think too much about it. "Yes sir. That will be done."

"One more thing before you leave." Ivan narrowed his eyes. "If this discussion ever goes beyond this tent, I will make sure that you end up with the natives in prison in Mombasa. That is a promise."

"That will not happen, sir."

"Good. You can leave now."

60

That night, there was no sign of the lions. Karim had no trouble thinking of ways to carry out Ivan's instructions. His initial hurdle was to find out who Kharak was, which was easily overcome by asking his two henchmen to snoop around and find the latest group of labourers who had arrived. From one of the new recruits, the henchmen obtained information about the section of the railway line where Kharak would be working and even managed to get a good glimpse of him the next afternoon.

Karim narrowed his options to two. The first one involved slaughtering a calf from the natives and sneaking the carcass outside the rear of his tent, with the hope that it would draw the stalking lion.

The other option was to furtively ambush him by drawing him to walk alone from his area of work in the evening and then beat him up.

For a reason that only he knew, Karim decided on the second option, to be carried out the next day in the evening. But there was one thing that neither Ivan nor Karim knew about, and that was Chand.

The previous evening, as Ivan and Karim were talking, Chand had been crouching outside Ivan's tent. It was Kharak's name being mentioned that had made him stop to eavesdrop. That night, not only did fear of the lions keep him awake, but anxiety at what he had heard. The conversation kept playing over and over in his mind. Eventually, he fell asleep three hours before the breaking of dawn, with no clarity in his mind.

In the morning, the Tsavo Bridge and the nearby area were blanketed by an unseasonal low-lying mist that lasted only an hour before the piercing sunlight melted it away. Narain was not very far from where the construction of the bridge was ongoing, measuring the rocks in preparation for chipping into the correct sizes. After looking around, Chand spotted him and walked down the slope of the riverbank towards him.

The conversation took a full ten minutes and, throughout, work became secondary as Chand confided in him about the conversation he had overheard the previous night in Ivan's tent.

"Where is Kharak?" Narain asked with a concerned look.

"Working on the other side of the river, lugging ballast."

"No wonder Ivan has put him to do this labour-intensive work, despite him being an engineer. He obviously hates him. But why?" Narain shrugged his shoulders.

There was a brief silence.

"You need to go and speak to him and tell him to be careful. Also, tell our close mates working on that side to look after him… especially when work ends." Narain paused. "I will speak with Colonel Patterson."

After the conversation, Chand felt a bit better, with some clarity about what he had to do.

The walk to where Kharak was working was a mile along the dusty, rust-red track that ran along the railway line. In the distance, Chand saw him shovelling ballast between the tracks. Not wanting to make it obvious to anyone observing that he had come to meet Kharak, Chand stopped to talk with his and Narain's friends as he slowly edged his way towards Kharak. Eventually, he grabbed a shovel that was lying a few feet away and joined him in shovelling the ballast. Sweating profusely and out of breath, Kharak did not say a word. Chand kept looking over his shoulder for Karim's stooges. He couldn't see any of them.

"Kharak, we want you to be careful here while you work."

Kharak stopped shovelling and gazed up towards Chand, resting his hands on his shovel. "What do you mean?"

"We have come to know that there are people here who have been instructed to cause harm to you." Chand lowered his voice.

"What?"

It took Chand a few minutes to tell him about the conversation he had overhead, and what he and Narain were planning to ensure that the plan failed. Kharak stood still with unease, his stare fixed on Chand, not knowing what to say.

"Why does Ivan hate you?"

Kharak took a deep breath. "It's too long a story to explain to you now, but I will tell you this evening." He broke his eye contact.

"I'll wait."

They both carried on shovelling in silence.

In that moment, Kharak felt lonely and missed Catherine even more. He wanted to be in Lahore with her, present around her, feeling her fragrant hair running through his fingertips.

The afternoon heat diminished and the light faded as evening approached. Chand had not left Kharak's side, working near him, keeping a watchful eye.

Luckily, nothing happened that evening on the way back from his work site. Chand and a few of his close friends accompanied Kharak to his tent. They knew that, once there, he would be safe as their tents were close by.

As darkness fell, everyone's fear resurfaced. The terror at the thought of being the next victim of the lions was real. Bonfires were lit at various points within the campsite in the hope of scaring them away.

After the evening meal, a slim, bearded man wearing an ivory-coloured turban sat next to Narain on the low wooden bench near the firepit. He picked his mug of milk, turned his head and whispered to him.

"Karim and his stooges are planning to lay a trap for Kharak after the midday break tomorrow. One of them will ask him to accompany him to collect some stones from the quarry and along the path, he will be set upon."

"How sure are you?"

"I'm certain. I heard their plan."

Narain had known Jammu for a while as he had worked under his supervision at the bridge. He was confident that he could be trusted.

"Thank you for your information."

"It's time that Karim is put away for good. He is a bully and a menace to everyone," Jammu said.

Narain nodded in agreement. He stood up, patted Jammu's shoulder and walked in the direction of Chand and Kharak. The mood all around was solemn as the coolies sat in little groups, fearful of going into their tents. Chand and Kharak were sitting alone on a canvas mat around another firepit when Narain joined them.

"My friend, it seems you have made enemies as fast as I can say your name." Narain smiled at Kharak, trying to lighten the mood as he sat beside him.

Kharak forced a weary smile.

"Now, you need to tell us what is going on and why; we have the whole evening to listen." Narain placed his hand on Kharak's shoulder.

Kharak took a deep breath and started to share his story. He began at Lahore Station the day Catherine had nearly tripped over, the day he had first met her and their paths had crossed. It had started as an ordinary day and never had he thought it would lead him to this. That day was vivid in his mind, unforgettable.

61

The group sat astounded as Kharak disclosed the events that had brought him here. He told them about Catherine. In silence, they looked at him, staring without purpose at the flickering flames. They got a tiny sense of his predicament.

Narain put his arm around his shoulder. "That's terrible, my friend… We are all together here, all of us."

Kharak shifted his gaze from the flames. "Thank you."

Narain got up. "I need to see Patterson Sahib. There are things that need sorting."

"Really? Are things that bad?" A confused Kharak looked up.

It was then that Narain and Chand revealed to him what Karim was planning for the next day.

"I'll sort him out, whoever he is." Anger was surfacing in Kharak's voice.

"It will be fine…" Narain tapped his shoulder. "We have

to be smart. Patterson Sahib is going to help us deal with this. Karim has tried the same with him previously, so the chances of a severe punishment are great."

Kharak took a few deep breaths to calm his nerves. Narain walked away towards Patterson's tent.

That night, Kharak did not sleep. Not knowing how the next day would unravel kept his mind galloping and so did the thought of ghostly, piercing lion eyes peering from the dark wilderness. Outside, there were no signs of the prowlers, only a grazing herd of harmless gazelles.

The morning routine was the same but the lack of sleep made Kharak feel fatigued. He caught up with Narain and Chand, who were waiting for him at breakfast. Beneath the cloudless sky, they briefed him on what to expect during the day and what to do.

As the morning progressed, Kharak was constantly looking over his shoulders at the coolies working nearby. It all seemed normal, just like the previous days.

At the other end of the camp, Patterson picked up his rifle and, together with Narain and two other stocky labourers, walked off into the bush without attracting any unwanted attention. They were heading off towards the quarry using a longer, untrodden path, ready to set up an ambush.

With the heat intensifying, midday was not far off. Sweat dripping from his forehead, due both to the heat and apprehension regarding the approaching break, Kharak straightened to stretch his back, which was cramping with the monotony of shovelling.

The metal rod striking the metal ring was a welcome relief to most as it was the signal of their midday break. A hundred yards back, under the tall acacia tree, was the spot where the men ate their lunch every day. Kharak dropped his shovel and was about to walk across, when he heard his name being called. He turned and saw a coolie waving a sheet of paper, hastily walking towards him. Kharak had seen him around at the site.

"Kharak," the man called as he approached him. "Freeman Sahib has directed you to go and ensure that the stones to be delivered from the quarry are properly loaded into the rail carts."

"I've never done that before." Kharak played along, realising that the plot Narain had warned him about was being played out.

"Here, this is the note from him."

Kharak read the note.

"Fine, let's go."

As planned, Kharak was going to take his time walking to the quarry. He wanted to make sure that everyone was in place. To the dismay of Karim's henchman, Kharak walked to the acacia tree, washed his hands, then grabbed a chapatti before joining the man in his walk towards the path that led to the quarry. No one saw a tiny man sneaking off towards the quarry the moment Kharak was approached.

The path towards the quarry was undulating, with boulders on one side and a steep slope rising above the Tsavo River on the other. Dwarf acacia trees sprouted amongst the tall blades of the savannah grass. Alone, this would be a very intimidating place, especially for Kharak, knowing that three other men were walking a few steps behind him, of whom one was Karim. A mile from the railway line, the path widened to a clearing.

"Stop here for a minute," Karim instructed.

After a quick glance around, two of his henchmen slowly surrounded Kharak. Karim walked towards him, brushing his palm through his black hair.

"Empty your pockets."

"I don't have anything in my pockets," Kharak replied. The two men then grabbed his arms in a lock behind his back. As he struggled, pain shot across his shoulder blades. It was immobilising and he gave up fighting. He had to wait.

Karim walked up to him, squaring his face with Kharak's, and placed his hand on Kharak's trouser pocket.

"What's this?"

"Nothing." Kharak was getting agitated.

Karim was hoping it was coins hidden away in a handkerchief. This was what most people did. He forced his hand into the pocket and pulled out Catherine's white glove.

"What's this?" He sniggered. "Why do you carry this rubbish?"

"None of your business," Kharak snarled back. "Just leave that."

"Perhaps I should throw it down the ravine."

"Don't you dare..." Kharak kicked out at Karim's shins.

Karim's reply was sudden and swift. A punch to Kharak's solar plexus took the wind out of his lungs, causing him to slump to his knees, clutching his stomach.

A gunshot cut through the silence in the wilderness. Startled spotted cuckoos flew off from the branches of the trees. The echo of the shot resonated around the shallow quarry. Faces emerged from behind the boulders.

Patterson stood up from where he was lying in the tall grass a few yards up the path. Six men emerged and surrounded the open space.

"Karim, I warned you that the British sepoys would take care of you, but you have not listened." The colonel strode towards him, holding his rifle. "This time, I will have to lock you up until they arrive to take you away to Mombasa. I know and I've seen it all with my own eyes, not once, but twice. You deserve to be locked up."

Karim stood frozen with panic, knowing that he had been caught out. The thought of being transferred to Mombasa and locked in a rat-infested cell amongst the African prisoners was hellish. Kharak, meanwhile, staggered upright and whisked the glove back from Karim's hand.

Karim's henchmen already had their arms raised in surrender and were blaming him for forcing them to do what they had done. The tables had turned against Karim; the plan had backfired with his very own stooges now speaking out against him.

"It was Freeman Sahib who told me to do it!" Karim tried to deflect the conversation as he took a few steps back.

"I am aware of all that has happened, so don't try to take advantage of me again—"

Before Patterson could finish his sentence, Karim made a huge leap from where he was standing near the edge of the path down the slope, losing his balance in the process and rolling down, kicking up red dust. He reached the bottom of the ravine and was seen running off into the wilderness.

"Should we follow him, Sahib?" one of Patterson's men asked.

"No, let him run. The middle of nowhere is a perilous place to run to."

They all fixed their eyes on Karim, as they watched him disappear.

It was Kharak who spoke first. "Thank you all for helping me." He squeezed Catherine's glove in his hand.

Karim was never seen again. What became of him remained a mystery. With no sign of him, his tent was eventually pulled down and his belongings burnt in the pit. To be running around in wild Tsavo was sheer madness, especially with the roaming 'devils' not caught. No one saw him at the campsite or the railway tracks, and it became a common belief that he had not made it.

Knowing what had happened, Patterson relocated Kharak to work at the bridge as his technical knowledge and ability to speak English, Hindi and Punjabi were desperately needed there. The construction of the bridge was already behind schedule.

Karim's henchmen were never the cause of trouble at the camp again. The only trouble, after two days of peace, was another night-time attack by the lions. This time, with sheer audacity, they attacked and carried off not one, but two coolies. Their boldness seemed to have kept on growing and this was starting to affect the morale of the coolies.

Ivan managed to keep a low profile for only two days before his vindictive nature boiled over again. It was the arrival of the train from Mombasa on Friday that stunned him, shaking his fickle sanity again.

62

Mombasa

Catherine's heart had never felt this way before; it fluttered with anticipation and anxiety. The warm, salty morning air caressed her face as she stood on the wooden veranda outside the port master's office in Mombasa, overlooking the turquoise waters of the Indian Ocean. On this Friday morning, she had finally made it to Mombasa.

She looked around, yearning to see Kharak's face. She knew he wouldn't be lingering at the port, but she couldn't help but glance around for him – to no avail. After the three weeks at sea, it was a relief to be on land, and she was even gladder that Lal was there to support her.

From the swaying palm trees with their rustling, reedy leaves emanated the whispering and soothing sound of the sea breeze.

The completion of her paperwork was easier than she had anticipated. As planned with Lal during the voyage, she stated that she had come to visit Ivan Freeman on his invitation and that he was her very close friend, who was posted briefly in Tsavo. She also pointed to Lal, stating that he was hired and given the duty by Ivan to accompany her along the journey.

Their paperwork was promptly stamped and tickets to Voi issued by a chubby man with a receding hairline, who, with a disquieted look, said, "Beware of the lions!"

"I beg your pardon?" Catherine asked.

"John O'Hara was killed by a lion a few months back in March, only twelve miles from Voi. His wife and two little children were lucky to survive the night in the tent." He paused as a mark of respect. "And now, news is that lions are terrorising the camp in Tsavo." He lowered his voice and furrowed his eyebrows.

"Really?" she asked, her voice full of concern, thinking immediately of Kharak.

"John is buried in the cemetery here in Voi."

Not wanting to talk any more about this, Catherine thanked the man and walked out of the room and towards the waiting area.

With calmer seas over the past few days around the horn of East Africa, their ship had docked ahead of schedule and this eliminated another hurdle of having to find a place to sleep as they would if they had arrived later in the evening as scheduled. Now, all that remained of their journey was a two-hour wait at the railway station for the UR35 train to Voi.

TSAVO

Earlier that morning, dawn had not yet broken across the eastern sky when Kharak's eyes flickered open earlier than his normal waking time. Apart from the early-morning starlings tweeting, silence still pervaded the camp.

As he lay, his eyes adjusted to the lack of light and his mind wandered back to that rainy day in Lahore, seated in the rickshaw under the pouring rain, with Catherine resting her head on his chest. *Ever since, she has been my last thought before I go to sleep and my first thought upon waking,* he thought. *Missing her is painful, a beautiful kind of pain...*

He closed his eyes.

MOMBASA

Catherine was aware that from here on, the train journey to Tsavo would be in the carriage with the labourers working on the railway line. This did not seem to bother her.

There were a few curious colonial eyes staring at her as she waited in the tiny waiting room while Lal stood outside. Those two hours seemed the longest for her, with eyes darting left and right in expectation. Eventually, the whistling of the steam engine cut through her tortuous wait as it pulled slowly into the platform.

It wasn't long before Lal had the luggage in the carriage and helped her in as she settled by the window. Another half hour dragged before the train started its slow and noisy departure from Mombasa Station.

TSAVO

At this very moment, over a hundred miles of wild bushland lay between Catherine and Kharak.

The support pillars had risen from the riverbed in readiness for the steel girders that were to be placed across the Tsavo River. Wooden scaffolding wrapped the pillars and a flimsy pathway had been constructed over and across, spanning the width of the river.

Kharak stood on this wooden pathway and began to examine the spacing where the girders were to be placed over the coming days. On either side of the makeshift bridge, the glaring, low-lying morning sun reflected off the shining railway tracks. Since being transferred by Patterson to work at the bridge, he felt appreciated.

Voi, British East Africa

With eager eyes, Catherine saw the train roll past the causeway with views of green mangrove trees at the edge of the ocean. The gentle uphill track went through the coconut trees and past the Rabai Hills before the landscape flattened into an open, grassy savannah plain. And that was when she saw her first glimpse of the teeming wildlife. Herds of zebras grazed amongst the giraffes that rose high above them. As Voi Station approached, she was mesmerised by the size of the elephants, with their coating of terracotta-red dust, flapping ears and huge tusks, standing not very far from the railway line.

A few minutes later, the train slowed as it approached the dusty station. Catherine looked out at the tiny platform with its corrugated iron shed. Painted on the wall was the name *Voi Station*. She got a bit nervous getting off the train, thinking about what the balding man at Mombasa Station had said about the lions.

It wasn't long before they were directed to the single dusty carriage that stood stationary at the far end of the station. With Lal helping her carry the luggage and with an ungainly step, she boarded the carriage. Unlike the other carriages, this one had basic wooden benches. As she was the memsahib, the coolies allowed her to take up one whole bench for herself. Before she sat, one of the labourers used his sleeve to wipe the bench clean of the infamous red dust as Lal placed her luggage on the side.

She felt like an outsider; not only the only woman, but also a white British woman in the middle of nowhere in wild East Africa. There was only one thing that spurred her on: her desire to reunite with Kharak.

The rattling carriage started to move.

With the midday break approaching within the hour, Kharak had only measured and marked a quarter of the spacing on the bridge, despite having five other coolies helping him. Narain was busy with the stonework on the pillars below, together with fourteen other workers. Chand was posted a few hundred yards away, to add another wooden ladder to the tall structure that held the water tank next to the tiny tin-roofed office that was Tsavo Station.

Chand was too engrossed in his work to notice the resident stationmaster walking out with his flag. The supply train with its single seating carriage whistled in the distance as it approached Tsavo, a cloud of steam accompanying it. This did catch his attention.

The midday break was due soon and Kharak was in two minds as to whether to complete what he was doing now and to go for a break later or not. He chose to delay his break.

The commotion escalated rapidly in the normally quiet and empty station as twenty-seven newly arrived workers got out of the carriage. Catherine remained inside, her heart racing as she gazed out through the horizontal bars of the window. She and Lal were the last ones left in the carriage.

"Time to get off. We have reached Tsavo." Lal lifted the luggage and tilted his head sideways.

Nervously, Catherine slowly stood up and followed him out.

Chand, who was fifteen feet up on the water tower, was observing the new arrivals when he spotted a white British woman stepping off the carriage and onto the dusty planks of the station to stand with the rest of the workers. This was very odd to him and his curiosity led him to climb down to find out more.

The coolies were being directed where to go by the flag-bearing stationmaster. Lal approached him and asked in Hindi whether he knew where a man named Kharak was working.

Rolling his head, the man replied, "They are all working there." He pointed.

Chand, who by now was only a few feet away, widened his eyes when he overheard Kharak's name. He took a few steps forward.

"I know him," he stated proudly. "He works at the bridge not very far from here."

Catherine felt solace in what she had heard. *He is here.* Her pulse quickened.

"Where?" Lal asked.

"You'd better follow me. I will take you to the campsite."

Seeing Lal fumble with the luggage, Chand decided to help him. He picked up one of the bags and, for the first time, glanced directly at Catherine.

"You must be Catherine, memsahib?" He bowed.

This surprised her. Here she was in Africa, in the middle of nowhere, and yet here was this stranger who knew her name. She was astonished.

Seeing the surprise on her face, Chand smiled. "Kharak has told me all about you and, believe me, he will be shocked to see you, memsahib." He started walking towards the camp.

"How is he?" she asked with a coy smile.

He paused and turned around. "I think he misses everyone... especially you. I sense this in his silence, and in the poetry he reads and recites around the fire in the evenings."

"Poetry?" Catherine asked. "What's this, Lal? You never said that he has a new pastime."

"I just forgot about it," Lal said, rather amused.

Eager to know more about the thoughts that occupied Kharak's mind here, she asked Chand, with a twinkle in her eye, "I would like to hear some of it. Could you recite something, please?"

Chand hesitated as he gathered his thoughts. He was enjoying being in the limelight. He then spoke out loud.

"Hidden from all, I will speak to you without words, for only you will hear my story, even though I will say it in the middle of the crowds."

Catherine repeated the words under her breath. She wanted to remember them and, for a moment, in silence, she felt their deeper, underlying meaning. She took a deep breath and applauded. "That's wonderful."

Although it was a short walk of a few hundred yards, it was an arduous path in the overhead sun, with the stumpy acacia trees and the golden, three-foot-tall savannah grass on either side. Halfway along the path, there was a natural oval-shaped clearing where the surface was chalky and sandy. A secondary, less-trodden path began. There were weathered boulders on the western side that rose above the grass. Catherine stopped to admire the area.

"It's not safe to wait here unnecessarily. This is a wild place."

Without questioning further, they followed as Chand led them straight along the main dusty path.

Moments later, the sounds of activity grew louder and clearer as they approached the campsite. The workers who had travelled with them that morning were a hundred yards further ahead and were directed to a registration tent.

As they gingerly approached the group who were ahead of them, there were a few coolies who were busy with routine chores around the campsite and they all stared at Catherine. She did feel a bit uneasy.

"Just wait here for a minute," Chand directed as he walked over to two coolies who were stacking firewood next to the tent.

She scanned the area around her and could see the tents pitched orderly around the central firepit. The constant buzzing of insects that came from the bush in the middle of the day astounded her. Further away, she could see the outlines of men seated on the ground, busy having their lunch. She looked at her boots and they were covered with a layer of the infamous red dust. It was everywhere.

Chand wasn't gone long before he walked back and interrupted her thoughts, saying, "Kharak is at the bridge. I'll go and call him—"

"No," Catherine interrupted hastily. "I would like to surprise him." She took a deep breath. "Where is the bridge?"

63

Chand pointed in the opposite direction. "There… if you look, you can see the wooden scaffolding."

Catherine cupped her hand over her forehead, brushing her curls away, and squinted in the direction he was indicating. She could make out the outline of a single man kneeling and facing in the opposite direction. Despite the convectional haze above the ground in the distance, and without taking a second look, unmistakably, she recognised Kharak.

Her heart started racing, her body leant forward and her feet took the first step towards the bridge. Her fingers let go of her bag. It landed on the red dust of Tsavo. Her first step became two, then three and, within moments, she was rushing towards the bridge.

Lal and Chand stood still and watched her go, unable to imagine how she felt.

Kharak had a few measurements to carry out before he could join the rest for his lunch break. Two stones sat on either side of the paper on which he had written his measurements, preventing it from flying away in the breeze. The edges flapped and rose with the rising wind. He was too engrossed to have noticed anyone approaching. In Tsavo, alertness was necessary, but on this occasion, it didn't matter. He never saw Catherine approach the wooden support bridge where he was kneeling, deep in concentration, facing the opposite direction.

It was him. The face she adored, the person she had taken this voyage for, the reason why, at this very moment, her heart fluttered with eagerness all of its own accord. She was a few feet away from him now.

There was a momentary loss of concentration as Kharak's mind wandered away as he stared blankly at the sheet of paper. He felt a sudden, warm flush across his face. A presence behind him urged Kharak to turn around.

Catherine stood a few feet away and he slowly stood up. He blinked twice before his eyes widened and his jaw dropped. He stood, speechless.

It was Catherine who broke the beguiling silence that encapsulated that moment over the waters of the Tsavo River, which flowed beneath them.

"Hello, Kharak."

Kharak stared at her, not believing what he saw. *Am I dreaming?*

The breeze blew her wavy hair across her enchanting face with its mesmerising smile as she spoke. "I have missed you."

He let go of the pencil he was holding and took a step towards her, still unsure whether his eyes were deceiving him. At the same time, she darted towards him on the wooden support bridge. He took steps towards her. An instinctive urge led them both to open their arms as they got closer. The tight embrace that followed soothed both of them, their hearts trembling together. Catherine felt her tears of joy glide down her rosy cheeks, while the corners of Kharak's eyes moistened as he felt her soft hair on his cheek.

Still holding the embrace, they leaned back and gazed into the depths of each other's eyes.

Kharak finally spoke. "Ever since the day we stood in the rain in Lahore, you have been my last thought before I sleep and my first thought when I wake."

Catherine inched her face closer to his and their lips locked. For the next few moments, their eyes were closed. Nothing else mattered.

Eventually, Kharak took her hand, their fingers intertwined, and led her away from the bridge towards the campsite.

"I'm astounded! How did you make it here?" He looked in her laughing jade eyes.

"Lal helped me accomplish my plan. He is here, just as he intended." She smiled.

"How did your parents allow you to travel by yourself?"

She paused. "I didn't tell them."

"You ran away?"

"Yes, I did."

He raised his eyebrows and squeezed her hand. "I can't believe that you are here."

"I had to… I could not restrain my feelings for you. I tried, but failed, and each day that has gone by since I last saw you, that fateful afternoon, there has been an emptiness that was made worse by the beautiful, touching note you left for me. I then decided, after reading it, that I had to meet you again. And here I am."

"You didn't have to follow me," he stated hesitantly.

"Right now, here, you are my everything," she said, gazing softly into his eyes before resting her shoulder on his upper arm as they ambled along the gently ascending path beside the rocky outcrop beyond the bridge.

In these moments of blissful silence as they walked, the responsibility he now had for Catherine dawned upon Kharak. Amongst the coolies, and the wilderness with its harsh living conditions, he had to look after her. He put his arm around her and held her closely.

Two hundred yards away, a pair of furious eyes observed the pair. For clarity, Ivan got his binoculars out to confirm what he was seeing. His whole body trembled with uncontrollable anger and a rising intensity, which led him to stagger into his tent.

The first thing he caught sight of was the hurricane lamp on his table, which he grabbed and smashed on the floor. His arms swept across the table, sending his books and papers fluttering across the tent. His kick sent the chair flying to the other end of the tent. He stood, bowed, with his hands clutching his head. He let out a howling, wrath-filled scream.

64

In the distance, Kharak saw Lal, with his broad smile, waving. As they approached the workers, Catherine and Kharak let go of each other's hands. The midday break was almost over and curiosity led some of the coolies to stare at them.

Lal greeted Kharak with smiles and a manly hug.

"You made it, brother." Kharak tapped his shoulder. "And thank you."

"For what?"

"For looking after Catherine along the way."

"It was her great plan to do this. Even I was sceptical about it, but she pulled it off... for you."

Catherine smiled coyly.

Chand stood still, watching in awe all that was going on around him and pleased to be part of it, although he knew it was a small part.

With the gathering getting larger, the curious coolies

were intrigued not only by seeing a British woman there in the wilderness, but noting that she was a very close 'friend' of their Sikh colleague. Muttering amongst them could be clearly observed.

The wind had picked up, swirling the red dust through the dwarf acacia bushes. From his tent, Patterson noticed that the number of workers had increased around the centre of the camp. This was uncommon at this time of the day and he decided to inspect the situation. He put on his beige hat, picked up his favourite rifle and strode out of his tent.

From the corner of his eye, it was Kharak who first spotted Patterson strutting towards them with his rifle. The joy of being with the person whose feelings for him matched his for her became tinged with worry at the sight. It triggered thoughts of the prowling lions, sending a wave of nervousness through his stomach. *Damn.*

Patterson soon reached the group with a bemused look.

"Good afternoon, young lady." He took off his hat.

"Good afternoon. I'm Catherine."

"I am mighty surprised. What brings you here to this desolate place?"

There followed a cramped silence.

Catherine plucked up her courage. "I came to meet Kharak." She clasped her hands together in front of her.

"Ah… the same Catherine you adore?" Patterson raised his brow as he looked at Kharak, waiting for a response.

"Yes, sir, she is *the* Catherine." A stunned Kharak furrowed his brow. *How did he know?*

Patterson paused and turned to face the other coolies. "Everyone, back to work. There is nothing to look at. Quickly!" He gestured with his hands.

Narain, who had just joined the group, promptly translated

his direction. Immediately, the men dispersed, still chatting away.

"You two." Patterson pointed at Catherine and Kharak. "I want to speak to both of you in my tent, now." He turned around and walked away.

Narain saw Catherine and realised that she was the one whom Kharak had mentioned before. He walked closer and whispered into his ear.

"She is worth fighting for. In her eyes, I see the joy of your presence." He grinned as he patted Kharak's shoulder. "Go and see Colonel Patterson. I told him about the two of you, so don't worry too much."

The afternoon sun baked the ground hot and there was an arid smell of dust hanging in the air as they strolled apprehensively towards Patterson's tent.

His large tent had an old wooden reading table with an oil lamp on one end and layers of papers and books on the other. In the centre was a pipe holder and next to it were two pencils, a pot of ink and a pen arranged in an orderly manner. Patterson sat on the wood-framed foldable canvas armchair, twiddling a foot rule in his hand.

Kharak let Catherine enter the tent first. Patterson stood up and pulled up another canvas chair and, following custom, asked her to sit.

"Now, can someone tell me what is happening here?" Patterson relaxed back in his chair.

Kharak and Catherine looked at each other in unison.

What followed over the next twenty minutes laid bare to Patterson the events of the past few weeks, right from the first day Catherine had arrived at Lahore Station up to her undisclosed and difficult trip to Tsavo. He instantly admired Kharak's sacrifice and her valour. *This is what love makes you do*, Patterson thought as he stood up and placed his pipe in his mouth, which was unusual for him at this time of day – usually he only smoked in the evenings.

Catherine, for the first time, recognised how naive she had been, not realising that, all along, Ivan had been the reason why Kharak was forcefully sent away from her, and how he had manipulated her father's disdain for Kharak. Now, she did not know whom she loathed the most, her father or Ivan.

She felt an urge to embrace Kharak at this moment. Though they were seated close together, she still couldn't, but she lifted her dainty fingers and touched his in devotion.

Patterson's eyes gazed up in contemplation and, after thinking deeply, he spoke. "We need to organise a suitable place for the lady to sleep... not a tent. As you already know, the danger from the lions is real. I want you and Narain to partition off and construct a makeshift cabin in that old carriage that lies on the disused side of the railway track."

"Yes, sir." Kharak nodded.

"Secondly," he paused, "the next work carriage back to Voi is on Monday morning and Catherine will have to take that back to Mombasa, from where she will return to Lahore."

Catherine's face crumpled with disappointment.

"But..." Kharak couldn't finish his sentence.

"I will sign you off with an official letter stating that your short work here has been accomplished successfully and that you will be escorting Catherine safely on her journey back to Lahore on behalf of the British East Africa Company. However reluctant I may feel about it, she needs to get back safely."

Kharak's jaw dropped, while Catherine's eyes widened.

"And that should be sufficient for you to go back to working with the Indian Railways."

There was an eruption of silent joy within Kharak's chest; it felt like a huge, heavy burden that had been suffocating him had finally been lifted off.

"I'm indebted to you, sir," he stammered with inner jubilation.

Patterson silently inhaled a puff from his pipe. This was the last complication he needed right now. The construction of the bridge was behind schedule and the pressure was mounting; the lions were terrorising the area, affecting morale; and now this cross-continental romance was an unnecessary inconvenience.

Catherine, who had listened quietly, finally spoke, "Your kindness is much appreciated, Colonel Patterson." She took a breath before adding, "What about Ivan?"

Patterson removed the pipe from his mouth, stood up and folded his free hand behind his back. "You needn't worry. I will keep an eye on him... and it's only a couple of days and then you will be gone."

"I misjudged him, despite all the hints he was giving."

"Unfortunately, Catherine, I am not able to comment on that. But it is important to me that you return safely to your family." He paused and stared at Kharak. "Let her know about the dangers of wandering out here in Tsavo... I mean, the lions."

"I will, sir."

Catherine looked up at Kharak with a concerned expression.

"You may leave now, as you have a busy afternoon ahead preparing the cabin for this young lady."

And with that, their conversation came to a close. Having thought the worst before entering the tent, they were both elated with the colonel's decision. They were going back to Lahore together and that was what mattered. Life was finally turning around. It felt beautiful.

65

It did not take long for Lal to get his papers in order, together with a designated space for pitching his tent. By now, Chand and Lal had forged the beginnings of a good friendship, with Kharak as their shared bond.

Lal, Kharak and Catherine sat together on wooden stools to have their late lunch under the restful shade of a tall acacia tree. Despite the exhaustion of her long journey, Catherine felt invigorated as she sat beside Kharak, often gazing into his hazel eyes. He still could not believe that she was here with him.

Not very far away, Kharak spotted Narain, whom he had sent for through Chand. They both joined them even though they had already had their break. They all felt a common sense of belonging.

Two hundred yards further away towards the left, dust was rising. Six coolies and three African natives were seen stacking the grey, thorny acacia branches five feet high. The alignment meandered and almost represented a boundary.

"That's something new, Narain. What are they up to?" Kharak asked.

"They are building a native fence called a boma. The Africans use them to protect their cattle from wildlife and the colonel has ordered them to build one to protect the camp from those lions."

"Those lions?" Catherine furrowed her eyebrows. "What do you mean by *those* lions?"

Kharak and Narain narrated to Lal and Catherine the happenings at the campsite over the past few weeks, and how the marauding lions had been terrorising the area and had caused fatalities. It was when Ungan's death was mentioned that Chand rolled his eyes and got visibly upset as he was assailed by flashbacks to that fateful morning.

Feeling perturbed, the fear that now hung in Catherine's mind clouded her earlier thoughts of the wild beauty of Tsavo. She nudged herself closer to Kharak.

"That is why you will sleep in the old carriage and not in a tent. It's too dangerous," Kharak said.

"Saying that, we'd better go pick up the wood and get working on the cabin for memsahib. We don't have a lot of time." Narain straightened his shirt as he got up.

"I shall come with you to the carriage," she stated as she pushed her curls behind her ear.

"Perhaps you could rest…"

"I want to be with you. That's why I'm here." She lowered her voice.

Lal winked at Kharak. "I think she is right," he added.

The lonely carriage had been left behind at Tsavo when the train had encountered some issues and was unable to pull all of the carriages. One of them had to be unhitched and, ever since, it had stood still on the service rails that emerged very close to the campsite.

Inside, Kharak and Narain wrenched out the wooden benches from half of the carriage in no time, creating enough space. A wooden partition that bisected the carriage was constructed, which ended up becoming one of the walls of Catherine's cabin.

Despite the sawdust being kicked up and the hammering of nails, Catherine sat on a Masai stool in one corner of the carriage, observing Kharak. In a peculiar sort of way, she felt as though he was building her home, a place of refuge in this otherworldly place. She watched intently as beads of sweat formed between the freckles of sawdust on his forearms.

The wooden benches were rearranged side by side and fixed together to form the base of her bed, upon which two blankets, together with pillows provided by Patterson, would provide downy bedding. After sweeping and mopping the floor of the carriage, two strips of rope were attached spanning the length of each of the two opposing windows, on which muslin sheets were hung as curtains. An oil lamp was positioned on the stool, which was placed by the bed. The carriage door had a working latch on the inside that would secure it.

Catherine stood up, walked towards Kharak and embraced him. "Thank you."

He felt his cheek against hers. She didn't care about his sweaty face, the sawdust or that she would get dust on her. It did not matter. She just wanted to hug him and not let go. But with Narain present, the embrace was short.

"Now, we need to sort out your washing space." Kharak smiled.

"Really?" Catherine giggled.

Standing at the corner near the carriage door, they both observed the space in front of them. It looked liveable, cosy and secure. Narain had already stepped out, feeling awkward being present with them.

Outside, they walked around the carriage to the other

side that faced the bush. There, they constructed a three-sided wooden frame six feet high, onto which sheets of old canvas were nailed, forming an enclosure that would be used as a washing space.

Looking rather bemused, Catherine said sheepishly, "How would I use this as a bath area?"

"With a bucket and an empty tin." Kharak grinned. "Hot water would be brought to you in a metal bucket… like that one." He pointed. "It would probably be me who would bring it to you."

He could not help but wink at her. Catherine responded with a shy smile.

"Then you would use a metal tin like this and wash yourself." Kharak showed her.

"That's surely new to me, however, I shall succeed," she laughed.

The sun had started its descent towards the horizon, causing a change in the shade of light, as early evening approached. The slate-grey branches of the acacia bushes took on an orange tinge. It wasn't long after Kharak had helped Catherine with her luggage into the carriage. While there was still light, he prepared some hot water over the fire and brought it to her so she could wash and feel relaxed.

On the other side of the camp, with light coming through the opening of his tent, Ivan was seated in his chair with the butt of his rifle in his hand.

His eyes wide, he was furiously cleaning the barrel of his rifle. He could not get the image of Catherine and Kharak out of his head.

66

Embers glowed as the fire crackled in the African evening. Most of the birds were silent, nestled away, but as usual, the crickets were busy with their nightly calling and the odd hooting of the Verreaux Eagle owl was heard.

The evening meal of potatoes and lentil soup was simple, but Catherine still relished it. Having freshened up, albeit a little awkwardly, her body felt relaxed with the need of rest, but her mind was excited and unable to unwind.

Seated as a small, close-knit group around the fire, the topic of conversation was their home in Punjab and what they missed about it. Even she could relate to their memories of the place and the people there, as she herself had made some wonderful memories in Lahore. Beyond them, dots of light from the oil lamps outside the coolies' tents glowed as darkness overcame the sky's pale tint of orange.

As fatigue gradually overwhelmed Catherine, she started to

lean towards Kharak until she rested her head on his shoulder. She shut her tired but happy eyes. He turned his head and watched the fire casting light upon her contented, seraphic face. He had never seen anything as beautiful as her. Not wanting to disturb her, he didn't move his shoulder at all.

It was half an hour later when she opened her eyes, feeling groggy. Her head still rested on his shoulder.

"Sorry, I fell asleep."

"I think you need to retire to your new cabin for the night. It's been a hectic day for you."

Catherine slowly lifted her head, arched her back and stood up. "Please excuse me."

"I'll walk you… remember, this is Tsavo." Kharak stood up.

Lal nodded at him silently.

"Goodnight, my friends. Thank you for a warm welcome and a lovely day, and I'm sorry that I cannot provide you with company," she said with droopy eyes.

The rest of them sat and watched as Kharak led her along the meandering hundred yards towards the carriage, their path lit dimly by the hurricane lamp in his hand. Hanging from his belt was a sheathed machete. It was a dangerous time in Tsavo.

Kharak was glad that Patterson had come up with the idea of using the carriage as Catherine's personal lodgings. *She will be safe there*, he thought as they reached it.

He opened the door for her. She turned around and, with dreamy eyes, kissed him on his lips and hugged him.

"Goodnight, Kharak."

"Goodnight. Don't forget to lock the door…" He paused. "Ah, I forgot." He fumbled in his pocket and retrieved a whistle. "Take this whistle and if you need any help whatsoever during the night, blow it. I'm here for you."

"I know it, Kharak. You don't need to say it… I feel it." She squeezed him tightly.

"See you in the morning."

And with that, she grabbed the railings and stepped into the carriage. He waited for the door to shut and did not move until he heard the latch clicking. He stood in silence, staring without blinking at the dusty door for a couple of minutes.

He placed his palm on the door and, under his breath uttered, "I love you."

He then turned around and walked back to his mates. With the perils that had lingered in Tsavo over the past few weeks due to the man-eating lions, it was not long before everyone was in their tents, hoping that another night would pass without incident. Every night, attempts had been made to secure the flimsy openings of their tents with rope fastenings. Also, the fire was left to burn all night, surrounded by thick logs, in the hope that it would scare any animals away. Some coolies slept with wooden sticks by their sides for protection.

As Kharak's was a larger tent, Lal shared it. After chatting for a few minutes, Kharak got no response from Lal. On raising his head, he heard subtle snores. Tiredness from the journey and the heat had worn him out. Kharak rested his head back on his pillow and stared at the canvas ceiling of his tent. His mind wandered to Catherine, with only an annoying mosquito to interrupt his thoughts. It took him over an hour of tossing and turning before he finally dozed off.

At two o' clock in the morning, in the tent twenty yards opposite, Chand and Narain were fast asleep. All was quiet in the still, cloudless night; even the earlier breeze had died down, with only the occasional brown bat flying over the tents. Dull, silvery light from the half-moon pervaded Tsavo. The firepit was still burning.

From the north-west side of the camp, a shadowy outline moved stealthily in the direction of the tents with emotionless eyes.

It happened again. Kharak was in the same dream. *He was lying flat on his stomach, on the bridge across the river, his hand reaching through the gap caused by the broken planks. Catherine was dangling from his hand!*

A twig broke under the weight of a foot. It was Narain who woke up, not sure whether he had dreamt the sound or heard it. Then, he heard a brief, soft thud on the dusty ground not far from his tent. This made him sit up and he rubbed his eyes wide open. He leant forward and cocked his head towards the direction he had heard the sound coming from. His heart was pounding. Turning his head, he saw the outline of Chand, still fast asleep. He silently crawled towards the secured flap of the tent.

With his fingers, he separated a tiny space in the canvas opening and positioned his left eye to take a peek outside. He scanned from one side of his periphery. The fire was still burning in the pit and there seemed to be no movement in and around the tents that were pitched on that side. He rolled his eye to scan the other side of the periphery.

At first, he thought that his mind was deceiving him. To make sure, he adjusted his position and narrowed his eye. There was a shadowy figure of a person hunching in stealth. There was something in the figure's hand. Narain inched closer to the opening and narrowed his eye further to identify the silhouette. The tent that was nearest to the figure was Kharak's. *What the hell is happening?* Narain asked himself.

The figure took two steps forward. It was then that Narain realised that a rifle was slowly being raised. His heart was thumping now. His mind was racing with images of people he knew and worked with in an attempt to recognise the person.

Then, it came to him. The more he thought, the more certain he was. There was now no doubt in his mind who it was: Mr Freeman. From where Narain was, he seemed to be pointing the barrel of the rifle towards the tent where Kharak and Lal were sleeping.

As the waters raged beneath Catherine, her grip got weaker and weaker until she could hold no more, and she plunged into the river—

At that moment, Kharak's nightmare was cut short by the taut voice of Narain ringing in his ears.

"Who are you? What are you doing there?"

Narain had grabbed a Masai spear and shouted as he opened the flap of his tent.

"Who are you? What are you doing there?" He decided to act as if he was unaware of the man's identity.

Ivan froze and lowered the rifle. By now, Narain had stood up outside his tent. His voice had roused almost everyone in the nearby tents and it wasn't long before panic-stricken faces emerged from them, expecting another lion attack.

Kharak sat up with sweat pouring down his face and his heart racing. It took him a few seconds to realise that he had had the dream again. He then heard voices coming from outside and was sure that he was not dreaming now. He turned around and heard Lal's heavy breathing; he was still asleep.

Without waking him, Kharak picked up his machete and crawled out of the tent apprehensively. In the cool night, and as the sweat evaporated from his skin, he felt a chill in the air. Looking around, he recognised Narain standing outside his tent. Three other coolies walked towards him with oil lamps in their hands. From the corner of his eye, he recognised Ivan in the faint orange light from the lamps, with his rifle under his armpit.

"I heard the growl of a lion from my tent," Ivan lied. "There is nothing of concern as I have checked the area, so I want all of you to go back to sleep." He flapped his hand at them.

Another lost opportunity to settle my score. Damn these foolish, sleepless Indians, he fumed. His eye twitched.

371

Narain was not convinced by his reason for creeping around the tents all by himself with his rifle pointed, particularly at Kharak's tent. He knew his eyes had not deceived him. This rivalry and animosity had become parlous.

Two coolies added more wood to the fire to build up the flames in the hope of scaring off the lions if they were prowling around. Kharak strode over to Narain, walking past Ivan. At that moment, in the dark, no one saw the ferocity of envy in Ivan's eyes. Having heard what had happened, Kharak turned his head in the direction of Catherine's carriage, which wasn't very far off. It was still dark and it seemed that she had been too tired to be woken up by the minor commotion.

"What's all this about?" Kharak quietly asked Narain.

"I don't trust Ivan," he paused. "He hates you fanatically."

"It's worse than you think." Kharak raised his eyebrow.

Ivan strutted away towards his tent with only one thought in his mind. *I will get another chance.*

"He was near your tent with his rifle pointed straight at it... I dread to think what was on his mind," Narain said.

"Another two nights and we will be gone." Kharak patted his shoulder. "But I will miss you, my friend."

"You don't belong here and I'm glad that you will be back in Punjab by next month."

The coolies had dispersed back to their tents, still worried as it was the dead of night. Yellow flames rose as the fire crackled on. Having borrowed a lamp, Kharak didn't walk straight back to his tent; he headed for Catherine's quarters.

There was no sound from the carriage and it was still dark inside. The door was shut properly. Using the light from the lamp, he scanned the dusty ground as he walked around the carriage. He was glad that he didn't see any pugmarks. Relieved, he walked away, knowing that Catherine was in deep sleep.

He stopped and turned around, just to have another glimpse

of her carriage. *There she is. She travelled all this way, just to see me. She feels the same as I do*, he thought.

The night beetles were bustling in the bushes beyond as he carried on walking to his tent, with his machete in one hand and his lamp in the other.

67

Golden rays of sunlight poked through the space between the muslin that hung as makeshift curtains across the carriage windows and highlighted Catherine's cheek. The warmth was soothing.

She blinked as she attempted to open her eyes in the morning brightness. It took her a few moments to realise where she was. She squeezed her eyes shut before opening them again. Distant sounds of stone being chipped could be heard. As her eyes grew accustomed to the brightness, she parted the curtains slightly with her fingers and had a peep through the window. All she saw was the backdrop of the unclouded blue sky against the distant grey hills that rose above the dry acacia thorn trees. She took the view in before rolling off the bed and staggering towards the opposite window to take another peep through the curtains. She scanned the little gap for Kharak.

The campsite was less busy than the previous day, but there

was a constant stream of workers carrying chiselled stone in shallow iron buckets over their shoulders, heading towards the tree-lined river. As she looked towards the right side of her window, near what seemed like a wooden storage shed fifty yards away, she saw Kharak standing and directing the coolies with shifting wooden poles. She noticed that every other minute, he turned around to glance towards her carriage. She timed his next glance and, as soon as he looked, she parted the curtains and waved at him.

Kharak was delighted when he saw Catherine. After giving the workers further instructions, he walked towards her carriage. He knocked on the door and, instantly, she opened it, still in her long-sleeved cotton nightgown. Even straight out of bed, he found her beautiful as her wavy hair drooped across her forehead, enhancing those soft eyes. She smiled at him and he felt like a lost traveller who had just found a path home.

"Good morning, Kharak." She tucked her curls behind her ears.

"Slept well?"

"Like a baby. I was so tired."

He gazed thoughtfully into Catherine's eyes. "I'll organise some hot water for you to wash up."

"That will be wonderful."

"I'll be back." He turned around.

"Kharak," she said, stopping him, "I'm glad I travelled here to see you." Her face tilted with a coquettish glance.

He smiled back. "I cannot describe the immense joy you brought me when I saw you." And with that, he marched off to collect the metal barrel to heat the water.

Having to freshen up with a bucket and jug was more amusing than a hindrance to her. Washing beneath the warm, open sky was a refreshing experience, despite having always used baths in the comfort of privacy.

Nearly an hour after waking up, refreshed, Catherine sat on

the edge of her bed in the carriage and brushed her hair. She felt like pinching her arm to remind herself that she was in Africa and that she had made that journey. *How did I do this and where did I get that inner strength from? What is this incomprehensible force that has made a man named Kharak matter this much to me that I feel his presence in everything I see around me?* She questioned herself as she blankly carried on brushing her hair.

Dressed in the straw-beige skirt suit she had bought from Brown's in Lahore, she looked at herself in her hand mirror. Over the last few weeks, she had noticed she was developing a tan, and admired the glow it brought out in her skin. She carefully adjusted her hat and curls. After putting her things away in her bag, she stepped out of the carriage and realised that although she had not eaten since the previous evening, she had no appetite. Her stomach felt knotty with the elation of being around Kharak.

On Saturdays, work at the bridge was never as intense as on weekdays and the workers were allowed to stop work in the afternoon. Also, Christian tradition was upheld and no work was carried out on Sundays.

It was past lunchtime and the overhead sun was blazing as Catherine walked towards the centre of the campsite. Out of the corner of her eye, she spotted Ivan walking in her direction. She pretended not to see him and shifted her gaze to the opposite side, hoping to avoid him. Now that she knew his true nature, she loathed him and didn't want to talk with him.

"Oh, Catherine?" He raised his voice from a distance.

She carried on walking, choosing to ignore him, but grew apprehensive as he closed in on her, knowing that their paths would converge ahead. Soon, he was only a few feet away from her.

"Hello, Catherine. This is a surprise! I never realised you were here," Ivan lied as he took a step in front of her, blocking her path. "It's fabulous to see you," he grovelled.

She remained silent, not looking at him as she was forced to halt.

"Do your parents know that you are here?" He stared directly at her.

Catherine felt ill at ease as he stood in her way, wanting to talk to her. She folded her arms.

"It's not your matter to be concerned about," she snapped.

"You shouldn't have travelled into the wilderness by yourself... and for no reason."

"If you'll excuse me, I need to go."

Ivan smirked. "Go? Where to, in this inhospitable place? Meeting that lowlife brown Indian again?"

Catherine's eyes widened and she pursed her lips. "Keep your nose out of matters that don't concern you. And remember this," she paused for effect, "in my eyes, he will always be above you and neither you nor anyone else can change that. And yes, he is the reason why I came here." She stared directly at him.

Ivan's eyes narrowed and his nostrils flared. This rejection hurt; he knew that his obsession with Catherine controlled him and took his mind to a twisted, miscreant state.

"You should be aware that I adore you more than he does." He took a step towards her.

"To you, I'm an object to possess, and what you forced Kharak to do is unforgivable in my eyes. I have no feelings for you and I never shall. You have to live with that," she said, without blinking. "And I will be going back... with him... in two days."

Hearing what he had never wanted to, Ivan's fury frothed within him and he began fidgeting with his ring as his face turned red. He knew that if it were someone else in front of him instead of Catherine right now, he would have nearly strangled her. *Even when she is angry, she bewitches me*, he thought. *And that Kharak, he has to lose... whatever it takes!*

Suddenly, someone called Catherine's name. She had never

been as glad to see Lal, who was calling her from the nearby medical shed. He had been watching her and Ivan from a distance and had seen the squabble brewing. Knowing what Ivan was about and seeing the discomfort on her face, he had shouted for her.

Without any courtesy, but with immense relief, she walked away from Ivan without uttering another word, leaving him to grapple with what she had said. He ogled her as she walked away along the gently sloping, dusty path in the direction of the medical shed. Meeting Ivan troubled her and what upset her more was the uneasy feeling she had.

The medical shed was a large wooden structure that contained six beds for any ill and injured workers. Hanging cotton sheets separated each bed. A whiff of iodine hung in the air and glass bottles of this brown liquid were seen on the shelf nearer to the door.

"Is everything all right?" she asked Lal as she approached him.

"Ah, yes. Just came to get some iodine to dab on this insect bite." He rolled his sleeve up to reveal a red blister on his forearm.

"That looks dreadful."

"What was he up to?" Lal nodded his head.

"Nothing... nothing good to say about Kharak or us." She paused. "Something else worries me about Ivan... his intentions; I don't feel comfortable about them. Deep down, it unsettles me."

"So, he is Ivan... don't worry. And by the way, Kharak asked me to pass by your carriage and ask you to go to the kitchen shed. I think he is packing lunch for the two of you by the river."

She smiled. She always did when Kharak's name was brought up in a conversation.

68

It was not Lahore, nor was it the River Ravi. Still, for Kharak, sitting on the bank of the comparatively tiny Tsavo River with Catherine was joyous. The sparkle of the sun's rays hitting the ripples, together with the herons resting on the tall, yellow-barked acacia trees on the opposite bank, was glorious. They sat well away from the river and close to the temporary wooden bridge. Kharak was aware of the dangers that lurked in this area. Although no one had seen any crocodiles here, the natives swore that the water-dwelling demons lived upstream.

He had made two makeshift stools out of rocks, on which they both sat. A thick log acted as their table, which they covered with a cotton cloth and on it placed their steel plates, flatbread, earthen pot of lentil soup and mangoes. There was no wine, just plain spring water. By Kharak's feet was the machete that he had started carrying with him.

"I see that you have taken a liking to your new friend, the machete," Catherine giggled.

"He is a good old reliable friend, always ready to help out." Kharak lifted the machete and admired it. He then grew serious. "This place is dangerous and it's not just the people. The terrorising lions around here seem to be notoriously cunning and have put fear into all of us." He took a deep breath. "That's why we are here by the bridge, where people are around us."

"Enough of the worry. Shall we have lunch? I'm starving," Catherine said, seeing the concern on his face.

The warmth of the afternoon sun soothed their faces as they smiled and giggled at each other while they had their leisurely lunch. A flock of herons flew from the branches to be replaced by twittering African sparrows. The usual palm trees with broader leaves formed the backdrop along the opposite riverbank. The occasional herd of zebras interrupted them as they came to lap the water.

As the afternoon faded, they sat gazing into each other's eyes, their leaning shoulders supporting one another, feeling uplifted in each other's presence. This bliss was often interrupted by Kharak's keen, observing eyes darting around, looking for any element of danger. He had learned from the coolies who had worked there the longest that it was when the wilderness grew quiet, with no birdsong or grazing animals around, that it was most dangerous.

Before the fading of the sun transformed the afternoon into early evening, they got up and ambled up the gentle path from the riverbank. They held hands with fingers entwined until they got above the bank, at which point, they let go as they approached the wandering workers nearby.

"Let's walk over the bridge. I want to see the majestic view of the river from there," Catherine suggested.

"I don't think it's a good idea." He screwed up his face.

"Why?"

He hesitated as the visions of his dreaded nightmare resurfaced. "It's still being built and it's not safe."

"It'll be fine." Catherine tugged his hand. "Come on." She took a step. "I want to see where you are working."

A feeling of dread washed over Kharak. *It was only a dream and I shouldn't take it too seriously... but it is a recurrent one. What if—*

"Walk with me," Catherine interrupted his thoughts.

Kharak did not want to take her across the bridge, but he was unsure how to convince her. As his mind struggled for a way out, that minute seemed like an hour.

From the camp side, they heard Chand shout. "Kharak!"

They turned and saw Chand waving and running towards them. A part of Kharak was glad of this timely distraction. He quietly hoped that Catherine would be distracted from wanting to walk over the bridge. The other part of him was concerned about the urgency of Chand's actions.

Chand's forehead was sweaty and he was gulping deep breaths by the time he reached them. He could hardly speak as he tried to get his breath back.

"Is everything all right?" Kharak asked.

"Your tent is on fire!"

"What?"

Chand pointed his hand in the direction of the campsite and they all saw faint wisps of grey smoke rising above the acacia trees.

"I thought it must have been the campfire, nothing more," Kharak replied.

"No. It's your tent."

Kharak's eyes widened in bewilderment. Immediately he put his hand in his trouser pocket with a concerned look and his fingers fumbled for a moment. He still had the glove and he was relieved.

"I'm heading there." He squeezed Catherine's hand. "Chand, stay here and accompany Catherine back to the camp. I'll meet you there."

He turned and sprinted off along the dusty path towards his tent and left them both scurrying behind him.

Two minutes later, Kharak saw the smouldering canvas with half a dozen coolies busy around it. Some were shovelling dirt onto it; others were bucketing water over it. It was evident that someone had pulled the rope that had been holding the tent, thus bringing it down. This had kept the fire from razing through all of the bedding and the few belongings that were in the tent.

Ivan was already there, standing a few feet away with feet shoulder-width apart, arms folded and a face marked by disappointment. For him, it was frustrating to see that the tent was not fully burnt, all because two workers had been resting in a nearby tent. Their quick actions had scuppered his plans. Kharak and Lal's belongings had been salvaged in time and dragged away from the smouldering tent.

It did not take Colonel Patterson long before he came to investigate the commotion. After an hour of questioning everyone around, he was no clearer as to what might have caused the tent to burn down. No one seemed to have seen anyone light the fire.

By now, Catherine and Chand had joined the group. When it was safe, Kharak and Lal retrieved some of their belongings that had been saved. Kharak discovered that one of his bags had been destroyed by the fire, but, luckily, his other, which was kept at the far corner of the tent, survived. They reeked of smoke. While searching through his belongings, he thought that an ember must have drifted into the air from the fire, causing the tent to burn down. Occasionally looking up and around, the only thing that troubled him was Ivan standing in the background, glaring and leaning on a shovel. Kharak's instinct kept pointing towards him.

On another day, this would have bothered him, but he knew that this inconvenience was only for another two nights and then he would be on his way back to Lahore with Catherine. This reassuring thought took a lot of his grief away as he glanced at Catherine, who met his gaze with a soothing narrowing of her eyes, before moving closer and clutching his upper arm.

It wasn't long before another tent was obtained from the store for them. By the time it was pitched, the sun had moved in the western horizon and the evening scent of wild flowers had blended with the settling early-evening dust as the air cooled under the clear sky.

The burning of the tent did not quench Ivan's thirst for vengeance, nor satisfy his vindictive nature that was made worse by seeing Catherine by Kharak's side. In his tent, he sat in solitude with his flask of whisky to accompany him.

Like a cat, he seems to have nine lives, Ivan thought as he took an inebriated sip.

"I should just take this rifle and fire a bullet into that bloody Indian's head. Who cares if the rest gang up on me, which I doubt, but at least he will be out of the way, like an irrelevant fly… I need to swat him like a fly," he mumbled to himself.

Again, he had tried to make Kharak's life hellish. Earlier, at the centre of the campsite, using the shovel, Ivan had carefully ensured that no one was around before taking some embers of coal from the fire and hurling them furtively onto the roof of the tent as he walked by. He was one of the first to rush towards the burning tent when the two workers raised the alarm.

69

That evening, despite the burning of the tent in the late afternoon, the routine in the Tsavo camp was the same. The fire was glowing and everyone sat around it. In any other place, at this time, watching the flames crackle would be serene and soothing, but in Tsavo, there was an edge of worry that hovered in the background. Any sudden sound startled everyone.

It had been nearly a week of undisturbed routine. There had been no sign of the marauding lions that had terrorised the camp. There had been whispers among some of the coolies that the lions must have moved away and found another village to attack during this time of drought. The building of the boma fence from the thorny branches of the acacia trees had not yet been completed, but still its ongoing construction had given some workers a false sense of safety. However, for some labourers, like Chand, the lions had inflicted permanent emotional scars after the ordeals of the previous weeks.

"You all keep talking about the lions, but all seems fine here," Catherine said to the group.

"We have only been here for a couple of days and, fortunately, they have not attacked in these days, so they tell me," Lal said.

"Let's not talk about them at this time," Kharak urged as he poked the embers with a stick. "Fire seems to be the greatest hazard right now." He sniggered.

The sky was clear and, with the change in the wind's direction, the night was cooler than previous nights.

The conversation wandered from the local tribes who lived in the Nyika Plateau to the Arabs with their influence at the port town of Mombasa. Time drifted. It was Narain who realised that it was getting late and excused himself first, and soon after, the rest of the group of five began to feel nervous at the prospect of being the last to leave.

"We'd better call it a day," Kharak said.

He stood up, which not only prompted Catherine to follow, but Lal and Chand as well.

"Goodnight, chaps," Kharak said.

"See you tomorrow," Chand replied.

Kharak's right hand ensured that his machete was in its sheath under his belt. After a nod and a goodbye, he and Catherine left and the whole group dispersed towards their tents.

Not too far away, the outline of the carriage was visible under the clear night sky. They walked along the path behind the yellow light of the hurricane lamp in Kharak's hand. Dust disturbed by their steps gathered on their boots. As they walked close together, their shoulders touched and Kharak took hold of Catherine's hand. She squeezed his fingers.

They approached her carriage.

"I want to show you something," Kharak said.

"What?"

Instead of walking straight to the steps that led to the carriage door, Kharak led her around the carriage to the front.

"Fancy climbing up onto the carriage?"

With impishness in her eyes, she gazed at him. "With you, I'd go anywhere." She narrowed her tender eyes.

Kharak reached his lamp forwards to illuminate the front of the carriage, which revealed the metal ladder that went up to the top.

"I'll climb up first with the lamp, then you can grab my hand and I'll help you."

Catherine nodded and let go of his hand. He climbed up and placed the lamp on the edge of the carriage roof. Supported by his other hand, he reached down and grabbed hers. She took the first difficult step onto the ladder and, soon, they were both on top of the carriage. He held her hand and, with the light of the lamp, gingerly led her to the centre of the flat carriage roof.

There, they sat down with their knees bent. He dimmed the light until it was as low as could be.

"Lie down on your back," Kharak said as he lowered his back onto the carriage roof. Catherine followed him.

"Look at the sky," he said.

She gazed towards the clear sky.

It was like diamond dust had been sprinkled across the clear night sky. A central cluster of sparkling stars spread outwards, emanating distant white light directly above them in this spellbinding moment.

In the enchanting quietness, they held hands tightly. Catherine broke the silence.

"I love you, Kharak."

He squeezed her hand caringly.

"I fell in love with you for who you are." She shifted her gaze from the stars towards him. "I was always drawn towards you, but ever since that day when we sat by the fountains at the Shalimar Gardens, I felt your presence grab hold of my heart and it shook my inner self… I was powerless to stop it."

Kharak turned towards her, leaned forward on his elbow

and gazed at her satiny eyes, which contained his reflection and those of the stars in the background. With his fingers, he gently pushed aside her hair from her forehead.

He whispered to her, "That day when you arrived in Lahore and I accompanied you home with your mother in the carriage, I had hoped that I would meet you again – and when you asked me to show you around," he took a deep breath, "I could not believe it. But I was also afraid that there was a chance that my life would never be the same." He paused. "I kept falling in love with you every day... over and over again."

"Ssh..." she whispered.

They kissed under the canopy of stars.

The breeze that blew over the carriage was brisk. In the distance, the strange 'laughing' of a hyena sounded uncanny. They sat cross-legged, observing the dark outline of the hill in the distance. Even in this harsh place, they felt contented. With the chill in the air, Kharak wrapped his arm around her as Catherine rested her head on his shoulder.

"What happens when we reach Lahore?" he asked.

"An irate mother and father to go to." She forced a wry smile. "But I will be with you at each hurdle."

"Let's reach Lahore and I'm sure things will turn out for the better. As I've always been told, life has a habit of revealing itself."

"You have a way with words; even Lal said to me that you admire poetry. Go on, quote some to me. I'd love to hear."

Kharak grinned. "Really?"

"Yes."

"Having read the work of a couple of great poets, Hafez and Rumi, I have realised that the same phrase of poetry spoken to different people will have a different meaning for each. That's its beauty."

"Alright then... I'm still waiting to hear something." She nudged his elbow playfully.

There was a silent pause as Kharak gathered his thoughts. He wrapped his arm tighter around her shoulders.

"*Lovers find secret places inside this violent world where they make transactions with beauty.*"

"That's powerful and beautiful… Any more?"

"I can think of one more that is relevant for us after I left Lahore."

"Which is…?" There was eagerness in her voice.

"*The breath of love is unrevealed until the hour of separation.*"

"I am in awe. That is so true and I can't explain why I felt the way I did when you left Lahore. I just had this urge to be with you."

Catherine put her arm around Kharak as they silently gazed at the stars on the horizon, both drowned in the blissful moment.

"Is there a favourite verse of poetry you have?"

Kharak paused for thought. "Yes, I think." He smiled. "It's one by Hafez…"

"And…?" she asked impatiently.

She saw his smile under the brightness of the stars.

"You will know it in time."

"That's not fair."

"You just have to trust me."

She smiled.

The moments passed by. In the background, only nature spoke: the crickets chirped, there was an occasional hoot from an owl and the faint sound of the Tsavo River trickled in the background.

It was half an hour later when Kharak realised that it was foolhardy for them to be out alone when everyone else had retired to their tents.

He prompted Catherine and they got up. Kharak turned up his lamp and scanned around for any animals in the vicinity of the carriage before climbing down the ladder first, then helping her down. The sky was still cloudless.

"I want to show you something," Catherine said as they reached her door. She climbed the steps, opened the door and stood facing Kharak. "Come on." She offered her hand to him.

He stepped up and into the carriage.

"This is my room."

"I know that."

"Look." She took two steps and peeked through the cloth that acted as the curtains, and gazed out of the carriage window.

Kharak walked towards her to the exact spot where she was looking out. Getting close to her face, he rested, feeling his cheek on hers, and looked at what she was pointing at.

"Look there." She wore a cheeky smile. "It's my turn to show you the stars."

He laughed out loud. She laughed, too. They both laughed until their stomachs hurt. They would glance at each other and the laughter would start again. It was wonderful.

As the laughter subsided, he took a step back. She clasped his hand and drew closer to him. She gazed deeply in the eyes of the man who was her world.

"What was your tent, is now ashes..."

"I know."

"Don't leave." She took a deep breath. "Spend the night with me, Kharak."

A closeness drew them together. He felt her warm breath and, before another word was uttered, their lips locked and their embrace grew tighter.

In the dimmed light of the hurricane lamp, two naked silhouettes of bodies came together as one with every breath they took. Heaven seemed to have moved down into the carriage from the stars that gazed from the sky above them.

With hearts fluttering, they made love.

70

The tweets of the birds were fewer than normal and, like a ritual, started just before dawn broke in Tsavo on the Sunday morning. Kharak opened his eyes in a daze. With the lamp unlit, it was still dark as his eyes adjusted. The fragrance that lingered around him was very comforting and he felt Catherine's hair caress his face, her warm body lying beside him. He tenderly ran his fingers through her hair that had curled around the nape of her neck, which prompted her to sleepily put her arm around his neck. How someone could mean so much to him, he had never envisaged. Now more than ever he knew that she was his life. The feeling was overwhelming, in a beautiful way.

He kissed her lips.

"Catherine," he whispered as he stroked her angelic face with his finger. "I've got to go back to the tent before dawn breaks."

"Ah…" she mumbled. She smiled with her eyes still shut.

"I've got to go before anyone sees me."

"Do you have to, Kharak?"

"Yes."

"So be it," was her reluctant reply.

He fumbled out of the bed and sat on the edge, before parting the cloth covering the window slightly and sneaking a look out. The sky was inky with clouds that had blanketed the stars that had been visible earlier. On the eastern horizon was the amber speck of dawn. *One more day here and we will be gone*, he thought.

Catherine caught his arm as he stood up. "I love you."

He turned, leaned down and ran his hand over her face gently, stopping at her chin before kissing her lips.

"I love you. Don't get up yet. Sleep and I will see you later today."

With that, he stood up, got dressed and headed for the door. He blew her a kiss and left.

The door was shut quietly. Outside, a gentle wind added an edge of coolness. Having deliberately left the lamp in the carriage, he knew that the walk to Lal's tent was not going to be quick.

Kharak neither noticed that the early-morning chirping of the birds was subdued, nor the eerie silence that pervaded the wilderness. He headed towards the firepit and from there got his bearings for the tent. He wanted to sleep for another few hours; after all, it was Sunday and there was no serious work to be done.

Early that morning, for the first time since he had met Catherine in Lahore, Ivan dreamt about her. *She stood at the door of her house in Royal Crescent in Bath, smiling fondly at him as he stepped off his carriage onto the cobbled road. It was early summer and the grass of the gently sloping lawn opposite was an intense green. He opened his arms towards Catherine and she walked towards him, as her father and mother peered through the window...*

It was at that moment that Ivan woke up and, to his dismay,

realised that it was just a dream. He tried to force himself to fall back to sleep, hoping that his dream would return, but it was to no avail. The dream was so vivid and perfect.

He opened his unforgiving eyes and it struck him that her parents must have been concerned about her. Had she told them where she was going or had she run away? Was Gilbert going to follow his daughter here and take her back? *Maybe I should send a telegraphic message to him saying that I have found her and that I can bring her back, after somehow getting rid of Kharak, of course.*

The tin-roofed stone building, which was the small and newly constructed Tsavo Station, built a few weeks back, housed the local telegraphic equipment. Whether it worked, he was not sure, but Ivan knew that he could attempt to send a message to Lahore and wait for a reply, hopefully by the end of the day. It would give him time to think.

This was the reason he needed to be out of his tent. There was not much time left.

LAHORE

Three weeks earlier in Lahore, the morning when Catherine's parents had found her note, Gilbert had gone to Lahore Station and attempted to send a message to Ivan via Mombasa, but he was informed that due to problems at Zanzibar, it could not be sent. Without hesitation, muddled by anger and guilt, he had taken the next train to Bombay in the hope that he could find Catherine at the port and, if he did not, he was going to take the next ship to Mombasa.

While there, he was taken ill with what turned out to be malaria and ended up recuperating at his close friend Thomas Hamilton's home.

It was that morning in Tsavo that it happened.

71

Tsavo

Low-lying grey clouds still occluded the sky, creating an oppressive atmosphere. An unusual silence hung in the wilderness. Even the herons that perched on the branches of the duom palm trees that clustered across the bank of the Tsavo River were not to be found that morning. The herd of zebras that were always spotted amongst the savannah grass on the eastern side of the railway track were absent too.

At around nine o' clock that morning, Ivan strode along the red dirt path through the thorny three-foot-tall shrubs that led to Tsavo Station. A few minutes later, the bush opened up and the tin roof of the station and the adjacent water tank came into view.

The bearded stationmaster was busy with the weekly clean of 'his' place when Ivan stepped inside. The discussion was one-sided and he rudely gave the details, instructing the stationmaster to send a telegraphic message to Lahore. Ivan hoped that if the earlier problems with the telegraph had been rectified and all went smoothly, he should receive a message in reply well before the end of the day.

After the stationmaster acknowledged that the message had been sent, Ivan headed out onto the veranda of the station. With his mind still hurtling around, he failed to notice the lanky Indian scurrying under the veranda towards the entrance of the building. The screech of a lone baboon from a rocky outcrop a hundred yards beyond the station was sudden.

He saw the man attempt to run into the station.

"You there. Can you not see me walking towards you?" he shouted at him.

The thin man stood at the door. He kept glaring at the rocky outcrop with nervous eyes.

"No... no, sahib," he stammered. He took another look at the outcrop.

"Then you must be a fool."

"Sorry, sir, I'm afraid for my life." He paused, with a flustered look. "The lion... it's the *sher*! I saw it in the distance, beyond the rocky outcrop!"

"Lock the door," the stationmaster shouted in Hindi from inside his makeshift office. "Hurry!"

This shook Ivan and he changed his tone. "Where did you see the lion?

"In that direction." The man pointed his hand, with one foot at the door.

Ivan took out his binoculars from the leather case that hung around his neck and raised them to his eyes. He focused on the distant rusty outcrop, dotted with acacia trees. At first, he saw the thorny, golden-brown shrubs growing at the top, but as he scanned carefully, he spotted what looked like a cobra with its hood flared. He paused and fixed his stare on it. He then spotted two flapping protrusions that disappeared into and reappeared from the golden grass.

Then, he saw it: the unmistaken outline of the face of a large feline. The hood he saw was not that of a snake, but the lion's tufted tail as it waved amongst the dry grass. The sandy hue of its fur was the perfect camouflage. It was the lion!

Eight hundred yards away at the campsite, there was a knock on the carriage door. Catherine opened it, hoping to see Kharak, but instead she saw a tiny man with a receding hairline.

"Sorry to disturb you, memsahib." He bowed his head. "Patterson Sahib would like to see you now."

"Oh… I'll be a minute."

She wondered what he wanted to see her about. A few thoughts crossed her mind, but she chose to ignore them as she stepped down from the carriage. There was no sign of Kharak when she glanced around.

At that precise moment, Kharak was with Mistry, the chubby man in charge of materials, in the metalwork shed that was located at the south-eastern edge of the campsite, not far from the bush path that led towards Tsavo Station. Before leaving for Lahore, he wanted to leave a plan for the next responsible person of what work had been completed so far and what needed to be completed. This task itself was nearing completion.

The man-eater! This was the first thought that crossed Ivan's mind as he maintained the 600-yard visual contact through his binoculars. His shoulder felt light; he had left his rifle under his bedding in his tent. A wave of coldness seeped down his back, but he still kept watching.

As he stood still, his rancorous and muddled thoughts gained the focus he was looking for. This was the opportunity he had been waiting for and, right now, in front of his very eyes, was the right set of circumstances for retribution. His vengeful eyes narrowed as a malicious grin appeared on his lips.

He needed to get back to the camp immediately. He turned around and scrambled back along the path. After the first fifty yards, he stopped, turned around, raised his binoculars and observed the rocky hill that rose in the background above the grey thorns. It was still there.

After a further hundred yards of hurried walking under the grey sky, the water tank at Tsavo Station had disappeared in the distance behind the bush. He stopped suddenly and decided to take another look at the lion. This time, it was standing motionless with its gaze fixed in his direction. The next moment, it crouched lower and flattened its ears, still maintaining its gaze.

Without hesitation, Ivan, his heart racing, started to jog back towards the camp. He knew what he had to do and he hoped that this time his scheme would work.

What he had not seen was that the lion had started to track down the rocky hill.

72

Outside the dust-coated metal shed, with the task of preparing his plan complete, Kharak hunched over and talked with Mistry, who poured water from a metal jug onto Kharak's hands to wash the dirt off them.

Ivan approached the perimeter of the camp, out of breath. On his left, beside the shed, he spotted Kharak chuckling with Mistry as he wiped his hands on his trousers.

This could just work out, Ivan thought as he reminded himself to show apparent concern. *Come on, Ivan. Do it or forever remain silent.*

"Kharak!" Ivan shouted as he waved from a distance.

Kharak turned his head and was extremely surprised to see Ivan striding briskly towards him. He didn't take a step and waited for Ivan to get to him.

"Catherine has broken her arm… she is asking for you."

"I beg your pardon?"

"She had gone to send a telegraph to her parents in Lahore and she slipped over the step, fell and landed on her arm."

"Where?" Kharak asked, with a sceptical look.

"At Tsavo Station. I was going to inspect the repairwork to the water tank when the stationmaster informed me halfway there. She needs the doctor... I'm going to get Dr McBride."

"Why did she go all alone?"

"I'm not the person to ask. When you see her, you could ask her." Ivan bit his inner lip in frustration. "You'd better get to her while I get the doctor and a number of coolies to help bring her here on a makeshift stretcher." Ivan walked off in a hurry towards the centre of the camp. He stopped a few yards away, turned around and yelled, "She is waiting for you. She calls for you. Go!"

Kharak stood there, not knowing whether to believe him or not. Mistry stood in front of him and noticed his concerned frown.

"I'll check at the camp for you."

"I'm worried about all this... I hope she is all right." His hand brushed his belt to ensure he still had his machete. "I'm going to find her." Kharak hurried off along the path towards the station. Mistry headed in the opposite direction.

Kharak had walked 200 yards along the bushy path when, from nowhere, the same lanky Indian whom Ivan had spoken to came dashing through the acacia bushes, startling him. The man had a red, flustered face, and was petrified and unable to speak. Disorientated, he kept pointing towards the station as he staggered towards Kharak. The merciless thorns had not only torn the sleeves of his shirt, but also scratched his arms, with bloodstains visible on them. Out of breath and still unable to speak, he passed Kharak and kept on running towards the camp.

"*Sher*... Lion?" he managed to say.

Hearing that, fear filled Kharak. His pulse quickened as he thought of Catherine. He moved on with urgency.

Catherine walked out of Colonel Patterson's tent after a formal discussion with him. He wanted to get a true picture of what had happened in Lahore and how she felt about Kharak accompanying her back there. She was relieved to be going back with him, but knew that she would face stern consequences from her parents for her actions. In her mind, she had run through these consequences over and over again.

She stood outside under the grey sky – to her, it was magnificent and she imagined the sunlight cutting through the clouds. The world seemed beautiful. She spotted a coolie whom she had seen around the camp rushing towards her.

"Memsahib, you are here and your arm is fine?" Mistry said with a puzzled look.

"I don't understand what you mean."

"Mr Ivan met us," he pointed in the direction of the metal shed, "and he said that you were at Tsavo Station and that you had broken your arm and were asking for Kharak."

"What?! Ivan said that?"

"Yes."

"Who was with you?" Catherine asked, a little bewildered.

"Kharak."

"Where is he now?"

"He has gone looking for you, towards the station."

Catherine paused and stroked her eyebrow. This situation didn't feel right. "Is that the path?" she asked him, pointing her finger.

"Yes, but you shouldn't—"

"I'm going to the station."

"But memsahib—"

"Listen… erm…" She did not know his name. "Go and find Narain and Lal and explain to them what has happened, and tell them to come to the station. I'm heading there." She started to head towards the path.

"Yes, memsahib."

"One more thing," she shouted. "Where did Ivan go?"

"He said he was going to the clinic to get help."

"What a liar," she fumed. She turned around and started running, her heart thumping.

Catherine had run a hundred yards when she encountered the scared and confused lanky Indian, dashing along and waving his arms frantically.

"*Jao… vapas jao!*"

Catherine stopped and caught her breath. "What's the matter?"

The Indian stammered, barely coherent, "*Sher!*"

"What?"

Taking gulps of air, with eyes wide, he pointed ahead.

Panic was setting in as she asked, "Have you seen my Kharak?"

"*Khaun?*" he asked in between breaths.

"The Sikh man named Kharak."

He bent down, his hands holding his quivering knees, inhaling vigorously. With barely enough strength, he pointed ahead. "*Sher…Vapas jao.*"

Catherine's instinct told her something was not right. She was filling up with panic, her heart racing at the thought of Kharak in peril. She did not bother to reply. The man straightened up, turned his neck and watched her run ahead.

"Kharak… Kharak!" she called as she ran.

A hundred yards ahead, Kharak stood still on the dirt path as he gazed around where the path opened up. Another ominous baboon screech shattered the strange silence in the wilderness. All around, the thorny grey bushes seemed to be watching him as the top of the water tank of Tsavo Station could be seen in the distance.

It was then that he heard a distant, muffled voice. Barely audible, he heard his name being called out from behind. He recognised the voice, but it resonated with fear.

"Catherine!" Kharak yelled as he turned around. Further away, he caught a glimpse of her darting through the bushes towards him.

"Turn back, Kharak. Don't go ahead." Her voice grew louder as she got nearer. He sprinted towards her, befuddled but glad to see her unhurt.

With open arms, they met and embraced tightly for a brief moment. She was out of breath as he kissed her forehead.

"We need to get out of here quickly," Kharak said as he held her hand tightly.

"He lied, Kharak, he lied. What an evil man."

"Ivan's cruelty has no bounds and he's been doing this since Lahore."

"He really can't bear to see us together and he hates you."

Catherine had barely got her breath back when a twig cracked.

"We need to be careful." Kharak scanned around the bush as he held her closer. "Keep a lookout on your left and I'll do the same on the right."

They took a few steps back the way they had come. He continued to hold her hand tightly. She never knew how his heart thumped with fear – fear of something happening to her.

From only yards away, a pair of piercing feline eyes observed them through the prickly thorns amongst the surrounding golden savannah grass. It provided the perfect camouflage for the lion.

It was from the corner of her eye that Catherine noticed the acacia bush sway. There was no breeze. She tugged Kharak's arm and lurched closer to him, putting her arm around his waist. Instinctively, he stood in front of her, shielding her with his left arm behind his back, holding her. His right hand drew his machete from its sheath dangling from his belt. Their eyes locked on the bush.

The lion made a feigned charge towards them. It leapt forward a few feet through the bush before stopping in front of them, growling. A large, sand-coated lion with a sparse mane crouched with saliva drooling through its huge canine teeth. Its fierce eyes were transfixed upon them and its growl was paralysing.

In that moment, all sense of time appeared to have slowed and elongated.

"Kharak!" Catherine screamed, overcome with fear.

Their palms were sweaty and their bodies were rigid with fear; it felt as if their hearts were thumping against their ribs.

"Stay behind me." Kharak waved his machete in front of his body.

Inside, he was trembling. In in a blink, thoughts of their last few weeks in Lahore surged across his mind. Then, the dreaded vision of his recurrent nightmare of Catherine dangling from his hand over a bridge flashed once more. *I can't let go! Never.* He gathered all his strength, grit and fury.

His face turned red and sweat appeared on his forehead as he held her hand and the machete tighter.

"*Kharak!*" Catherine yelled again.

"Stand behind me."

Suddenly, the sound of metal striking metal was heard coming towards them from the distance, along with the shouts and screams of people.

In that instant, the startled lion charged towards them. At the right time, Kharak, protecting Catherine, took two steps back. Catherine yelled. The lion took a swipe with its paw, tipped with razor-edged claws. Kharak felt a lacerating pain in his inner thigh. The loud snarling was frightening as dust rose from the ground.

For whatever reason, the lion chose to take a step back before it attempted another lunge. This time, Kharak swung his machete towards the lion. The tip brushed through the creature's short mane and opened a wound on its leg near its heel. Kharak swung once more. The lion swept its paw and came into contact with his hand holding the machete and deflected it back to Kharak. He felt a sharp, splitting pain.

At that moment, a crowd of about twenty noisy coolies, running and banging barrels with steel rods, reached them, led by Narain and Lal. A gunshot echoed as Patterson fired into the air. This startled the lion and it scurried off into the thorny bushes and disappeared.

As everyone's eyes turned towards Kharak, they were horrified to see blood gushing from his thigh through his torn trousers, as well as from a cut on his hand and a slit on the side of his neck. With cold sweat across his forehead, he felt light-headed and fell to the ground.

"*Kharak!*" Catherine screamed.

Narain was the first to act. He ran over to Kharak where he lay on the ground and tore the remnants of the upper part of Kharak's trousers to make a tourniquet around his upper thigh. This helped to stem the profuse flow of blood from the deep gash.

Colonel Patterson took aim and fired another shot in the direction of the bush. He reloaded his rifle and fired again, hoping to hit the lion if it was still nearby. Cautiously, he prowled forwards towards the bush, pointing his rifle ahead of him.

Lal quickly took off his shirt and pressed it against Kharak's neck wound, which had been caused by the deflected machete.

"Quick, we need to carry him to the clinic as fast as we can." There was urgency in Narain's voice. "We need eight of you to hold your hands under him and lift him like a stretcher, move as fast as possible. We'll hold his wounds together." He barked out instructions.

"Run ahead and get the doctor ready at the clinic," Lal yelled to a coolie who was standing nearby, watching.

Catherine was pale, dazed, in a state of shock, with heart pounding as she knelt beside Kharak, holding his hand. Everything was happening too quickly around her. They lifted his prone form and started walking, while Patterson followed with the other workers as he scoured the bush for the possibility of the lion returning.

Catherine held Kharak's hand in her trembling hand and kissed it often as she walked beside him.

In his state of semi-consciousness, Kharak could feel her velvet hand holding his. Her voice seemed faint and distant, but it was the most beautiful sound he had ever heard. The intensity of the pain began to overwhelm him and he felt limp and unable to move.

He continued to fall in and out of consciousness.

73

By the time they reached the clinic, a bed had been set up for the wounded Kharak. Makeshift cotton sheets acted as curtains, which separated his bed from the rest of the occupied beds. Dr McBride, the Scottish doctor in charge at the camp, was ready in his apron, setting up his equipment and the iodine solution.

The eight men rested Kharak on the bed and the doctor quickly assessed him. The explanation was brief and to the point, after which Lal and Narain were asked to remain in the clinic to help Dr McBride. Despite the doctor asking Catherine to leave the room, she refused to comply and insisted on being by Kharak's side. There was no way she was going to leave him.

With no time to argue, the doctor warned her about the stomach-turning sight she would witness, then began the procedure to stem blood loss and stitching the wounds.

As it began, Catherine whispered into Kharak's ear, "I'm here with you and it will be fine. Hold on." She kissed him on his forehead.

Dr McBride's efforts took over two gruelling hours. During the entire task, Catherine did not flinch, but on the inside she was concerned, though she chose to cling on to hope. She didn't care what anyone thought of her as she frequently spoke to Kharak and held his hand as the clinical procedure progressed.

The lacerations on his thigh, hand and neck were stitched, but they still bled. In the hope of improving the outcome, the wounds were bandaged. After completing the operation as best as he could, the doctor led them out of the tin-shed clinic.

"I have done what I could. The wounds are very deep and with Kharak having lost a lot of blood, the outcome is extremely uncertain. I can't say, but it could go either way," the doctor said slowly as he lowered his head and cleaned his hands with soapy water.

It was then that the reality of the situation hit Catherine. The rush of adrenaline had worn off and she felt all alone, standing by herself, not knowing what to do and how things would turn out. The corners of her eyes filled with tears and a lump in her throat made her unable to speak. Tears rolled down her face.

"I will be changing his bandages every couple of hours as the wounds are still bleeding. The artery in his thigh is severely damaged, but my main concern is the neck injury from the machete; it has touched his carotid artery. I'm worried about it rupturing."

Lal was visibly shaken, but Narain knew that he had to put on a brave face in front of Catherine and Lal.

"I'm not going anywhere," Catherine said as she wiped her tears. "I will be here by his side."

"It's not necessary… but I won't stop you," the doctor replied, when he realised how adamant she was.

No one had a sense of time. It was past two o' clock and low-lying grey clouds still blanketed Tsavo, threatening to let the rain loose. Narain offered to bring some lunch for them while they waited at the clinic, but Catherine declined as she had lost all appetite and it did not feel right to eat.

"I'm going inside," she announced. No one stopped her.

Kharak's bed was the furthest from the door, behind the hanging sheet that separated him from the rest of the patients. She pulled a rickety wooden chair from the corner and sat beside him. She looked at him lying there, serene, with those eyes that seemed to reflect his very soul shut. His face seemed pale but that did not matter to her; he was her Kharak.

She was about to adjust the sheet that covered him when she noticed an odd white cloth poking from his trouser pocket. At first, she didn't think much of it, but she decided to pull it out from his torn pocket. As she did that, she immediately realised what it was... it was her glove. The same glove she had dropped for him from the carriage after the wedding celebration.

Her face crinkled with emotion.

Oh gosh, he always keeps it with him... Her eyes grew moist as she held his hand and kissed it. Her breath shuddered. She felt helpless.

Time dragged on and it had only been an hour, but already Kharak's blood had seeped through his bandages. Although there was another hour to go before they were due to be changed, she summoned the doctor, who got another roll of bandage and changed Kharak's dressings. As he left, he again shook his head in despair.

"There's been no improvement."

This worried her. She wished she could turn back the clock and not let Kharak leave her carriage that morning. She didn't shift her gaze from his face as he lay in bed, but, instead, moved her chair even closer.

Getting closer to his face, she stroked his forehead, kissed it, then whispered in his ear, "I love you." She tucked her glove back into his pocket.

Kharak's innermost self was in a state of quietude. His reaching senses picked up the fragrance of Catherine; the soft, soothing touch of her fingers as they ran across his forehead; her warm, life-giving breath and her voice expressing her love for his soul. It was beautifully peaceful.

There was a calmness where all pain seemed to have dissipated, giving a light, levitating feeling. A wave of joy was picked up by his feeble senses and gradually swept through him, starting from his feet and moving upwards.

"I love you…" Catherine's voice, sublime and soft in Kharak's mind, was followed by brightness that finally led to nothingness.

74

Dr McBride came to check on Kharak and, after a few worried minutes of checking for vital signs, he knew the outcome.

"I'm sorry, Catherine." He took a long breath. "Kharak is no more." He rested his hand on her shoulder to comfort her.

In that moment, her life caved in. Her stomach twisted and knotted as she let out a howl of anguish and clutched his hand over her heart. Emptiness shrouded her as she broke down and cried.

Lal and Narain rushed inside to see what was happening. As they glanced at the doctor's glum face, he shook his head to signal Kharak's passing away. Even as grown men, tears rolled down their faces.

Lal could not comprehend what had taken place. Only a few hours ago, life was normal and now he had been told that he had lost his closest friend. He could see Kharak lying motionless in front of him. It was the most difficult moment of his life as he walked over to his bedside and held his feet, knelt and broke down. In the minutes that followed, their life growing up together in Lahore flashed through his mind: their ambitions, hopes and secrets all simmered to the surface.

He glanced at Catherine and saw her mourning, her face crumpled with tears and still holding Kharak's hand tightly. He broke down again.

Narain walked over after wiping his tears away to comfort them. He placed his hand on Lal's shoulder and patted it in solace, encouraging him to stand up. They both stepped towards Catherine to comfort her. She stood up and, instinctively, with tears in her eyes, hugged them. The pain was immeasurable.

Narain offered to go and inform Colonel Patterson of what had happened, and left the two at the clinic.

Soon, word had spread about the terrible incident within their own camp, as well as the camp at the railhead, leading to the workers congregating around the clinic.

Patterson was saddened by what had happened. After meeting the distraught Catherine at the clinic and discussing with Narain, who was looked up to by most of the workers, he instructed Lal and some of the other coolies to officially inform the camp of what had happened.

Mistry was the only person who had been present when Ivan had lied to Kharak about Catherine being in trouble. Mistry realised then that Ivan had planned this to happen and had deviously led Kharak towards the lions of Tsavo.

Circles of cigar smoke whirled from Ivan's mouth as he exhaled with deep satisfaction. He sat slumped in his armchair in his tent, gazing out at the bush. *What a great day*, he thought. *The thorn is out*. He removed his boots and tossed them to the side, letting the air cool his feet. *A few more weeks and I'll be back in England via India... and that Sikh will be a piece of history for*

Catherine and she will be with me. He savoured the essence of the cigar as a cruel smile spread across his face.

Later in the afternoon, Patterson visited Ivan to hear his version of events. When asked about the incident, Ivan blatantly lied with a straight face about his conversation with Kharak and denied Mistry's version of events. The conversation lasted a whole hour. As he walked away, Patterson was no clearer about what had happened.

It was Ivan's word against Mistry's, but the coolies believed Mistry and their hatred for Ivan simmered even more now.

Ivan decided to keep a low profile and informed Patterson that he had some matters to attend to at the railhead camp, and that he would be camping there for a couple of nights.

Needing someone to comfort and keep an eye on Catherine at this harrowing time, the only person whom Patterson thought appropriate was Lal, as he had accompanied her from Lahore and had been Kharak's closest friend. Kharak had even trusted him to look after her in Lahore when he was posted to Tsavo.

Catherine did not want to leave the clinic. She sat beside Kharak's body as it was covered by a sheet of cloth, as was the Sikh custom.

"This can't be real," she kept saying to herself. Inside, she felt like a mirror shattered into a thousand pieces that would never be joined back together.

The most difficult conversation Lal had with Catherine was when he had to inform her that the cremation would have to take place that late afternoon as soon as the funeral pyre was ready. She looked like a broken young woman who carried the heavy burden of the love she had lost.

75

As they were in Tsavo, with its hot climate and the risks of not only lions, but also hyenas, the cremation needed to be carried out as soon as possible. Ten coolies were delegated the task of getting the wood to set up the pyre in preparation for the late-afternoon cremation.

As per tradition, Lal, Narain, Chand and Mistry prepared Kharak's body for the funeral. A room at the rear of the clinic was designated as the morgue. It was there that they washed and dressed his body before placing it on a makeshift stretcher, which would be used to carry it to the funeral site for cremation. As per Catherine's wish, they made sure that they placed her glove that Kharak so cherished in his pocket. At the same time, the pyre was set up on a sandy stretch along the bank of the Tsavo River. The mood was sombre at the camp.

All that time, Catherine sat beside Kharak's empty bed at the clinic, refusing to budge, her mind in a muddle, somehow thinking that Kharak would walk through the door at any moment. Internally, she was screaming and felt trapped in a void.

The stratum of clouds across the sky had thinned by the late afternoon, revealing specks of amber sunlight. For Catherine, it did not matter; everything around her was dark and grey. Everywhere she looked, everything she cast her eyes on, had colour missing. Her eyes were swollen from continuous crying, but even her tears deserted her in despair as she followed the procession towards the cremation site from the makeshift hospital. The realisation that Kharak was no more was not sinking in.

Everyone at the camp was apprehensive about a woman being present at the cremation, as it was believed that it would be a traumatic experience for her. In spite of the anguish she was in and the apprehension of the others, she wanted to be there to say her final goodbye to Kharak and no one could stop her.

The procession reached the sandy riverbank where one of the coolies, having led religious ceremonies in the Punjab, led the final prayers.

Kharak's body was rested on the pyre and it was then that Catherine broke down. She felt crushed to see the man she loved, her everything, her meaning of life, lying there, never again to be by her side, never to gaze into her eyes. Her soul felt destroyed.

Lal comforted her as she cried. He now had to carry out his life's most excruciating task and light the pyre.

Minutes later, the pyre was lit and, with it, emotions of a thousand sorts erupted from within, sweeping and taking hold of Catherine's heart as she whispered Kharak's name. Under her breath, she uttered a heartfelt final goodbye before she walked away, with memories of him pouring through her mind. She couldn't take it any more.

Gradually, one by one, the coolies dispersed back to the camp as the light started to lose its strength. This was not a place where they wanted to spend more time than needed.

Lal stood by the banks of the river for a while, staring at the flames, thinking of Kharak's family and the devastation they would feel at this news. A lump formed in his throat.

It was not until Patterson called for him that he left the edge of the river, feeling broken.

Of all the deaths he had encountered in Tsavo, Kharak's affected Patterson the most. Despite having spent time in the armed forces, with all the toughness it brought, the death of Kharak saddened him.

As he sat slumped in his chair in his tent, reflecting on the circumstances, Lal approached.

"Come on in." Patterson gestured through the open canvas entrance.

Lal stood staring blankly at the zebra hide on the floor.

Patterson broke the silence. "With all that has happened here, and knowing that Kharak was a dear friend of yours, I want you to go back to Lahore. Accompany Catherine back to her family in safety. Kharak trusted you and she needs to return safely to them."

His voice still quivering, Lal spoke, "We would like to take his ashes back to Lahore so that his family can scatter them in the River Ravi." He felt his throat hardening.

"I agree with you."

"We will gather his ashes in the morning and later we will leave for Mombasa."

"I will organise everything for the both of you," Colonel Patterson said.

"Thank you, sir."

Lal turned around to leave the tent.

"One more thing," Patterson added, halting him in his tracks. "Lal… I want you to move your tent close to Catherine's carriage. She needs support and someone to keep an eye on her during this devastating time."

"I will see to that."

Lal turned again and walked out of the tent, and into the oppressive atmosphere of Tsavo.

76

Catherine gulped for air as she sat on the edge of her bed and sobbed. She felt hollow and empty as she recalled the last night she had spent with Kharak. She missed his face, his voice calling her name, the way he gazed at her with fondness… she missed his presence.

She was leaving Tsavo that morning and now she longed to go. The previous two days had been an infliction of pain on her soul. With no appetite, she had hardly eaten anything, and she had barely managed to sleep. The long nights were consumed by thoughts of despair. Her real desolation was not only in missing Kharak, but in the realisation that he was gone and would never be there again, missing and thinking about her at the same time. That was the loneliest moment of the night.

The light in her face seemed to have vanished as her puffy eyelids hid the eyes that had mesmerised Kharak.

It had been an hour since Lal, Chand and Narain had gone to the riverbank to collect Kharak's ashes in an urn. Catherine could not bear to go back there, so, with a heavy heart, she sat in her carriage quarters for the very last time, surrounded by her belongings, ready to leave the Tsavo camp.

It was Narain who knocked on the door to inform her that it was time to leave. With one final glance at the space where she had spent her last night with Kharak, she stepped out. Deep emotions stirred and, with no other outlet, her eyes seeped with pain when she saw Lal holding the plain earthen urn that contained his ashes.

Partly due to the fear of lions and partly due to respect, a procession of coolies accompanied them to Tsavo Station where the workers' train with its single seating carriage was waiting. The vast, clear, powder-blue sky made no difference to her mood and a heavy silence seemed to follow her everywhere.

The boarding of the carriage was a solemn affair. Chand, with both hands clasped in front of him, gave a little bow to her, which she acknowledged with a thank you. As she shook Narain's hand, she managed to utter a few words to thank him for everything he had done for her and Kharak before she broke down again.

Colonel Patterson was the last person she said goodbye to. "Thank you, Colonel Patterson, for being understanding and for doing all this." She paused to take a deep breath. "Thank you on behalf of… Kharak… he would have appreciated it…" She could not say another word as emotions overcame her.

Patterson removed his hat, held it under his arm, bowed and held her hand in both of his. "My dear," he looked straight at her, "time shall heal, just give it a chance. And go and see your family. I think you need each other."

Catherine wiped away a tear and, with that, boarded the carriage. Lal followed her to her seat and sat opposite her. In silence, he reached out his hands that held the urn.

"Hold him," he whispered to her.

With eyes still wet with tears and trembling hands, Catherine took hold of the urn with both hands and rested it on her lap. Torrents of grief coursed though her body. The train cranked forward and slowly started to move away from Tsavo Station.

She did not turn around to look back.

That night in Tsavo, the man-eating lions struck again. The incomplete boma fence that enclosed only three sides of the main camp by the bridge made no difference.

Just after midnight, beneath the dark, sable sky, the silent attack happened at a tent at the far end of the campsite. It was a sudden and the most ferocious attack by two lions, yet happened with such stealth that no one at the campsite heard it.

Feeling smug about how the events of the previous two days had turned out, Ivan had had an extra glass of his favourite whisky. This made his snoring even louder as he slept in his dreamy world. He never heard the twig break outside his tent, nor the scratching on the canvas.

One of the lions poked its huge nose through the entrance to the tent. Using its paw and the razor-sharp claws that retracted at will, the lion tore and unravelled the flimsily tied canvas. Without a snarl, but with a sudden pounce, it grabbed Ivan's leg and dragged him out of his tent in one snap movement.

As Ivan realised what was happening, but before he could react, the second lion grabbed hold of his neck, pressing down on his vocal cords. Ivan could smell the lion's breath and he stared directly into its piercing, ghostly eyes. His bowels opened in fear as he was dragged over the rugged ground in the pitch-darkness and the lion's canine teeth pierced even deeper. It was then he started to feel an immense pain all over his body, a pain he had never felt before.

The following morning when Ivan's assistant went into his tent, he saw the torn canvas and pugmarks all around, together with drag-marks tainted with blood leading out of the tent. He immediately raised the alarm and a search party, led by Colonel Patterson, was set up to search the surrounding area.

Nearly a mile further along the bank of the river, beside a ridge that was overgrown with savannah grass, human remains were found. It was a horrific scene, with blood staining the surrounding grass red. At the centre of a patch of flattened grass were the remains of a body. The abdominal cavity was torn open, the entrails had all been eaten and the limbs were gnawed down to the bone. The jaw was ripped open and it seemed as if the lions had licked the skin off Ivan's face. Only one of his steel-grey eyes was still in its socket. Beside his remains was his gold ring.

One Indian coolie who stood at the back of the search party uttered to himself in Punjabi, "The fruits of karma."

Lahore
Three Weeks Later 77

The amber sun was gradually rising higher in the Lahore sky, increasing the intensity of warmth. A flock of herons glided, skimming the surface of the Ravi River. As far as the eye could see, it meandered; there were no fishermen on that day as the rains over the past few days had made the waters choppy.

On any other day, it would have been perfect, but on this day, despite the sun shimmering over the surface of the river, the mood was dark. A group of men had gathered on the pier to perform the final rites. Kharak's father and younger brother were present, together with the majority of the men from his village of Rahmanpur, including Lal and Nandu, the rickshaw driver. Kharak's mother and younger sister, Neina, were at home as it was an emotional day and women tended to be absent from funerals. The whole family were torn, devastated and inconsolable at losing him.

Having lost Catherine for a few weeks, Ethel never wanted to lose her again. She had softened her stance and accompanied Catherine to the ceremony to scatter Kharak's ashes, offering comfort and support. They stood on the bank, a distance away from the men at the pier.

Catherine, dressed in a black dress and carrying a matching bag, glanced to her side and, not far away, saw the evergreen neem tree. She remembered it was Kharak's favourite spot by the river, where they had had an unforgettable afternoon. The image evoked her memories of that day and, inside, Catherine broke into a thousand pieces.

Having arrived in Lahore two days ago after a long, emotional and physically tough journey, Catherine found the city to be laced with emotional burdens. Everywhere she looked, she remembered Kharak, right from the moment she disembarked from the train and walked through the station entrance, where she had met him for the very first time. That broke her spirit again.

She had made up her mind to leave Lahore at the soonest possible opportunity.

On the pier, the Granthi recited a prayer and, afterwards, Kharak's father and brother slowly scattered his ashes in the river. Within moments, they rippled in unison with the water before disappearing into the fast-flowing river.

On the bank, Catherine's heart sank as she stood with her mother, emotionally lonely. The pain of separation was crushing her.

Minutes later, the villagers started to disperse after consoling the close family members and the tiny pier was soon empty. Catherine ensured that she kept an eye on Lal as she wanted to speak with him before she left Lahore for Bath.

From the pier, Lal took the opposite path to the rest of the men, walking along the bank of the river towards her. Catherine excused herself from her mother and told her that she would see her in the waiting carriage as she had to talk to Lal briefly.

Ethel did not object and walked towards the carriage along the upward-sloping path, occasionally turning back to look at Catherine with concern as she saw Lal approach her.

"Thank you for doing all this for Kharak and me." She felt a lump in her throat.

"He was more than a brother to me."

She lowered her face to wipe a solemn tear. "I'm leaving for home tomorrow."

"Is there anything I can do? Arrange transport, perhaps?"

"That is done." She paused. "However, there is one thing I want you to do for me."

"Yes?"

Catherine retrieved a blue velvet pouch from her bag and opened it.

"This is for Kharak's family." She loosened the neck of the pouch and took out her gold necklace and two ruby-encrusted bracelets.

"I don't know what you mean."

Catherine sighed deeply. "They have also lost everything… and it's my way of supporting Kharak's family on his behalf."

"They won't accept these—"

"They will if they think they were Kharak's," she interrupted him. "Sell them and tell his family that the money was his savings that you kept for him."

"That's difficult."

"Please, you must. If not for my sake, then at least for Kharak's. He sacrificed everything." Her eyes welled up again.

Lal palmed his face with both hands.

"You are the only person I can trust to do this."

He took a long breath and accepted the pouch from her. "I promise that I will do that for you and for Kharak."

"Thank you." Catherine felt relieved.

"When does your train leave?"

"Tomorrow at four o' clock in the afternoon."

Lal thought for a second. "Will you ever come back to Lahore?"

Catherine shifted her gaze over his shoulder to the neem tree in the distance.

"No. This will be my only trip here." She let out a sigh. "I take with me memories of love and pain. Those of love, I wish not to ruin, and those of pain, I wish not to endure again." Her voice was full of emotion.

He rolled his head in agreement.

"Thank you, Lal, for all that you have done for me... and Kharak. I'm indebted to you."

"Don't say that."

Catherine wiped away a tear.

"I have to go with his family now to his house." Lal paused. "Have a safe journey and Punjab will always be happy to have you." He tightened the thread at the neck of the pouch, closing it tightly.

"Thank you and goodbye." Catherine shook his hand.

Lal tucked the pouch safely into his pocket, buttoning it, turned around, waved and, with that, hurried to catch up with the group of men walking away from the pier.

Catherine headed for the carriage where her mother was waiting for her, before boarding it and riding off to the family home.

78

Catherine chose not to speak to her father. To her, he had to bear some responsibility for sending Kharak away to East Africa. There were times, after she returned to Lahore, when she would walk out of a room as her father walked in, to his annoyance. He had not yet fully recovered from the bout of malaria he had suffered a few weeks ago and still felt weak. But Catherine was hurting and in no mood for forgiveness or trivial talk with anyone.

After the events of the past few weeks, including his ill health, Gilbert handed in his letter of resignation from his post at the medical unit at the Punjab University and decided to go back with Ethel and Catherine to England.

Late that evening, Catherine took a stroll around the garden for the very last time. She wandered aimlessly, just like her thoughts, never fully taking in the serenity and the sounds of the rock buntings that she so admired. Vadu briefly observed her through the kitchen window. She had lost weight.

That evening, as she did every evening, she went up to her room at dinnertime to avoid sitting with her parents at the table. She sat on her bed, propped up against the upholstered headboard, and ate a tiny amount of the food on her plate before her appetite deserted her. In the corner of her room were her belongings, packed away in suitcases. In a way, it seemed as if it was only yesterday that she had arrived and her suitcases had been waiting in the same place, waiting to be unpacked.

She felt sad.

A knock on the door jolted her from her distant thoughts.

"Come in."

The door opened gently and Vadu stepped in. "Can I get you anything, memsahib?"

"Not at the moment. But you can take my plate to the kitchen."

With his head lowered, he walked and picked up her dinner plate, which was resting on the bedside table.

"What happens to you when we leave?" she asked him.

"Memsahib, in a few days, the next family appointed by the establishment will move in and our lives will go on."

"There must be a lot of adjustment for all the staff here."

"Yes, memsahib." He carefully lifted the tray and walked towards the door. At the door, he turned around and bowed his head. "I'm very sorry for your loss, memsahib."

Leaning against the bed, Catherine lifted her gaze and said nothing.

"He was a good man," Vadu added.

There was a brief silence.

"Thank you."

Vadu turned around, opened the door and left.

After another seemingly long night, the morning flew by, with time spent on supervising the servants as they brought the baggage downstairs into the front room and cleared the rest of the rooms.

The carriage arrived and Catherine was the first to step into it and sit by the window. Gilbert and Ethel sat on the opposite seat, engaged in conversation about their bags and the journey ahead. Catherine did not pay any attention to them. In silence, she sat gazing out as the carriage slowly left the house and moved along the tree-lined Victoria Avenue. The yellow Amaltas trees stood out. Catherine shut her eyes to stop her tears forming, but it didn't help.

Bath

October 1898

79

Autumn was in full swing, with magenta, orange and yellow colours erupting on the trees on the hill that formed the backdrop to the lush green grass that overlooked Catherine's first-floor bedroom window at Number 2 Royal Crescent. The early-morning frost had melted away with the warmth of the rising autumn sun that hit the leaves, augmenting their mosaic of colour.

Three months had passed since she had arrived back in England from Lahore. At the end of her room, near the wardrobe, lay the three suitcases that she had travelled with, still untouched on the rug. Catherine had not yet allowed the maid to unpack her belongings. For her, the closed suitcases contained precious memories that were tucked away safely, and by opening the cases, she felt that these memories would escape.

Three days after arriving in Bath, Gilbert had suffered a stroke. Some doctors said it was due to the long journey, whereas Ethel thought that the strain of his fraught relationship with his daughter might have contributed to it. He survived, but was paralysed down his left side and in need of care, and a nurse had been engaged to look after him. As a result, he was moved to the room on the ground floor where he spent most of his day.

News of what had happened to Ivan in Tsavo reached the family when a news article of the event was written in the Bath Chronicle. Catherine did not flinch or show any emotion when her mother told her what had happened. Deep down, she was glad of the manner in which Ivan had met his death. Still, to Catherine, every moment she spent thinking of Ivan would be a moment lost in thinking of Kharak. She went to the extent that she never uttered Ivan's name; to her, it was a breath wasted.

Catherine sat on the velvet armchair by the window in her bedroom, sipping her mid-morning Earl Grey tea and looking out onto the cobbled road that ran around the crescent, separating the houses from the expansive green common lawn. She still missed the Darjeeling tea she used to have in Lahore. A well-dressed young couple ambled, arm in arm, along the footpath, the woman giggling affectionately at her suitor. Catherine gazed intently at the couple, who seemed obviously in love, until they were out of sight. A warm tingle ran through her.

After taking another sip of tea, she turned her head and stared at her suitcases. She stood up and walked towards them. The leather straps were just as secure as they had been the day she had left Punjab. She gently ran her hand over the top of the smallest suitcase. Taking a deep breath, she lifted it, set it on her bed and slowly started unfastening the straps, one at a time.

Moments later, with a tremble, she lifted the top of the suitcase. Lying at the top was the blouse she had worn that last night; the night they had watched the stars from the carriage; the night they had spent together. She gently lifted it, for it was precious to her… and she knew that she would never wash it. Bringing her nose to it, she sniffed it, hoping to get a scent of Kharak. She felt hollow.

At the corner of the suitcase, with only an edge visible, she spotted the carved wooden jewellery box that Kharak had given to her. Memories came flooding back. She caressed it with her hand before lifting it. Holding it carefully, she walked back to the chair by the window and sat down, placing it on her lap.

Through the window, an angled stream of golden autumn sun landed on her lap. The tiny hinges of the jewellery box glistened in the light. *He wrapped it in brown paper the day he bought this for me*, she thought with a heavy heart. She stroked the box's surface, feeling its every detail, her fingers moving over the intricate carved design.

It was at that instant that it struck her out of the blue. The secret compartment at the side of the jewellery box.

Her heart started racing wildly. Opening the box, her favourite pearl earrings were there next to Kharak's note and the map he had drawn for her. But that was not why her heart was racing. She felt for the little protrusion at the corner of the box and pressed it.

With a click, the tiny compartment was released on the outside. With trembling fingers, she slowly pulled it out fully and there it was. She had forgotten about it: Kharak's second envelope, which he had left for her when he left Lahore! Her heart was thumping and her breath was rapid. She read his instruction on the envelope once again:

Only open in the future when life throws at you seemingly dark days or moments.

Catherine stared at the envelope and at his handwriting, feeling numb as waves of emotions rose from within her.

With trembling hands, she delicately opened the envelope.

Inside was a small piece of folded paper. She slid it out and unfolded it. She read his written note.

I may be far,
But every time I shall whisper your name,
I will feel you beside me.
And I wish I could show you,
When you are lonely or in darkness,
The astonishing light
Of your own being.

Kharak

As her heart thumped against her ribcage, she felt a warm, glow spread through her body and grab hold of her beating heart.

She felt his presence and yearned to call out his name, but she was speechless. It was like Kharak had wrapped his arms around her, holding her close to him. She could feel his beating heart. There was pain in her soul, but this time it felt a bit different, as there was also love wrapped within that pain.

Memories in the form of tears spilled from her soft eyes and down her cheeks, and she began to cry.

They were the most cherished words that she would ever read. That moment was etched in her being forever. She kissed the note before holding it next to her heart.

It was then she realised that Kharak was only a whisper away, and as long as he lived in her mind, thoughts and heart, he would never die.

She knew that it was not going to be easy moving forward from all that had happened. In times to come, there would be sights, sounds and scents that would waft in the air unannounced and rekindle her memories. With each memory, she would miss him dearly, but with his written notes to her, she would always find comfort in the fact that in each of those brief moments with him, a thousand joys resided.

With the note in her hand, she stood up, walked to her bed and sat down and read it again. The sun had slipped further along the sky, shifting its rays from the floor and onto the corner of her bed, highlighting the embroidery on the cover at the edge. She lowered herself onto the bed and lay on her side, resting her cheek on the soft pillow as she stared at the note held in her hand. She closed her eyes.

She whispered his name.

Author's Note

Roshan, an Indian foreman working in Tsavo in 1898, wrote an epic account of his time there. An extract from his diary states:

> ... Because of the fear of those demons, some seven or eight hundred of the labourers deserted and remained idle... And because of fear for their lives, would sit in their huts, their hearts full of foreboding and terror...

Over a period of nine months to 29th December 1898, it is believed that 135 people were killed by the two man-eating lions of Tsavo before Colonel John Patterson, who was commissioned by the Railway Committee to build the bridge, managed to kill them, with the utmost difficulty.

These lions have the infamy of being the only animals to have ever been the cause of debate in the Houses of Parliament at Westminster in London.

Today, they can be seen displayed at the Field Museum of Natural History in Chicago, USA.

As one walks into the Nairobi Railway Museum, a small stone building with a corrugated terracotta roof located off Haile

Selassie Avenue in Nairobi, Kenya, in addition to the trains that ran during the period in which this story is set, one can see a wooden desk that has a drawer with no markings. Stored inside this drawer is a tiny box. In this box rest three huge claws that belonged to the man-eating lions of Tsavo.

The area of the old railway bridge across the Tsavo River can still be observed today as one travels from Nairobi to Mombasa by road. Even today, the place has an eerie feel about it and has been aptly named 'Man-Eaters'.

In 1981, the Shalimar Gardens in Lahore were designated as a UNESCO World Heritage Site.

At the turn of the 20th century, in the year 1900, the population of Sikhs living in Lahore was around 40,000. During the Partition of India, which divided India and incorporated the region of Punjab into Pakistan, fourteen million people were displaced and an estimated 200,000 to two million people were killed as a result of religiously motivated violence that erupted as families moved.

The current population of Sikhs in Lahore, now in Pakistan, is less than eighty.